STARSEA INVADERS:
SECOND
CONTACT

by

G. Harry Stine

P9-CNI-179

A ROC BOOK

ROC
Published by the Penguin Group
Penguin Books USA Inc., 375 Hudson Street,
New York, New York 10014, U.S.A.
Penguin Books Ltd, 27 Wrights Lane,
London W8 5TZ, England
Penguin Books Australia Ltd, Ringwood,
Victoria, Australia
Penguin Books Canada Ltd, 10 Alcorn Avenue,
Toronto, Ontario, Canada M4V 3B2
Penguin Books (N.Z.) Ltd, 182–190 Wairau Road,
Auckland 10, New Zealand

Penguin Books Ltd, Registered Offices:
Harmondsworth, Middlesex, England

First published by Roc, an imprint of Dutton Signet,
a division of Penguin Books USA Inc.

First Printing, March, 1994
10 9 8 7 6 5 4 3 2 1

 REGISTERED TRADEMARK—MARCA REGISTRADA

Printed in the United States of America

AUTHOR'S NOTE AND DISCLAIMER: This is a work of fiction. However,
the surnames of some of the fictional characters are those of the pioneer aviators
of the United States Navy and are used herein to honor their memories.

To:
Martin Caidin,
who would rather fly than dive
(but so would I).

"My biggest satisfaction comes from directing smart, capable people. Every submariner undergoes extensive screening, and most attend difficult schools to get here. All are volunteers. . . . Motivating them is my number one priority."

—Anonymous submarine commander,
United States Navy, circa 1989.

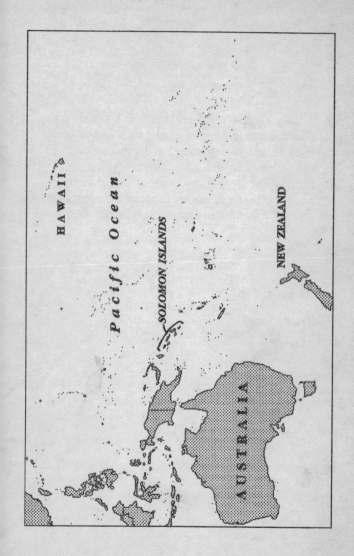

1

"Dive! Dive! Dive!"

No other command in the submarine service of the United States Navy is as intense or fraught with potential danger.

When Captain William M. Corry gave that order, it was always triply redundant so no one could possibly misunderstand it.

It signaled a course of events that was to sink the 390-meter SSCV-26 U.S.S. *Shenandoah*. Corry's command converted the *Shenandoah* from an aircraft carrier to a submarine.

Aye, aye, sir! Dive! Dive! Dive! echoed the Executive Officer, Commander Arthur E. "Zeke" Braxton both verbally and on the N-fone net.

And this was repeated in turn by the diving officer of the watch, who was also the boat's First Lieutenant, LCDR Mark Walton.

Even in the twenty-first century, people who went down to and under the sea did *not* turn over to machines and computers the entire control of a naval vessel. A carrier submarine is large and complex. It offers ample opportunities for something to be forgotten or to go wrong. The deadly sea beyond the composite pressure hull will kill quickly if a mistake is made or if a computer or automatic control fails to function properly.

Thus, even in the futuristic control room of the *Shenandoah*, orders were passed verbally as well as by neurophonic units and other telecommunications means. And orders were repeated back for redundancy. In the sea, redundancy is safety.

The huge submarine slipped beneath the Pacific Ocean silently, stealthily, and with little disturbance of the blue waters. The days of brute force naval engineering had passed. At one time in the submarine service, silence was golden and just about as valuable. As a result of technological progress and maturation, the "Silent Service" became truly silent and even more mysterious.

Zeke Braxton's thoughts were glum as he watched the situation displays of the dive. He wondered why the crew of the *Shenandoah* hadn't been let in on the mystery this time. The world situation was going to worms by the hour. The crew knew they were being sent on a sea control mission. But why were they headed where the action probably wasn't?

Corry knew but wasn't telling. He *couldn't* tell them yet.

The mission was too sensitive.

And although the Captain of the carrier submarine didn't know it, he didn't have all the details yet himself.

As a result, the control room snapped with tension. The crew *knew* their skipper normally didn't keep them in the dark. As a result, everyone was on edge, thinking that the mission probably was more hazardous than usual.

Thus, the center of the massive ship's brains and nervous system was unusually quiet during the dive.

Sir, we are level at one-zero-zero meters. We have a steady bubble. Heading one-three-five, came the report from the diving officer.

Without hesitation, CAPT William M. Corry gave the quiet order, *Come to best depth for high-speed long-range cruise. At depth, come to best long-range cruise speed. Come to new heading two-three-five.*

And without hesitation, Zeke repeated the new orders, which were promptly echoed by the ship's First Lieutenant seated behind the ship's control panel.

"Sir?" LCDR Natalie B. Chase, the Navigation Officer, voiced in a single interrogatory word a whole series of questions not only in her mind but that of the crew as well. She didn't use the N-fone. She merely turned in her seat and asked the Captain directly. "Destination?"

"Latitude zero-zero-eight south, longitude one-six-two

east. Those coordinates will do for now, Commander," Corry responded.

"The Solomon Islands?"

"You keep charts in your head, don't you, Natalie?" Corry asked her rhetorically.

"Yes, sir. A professional athlete has to know the playing field," she replied and got busy at her job of navigating the huge carrier submarine to its new destination. It didn't bother her that the course and destination had abruptly and radically been changed by the Commanding Officer. She wasn't running the U.S.S. *Shenandoah*, just telling the crew where to steer the ship to get where the Captain wanted to go.

"I was sure nothing was happening around Cape Horn," muttered SCPO Carl Armstrong, the Chief of the Boat. That's where the original course line would have taken the carrier submarine as she was dived once clear of Pearl Harbor and the Hawaiian Ridge.

Natalie had the new course up on one of the control room display panels within a minute. The vast expanse of the Earth's water hemisphere, the Pacific Ocean, lay between the ship and its destination. The data box on the display flashed the information, *"Present distance 2,963.14 nm. Estimated time enroute 74 hrs 5 min."*

Sir, we are level at one-seven-four meters. We have the bubble. Speed coming to forty knots. Heading two-three-five true, came the report from LCDR Mark Walton.

Corry stood up. *Steady as she goes, Mister Walton. Number Two, set the forenoon watch.* Corry used one of the two deck calls of his Executive Officer, the Number Two officer in the boat.

Steady as she goes, sir. Set the forenoon watch, Zeke repeated. Then he added verbally, "May I see you at your convenience, sir?"

"Certainly. Why am I not surprised that you make the request?" Corry told him lightly. "I'll be in my cabin."

"Now we'll get the ungarbled word," muttered the Chief of the Boat.

The COB didn't think Corry had heard him. But the Captain turned and added to Zeke, "And please bring Chief Armstrong with you."

The Chief's stepped in it! thought Natalie Chase, but

she was careful not to allow her thought to get into the N-fone circuit. She was wrong, of course. Corry rarely left anything for anyone to step in.

In spite of the size of the U.S.S. *Shenandoah,* even the Captain's cabin wasn't expansive. Corry had a small sleeping compartment, a minuscule head, and a cramped office that also doubled as a tiny conference room. His quarters weren't far from the control room. In any event, Corry had a terminal and display that allowed him to monitor the ship at all times from his quarters.

Zeke Braxton and Chief Armstrong found the Captain seated in the office when the door signaled them to enter.

"Sit down, Zeke. You, too, Chief," Corry told his two top people with a brief wave of his hand. "Before you do, help yourself to coffee there on the sideboard."

"Thank you, sir," Braxton responded.

"I'll get it for you, Commander. I figure after a dive we can always use a little turbo juice," Chief Armstrong put in.

Even in the twenty-first century, the Navy still operated on hot coffee, with cold bug juice running a close second. Polite formality was part of the ship's tight discipline, at least among the Ship Division officers and CPOs. The people in the Air Group had their own protocols. So did the all-male Marine Battalion. But everyone conformed to the ways of the Ship Division in briefings and meetings. Braxton was especially careful to do so. He looked forward to his own blue water command in a few years. The competition was tough. The twenty-first century United States Navy had a limited number of keels available for command. Only the best people rose to blue-water command.

"Warm your cup, sir?" Armstrong offered.

Corry shook his head. As Braxton sat down, the Captain began, "To anticipate your questions, Number Two—and to confirm your suspicions, Chief—CINCPAC never intended to send us to Cape Horn."

Armstrong set a steaming mug of coffee in front of Braxton and sat down himself, cupping his hands around his own mug. "I wasn't suspicious, Captain. Just echoing what's going around Rumor Control."

"Which you should be doing," Braxton reminded him.

"Yes, sir. Part of my job."

Braxton sighed. "I'd rather be hunting extraterrestrials."

"So would I," Corry agreed.

"Frankly, sir," Braxton admitted with candor, knowing that he could speak freely to Corry in the privacy of the captain's cabin, "I didn't like the way we were treated when we got back from the Makasar mission."

Off Makasar, the crew of the *Shenandoah* had discovered an alien extraterrestrial species that lived in the Earth's oceans and fished for human beings. They had gotten excellent data on the alien submarine spaceships. They'd even managed to capture an dead alien specimen and bring it back to Pearl Harbor frozen so it didn't decompose.

Then they were told to remain silent about it.

"Orders are orders, Number Two," Corry reminded him.

"Yes, sir. That doesn't mean I like it."

"Nor do I."

"Frankly, sirs, if the Chinks hadn't released their videotapes of the aliens and the UFO, all of us would probably be sitting at the North Pole Station right now," Armstrong muttered darkly. "Sorry, but I'm a little yanked by the Chinese claim that they made the discovery. . . ."

"The Chinese wouldn't have made the claim if Washington hadn't remained silent after the original Beijing announcement," Zeke said with some bitterness in his voice. "The United States didn't own up to having our videos and other data. And no one would admit we brought back a dead, frozen alien. I don't understand the reason for leaving the door open for the Chinese to claim the discovery."

If CDR Zeke Braxton was frustrated and baffled by the behavior of the civil servants and politicians who were the ultimate bosses of those in the armed services, he didn't say more. It wasn't proper for him to do so as long as he held a commission. But he was echoing the perplexity felt by the officers and crew of the ship.

"Sir, with all due respects, they don't know what to do with all of it. It's a hot potato," Armstrong told him. "It's not covered by the procedure manuals. So they treat it the same way they've treated UFO sightings and other close encounters for over a hundred years. They say nothing. It's safer than saying something and being hung for it later. We're the ones paid to take risks, not them."

"You're probably right, Chief," Zeke admitted and took a sip of hot coffee. "But why didn't the Sulawesi officials speak up? They were there, too. They saw that alien submarine take off and climb out of sight."

"And admit that carnivorous aliens were in their coastal waters fishing for humans? And ruin what little tourist trade they have left?" Corry put in rhetorically. "No, they kept quiet to protect part of their economy."

"That's deceitful." Zeke was a purist when it came to ethical behavior.

Corry shrugged. "It's their country, Zeke."

"It might not be for very long if the Chinese increase their expansionist threats in that direction," Zeke growled. "I take it that's why we're headed toward the Solomons—"

He was interrupted by the chime of the door signal.

The cramped little conference room hardly had room for another person, but Corry announced, "Come!"

It was CDR Terri Ellison, the CAG or Commander Air Group. She was still wearing whites from the on-deck departure formation. Zeke thought she looked good in anything she wore, especially any of the attractive naval officer's uniforms of the Millennium Navy.

Terri looked around. "Sorry, Captain. I didn't realize you already had visitors. I'll come back when it's less crowded—"

"Squeeze in, Terri," Corry told her. "I think you're here for the same reason Zeke and Chief Armstrong are. But tell me anyway."

"Sir, I'd like to know more about our mission," Terri said bluntly, getting at once to the point without any hesitation.

Corry expected this aggressive approach on her part. She was one sierra hotel naval aviator who had risen to command an otherwise non-offensive patrol squadron. She'd managed to shoot down a Burmese fighter that had hassled her on a patrol flight. No one in the Pentagon had ever considered that the P-10 Osprey was anything more than a patrol aircraft with only enough armament to defend itself. Terri Ellison had turned her P-10 into an offensive weapon by good flying, pushing the craft to the limit of its envelope, and audacious employment of the basic tactics of air warfare. She got on the tail of the Burmese Marut and stayed there until she shot it out of the sky. She gave no quarter.

But that was Terri Ellison's basic approach to life, anyway.

It often caused Corry some heartburn, but he'd gone to great lengths to make sure she'd been assigned as CAG in his boat.

When Corry didn't respond immediately she went on, "It's bad enough that the Air Group has to stand down for more than three days while we cruise to our new destination. My pilots like to fly. They get bored playing video games in the simulators. And we don't know what sort of games they should be playing anyway because we don't know what we're likely to be flying against when we get there. Chinese? Indians? Annamites?"

"All of the above, Commander," Corry put in. "You know the world situation as well as I do. East World is pushing at its limits. They're harassing the Russians on land. And they're pushing south and east at sea."

"Classical geopolitics, Terri," Zeke reminded her.

'So we're headed for the Solomons to stop something that's brewing there?" she replied.

Corry didn't get the chance to answer. The door chime sounded again.

"Bart Clinch, I'll bet," Zeke guessed.

"And no room at the inn," Terri added, looking briefly around the crowded conference room.

It was indeed the commander of the Marine battalion. He quickly saw that the room was full. "Sorry, Captain! I'll come back later."

Corry held up his hand. "Let me guess, Major. The change of destination has you concerned. You'd like to know what we're likely to get into, and you want the three days to get your batt in shape for it."

"Uh, yessir," Major Bart Clinch replied in his gravelly, rasping voice. He paused for a moment, then went on,

"The men are goddamned restless, sir. They know now we're not headed to Cape Horn. Galley yarns travel pretty damned fast in a carrier sub. From my point of view, I've got to shift gears. The Solomons are a hell of a lot different if we have to go out and be nasty to someone. Jungle warfare isn't the same fighting environment as Tierra del Fuego in the Antarctic. Different tactical approach, different weapons, different logistics. . . ."

"And I'm beginning to wonder if somehow we're being sent back into the area where we encountered the Awesomes," Terri said, using the nickname the crew had given to the aliens they'd encountered. "I'm still pissed off about the way we were treated when we got back to Pearl after the Makasar mission!"

The morale situation was worse than Captain William Corry had estimated. The crew of the U.S.S. *Shenandoah* was a tightly knit group of people who were no-nonsense submariners, aviators, and warriors. All three organizations aboard—the Ship Division, the Air Group, and the Marine Battalion—were made up of people who wanted to be where they were, who liked doing what they did, and who expected to be treated as professionals.

The people of the Ship Division were submariners with the sort of quiet familylike camaraderie that had always existed among the officers and sailors of the Silent Service.

The "brown shoes" of the Air Group were pilots and aviation specialists who had a love for the air and flying machines. They were different. They looked at the world from the unique viewpoint that has always identified those in aviation.

The Marines aboard were . . . well, Marines. They were gun apes. They were happiest when fighting. Some people are like that. The millennium culture of America had to make a place for them as it had done for the submariners and aviators.

The world was still a dangerous place. America needed the sort of people who were in the U.S.S. *Shenandoah*.

Corry had planned a briefing later in the day. But he decided nothing was to be gained by putting it off.

His senior officers had come to his quarters with the same concerns in mind. That convinced him to act.

Corry stood up. "Zeke, please call a meeting in the main wardroom in fifteen minutes. I want all group and division heads to be present with their lead chiefs. I'll pass the Ungarbled Word there." He paused. "At least, I'll tell you what I know and what I was going to tell you later. I think there may be more, but I don't know what it is right now."

2

The eighteen senior officers and their lead CPOs came to their feet when CAPT William Corry entered the wardroom.

Corry moved to the head of the table, motioned to them with his hand, and told them, "B-B-B-Be seated." He then took his chair, personally embarrassed that he'd let slip his control over stuttering. In only two short breaths, he had his speech impediment in check. This didn't stop him from pausing for a fraction of a second before speaking each time.

His officers and chiefs knew of their Captain's speech impediment, recognized what had happened, and over-looked it. CAPT William M. Corry was an outstanding commanding officer. He was a leader, was fair in his dealings with the crew, and always kept the welfare of the *Shenandoah*'s people in mind. If he stuttered occasionally, that was a minor shortcoming they could easily live with because it was the only one he had.

"Ladies and gentlemen, the nature of the orders I received from CINCPAC prevented me from disclosing them to you before we were under way," Corry began once everyone was seated. As he spoke, he briefly made eye contact with each of them and with the video camera that was transmitting his image to other parts of the boat. He offered no additional apology. It wasn't necessary, and his crew knew it. Orders were orders.

He opened the seam on his shirt's breast pocket, took out a folded paper, and resealed the pocket by running his finger over the seam. The wardroom remained silent as he unfolded the hard copy. The people in the U.S.S. *Shenandoah* were about to get the Ungarbled Word, so they listened.

Under normal circumstances, Corry could have keyed the terminal on the wardroom table next to him, retrieved the orders from the ship's computer memory, and caused the text to come up on the video screens throughout the ship. But the text was in a memory cube in his other shirt pocket. Before coming to the wardroom, he'd generated a hard copy on his personal system. He wanted to read the orders aloud to the crew. Corry preferred to exercise command on a personal level if possible. He believed modern telecommunications should supplement command, not place machinery between the commander and the commanded.

"I was ordered to maintain silence about our actual mission," he went on. "I did indeed receive orders to sail the boat to the vicinity of Cape Horn, where we would engage in patrol and sea control duties near that maritime choke point. Those orders were posted on the bulletin board of the ship's local network before we departed Pearl." He paused and smiled. "I know some of you personally had doubts about those orders. We know why the *Shenandoah* exists and why we sail her. The purpose of our boat and our training is to exercise power projection in peacetime. When a crisis or confrontation develops, our mission is to stop it from escalating into armed conflict. If we can't do that, our standing orders are to be tough bastards and bitches who go in there and win.

"We all follow the news of world affairs. We know the action won't be near Cape Horn. So we're going where the action may be.

"Yesterday, I was called to CINCPAC. I was personally handed classified orders. I was given a classified briefing."

Zeke Braxton looked at Terri Ellison. Together, they looked at Bart Clinch. Independently, the three of them had guessed the real reason for the Captain's quick trip ashore. So had Chief Armstrong and the other CPOs. They'd served in the Navy and Marine Corps long enough to know that the politicians, diplomats, admirals, and generals often played the game of "surprise-surprise."

They also knew what was happening in southeast Asia and the South Pacific.

Except among themselves, they'd remained silent about their doubts. Good leaders don't spread scuttlebutt among the junior officers and rates.

And they were good or they wouldn't be serving in the U.S.S. *Shenandoah*.

"I will read the classified orders to you," Corry said.

" 'This is an Execute Order by authority and direction of the Secretary of Defense. This order is classified Secret. On Sunday, August tenth, massive troop movements of the People's Liberation Army of the People's Republic of China along the border between Russia and China near Yining and Karamay were confirmed by observations by reconnaissance spaceplanes. Other troop movements of the People's Liberation Army of the People's Republic of China were observed in the Lesser Khingan Range near Aihul. Intelligence information indicates movement of ten armored and motorized infantry divisions of the Indian Army between Jaipur and the Rann of Kutch on the Indian subcontinent. Submarines and fast attack hydrodynes of the Indian Navy have been observed in the Strait of Hormuz, Bab el Mandeb, and Strait of Mozambique. Four attack submarines of the Navy of the People's Republic of China have been detected in or near the Malacca, Sunda, Lombok, and Torres straits. No submarines or hydrodynes are presently in Indian or Chinese ports. Chinese air interdiction and harassment of ships in the vicinity of the Spratley Islands in the South China Sea have increased in number and aggressive actions. On Monday, August eleventh, the ambassador of the People's Republic of China was recalled from Canberra to Beijing for consultations following breakdown of negotiations on the Sino-Australian nonaggression treaty. These movements of military and naval forces and the recall of China's ambassador to Australia have caused the National Security Council to place national defense elements in DEFCON Three.

" 'At twenty-two hundred hours Zulu on Tuesday, August twelfth, the National Command Authority directed the Joint Chiefs of Staff to issue JCS Execute Order zero-seven-dash-three-two-dash-four-seven November. This Execute Order was transmitted to CINC-PAC at twenty-two-thirty hours and is hereby transmitted by hand to Commanding Officer, U.S.S. *Shenandoah* SSCV-26.

" '*Shenandoah* will depart Pearl Harbor as planned and proceed in the direction of Cape Horn until the ship is dived. Commanding Officer is not authorized to reveal the existence or contents of this Execute Order before that time. After diving the ship, Commanding Officer will order course change. Ship will proceed to the Solomon Islands in South Pacific. Upon reaching this destination, *Shenandoah* will use on-board instruments and air operations to monitor and report position and movements of naval vessels of India and People's Republic of China. Observational stealth will be maintained. Extended surface operations are not recommended.

" 'Rules of engagement are standard defensive offense. Commanding Officer of *Shenandoah* will not initiate offensive action but is authorized to defend the ship and counterattack if required by nature of adversary's actions. Ship's aircraft may carry and utilize both defensive and offensive ordnance under the rules of engagement. Ship's Marine battalion may be used to board and seize any vessel of India or People's Republic of China that attacks *Shenandoah* or that *Shenandoah* discovers is bringing under attack other vessels of United States or friendly nation registry.

" 'Commanding Officer of *Shenandoah* will report actions and activities through normal channels to CINC-PAC using stealthy communications media.

" 'Commanding Officer of *Shenandoah* will execute JCS Execute Order zero-seven-dash-three-two-dash-four-seven November.' "

The faces of the officers and CPOs in the wardroom remained passive. Corry handed the hard copy to Braxton, then took a computer memory cube from his shirt pocket. "XO, please download these orders into the ship's computer. They may be displayed or printed out at any terminal on the ship. I request that all hands read these orders."

Zeke took the cube. "Aye, aye, sir!"

The Captain looked around the room. "Any comments? Questions?"

"Well, at least we're going someplace significant and we know more or less what we're going to do when we get there," Terri Ellison remarked. "But we don't know what we'll be up against."

"Mister Lovette, that's your department," Correy reminded LCDR Robert Lovette, the head of the Operations Department. "I want you to keep Mister Strader and his crew on their toes. I'll need the latest intelligence updates."

"Aye, aye, sir!" Lovette replied smartly. "I'll set special watches on the sensor suites."

"Don't ping. Use passive sonar and the masdet," Zeke reminded him. The U.S.S. *Shenandoah* was one of the few ships in the Navy big enough to mount the new mass detector developed by White Oak Laboratories. A completely passive sensor, it detected the presence of mass density change boundaries using some arcane aspects of modern twenty-first century physics. The WSS-1 mass detector was the most secret of secrets, although it was based on unclassified work done more than fifty years before by Dr. William O. Davis and CDR Pharis Williams. The "masdet" gave a submarine yet another set of eyes to use in the depths of the oceans. It also gave the Captain of the U.S.S. *Shenandoah* a definite edge over any adversary, especially one who didn't know that the masdet existed. The masdet had changed submarine warfare doctrine and tactics, and the crew of the U.S.S. *Shenandoah* had helped write the book. It turned the carrier submarine into the "one-eyed man in the country of the blind."

"Navigation Officer," Corry said to LCDR Natalie Chase, "please cross-check positions with masdet and gravitational anomaly data from Mister Lovette's shop as we cruise. I know you aligned and locked the inertial system before we dived, but I don't want to take any chance of running into a sea mount en route. Or after we get there."

"Captain, all three inertials are checking well within operational tolerances," Natalie reported with confidence. "And I downloaded the latest charts after we left Pearl and before we dived." The petite, dark-haired navigator was not only a math and computer whiz—she'd graduated Number One in her class at the Naval Academy—but she had a mental inertial positioning system of her own that seemed to be able to tell her where she was at any time. And her eidetic memory allowed her to carry charts in her head.

"Mister Lovette, make sure the SWC remains hot," the Commanding Officer reminded his Operations Officer. The SWC, or Scalar Wave Communications system, was another highly classified piece of equipment in the carrier submarine. It didn't operate in the normal electromagnetic spectrum of radio and radar but in the esoteric realm of standing waves that didn't obey speed of light limitations or have the restrictions of ordinary electromagnetic communications devices. The ship had continuous communication with CINCPAC at all times, although SWC had a band width that precluded its use for voice comm.

This request caused Zeke to ask, "Are you expecting additional orders, Captain?"

"Yes, XO," Corry replied frankly.

"I suspected as much," Terri Ellison put in. "That Ex Ord is very loosy-goosy."

"We're being positioned, Commander," Corry pointed out. "That Execute Order is indeed loose. It's precisely the sort of order I would expect to receive in a world situation like the present one. American power projection and defense assets are being positioned. As the situation develops, I full anticipate receiving additional orders. In the meantime, we will carry out the Execute Order."

"I'm not sure what we're expected to do in the Solomons except provide eyes other than those on Aerospace Farce hypersonic recce spaceplanes and snoopsats. So the Air Group won't relax during this cruise-out. We'll be ready to launch CAP, patrol, or attack birds as soon as water clears the flight decks when we surface," Terri said.

"My batt will refresh on boarding procedures," Bart Clinch added. "We'll also do a little research on how the Marines fought in the Solomons during War Two. I don't make the mistake of re-inventing the tactical manuals."

LCDR Natalie Chase started to say something, then paused. "Uh, sir . . ." She was very hesitant to speak her thoughts.

"Commander?" Corry prompted her.

On the urging of the commanding officer's prompt, she went on, "We're heading into warm, shallow equatorial waters again. It's a similar environment to the one in which we encountered the Awesomes." She used the phonetic of the unofficial acronym developed by the crew of the *Shenandoah* to refer to the underwater aliens they'd met off Sulawesi and in the Makasar Straits. This was verbal shorthand for "Alien Underwater Sea Monsters," or AUSMs. The term "Awesomes" caught on and had been used ever since. "Are you . . . uh . . . *sure* we're not being secretly sent out to fish for Awesomes?"

"Yes, I am," Corry replied quickly so that his rebuttal would be received as firm and positive. "Fishing for Awesomes is *not* the mission of the U.S.S. *Shenandoah*. We've been ordered not to discuss our encounter with the Awesomes. Nor are we to consider that our mission and that of this carrier submarine has been changed as a result of our encounter with the Awesomes. And that's that. Period." He paused. "However, it doesn't mean we shouldn't keep our sensors peeled in case we run into them again. You're right, Commander. We're going into warm, shallow equatorial South Pacific waters again. A definite possibility exists that we'll encounter the Awesomes there. If we do, we'll take action and data as we did before."

CDR Laura Raye Moore, the Medical Officer, shook her head slowly. "I keep hoping we'll run into them," she admitted. "I'd like to work with a live Awesome. All I got to do was autopsy a dead and frozen one. That's like trying to understand human beings by dealing only with cadavers. I'd like to get more data to supplement what I have."

Corry looked piercingly at her. "Doctor, did you turn over your data to CINCPAC as ordered?"

"Yes, sir. I did."

Corry had suspected this from scuttlebutt. But the

Medical Officer had now openly admitted it. "Did you withhold any data, Commander?" He deliberately used her naval rank rather than her professional title, a gentle reminder that she was a commissioned naval officer subject to orders.

"I withheld nothing, sir. But I kept copies of all the data available to me—verbal and written reports as well as visual documentation," she admitted. The ship's Medical Officer paused, then added, "The orders didn't say we couldn't retain copies."

"Commander, your naval career may be terminated if anyone outside this ship becomes aware of this," Corry reminded her. He was truly concerned. Laura Raye Moore was an excellent doctor. He didn't want to lose her. But he didn't want her to fall afoul of the naval hierarchy for willfully failing to carry out the letter *and* the spirit of an order.

"They won't, sir." She was confident. She knew the people who were the crew of the U.S.S. *Shenandoah*. The crew was a tight, unified "family." And everyone had been royally pissed off because they'd made contact with an alien race and hadn't been allowed to discuss it with anyone other than the debriefers from Naval Intelligence. No one in the ship would rat on anyone else in this matter.

Corry knew she was right. He turned to the others. "Did anyone else retain copies of their data?"

"Yes, sir," Zeke Braxton replied immediately. "We all did, sir. We turned over all the data we had. But the orders said nothing that would prevent us from keeping copies. We know the information is classified Top Secret. So we're treating our copies properly in that regard, sir."

"My medical data on the Awesomes are *not* in the ship's computer, Captain," Moore pointed out. "I have them in a very secure place under triple-encryption locks. I'm treating them with the same professional confidentiality as the crew's personal medical data. Sir, it's the prerogative of a ship's Medical Officer to keep such confidential records. In fact, the protocols of the naval medical service require it. If we run into other Awesomes, this data could be critical. Contact with an Awesome might result in medical problems for a crew member."

"It didn't before."

"And the first Plains Indians didn't immediately come down with smallpox when they encountered Lewis and Clark, sir."

After a long pause, the Commanding Officer of the U.S.S. *Shenandoah* said, "Very well. You didn't disobey orders, because the orders weren't specific about this. However, the Executive Officer has reminded everyone of the highly classified nature of the information. If it does leak, the consequences could be serious. Naval prisons are *not* country clubs. Please keep that in mind."

Corry didn't say so, but he, too, had his cache of personal data hidden where no one but he could possibly find it. He'd acted with the same motivation as his crew: Someday in some part of the vast terrestrial ocean, he stood a very good chance of encountering these underwater aliens again. And he didn't want to rely only on personal memories if it happened.

So he brought the subject to a close. "We have our orders for this cruise. You've heard them. Now that we're under way in a submerged stealth mode, you may access the computer and read the orders for yourselves. I repeat what I said earlier: We're on a power projection and patrol mission. However, the world may be coming apart. We may find ourselves in a critical position to hold it together. Or we may have to put it back together before it self-destructs. That's one reason why we serve in the United States Navy. This service has a long historical tradition of doing just those things. Therefore, we will cruise submerged until we reach our destination. What happens then depends a lot on what happens above the surface of the South Pacific Ocean.

"But, much as we would like to do so, we're *not* being sent out to fish for underwater aliens."

He was wrong on several counts, but he had no way of knowing it then.

3

A second-generation United States Navy carrier submarine running submerged in stealth-cruise mode is for all intents and purposes not there at all. Its condensing-steam hydrojets provide silent thrust with no wake thermal signature. The hull hydrodynamics not only prevent cavitation and boundary layer turbulence but actually suppress the minor eddies created by the hydrojet wakes. Its highly-engineered composite outer "skin" is sonar stealthy to the extent that no sonars except those of the United States Navy itself are good enough to separate the ping return from the background ocean noise. Even the most sensitive MADs (Magnetic Anomaly Detectors) couldn't sense the ship because of its non-magnetic structure. A mass detector would sense the presence of its 58,700 ton mass, but only the SSCV's of the United States Navy were equipped with the new and highly classified masdets.

So the SSCV-26 U.S.S. *Shenandoah* was a 390-meter human-built sea monster that wasn't there.

Inside, the ship was quite real indeed. And it was a world unto itself. Night and day existed only as people needed normal twenty-four-hour cycles. Its internal lights were constantly bright except in those sections of the crew quarters where people were off watch and sleeping. Otherwise, the crew lived by the clock as they always had.

In a submarine, as in surface ships, the five daily four-hour watches and the two two-hour dog watches were the important time units. Hours were only subdivisions of watches. Human beings had been living in these kinds of artificial clock-paced environments for more than a hundred years. The lessons learned in the submarine service had been critical for the design and manning of the deep-space stations, where similar conditions prevailed. In turn, some of the lessons learned in deep-space habitats had submarine applications. But the submariners had been there first. And they were fiercely proud of it.

However, the U.S. Navy learned from the deep-spacers when it came to mixed-gender crews. Although women had served aboard ships of the British Royal Navy until 1846, the admirals of the United States Navy had stood firm against women aboard naval combat vessels for decades. They should have known better than to take firm stands against women doing anything. All those admirals were married. They just hadn't connected between the two worlds. Most wives don't hear the word "no," although they can say it.

So women slowly worked their way into critical positions and ratings. What had begun in the twentieth century didn't stop. When twenty-first century biotechnology at last allowed both men and women to exercise voluntary control over their hormones, the final barriers standing against mixed-gender crews finally came down. A century before, no one would have believed it possible.

In the wake of the infamous Tailhook scandal, learning how to handle that aspect of biotechnology hadn't been easy either for individual naval personnel or the Navy itself.

The old saying claimed that time heals all wounds. But CDR Terri Ellison's version of that was, "Time wounds all heels." She hadn't stood around whining about feminine equality. Long before her plebe year at the Naval Academy, she'd always done an outstanding job at anything she tackled or was assigned. She assumed that respect would follow. When it didn't, woe betide the man who demeaned her. She allowed time to do its job. She wasn't a militant feminist person, but a feminine military officer.

She was being very feminine the first "evening" out of Pearl.

And she was being feminine with one of her favorite masculine companions, CDR Zeke Braxton.

That included amorous activities but not always sexual ones. She enjoyed being a woman with a man because she liked the sort of men who were attracted to the Navy's submarine service. The same could be said for most women who served in submarines. The question of equality no longer existed. The men and women of the *Shenandoah* were equal but different. They liked the difference. They knew that men and women do indeed think and behave differently and this difference was usually more stress-relieving than stressful.

This also gave the United States Navy a unique approach to naval operations. The teaming of men and women in American naval vessels resulted in atypical offensive and defensive activities that adversaries had difficulty anticipating. Or understanding.

CDR Terri Ellison's quarters were small. They were as Spartan as any in the *Shenandoah*. However, no one could have mistaken them for anything but a woman's quarters. A naval officer and author in the previous century had observed that a woman wants a "better-upholstered cave." To some extent, he was right.

Three stuffed animal toys sat on the shelf above her desk. One was a comic tiger with "VA-65" embroidered on it. The other was a small black panther with white fangs, a boat with a broken keel in its mouth, and "VP-35" on its silver collar. Stuffed animals given as presents by squadron commanders who served with or under her were nothing new or unusual. The third was obviously much older, a battered, scuffed, and disreputable cat with golden wings and patches sewn here and there to cover up what might be wounds from alley fights.

A color holograph of a naval officer standing on the bridge of an old surface aircraft carrier stood in a frame on the desk. Terri looked like him.

Six gold naval aviator wings were in a deep frame hung on the bulkhead above her bunk where she could see them while lying down. Three of them were so old that the tarnish could no longer be removed from their surfaces. The names engraved on the brass plates under each of them all ended in "Ellison." The dates went back to the early twentieth century. Terri's first set of wings was last in the queue.

On the crisply made bunk lay a small red pillow bearing the arms of the United States Marine Corps and embroidered with the words, "For Talking with Bart."

Zeke knew the meaning and relevance of all of them to Terri. One had deeper meaning to him, however. It was a red silk rose in a clear plastic hollow cube with two holes drilled in its top surface. Sealed inside with the rose as one of Zeke's calling cards. On it was written, "When in trouble on the road to Hell, stop a spell and take a smell." He had given it to her to help her bleed off some of the stress of the Chilean operation when she'd shot down her second aircraft. The board of inquiry later decided she'd only responded to excessively aggressive overt actions and hadn't broken the rules of engagement or disobeyed orders.

Terri didn't break the rules except when she was in a fight. Then it became a matter of "Nice people don't always win, and I always win."

She wasn't in fighting mode that evening. Neither was Zeke. And neither of them wanted to break the rules because they were senior officers who had to set an example. Although Corry had suspended Naval Regulation 2020 during the cruise-out to the Solomons, both of them were tired after days of getting ready to put to sea on a mission they *knew* would be full of surprises. This was the first time either of them had had a chance to relax from their duties. So they just wanted to enjoy one another's company and talk.

This didn't prevent Terri from being provocative. She was often as aggressive in love as she was in war. Tonight, she wasn't in aggressor mode.

"That's a very fetching outfit, Alley Cat," Zeke told her as they finished the supper the red jacket had brought up from the wardroom.

Terri cocked her head so her blond curls fell down one side of her face. "I'm glad you like it. It's comfortable for relaxing." The glistening white silk of her oriental pajamas cascaded over her trim body like liquid metal. Except for the form hugging "speed jeans" of her tailored flight suits with their built-in anti-g bladders, Terri didn't affect body-hugging clothing while off duty. She was a small, trim woman and had the knack of choosing and wearing clothing that covered while also draping in such a manner that it hid very little.

"Relaxing? You look ready for a cat shot and Mach six," Zeke said lightly.

She smiled and took a sip of water from the glass on the dinner tray. Looking over the rim of the tumbler, she replied with just a touch of coyness in her voice, "Maybe. But I always eliminate the tiger error factor. Then I close fast."

"I've noticed."

She held up her arm and the silk rippled down from her wrist. "Bought it in Honolulu. Glad you like it. And it feels damned good. It's Chinese silk."

"Trading with the enemy, eh?"

"No, the enemy is providing aid and comfort to me." she sighed and put down the water tumbler. In a rare expression of frankness, Terri said wistfully, "Why the hell does East World have to threaten us all the time? They're decent people. At least, the Chinese submariners we met off Makasar were civilized. I sort of hate to blow away people who can make things like this. They don't have to be so mean and nasty to get along in the real world."

"True, but neither do we," Zeke reminded her. He was enjoying just watching her move and talk. "We're a militant society, too. And if East World wasn't making trouble, we'd both be out of a job."

"Oh, I could find work driving a commercial hypersonic or even a spaceship," Terri decided. She smiled, looked askance at him, and kidded him, "I don't doubt you could find a garbage scow to command."

Zeke didn't rise to the bait. He turned serious. "No, I'd mount an expedition to fish for Awesomes. It bothers the hell out of me that we made definite, documented contact with extraterrestrials. And, dammit, it's being ignored!"

"It bothers me, too," Terri admitted. "But I've got to let someone else worry about it. I've got this bird farm that keeps me busy."

"We might learn a lot from them."

Terri shrugged. "Maybe. Maybe not. Their ship outran

the *Shanna,* but I didn't see any technology that would impact my ability to aviate."

Zeke paused before he asked, "You mean you wouldn't like to have an aircraft that could operate on both sides of the air-water interface? And accelerate into space faster than your Sea Devils can climb in full boost with throttles through the gates?"

"Okay, it might be nice to launch submerged," she admitted. "But getting back for a trap might be sporty. Finding a submerged vessel still isn't easy. You haven't flown any patrols with the Black Panthers lately."

"So we'll put masdets in the Ospreys."

"And give them hernias in the process?"

"Well, a hundred years ago the first radars wouldn't even fit in a ship the size of the *Shanna,*" Zeke said. "How many different types of radars to your chickens carry, and sometimes four or five in a single airframe?"

Terri snorted. "Too many. And they're small. Even my LSOs have hand-helds that let them check speed of aircraft coming into trap."

She paused for a long moment, then admitted to Zeke, "I've issued orders to all my flight crews to watch for *Tuscaroras.*"

Terri Ellison had used the slang term adopted by the *Shenandoah*'s crew to refer to an alien submarine-aircraft-spacecraft that they'd seen and photographed in the Makasar Straits. It was apropos. In the U.S. Navy, the U.S.S. *Tuscarora* is an imaginary ship that never makes port when you're there. Other naval personnel claim to have actually seem it or served aboard it. Usually, the U.S.S. *Tuscarora* departed the day before your ship entered port.

Zeke didn't respond at once. Finally he said, "Good! I'm glad you told me. Please keep me informed."

"I don't keep secrets from you," Terri responded quickly.

"I hope not. I don't keep them from you."

"Good! Care to tell me about the good time you and Natalie Chase had on Waikiki while we were at Pearl?"

"Not unless you reciprocate with details of your shore leave with Bart on Maui."

"Let me just say I was engaged in comparison testing."

"Oh? Between me and Bart?"

"Not necessarily. The differences between you and Bart Clinch are so obvious that I don't require a lot of comparison testing."

"I hope not!"

"Well, don't get the idea that you're Number One." Zeke grinned. "I'm here tonight."

"But maybe not tomorrow night."

"Would it help to properly initiate those silk pajamas? Harriett Gordon likes to do needlework to pass the time on a cruise. I could get her to embroider the Three Dolphin insignia on them tomorrow."

Terri leaned forward, put her elbows on the small table, and rested her chin in her hands. Looking directly at him, she said intensely, "Commander, if you really think you're up to it, I'd almost be willing to give it a try just to find out if you're right or not."

"Would you?"

She sighed. "Not really. I hit bingo fuel about two hours ago, Zeke."

He grinned. "So did I. But we could turn the cabin temperature down and keep one another warm."

"That might be fun. But you know what would happen—"

They didn't have to wait. It happened then.

The sound of the intercom wasn't intended to be pleasant. Its purpose was to wake the dead, if necessary. Terri often compared it to the sound of fingernails scraping on glass. Zeke didn't like to mention what it sounded like to him.

"CAG here!" Terri called out because it was her intercom unit.

"CAG, this is OOD, Lieutenant Brewer, on deck," the reply came. "Is the XO there?"

Barbara Brewer, the radar/lidar officer, certainly knew where to call for Zeke when his intercom in quarters wasn't answered.

"XO here. Go ahead, Lieutenant," Zeke spoke up.

"I need to inform you that Lieutenant Atwater reports an SWC message coming in from Pearl, sir."

The Navy's super-secret Scalar Wave Communications system was a surefire stealthy way to contact a submerged submarine also in stealth. Although the message couldn't be received or even detected without SWC equipment, its existence was so sensitive that the admirals used it only for high-priority can't-wait communications.

That always meant an SWC message was important.

"On my way to the bridge! XO out!" Zeke responded and started to rise from the little table.

Terri was already on her feet. "I'll be there as quickly as I can change into uniform."

"Not necessary for you to come," Zeke reminded her.

"Maybe not," she shot back, "but any SWC message could mean my chickens have to leave the coop. If that's going to happen, I damned well want to know as far in advance as possible! Go do your job, XO! I'll be right there to do mine!"

He knew she would.

Terri's cabin was farther from the bridge than his, which was almost as nearby as the Captain's. It didn't surprise Zeke to find Corry on the bridge when he got there. Nor did Corry reprimand his XO for arriving a few seconds after he did.

Zeke checked the telltales on the bridge bulkhead. The U.S.S. *Shenandoah* had been under way for seven hours and was 487 kilometers southwest of Pearl Harbor. The course screen showed the ship's present position, while another showed the bottom underneath. The ship's cruising depth of 150 meters ensured plenty of sea beneath her. The sensor scans, including the masdet pixel array, showed only targets that the standing watches in Sonar and Special Sensors had identified and labeled as "natural."

"Good evening, XO."

"Good evening, Captain."

Corry keyed the panel before his station. "The SWC message has concluded and it's in the computer," he observed. "Call it up on your screen."

The message had come through uncoded and unciphered. It was possible to broadcast in the clear on SWC, especially this close to Pearl.

SWC Transmission 24-04-44 from CINCPAC to CO SSCV-26. Subject: Amendment to Execute Order 07-32-47N designated 07-32-47N-A. By direction of the Secretary of Defense. SSCV-26 Shenandoah will proceed to Johnston Atoll and stand by to surface on command from CINCPAC to recover C-26 Sea Dragon carrying special projects team operation code Second Contact. Report ETA Johnston ASAP via SWC. Report arrival vicinity Johnston. Monitor SWC. Expect further orders at Johnston. Carry out DOD Execute Order 07-32-47N-A. 1ST Ind. Forwarded Kane CINCPAC. End message. End message. End message.

"Will we have to feed that Dragon?" Terri asked. She'd quietly slipped into her bridge position and was scanning the message on her screen.

"I don't know," Zeke admitted. "Doesn't say. Any problem if it needs refueling?"

"Only that it cuts into our fuel reserve. Let's hope we don't have to. A Sea Dragon has more than enough range to make it round trip to Johnston from Pearl."

"You assume it comes from Pearl," Zeke said.

"No other place it can originate. Doesn't have the range to get to Johnston from anywhere else in these parts. Remember: We're in the Earth's water hemisphere."

"Thanks for reminding me." Zeke looked at the hard copy again and then asked Corry, "What does this really mean, Captain?"

Corry shook his head slowly. "I don't know, Zeke. Surprise, surprise again. Whatever it is, we'll be ready to do it." He touched his N-fone behind his right ear. *Navigator, this is CO.*

Navigator here. GA, sir. LT Marcella Zar was on duty.

Plot a course, present position to Johnston Island.

Aye, aye, sir!

The days of laborious plotting on a chart board were long past. Zar keyed her computer terminal.

"PRESENT POSITION TO JOHNSTON ISLAND: STEER 278 DEGREES TRUE. DISTANCE 507 KM. TER 6 HR 50 MIN," the navigational computer reported on its telltale screen after spending 720 picoseconds

checking the ship's three internal inertial positioning systems, comparing the result with long-wave satellite positioning system data, and triple-checking the calculations.

XO, steer for Johnston. On arriving vicinity of destination, remain submerged. Report arrival, Corry said curtly.

Aye, aye, sir! Officer of the deck, steer course to Johnston Island. Come to a heading of two-seven-eight degrees. Maintain forty knots. Steady bubble.

Aye aye, sir! Come to heading of two-seven-eight. Maintain forty knots and a steady bubble, LT Barbara Brewer repeated back to Zeke.

Corry got up. He was used to having orders changed. He didn't know why the boat was being ordered to take on this "special projects team." Whoever was in charge of the contingent would undoubtedly be carrying new orders. In the meantime, he wouldn't fret about it because he could do nothing anyway. So he told his senior officers, "I suggest we all try to get a little sleep. We'll be recovering that Sea Dragon around dawn, if CINC-PAC tells us no East World recon satellites are over our horizon. That means fast action on our part. Terri, be ready to trap and turnaround quickly. I suspect we'll be on the surface only long enough to take this special projects team off the aircraft."

"We'll be ready, sir," Terri assured him.

"This cruise gets stranger by the minute," Zeke ventured to say.

"It could get even more so before we're through, whatever we're being sent out to *really* do!" the Captain of the U.S.S. *Shenandoah* guessed.

4

It's raining hard up here, CDR Terri Ellison reported from PRIFLY.

Roger that, CDR Zeke Braxton replied. They'd surfaced at Johnston Island in the rain shield of tropical storm Evan. *How's the visibility?*

If Natalie is right and we're five klicks off Johnston, we've got an estimated three klicks with five klicks between rain squalls. The sea gulls are walking, the CAG of the U.S.S. *Shenandoah* said via N-fone.

Do you have a visual on Contact Deuce yet?

Negatory!

XO, this is Radar. We have just received a single pulse with IFF modulation, came the call from LT Barbara Brewer in the radar room. *IFF code is seven-seven-zero-three. Bearing zero-eight-eight true. Assuming the pulse came from an APS-six-oh-four on a C-two-six, computer analysis of signal strength gives range estimate of twenty-two klicks.*

Thank you, Radar, Zeke replied.

Radar, CAG. I read your bogey on my repeater, Terri's N-fone "voice" came in. *We're looking. No joy.*

"This could be tight, Captain," Zeke said.

Corry was watching his screens. Long ago, he'd learned not to rely on a single report or datum point. So confirmation by "calibrated eyeballs" and other sensors was always welcome. "We have twenty-three minutes of surface time left. Let's see if we pick up another pulse, XO. That will give us a reading on closing speed."

XO, Radar. Another pulse. Bearing zero-eight-five. Range estimated one-seven klicks. The transmitter has just gone to three-pulse bursts.

"He's seen us," Zeke surmised. The C-26 Sea Dragon's pilot apparently had gotten two solid returns from the

Shenandoah's retractable island. So he'd switched to pulse bursts to get a more accurate reading of the closing rate.

LSO is initiating strobes, Terri reported.

XO, we have a lasercom signal, bearing zero-eight-five, the voice of LT Ed Atwater, the Communications Officer, came through the N-phone transducer behind Zeke's ear, sending an electronic signal directly to his auditory nerve.

Patch it up on verbose, Zeke told him.

"Star Ship, this is Contact Deuce. Distance eight klicks. Bearing zero-eight-five. Your strobes are in sight."

"Contact Deuce, Star Ship LSO, give us a light."

"Our lights are on *now.*"

"Contact Deuce, Star Ship LSO. I have you in sight. Cleared to land, area Bravo Two, rear flight deck. Ship is making eight knots in a following sea. Wind on deck one-four on the bow. Sea state Hotel One." The Landing Signal Officer gave the Sea Dragon pilot the information needed to help him land the cargo aircraft. The rest was now up to the pilot.

The PRIFLY videocamera was now centered on a bright pair of flashing white strobe lights.

The screen before Zeke flashed, *"19 minutes."*

"How many people to get off the Dragon, sir?"

"Five," Corry replied tersely.

"Captain, we probably have more time than nineteen minutes, and we may need it to debark five and their baggage. We've got maybe another ten minutes," Zeke reminded his commanding officer. "We're thermally stealthed. In these rain squalls, no East World surveillance satellite is going to get anything more than a smeared image of us at a very low angle through lots of atmosphere. When it dumps its data on the next pass over Asia, this will indicate only that something was north of Johnston."

"XO, my orders are to operate in stealth. It's bad enough we have to surface to pick up this team. Anytime we break the air-water interface, we've set ourselves up for detection," Corry muttered darkly. "We'll dive in eighteen minutes. The Sea Dragon could be blooming on someone's passive radar right now."

"Sir, even the masdet shows nothing within several hundred klicks except the skimmers we've been tracking since we dived off Pearl yesterday. And we got i-d confirmation on those from CINCPAC intel before we dived."

Corry sighed. "Zeke, someday you'll have a sea command. One of the reasons a heavy command isn't given to young officers is that they must learn caution. They must learn to refrain from making unwarranted assumptions on the basis of insufficient data. It comes only from experience. Yes, I've been guilty of breaking my own rule in this regard. But I did it only when the positives outweighed the negatives." He paused. "Since we don't know exactly what we're getting into here, I intend to be extra cautious."

Zeke nodded. "Yes, sir. I can appreciate that. I had only a moment to glance at that SWC message before I had to do something about it. I don't recall that it said anything about a possible change in mission."

"XO, always read orders carefully. Very carefully. Often hidden meanings lurk beneath the otherwise commonplace terminology of orders," Corry advised him in gentle tones. The Captain of the U.S.S. *Shenandoah* knew that an important part of his job was to train promising officers for future command. Zeke was one of those people who had the aptitude and background. Furthermore, he knew that Zeke ached for command. However, the man needed a bit more seasoning. And Corry believed he could help him get it. "You've got a few minutes now. To be exact, fourteen minutes before we have to dive. So pull up that SWC message on your screen and read it. Carefully."

Zeke shot a quick glance at the video screen, being cautious as Corry had just advised. He wanted to be sure everything was copasetic topside. The camera in PRIFLY revealed a scene that was nearly white-on-white. The C-26 Sea Dragon in its low-contrast color scheme blended with the off-white of the scudding rain clouds. The approach looked notional to him. Air Group's people had the Sea Dragon in sight and were on the job. So he followed Corry's gentle advice and pulled up the SWC message.

SWC Transmission 25-04-44 from CINCPAC to CO SSCV-26. Subject: Addition to DOD Execute Order 07-32-47N-A. By direction of the Secretary of Defense. SSCV-26 Shenandoah will surface five kilometers north of Johnston Atoll at 1732Z and stand by to recover C-26 Sea Dragon code Contact Deuce. IFF squawk 7703. Special Projects team will debark Contact Deuce. SSCV-26 Shenandoah must dive no later than 1759Z Special team members: CDR M. H. Smith USN, LCDR C. G. Zervas USNMC, Dr. E. Lulalilo NSF, Dr. B. W. Duvall NOAA, and A. H. Soucek Majestic Corporation. CDR Smith carries additional orders for CO SSCV-26. DOD Execute Order 07-32-47N-A, Addition 1. 1ST Ind. Forwarded Kane CINC-PAC. End message. End message. End message.

Zeke quickly turned to his dedicated terminal and queried the data base of the ship's computer. This was something he did routinely when new officers and rates reported aboard. He accessed the personnel file for CDR M. H. Smith.

He wasn't surprised at what flashed on the computer screen.

"Smith, Matilda Harriet, 523-36-8453. Office of Naval Intelligence. Further personnel records privileged.

He looked up LCDR Zervas and discovered the man was an M.D. specializing in cellular biology research at Bethesda Naval Hospital.

But the ship's computer couldn't access personnel files beyond those of people serving in the armed forces. So Zeke could glean no additional information about Dr. Lulalilo of the National Science Foundation, Dr. Duval of the National Oceanic and Atmospheric Administration, or A. H. Soucek of Majestic Corporation. He'd never heard of Majestic Corporation. This wasn't unusual because thousands of consulting firms and think tanks existed in the national capital area. Majestic Corporation could be one of those. When he queried the Standard & Poor's data base in the ship's computer about Majestic Corporation, the screen told him, *"Search unsuccessful. Push* ENTER *key to return to menu."*

Well, he'd learn soon enough, he told himself and cleared the screen.

Then the realization hit him. These people were scientists and they were accompanied by an officer from

Naval Intelligence. The mix was interesting—a cellular biologist, someone from NSF, and another from NOAA. Plus an unknown, A. H. Soucek.

"Captain," Zeke finally ventured to admit to his CO, "judging from the organizations these people represent, I wouldn't be a bit surprised that our mission has indeed changed."

Corry just raised an eyebrow. "Oh? Speculating again, Zeke?"

"Yes, sir."

"And?"

"We're taking aboard an exploration team, and we're going fishing for Awesomes."

"That's crossed my mind, XO." Corry watched the video screen that showed the Sea Dragon touching down on the aft upper flight deck. It wasn't a smooth landing. In sea state Hotel One, the *Shenandoah* was being hammered by waves. The huge ship was both rolling and pitching in a complex combination of motions. He knew he might have some seasick visitors on his hands. And he wanted to dive and get back to the smooth cruising at 150 meters.

Five people erupted from the aft ramp of the Sea Dragon. They were hunched against the driving rain. All of them were carrying or dragging containers. LT Paul "Duke" Peyton didn't waste any time. He and a dozen of his flight deck crew were at the C-26 immediately. Some helped the five passengers across the wet deck. Others became instant baggage handlers.

"Contact Deuce, Star Ship LSO. Need a top-off?"

"Negatory, Star Ship. We won't even ask you to clean the windshield. Wouldn't do any good in this rain anyway. Let me know when you're clear. I've got to get out of here ASAP and back to Pearl."

"Hot date tonight?"

"You got it, Star Ship! Half-price Happy Hour at the Club tonight! Time, tide, and companionship wait for no one!"

"Contact Deuce, you're clear. Ready for departure?"

"Contact Deuce is ready for liftoff."

"Contact Deuce, Star Ship LSO. You are cleared for takeoff. Climb to maintain your assigned altitude. Assume your return course heading."

"Roger, Star Ship. Good luck!"

"Fly low and slow."

As the videocamera showed the Sea Dragon lifting clear of the aft upper flight deck, Corry checked his telltales. *XO, clear the aft upper flight deck. Close watertight doors. Prepare to dive. We've got a twenty-fathom bottom. Dive to bottom. We're going to lay there until we learn what our new orders are.*

Aye aye, sir. Prepare to dive. When ready to dive, come to the bottom at twenty fathoms and maintain position.

Corry stood up and verbally told his Executive Officer, "Have Lieutenant Strader and Chief Armstrong escort our guests to the main wardroom. Commander Lovette is OOD, correct?"

"Correct, sir."

"Ask him to relinquish the conn to his JOOD. I'd like him to come to the main wardroom, too. Ask Commander Moore, Major Clinch, and Lieutenant Berger to join me there as well. When the CAG has secured her division and you've got the ship on the bottom, I'd like the two of you to come to the main wardroom, too."

"Aye, aye, sir."

Submariners rarely got wet except if caught topside without foul-weather gear in the rain when the boat surfaced. The five people who had arrived via Sea Dragon didn't have weather gear and indeed they looked like they'd been caught in the rain. This was in sharp contrast to the crisp, dry appearance of the officers of the U.S.S. *Shenandoah* in the main wardroom.

And the visitors weren't used to being in a submarine. It was obvious to Corry from the way they moved and their confused looks. They behaved like new officers and rates just arrived at New London for submarine training. Corry knew he'd have to spend some time acquainting these people with the niceties of living in a submarine.

In spite of the fact that she was wet, CDR M. H. Smith was a striking woman. Tall, statuesque, and mid-thirtyish, she had a no-nonsense look about her in spite of her black hair hanging wetly to her shoulders. She hadn't served at sea. Otherwise, she would have worn her hair in a shorter style that was far easier to manage and care for under shipboard conditions.

She was nearly as tall as Corry. He stepped up to her and extended his hand. She didn't salute; they were under cover. "Welcome aboard, Commander Smith. I'm Captain William Corry."

"Yes, I know," she replied bluntly. But there was a twinkle in her eyes as she went on, "We spooks pride ourselves in giving the impression we know everything that's happening around us."

That caught Corry off guard, so he replied in his characteristic brief fashion, "Yes." He started to introduce himself to the others when Smith did it for him instead.

"Captain, this is Doctor Evelyn Lulalilo. She was sent by the National Science Foundation." Smith indicated the short, dark-haired woman with Eurasian features. Corry noted that if Dr. Lulalilo would pay some attention to her appearance, she would also be a pretty woman in a way quite different from CDR Smith. Perhaps she was only showing the stress of a long journey and being caught in the rain.

"Doctor," Corry responded, taking her proffered hand. "And what is your specialty?"

"I'm a marine biologist," the scientist replied. "It comes from being born and raised in Hawaii."

"Oh? So was I. Oahu?" Corry questioned her.

She shook her head. Her wet, black hair was still plastered against her skull. "Maui," she replied curtly. Corry got the impression Dr. Lulalilo was awed by her surroundings and the officers of the *Shenandoah*. He was wrong, but he didn't find that out until later.

"Lovely island," Corry remarked politely.

"And this is Doctor Zervas," Smith went on.

LCDR Constantine G. Zervas, U.S. Naval Medical Department, was a small man with flashing dark eyes set deep and narrow on his face. He acted in an animated manner, although he looked weary. After he shook hands with Corry, he put in bluntly, "Captain, to anticipate your question, I'm the officer at Bethesda who's in charge of the frozen underwater alien carcass you returned from Sulawesi."

The purpose of this special team was beginning to fall into place. Corry hadn't wished to air his speculations, but Zeke had been right. "Really? Commander Braxton here was the one who shot it, and Doctor Moore took charge thereafter. I suspect you'll have a lot to talk about."

"Perhaps," Zervas replied briefly. It seemed he wanted to establish his turf right from the beginning. Otherwise, he was acting in a guarded fashion. "I read the reports. Do they know something that wasn't included? Or that wasn't revealed in the debriefings?"

"Not at all, Doctor," Corry interjected. "However we weren't encouraged to include speculation."

"Obviously, you've speculated privately?"

"It's difficult not to do so."

Smith took charge again. "This is Doctor Barry Duval, an oceanographer from NOAA."

The tall, blond-haired man had a thin face, a long aquiline nose, and an indifferent manner as he shook hands with Corry. "Yes, I presume you've been sent to advise us on bottom, currents, and temperature gradients in the Solomon Islands while the rest of your team hunts for Awesomes?" Corry wanted to get right at the heart of the team's assignment.

"Excuse me, Captain? Awesomes?" Duval asked.

"Our shipboard phonetic rendering of the acronym for Alien Underwater Sea Monster, A-U-S-M," Corry explained.

"Oh. Well, I haven't read the actual reports. I had time only to skim the abstracts. Forty-eight hours ago, I was vacationing off the Maine coast. Alien underwater monsters were the farthest things from my mind. In fact, their existence is so highly classified that I hadn't known of them at all until I was briefed by Mister Soucek on the flight from Washington," Duval admitted.

"I see."

"And the final member of the team, Allan Soucek of Majestic Corporation," CDR Smith introduced the fifth person.

Soucek had what Corry called one of the five "universal faces." In a crowd, he wouldn't have been obvious at all.

"And your area of expertise, Mister Soucek?" Corry inquired.

Diffidently and somewhat defensively, Soucek responded, "I'll assemble the data."

"So you're the tech writer for this team?"

Soucek shook his head. "No, I'm a synthesist."

"I see," Corry said, but he didn't understand the man. So he asked, "I'm not familiar with Majestic Corporation."

"We're a Washington-area consulting firm. We work for a variety of government agencies, especially when several agencies are tasked to work together on a given project. Our job is to even out the emphasis in the documentation so the information from all representatives of different agencies is given proper weighting."

"I take it, then, that such work requires some expertise in the task area?"

Again, Soucek nodded. Corry noted that the man appeared to be frightened. He acted furtively, and his eyes kept flicking around the wardroom. The man was uncomfortable. Perhaps it was airsickness or seasickness. Perhaps it was only the strange surroundings.

Corry didn't know the man, so he decided he might be wrong. He asked, "So Majestic Corporation has some expertise in extraterrestrial alien affairs?"

"Yes. It's highly compartmentalized security information. I'll have more to say in my classified briefing." The curt reply was all that Soucek was apparently willing to say at the moment.

Soucek's remark put the final brick into Corry's speculations about the purpose of the "special team" and also gave a rationale for why the DOD Execute Order and its subsequent amendments had been given as they had.

The U.S.S. *Shenandoah* was indeed going to fish for Awesomes.

But no one except the highest levels of the federal government knew it.

Corry wondered why the United States government apparently was scared about all this. Why was it classified above normal classification?

And what bearing would it have on the growing international crisis?

Corry wanted answers. Looking around the wardroom, he saw that his senior officers did, too.

He decided he'd get the answers as quickly as he could.

But he carried out protocol first. He introduced his officers. When he got to Chief Armstrong, he told the special team, "Chief Armstrong is the Chief of the Boat. He's my primary channel to the noncommissioned members of the crew. If you can't find me or Commander Braxton, Chief Armstrong can help you. Right now, Lieutenant Berger and Chief Armstrong will show you to your quarters so you can get into dry clothing. We'll reconvene here in one hour. Breakfast will be served then."

"Captain, I have hard-copy orders to deliver to you," CDR Smith said. She didn't like the delay.

Corry noticed that. "Are they time-sensitive, Commander?"

"No, but the sooner you're aware of them and we get under way, the better."

"Then give them to me now. I'll read them while you're getting settled in," Corry told her, extending his hand.

"Captain, I . . . uh . . . I would prefer briefing you as well."

Corry didn't withdraw his hand. "I see. Let me have them to read. I'll also let my officers read them. Then you can brief us during breakfast in one hour."

"Captain, these are so sensitive that they're hand-carried."

"And, Commander, you're in a carrier submarine lying on the bottom of the Pacific Ocean off Johnston Atoll," the Commanding Officer reminded her. "This is a *very* secure environment. While my officers and I are studying these orders, you and the special team can shuck those wet travel clothes, take a hot shower, and get into fresh, dry clothing. You'll feel better when you do. Those are standing orders for anyone in the *Shenandoah* who has been topside and gotten wet as a result."

He decided he'd try a little humor on her, as she had on him. "We submariners are a strange lot, Commander. We spend most of our service lives underwater, but we don't like to be wet!"

CDR Smith reached into her shoulder bag, extracted a long envelope, and handed it to Corry. The suggestion of a smile played around the corners of her broad mouth. "Neither do I, sir," she admitted.

"Lieutenant Berger, Chief Armstrong, please show these people to quarters and bring them back in an hour."

5

After the special team left, CAPT William Corry opened the sealed envelope in an old-fashioned manner. He tore off one end of it, blew into the envelope, and extracted the folded hard copy inside.

For the first time in his naval career, he stared at a handwritten order.

It was on the personal letterhead of the CNO, ADM George L. Street. Corry had been a plebe under Street at the Naval Academy and had served with him in the U.S.S. *Gilmore*.

"Zeke, please get Lovette, Walton, Chase, and Stocker here," he told his XO, then addressed his officers, "I presume most of you can still read handwriting. In any event, Admiral Street's is remarkably legible. Please read it with me."

Without hesitation, because Corry always shared orders with his subordinates when possible, he slipped the unfolded sheet into the slot of the document converter on the bulkhead behind him. The ship's computer scanned it, put the contents in memory, and projected the document in its handwritten form on the wardroom's screen behind Corry, who turned to see it.

Following the headings, it read:

Subject: Change of orders
1. JCS Execute Order 07-32-47N is hereby changed by this Amendment B. Copies may be placed in the ship's computer memory, but no copies exist in other places.
2. CO SSCV-26 U.S.S. *Shenandoah* will accommodate the five persons of the special team that carries this order.
3. SSCV-26 U.S.S. *Shenandoah* will proceed under stealth conditions to the Solomon Islands, South Pacific Ocean.

4. The overt mission is to maintain U.S. presence in southwest Pacific area during the current international crisis. However, the covert mission is to capture one or more underwater aliens and return it alive to Pearl Harbor.

5. Naval Intelligence representative will brief you on international aspects of this mission. Naval Medical Service officer will be responsible for maintaining the live alien or aliens when captured. NSF representative will attempt to establish communications with alien. NOAA representative has latest information on ocean conditions. Majestic Corporation representative will provide background information, including latest data on alien activities.

6. This mission has the highest possible security level. It is known only to two persons in the White House and the National Security Council. No data base or other written records exist. Act accordingly. Communications security will be maintained. Monitor SWC for additional information but do not transmit. Report only on completion of mission and ETA of return to ZI with alien.

/s/ George L. Street

At the bottom was a personal note: "Bill, only a submariner could give such an open order to another submariner. And only submariners could figure out how to pull this off alone with minimum guidance from above. As verification of this document, I'm sure you remember, 'Sir, you can't control by backing!' Good luck and good hunting! — G.L.S."

The officers of the U.S.S. *Shenandoah* were subdued in their responses.

"Capture an Awesome! Well, that's what we wanted to do in the first place!" Terri Ellison put in.

"The PTB had to make it complicated first," Laura Raye Moore pointed out.

"Took long enough for them to get around to it!" Bart Clinch growled.

LCDR Mark Walton and the others showed up, sat down, and read the projected orders. "Sir, what about control by backing?" the ship's First Lieutenant asked.

Corry reddened briefly, then told him firmly, "A private incident from the past, Commander. But it verifies the order was written by Admiral Street because only the two of us could possibly have remembered it. And I intend to leave it at that."

Walton didn't press it. He had skeletons in his closet, too. So did everyone aboard. They'd made mistakes in their naval careers. Most remembered them well because they'd become better officers as a result. But they hoped other people had forgotten.

The revelation of an embarrassing mistake reinforced the officers' belief that Corry was one of them. He was the CO but also a human being who'd made and learned from stupid but non-lethal mistakes.

Few mistakes in the submarine service are non-lethal.

"Navigator, what's the bottom in the Solomons area?" Corry asked Natalie Chase.

She thought about this for a moment before answering, "On the Solomons tectonic plate, the bottoms range from shoal waters to about a thousand fathoms. In the Solomon Sea west of Bougainville, the Solomon Basin goes down to about five thousand fathoms. The area is tectonically active. Earthquakes and seaquakes are common. So are volcanoes, fumaroles, and other geothermal features. The region is part of the so-called 'ring of fire' that circles the Pacific Ocean."

Corry turned to his operations officer. "Mister Lovette, the Navy's submarines have operated in those waters for more than a century. Please recover this operational data from the ship's computer and transfer it to a macro for rapid access." Corry knew Lovette would put LTJG Ralph Strader, the Intelligence Officer, on the job right away.

"Aye, aye, sir."

Zeke realized that Corry was slowly formulating an operational plan in his mind. The Captain was asking questions and giving orders that would provide him with information. The Executive Officer knew that an open-ended order such as the one still displayed on the screen was extremely difficult to carry out. This was particularly true considering the paucity of information in hand. Specific orders were easy in comparison because they *were* specific: "Go there, then do this on this time schedule under these rules of engagement and against this background information." But the handwritten order was broad, general, non-specific, without time limits, and stated only a goal.

But the Executive Officer had noticed something else about the order. "Captain, are we to presume that this special team is only advisory and not in charge of this mission?"

"Yes," Corry replied with only his normal hesitation while he formulated his words. "None of the orders or amendments received so far has indicated to me that someone else is in command of the mission. Perhaps a member of the special team has some other ideas, but they aren't reflected in my orders."

"So you're running the show, sir?" Terri Ellison asked. Perhaps it was an unnecessary question, but by asking it she would get an unambiguous reply.

"I am. As you can surmise, my big problem is determining how to carry out these orders."

"Well, Captain, we didn't know how to hunt for Awesomes when we went to Makasar, either." Zeke pointed out. "We knew only that American and other visitors to Sulawesi were disappearing. We lucked onto the Awesomes when we went scuba diving on liberty. Are we being sent to the Solomons because people have been disappearing there, too?"

"I don't know, XO. When the special team returns in a few minutes, we may get the answer to that."

"And a lot of other answers, too, I hope." Zeke remembered their first action with Awesomes off Sulawesi. So he added, "It might be a mistake if we operated on the assumption that all the Awesomes were fishing for humans. It looked like we ran into two groups of Awesomes: one fishing for humans and the other being game wardens. At least, they acted that way."

"We only know that one contingent was friendly and the other one definitely was *not*," Natalie Chase added. She'd been snared by an Awesome underwater trap while scuba diving.

"Damned right they weren't friendly!" Bart Clinch snapped. "They injured some of my Marines during that last fight in the rocks off the beach. Those blue beasts were *not* happy fish!"

"They aren't fish," Laura Raye Moore put in. The Medical Officer had spent a lot of time studying the frozen carcass of the captured Awesome until it had been taken away from her at Pearl Harbor. "Semi-mammalian, maybe. But the one I studied didn't belong to any terrestrial phylum. It was alien, period. And fascinating."

Corry let his officers talk. He couldn't do much until the special team reported back to the wardroom. He looked at his watch and turned to Zeke. "Mister Vice," he addressed the XO who was also vice president of the officer's mess, "although it's only oh-six-hundred, could you ask the chief steward to serve breakfast early? Say, in a few minutes?"

"I'll see to it, Captain. How about the special team?"

"They'll be back here shortly. I suspect they haven't eaten since Pearl, and maybe not then. And their circadian rhythms are all out of synch with ours." Corry paused, then added, "Nothing like a hot breakfast to help remedy that. In the meantime, mugs up. I'd like some hot, black coffee, please. This could be a long day."

Dr. Evelyn Lulalilo was the first member of the team to return to the wardroom. She went immediately to Corry, who motioned her to take the chair on his right at the table. "Thank you, Captain. Is that breakfast I smell?" she asked pleasantly.

Corry nodded and said, "A good, hot breakfast does wonders for jet lag."

She smiled shyly. "Fortunately, I don't have the same problem as other members of the team. I had only to get to Pearl Harbor from the Aquatic Mammal Research Institute on Kauai. A short plane ride last night. However, I had little chance to sleep before boarding the airplane for the flight to this ship."

Evelyn Lulalilo was a woman who possessed natural beauty but seemed not to care. The Captain was a gentleman, so he asked his Engineer Officer, "Mister Stocker, would you be kind enough to get a breakfast tray for Doctor Lulalilo, please?"

Stocker normally didn't take notice of much of anything except his machinery, but he'd been distracted by Evelyn Lulalilo. Corry had noted that, which is why he'd asked the Engineer Officer. It served to remind Stocker that he was more than just an engineer; he was, by act of Congress, an officer and a gentleman. Corry's request galvanized him into action. "Aye, aye, sir!"

Corry noted that Dr. Lulalilo had refreshed herself with remarkable speed. "May I compliment you on your quick job of drying off and getting into fresh clothes?"

"Thank you, Captain. I swim with dolphins several times a day. I've learned to become a dry land animal in a hurry," she explained.

"So," Corry replied in his typical brief manner. "Do you expect to swim with Awesomes on this trip?"

"Awesomes?"

Corry explained the derivation of the name.

"Yes, they are awesome. At least, they seem that way, judging from the photos I've seen. I can't wait to meet one."

"Doctor Lulalilo, some of my officers have met Awesomes in the water. They may not be as charitable or scientific as you when it comes to thinking of Awesomes as friendly," Corry told her, pouring her a cup of coffee.

"Captain, the use of my formal honorific may be proper protocol, but I think it's a bit pretentious. Please call me Eve."

Corry nodded. "As you wish, Eve. How long have you been planning for this mission?"

"Planning?" She gave a little laugh. "Yesterday at this time, I was looking forward to spending several weeks working with my brightest dolphin friend. We were making some progress in communicating with one another. When I got back to the office, Brad popped this on me and told me the National Science Advisor wanted me to go on this scientific expedition. I didn't learn what it involved until Commander Smith briefed me at Pearl Harbor late last night. Or maybe it was early this morning."

"It's my understanding that you're representing the National Science Foundation." Corry got the fleeting impression that Evelyn Lulalilo was very much like his wife in the way she moved and acted. Certainly, her body language was similar. LTJG Judith Corry had taken on a formidable career, just as Dr. Evelyn Lulalilo had. Corry liked Evelyn Lulalilo.

She shook her head, her short black hair barely moving. "No, I think NSF is funding me. I don't know. Frankly, when funding comes in an unsolicited package, I'm delighted to accept it. This is a dream project. I can be a *scientist*. I don't know how much money is involved, so I don't have a budget to restrict my activities. I don't know what the answers are going to be, so I can ask anything of the universe without being considered stupid by my peers. In fact, it's refreshing to work on something where I *don't* know the answers in advance. In that regard, Captain, modern scientists have strayed from the principles of the patronized scientist of old."

"I'm afraid I don't understand the workings of the scientific community, Eve," Corry admitted.

"Oh? Well, scientists in every age have always had to work with the financial support of patrons," she explained. "Kings, companies, wealthy dilettantes, or governments, they were all the same. A very large percentage of my time—and it's the same for most scientists—involves searching for financial support, writing grant proposals, and producing reports to prove I've actually spent the money properly. Captain, I'm really two persons. Basically, I search for the answer to the question 'why.' The other side of me is a beggar who goes from door to door seeking means to carry on my hobby. I'm forced to do the latter so I can be what I am. But I really don't consider it a hobby any more than you consider that your hobby is commanding a carrier submarine."

"No, but it's what I want to do," Corry confided. "You'll discover that everyone is aboard because they want to be. Submariners are like that."

CDR Ray Stocker set a breakfast tray before her. On it was a steaming cup of black coffee. she looked up at him and smiled. "Thank, you, but do you have some tea?"

"I think we do," Stocker replied, somewhat taken aback. Then the Engineer Officer realized that the lovely young woman wasn't aware of the life-style of submariners. So he explained, "Doctor, in a carrier submarine or any other Navy ship, you're going to find coffee but perhaps not tea."

"Oh? Why?" Lulalilo didn't take things for granted. Her career involved asking questions.

"I don't know, ma'am," Stocker replied.

"It's a custom that dates back to the late nineteenth century," Corry explained, calling upon his knowledge of naval history. "The United States Navy's roots go back to the British Royal Navy. Jack Tar counted on his daily ration of grog, which is rum diluted with water. In the United States, the temperance movement forced the Navy to forgo alcoholic beverages aboard ship. So the Navy substituted coffee for grog."

"Fascinating!" Lulalilo said brightly. "We have so many human traditions! It would be wonderful to learn the traditions of dolphins. Or the Awesomes."

"You presume the Awesomes have a culture," Corry remarked.

"Oh, they do! They must! But it's probably nothing like human culture. I'm not even sure we'd recognize it as such when we first encounter it! In fact, you may have encountered it already and not realized it. I certainly didn't expect the dolphins to have a culture of their own."

"This also presumes that dolphins are intelligent."

"Oh, they are! But we didn't recognize it as intelligence."

"The Doctor is right." CDR M. H. Smith had re-entered the wardroom during the conversation and now sat down on the other side of Corry. "It's well known that four forms of intelligence exist: human intelligence, animal intelligence, machine intelligence, and naval intelligence. Not necessarily in that order. Depends on whether or not I have a good day."

Smith had donned tropical whites. On her, they looked good. Zeke seemed to materialize immediately on the other side of where she sat. "I'll do my best to make this a good one," he told her.

"That depends in which of the first two categories I

decide to place you, Commander." Smith was sharp, pleasant, and had a disarming sense of humor.

This didn't distract Corry from the fact that she was Naval Intelligence. He suspected she used her likable personality, sense of humor, and appearance to help do her job.

"As any of the ladies in the boat will affirm, I always fit into the first category," Zeke told her with a grin.

"Well, Naval Intelligence has ways of confirming that," Smith responded quickly.

"I'll try to see to it that your efforts aren't hampered by Rule Twenty-twenty." Zeke referred to the naval regulation that prohibited physical contact between naval personnel except as required for official Navy business. The regulation was more complex than that, of course. Everyone in the *Shenandoah* knew the entire regulation word for word by heart. And they obeyed it. The Captain had the prerogative of invoking Regulation 2020 at his discretion and going to "monastery mode" if things got out of hand. So no one let them get out of hand. No one wanted to screw up a good thing.

Mixed-gender crews had been a long time coming in the United States Navy. Some admirals and congresscritters still objected to the concept. However, the mental and physical health of naval personnel was much better than at any previous time in history. All-male crews on long voyages had always faced problems. And with the rise in behavior-vectored diseases, the squeaky-clean Navy crews knew they'd stay squeaky-clean under Regulation 2020. They no longer tended to patronize questionable shore establishments where they stood a very good chance of picking up one of the new viruses that kept cropping up around the world.

"Thank you for reminding me of that," Corry remarked as LCDR Zervas, Dr. Duval, and Allan Soucek came into the wardroom together. "Commander Smith, I'm sure that you and Commander Zervas know about Naval Regulation Twenty-twenty."

Smith nodded. "Of course, Captain."

"It's specifically applicable in a hospital environment, Captain," Zervas added.

"Do the civilian members of your team understand it?" Corry looked at Lulalilo, then at Duval.

Soucek nodded and remarked briefly as he took an empty chair at the table, "I do."

"Regulation Twenty-twenty?" Duval asked, seating himself next to Soucek. "No, I'm sorry, I don't know of it."

"It's rather like some of the civil service regulations pertaining to sexual harassment," Zervas remarked. "Captain, if that's breakfast, I'll have some, please."

"Please serve yourself from the sideboard, Commander," Zeke advised him. It was apparent that Zervas hadn't been in a submarine, either. The Captain was the only person aboard who automatically rated being served in the wardroom. Everyone else fended for themselves.

"Oh! Sorry! Thank you, Commander! I'll adjust to your protocols eventually," the naval surgeon remarked.

"Zeke, I suspect none of our guests have been in a carrier submarine before," Corry said. "Would you issue each of them a copy of OpNav Two-oh-two-dash-seven?"

That was the little blue-covered booklet entitled *Carrier Submarine Protocols and Procedures.* Because of the cover color, it was simply known as "the blue book" by submariners.

Commander Smith had resumed her seat alongside Corry after picking up her breakfast tray. "I already have mine, Captain. As the leader of the special team, I'll brief my subordinates."

Allan Soucek paused as he rose to his feet to go after breakfast. "Commander, I believe you're mistaken. I'm in charge of the team."

6

"On the contrary, Mister Soucek, I was specifically told by Admiral McCarthy, the chief of Naval Intelligence, that I'm in command of this team," CDR Matilda Smith snapped back at once with strong conviction and some irritation in her voice.

"May I see a copy of your orders, Commander?" Soucek responded just as quickly and sharply. The man seemed to be under enormous emotional pressure.

"No, you may not, even if I had written orders! You know I'm with Naval Intelligence. And you know that Naval Intelligence rarely gives its personnel anything as potentially incriminating as a written order!" Smith informed him.

"May I see your travel orders?"

"No."

"Why?" Soucek was very terse in his snapped words.

"I don't have any. If you really want to know, I came to Pearl directly from Patuxent. Op-thirty-two doesn't use MAC in situations like this." The woman from Naval Intelligence paused for a moment, then went on before Soucek could say anything, "However, I'd like to reciprocate your request. Please show me your travel orders, Mister Soucek."

The little lean-faced man didn't even blink. He opened the attaché case he'd carried since coming aboard. Without a word, he tossed an airline ticket envelope in front of Smith. When she opened it, she saw it contained only a one-way economy coach class airline ticket from IAD to HNL. No travel agent had been involved; it was a direct reservation. It had been paid for with an American Express corporate card issued to Majestic Corporation.

CDR Smith handed it back.

"Satisfied?" Soucek snapped testily.

She glared at him. "No. I want to know more about you, Mister Soucek."

"What were you told about me?"

"Nothing. Admiral McCarthy advised me that you would be on the team. But I was given no further information about you or the Majestic Corporation. What *is* your function on our team, Mister Soucek?"

"I'm in charge."

Smith sighed again. "Saying so doesn't make it so, Mister Soucek." She turned to Corry. "Captain, the matter of team leadership and command is of utmost importance. This must be settled at once. Will you please contact CINCPAC so I can get a resolution of this?"

Corry had sat quietly and listened while this heated exchange had gone on. Now he leaned forward, put his arms on the wardroom table, and folded his hands. With one finger, he massaged his class ring in an absent fashion. It was time he brought to an end this squabble over command. Insofar as he was concerned, the issue was moot. "No, Commander, I won't."

"Sir?"

He turned and toggled a control recessed on the wall behind him, then faced her again. Copies of his orders were projected on the briefing screen behind him. "I have my orders. You may read them on the screen at your leisure. Commander Smith, can you read and do you understand those orders?"

She nodded. "Yes, sir."

"Please note that I cannot break comm stealth," Corry said. Then he turned to the little, thin-faced man from the unknown corporation. "And you, Mister Soucek, do you understand what they say?"

The strange man snapped back quickly, "Yes, but they don't contravene my orders. I'm in charge of this mission."

"No, sir, you are not," Corry assured him. He paused, got his breathing and stuttering tendency under control, then went on in quiet but assured tones, "As commander of this vessel I cannot relinquish command of the operation to anyone who cannot show me specific written orders instructing me to do so. Mister Soucek, if Washington wanted you or Commander Smith to be in command, the orders I received through CINCPAC would be specific in that regard."

Soucek suddenly became agitated. Corry's words had irritated him. It appeared that he wasn't used to being spoken to in that manner. He quickly reached into his case and withdrew a leather bi-fold wallet. As he opened it, he stated, "Captain Corry, I had hoped that I wouldn't have to pull rank on you. However, I'm the senior officer present, and I'm therefore assuming command."

He handed the wallet to Corry. Inside was a machine-readable card with Soucek's photograph on it. It was his military ID.

It listed him as Allan H. Soucek, Captain, United States Naval Reserve. His date of rank placed him a year ahead of Corry.

The Commanding Officer of the U.S.S. *Shenandoah* calmly handed the wallet back. "I'm very sorry, sir. You're Naval Reserve, not a line officer on active duty. I've seen no orders mobilizing you to active status. Therefore, although I shall accord you the protocol and privileges of a four-striper while you are in this ship, I must treat you as another civilian member of the special team. Naval protocol further restricts me from the usual courtesy of unofficially upgrading you to the rank of Commodore while aboard because you are not on active duty and have not been given command authority."

Soucek rose to his feet. "Captain, I outrank you."

Corry appeared to remain calm, although he was angry. "Mister Soucek, please sit down so we can discuss this cruise and get under way again."

"I am in command, sir!"

It was time for Corry to bring this to an end. Whatever Soucek's naval background was, Corry knew the man had never exercised blue-water command. Soucek had directly challenged the authority of the captain of a ship without documentation to back it up. Corry didn't intend to allow that to pass without confronting it and taking action. Looking Soucek directly in the eyes, Corry told him with a steel edge on his voice, "Mister Soucek, you are an inactive reservist. You have no authority, written or otherwise, to assume command. You have attempted to do so nonetheless. I shall continue to treat you as a guest in this ship, but your behavior has forced me to place you under detention, charged with attempted mutiny. Mister Braxton, will you and Chief Armstrong please escort Mister Soucek to his quarters and arrange for him to be confined there until further notice?"

The XO and the COB got to their feet without hesitation. "Aye, aye, sir," Braxton replied.

Dr. Barry W. Duval spoke up for the first time using a conciliatory tone, "Captain, Captain, do you really need to do this? After all, we're all in this together. Can't we get along and work this out between us?"

Corry looked at him and asked, "Doctor, is this the first time you've shipped with the Navy?"

"Yes, but I know something about nautical matters. I own my own ten-meter sailboat and I've been aboard several of our NOAA oceanographic ships," Duval explained. "When disputes have arisen on the water, we've always managed to achieve closure and a consensus between us. May I suggest that might be the best approach here?"

Corry shook his head. *Damn, why had they saddled him with this bunch of undisciplined scientists and shore establishment types who were trying to take over the boat?* "Doctor Duval, you are in a ship of the United States Navy. We don't run naval vessels by closure and consensus. This is basically a warship. We've been ordered into an area where we could encounter Chinese or Indian submarines. Given the world situation, I must consider that we may become involved in hostile actions."

"We're not at war, Captain Corry," Duval reminded him. "I fail to see why we can't work together. This isn't the *Bounty*. You've been ordered to provide a service for a scientific expeditionary team. I see no reason for you to incarcerate one of the members of this special team."

"Would you like to join Mister Soucek in detention, Doctor? If not, then kindly do not try to tell me how to carry out my duty. I am always willing to entertain suggestions and recommendations, but I will not and I cannot allow this ship to be run by a committee. I have definite responsibilities under naval regulations, and I have the authority to detain those who challenge them. And I have just done so." Corry didn't try to answer the question of what he would do to carry out his orders if all or most of the special team were confined to quarters for refusal to acknowledge his command authority. He had to deal with one element of the situation at a time, and it didn't seem to be improving. These scientists were *not* used to the tight sort of discipline that *had* to be maintained in a carrier submarine. And he had to emphasize the serious nature of their independent, committeelike suggestions.

After all, within the bounds of naval regulations, the Uniform Code of Military Justice, and various federal laws and regulations that Corry knew in detail, he was one of the last of the absolute monarchs. Soucek and Duval obviously didn't understand this or realize that Corry would and had to act to preserve this responsibility.

It was a tense moment in the wardroom.

"Captain," CDR Smith put in quickly, "may I request a delay of your disciplinary measure?"

"Why?"

"It's apparent that protocols and procedures were overlooked in the haste of putting together this special team," the officer from Naval Intelligence went on, speaking in the careful and stilted terminology of formal naval activities. It was obvious to Corry that Smith wanted to break this deadlock of wills in a manner that didn't jeopardize whatever the special team was supposed to do. So he listened as she went on, "In view of the apparent urgency that resulted in the hasty selection and transportation of the team, the confusion of command authority wasn't resolved. I have no intention of challenging your command authority, sir. However, in view of our various assignments, I would like to resolve the matter of team purpose and objectives. In order to do this, it might be well to query the individual team members at this time. Perhaps we'll discover what we as a team are really supposed to do. If Mister Soucek isn't available to participate in this, we could miss some important datum point. Once we bring everything to the surface, perhaps the course of action will become clear. Then you would be able to act on the basis of the best and most solid information available, Captain."

Corry knew she was right. She'd phrased her mediating request in careful words that would offend no one involved. He realized she was one very smart person. Acceding to her request would cause him no loss of command authority right then. He'd acted because he had to bring matters to head. It had worked. Smith's request gave him an alternative without compromising command authority.

When he returned from this cruise, Corry intended to lodge a strong but unofficial gripe with Admiral Richard Kane at CINCPAC. Someone at CNO should have known better than to saddle him with this special team having no orders, no leadership, no command structure, and no specific objective other than to capture a live alien. He'd known his orders were loosy-goosy when he first saw them. He hadn't anticipated that orders given to other people might be even more loose. It complicated his life as a commanding officer.

Smith was also right in her suggestion that things should be straightened out before going any further. This cruise could have a very high pucker factor indeed, given the world situation and possible action by the Chinese or Indian navies in the Solomon Islands area.

"XO, Chief, as you were," Corry told them. When the two of them and Allan Soucek resumed their seats, he went on, "Very well, Commander Smith, please tell us what you know about this operation."

"Is everyone here cleared for Top Secret, Captain?"

"Commander, we're all inside a composite hull thirty meters below the surface of the Pacific Ocean. We have no communications with the outside world," he pointed out, not mentioning the SWC system; he didn't know who on the team was aware of this classified communications system. "Security is a moot point. The people in my crew are cleared and know enough not to violate the various national security acts. Before this cruise is over, everyone will be advised concerning what they may and may not discuss openly with others. I do not keep secrets from my officers and crew members except when specifically ordered to do so. Consider everyone in the boat to be cleared."

"Not without seeing their security clearance documents," Soucek put in. "Captain, if you're going to insist on strict adherence to regulations, I'm afraid I'll do the same."

Corry realized that this little man could be a continuing source of trouble for him. But he didn't know what was chewing Soucek apart at the moment. "You will have full access to the ship's computer data base, Mister Soucek. If you're concerned that the existence of the Awesomes may carry a national security classification so high that only a few people in the White House and DOD know of their existence, please remember that we were the ones who first encountered the Awesomes off Sulawesi. We fought them. We recovered dead ones. We saw their vessels and observed what their technology is capable of doing. We're the source of the data and reports you've read. We may know more about the Awesomes than any of the special team members."

"I doubt that you do, Captain, but I'll keep in mind that you and your crew indeed know something about these underwater aliens during my briefing," Commander Matilda Harriet Smith said levelly with no challenge in her voice. She understood Captain Corry's authority and knew he wouldn't hesitate to use it. However, she still had that aura of informational superiority that affected most Naval Intelligence people.

"You don't need to brief us on what the *Shenandoah*'s crew discovered around Sulawesi, Commander," Corry said. "We know what we saw and did. So please tell us what you know about this mission and what you expect of the officers and crew of the U.S.S. *Shenandoah*."

Smith paused and looked around. "The mission of this special team is to capture one or more live underwater aliens and return this catch alive to Pearl Harbor. Thanks to what all of you did on your last cruise to Makasar, we've added a great deal of information to our alien data base. This resource is extremely extensive and goes back more than a hundred years." She paused. She got no response from the attentive but passive faces of the naval and Marine personnel in the wardroom. They were behaving as professionals intent upon learning additional information that might help them carry out the mission, whatever it might happen to be.

CDR Smith went on, "To clarify what I just told you, various DOD and civilian intelligence agencies have maintained a constant but passive data collection operation since well before such announced twentieth century cover operations as Project Blue Book. The data includes artifacts and deceased extraterrestrial biological specimens. However, your discoveries revealed the first underwater alien species. Congratulations."

When Smith paused for effect, the ship's Medical Officer added, "We discovered the first aliens that apparently like to eat us."

"What makes you think they like to eat us, Doctor?" LCDR Constantine Zervas from Bethesda put in.

"Their DNA is compatible. I found that fascinating in view of the varieties of organic life molecules possible in a large universe," Laura Raye Moore stated.

"I take it then that you attempted an autopsy. I found indications that tissue samples had been taken."

"I didn't autopsy, Doctor, but I took those samples you mentioned," Moore admitted to Zervas.

"May I ask why you disturbed the specimen?"

"Frankly, I was curious."

"I can understand that. Thank you for not disturbing the corpse to any greater extent. You might have caused me to miss the most important finding I uncovered in my autopsy and biopsies."

"And that was . . . ?" Moore prompted him.

"They don't eat us."

"Really? Then why do they fish for us?"

"I don't know yet."

"That is what I intend to find out," Smith put in.

"Doctor, as you know since you've identified that the aliens have similar DNA to ours—it turns out that DNA is DNA in all the terrestrial and extraterrestrial species that we've examined—one would expect to find similar biochemistry as well," Zervas lectured her. That was a mistake. No one lectured Doctor Laura Raye Moore on a subject about which she knew a great deal.

"Certainly! They were fishing for humans!"

"But not to eat us. The similar biochemistry to support your hypothesis isn't there. This led me to hypothesize that the EBEs—extraterrestrial biological entities, that is—were harvesting something else from human bodies."

"They aren't the first alien species we've encountered that needed something biological from human beings," Allan Soucek suddenly interjected. He seemed unusually anxious to talk for the first time. "A particularly rapacious alien species was here in the last century. They wanted human reproductive organs, blood, certain body tissues, and endocrines. Majestic Corporation has identified their star origins and has hypothesized that their biological shortcomings were caused by radiation damage from a supernova in their region. We haven't seen that supernova yet, which means the aliens have faster-than-light transportation. Our first evidence of their needs came from mutilated animals and kidnapped humans who were returned. Those aliens also made mistakes. Their ships crashed occasionally, and we recovered the dead occupants." Soucek stopped and wiped the sweat from his face and eyes with a handkerchief. He was shaking.

Corry studied the man carefully. Allan Soucek acted as if he wanted to present a briefing, but he appeared unable to get his thoughts together well enough to present a rational story. Corry had seen naval officers bilge a briefing the same way. Those officers had been insecure, scared, or simply incompetent.

In spite of the fact that Soucek had interrupted Smith's briefing, the Naval Intelligence officer didn't attempt to regain control. Apparently, she was hearing new information, too.

"I want all of you to realize that what I'm telling you is extremely classified," Soucek went on. "I'm telling you even though you may not be cleared to hear it. That's a big risk, but I'm willing to take it. I've decided that you do indeed have a need to know. And I'm sure you'll understand why this information has remained classified for nearly a century."

"How can something remain a secret for that long?" Major Bart Clinch wanted to know. "Hell, our nation's capital runs on leaks. It's part of politics!" He said it with obvious distaste. As a Marine, Clinch was bound by oath as well as personal conviction to protect and defend that system of politics, but that didn't keep him from bitching about it.

"How was it kept secret, Major? By using the usual secrecy tactics: It was turned into a joke. People who wouldn't keep quiet were destroyed by character assassination. In some cases, *covert* assassination was actually used," Soucek explained with distaste.

Corry thought that perhaps Soucek was afraid those tactics would be used on him.

CDR Smith nodded and confirmed, "Those are classical tactics in the intel community. I'm not proud of the tactics, nor do I endorse them, but intelligence work simply could not exist without them. Mister Soucek, please go on." It was obvious that she wanted Soucek to talk and reveal what he knew. It kept her from having to reveal what *she* knew.

"Thank you, Commander. You're absolutely correct," Soucek said. "Please be advised that everyone here is subject to that sort of treatment—or worse—if this information is revealed to anyone else. It cannot be declassified as long as it involves a long-term threat. It's a very deadly game, and we must play it for keeps."

"It sounds like a war," Terri Ellison remarked. She'd heard of various airborne encounters with UFOs, but she never placed much credence in them. And she was having trouble believing Allan Soucek now. She didn't openly challenge him. She was hoping he'd either verify what he was telling them or stumble so that she could attack and destroy him as a paranoiac.

"It is," Soucek replied simply. "I must give you some deep background here. This has been going on for a long time. Few people know that extraterrestrial biological entities or EBE initiated contact with humans in 1964. The meeting took place on the old missile test range in New Mexico. Over the next few years, the

United States government cut a deal with these aliens—not the same ones you encountered, unfortunately, which is one reason for this mission. In 1971, the government agreed to swap technology with the alien species. It turned out that we were better biotechnologists at that time. Therefore, the American government agreed to solve the aliens' biotechnology problem if they'd pass the results along to other aliens in the affected galactic sector and stop harvesting those biochemicals here. The aliens wouldn't share their energy technology but they did agree to teach us their materials technology and certain aspects of mathematics that helped us in computer design and programming. We know now that it wasn't a good deal. But this country was in a Cold War with the Soviet Union then, and it was feared that the Soviets would cut a deal instead. So EBE contact and the agreement was treated as a very high national security matter. After the end of the Cold War, it was planned to announce the arrangement with the aliens sometime around the turn of the century. But before that could be done, people had to get used to the idea of extraterrestrials. Look at what was being shown in the motion picture theaters and on television at that time. It was one of the most difficult social engineering tasks in history because Majestic Corporation could *not* reveal that it existed and was manipulating Hollywood, the television networks, the news media, or the bankers. We almost succeeded."

Soucek stopped. It was almost as if he had said too much. The officers and crew of the U.S.S. *Shenandoah* got the distinct impression that it was very difficult for the man to talk about this. Most of them attributed this to the fact that Soucek had *never* spoken of this to such a large number of people whose security clearances he hadn't confirmed. CDR Laura Raye Moore and the ship's Chaplain, LT Tom Chapman, saw it differently; as both later confirmed to one another, it was a catharsis or confession on Soucek's part, getting something off his mind that had bothered him for a long time because he'd had to remain silent about it. Now he was going into a personal situation where he would actually have to confront what he'd only studied in the past. So he'd unloaded.

When Soucek didn't proceed, Corry asked quietly, "Why didn't you succeed?"

"The aliens broke the agreement. And we fought the first interstellar war, one that none of you ever heard about."

7

"Interstellar war? What interstellar war? I don't know a damned thing about being involved in an interstellar war!" Major Bart Clinch interrupted the man from Majestic Corporation. "Mister Soucek, I'm a professional military man. I know military history. I follow all the current journals and professional publications. If we'd been involved in an interstellar war, I sure as hell would have learned about it—if not from the literature, then from scuttlebutt!"

"I agree with you, Major," Terri Ellison added. "I keep track of technical developments in the aerospace field. We don't have starships. And nothing has happened in the Earth-Moon military theater, or I would have heard about it." She paused, then went on to amplify her statements. "Mister Soucek, I have deep sources of my own. I guarantee you I would have known about any interstellar war."

Terri indeed had such sources. The naval background of her family went back for over a century. She had family, friends, and colleagues not only throughout the naval establishment but in the other armed services as well.

Soucek let the two of them unload while he kept a passive face. Finally, he wiped his face again with his handkerchief and asked, "How many of you have heard of Dulce, New Mexico?"

CWO Joe Weaver raised his hand. "I spent a tour at the Special Weapons Laboratory at Los Alamos," he explained. "Did some skiing around Chama. As I remember, Dulce was a wide place on the road between Chama and Farmington."

Soucek nodded. "The first joint American-alien biotechnology lab was established near Dulce. American biotechnologists worked side by side with the aliens for nearly ten years in that subterranean lab."

"That sounds very much like one of those mid-century science fiction novels," Zeke recalled. "I remember one that was about a biotechnology invasion. Took place in an underground lab."

"Yes. It was called *The Andromeda Strain*. It was made into a motion picture, too. It was part of the 'love the aliens' plan that was to culminate around the turn of the century ... and would have if it had not been for the war." Soucek had acted like a scared brahmin among the unwashed to that point, but now sadness crept into his voice. "In June 1979, a disagreement occurred between the American biotechnologists and the aliens. The biotechnical staff was taken hostage. A team of sixty-six men from the Fifth Special Forces Group was sent in to rescue the biotechnologists. They were killed in the fight. So were the other humans in the lab and the aliens as well. The aliens were trapped, so they self-destructed the lab and all its records. They used something like the subnuclear explosives we have today. No radioactive aftermath, and the explosion was so small that it hardly jiggled the seismographs in any of the earthquake labs. My grandfather was one of the Special Forces team and perished there. I discovered that only after I went to work for Majestic Corporation."

He turned to Terri Ellison and told her, "Commander, you aren't the only one here with a long family history of service to our country."

"I thought your name sounded familiar, and I was going to ask you about it at some point," Terry replied. She'd been hostile toward this enigmatic little man, but now sensed a bond that hadn't been there before. Soucek had done his homework. He'd run a preliminary check on the major officers of the *Shenandoah*. He knew their backgrounds. So he'd deliberately made that remark in hopes of getting her on his side. Because he'd gotten off to such a bad start with Corry, Soucek intended to do something similar with the Captain at a later time.

"One underground battle on Earth doesn't make an interstellar war," Major Bart Clinch growled.

"It wasn't the only one. Other Special Forces teams went into other labs near Pietown, New Mexico and Site Fifty-One in Nevada. But by the time they got there, the aliens had left, taking the biotechnology data, the biotechnologists, and some tissue banks with them. Several skirmishes followed over the years. They occurred on Earth, even though one of the adversaries was an interstellar species. We later learned from other alien species that the Mantids, as they were called, returned to their home worlds near Zeta Reticulae and set up a monopoly on the biochemicals needed by other alien species in that sector."

LCDR Natalie Chase nodded and muttered, "Zeta Reticulae. Southern hemisphere constellation. Sort of obscure. No star brighter than about third magnitude."

"Are you an amateur astronomer, Commander?" Soucek guessed.

"No, I'm the Navigator." She tapped her mop of dark hair. "I carry ocean and star charts around up here."

"Mister Soucek, you just mentioned 'other alien species,'" Zeke put in. The man's story was becoming more bizarre by the moment. He didn't know whether to believe it or not. Had he not encountered an extraterrestrial species himself, he probably would have dismissed the man as a certifiable nut. "We've found one of them. But not the species you talked about. Are there others?"

"Seventy that we know of."

"*Seventy?*"

"The universe teems with self-aware life-forms, Commander Braxton."

"Frank Drake was right," muttered Natalie.

"Don't forget the Bible," the ship's Chaplain reminded them all. "John, chapter fourteen, verse two. 'In my Father's house are many mansions . . .'"

"So we discovered Number Seventy-one?" Zeke asked.

"It would seem that way. And, contrary to a commonplace fixture of a lot of science fiction stories and television shows, no 'galactic federation' exists. Those seventy-one alien species have alliances and adversaries. They compete. It's a deadly game. And we're now part of it, whether or not we participate in space or here on Earth. Consider us as Galactic Species Seventy-two. *That's* why we must learn more about Species Seventy-one, the things you call the Awesomes. They're a new wild card in the game."

Corry sat forward, placed his forearms on the wardroom table, and folded his hands. "Mister Soucek, do you mind if I ask you the source of the story you've just told us?"

"Yeah, it's a pretty wild-assed story." Bart Clinch wasn't one to mince words. In a social setting, he could indeed be an officer and a gentleman. But when it came to his profession, he was a first-class brass-plated sonofabitch. He was a Marine. "One alien species I can believe. I've fought it. But this whole cockamamie yarn about interstellar wars sounds like a crock. I've got to be honest with you, Soucek. I don't believe you."

Soucek merely replied briefly to Clinch, "And that's both the secret of how this has been kept secret and the reason it's highly classified. If you won't believe it, do you expect the public to do so, Major?"

Without giving Clinch the chance to respond, Soucek told Corry, "Captain, less than a dozen people know what I just told you. Two of us—myself and my CEO, Newell Carew—are in Majestic Corporation. The company is a legitimate corporation registered in Delaware. It was formed decades ago for the specific purpose of serving as a covert long-term repository of information and analysis relating to EBEs, UFO, ETs, and other extraterrestrial manifestations and phenomena. I did not even know the full extent of our data base until I was given a full briefing by Mister Carew only hours before I left to come on this mission."

"How do you know that seventy ET species exist?"

"We were told by at least three alien species."

"You've established communications with extraterrestrials?" Dr. Evelyn Lulalilo put in. It was apparent that she had been shocked at all this and didn't believe him.

"Yes. Doctor Lulalilo, I know your specialty is communication with aquatic mammals. I know that not much progress has been made in your field for a long time.

And I know that you're trying very hard," Soucek tried to explain to her. "However, it's unlikely that any meaningful communications will ever be established with aquatic mammals. There's a reason for this. A dolphin's brain may be self-aware, but its communications abilities are primitive compared to ours and the alien species we've contacted. The research in aquatic mammalian communications has been kept alive all these years *not* because there's any real hope of human-dolphin communication but to support a cadre of experts who know *something* about extra-human communication. From time to time, such as in the present matter, this has been useful."

"Why wasn't I told these things? Why have we been forced to work for decades in ignorance? Why ... ?" Evelyn was indignant.

"Because you did not have Magic security clearance and a need to know. You are a scientist, Doctor, and you must operate with the 'publish or perish' protocols."

"Of course! That's the way of scientific research! What you've just told us means that most of my life's work has been meaningless! While you've been communicating with totally alien species, I've wasted my time trying to talk with a terrestrial life-form that you claim is too stupid. Why did you do this to me?"

"Because you would have published."

"Yes, I would have! So what difference would it make if the world knew that seventy extraterrestrial intelligence life-forms existed, three of which we've talked to?"

"Sheer worldwide panic would have resulted, Doctor."

"I think you're wrong, Mister Soucek."

"That's not for me to say. These security rules have been placed on this matter from above. And they're long-standing. The policy is supported by continual surveys of public attitudes. But don't be so angry, Doctor. You're on this special team because you probably have the best chance of establishing communication with this alien underwater species."

"I'm not so sure I want to get involved if I can't talk about it to other people in my profession!"

"That's your decision, Doctor. If you want out, say so. However, you'll have to stay aboard while the rest of the team tries to find and capture a live underwater alien. Regardless of how you decide, what I've told you this morning is highly classified. If you reveal it to unauthorized persons, you will be punished under the laws of the United States. Or worse. You don't have to give me your answer right away. The ship won't get to the Solomon Islands region for several days."

CDR Matilda Harriet Smith sensed that Soucek was in fact taking over leadership of the special team. She wanted to stop that right away. Besides, if what Soucek had told them was right, she had some complaints of her own that needed to be brought forth. And this seemed like the time and place to do that.

"Soucek," she snapped, deliberately using only his last name, "I was thoroughly briefed at the highest security levels by Naval Intelligence before I left Washington. I got the full rundown on Operation Snowbird and Project Black Star, to name but two. I got a full data dump on everything that Op-thirty-two knows about ETs and UFOs. This is the first I've heard about actual contact and communication with aliens. And the first I've heard about Dulce and your interstellar war. And about seventy alien species. Why the hell have you kept it from Naval Intelligence, sir?" Her clear blue eyes sparked. She was angry.

"Majestic Corporation didn't keep it from Naval Intelligence," Soucek replied. "In fact, Op-thirty-two has been one of our sources. So have the intelligence departments of the other armed services along with DIA and CIA. But each has only part of the overall picture. Majestic Corporation was tasked to collect, collate, study, and integrate all the information. We are also under orders not to reveal the total picture to any other intelligence agency. I haven't been told the reason for this, Commander. The order is very old and came from the highest office in the land. It's never been changed. No new Chief Executive has seen fit to change the basic secrecy order."

"And what is your position in Majestic Corporation, Mister Soucek?"

"I am Executive Vice President of Field Operations, Commander."

"And by whom was Majestic Corporation tasked?"

"The White House."

"For this operation?"

"Yes."

"Who in the White House?"

"I don't know. I was not told."

"Who chose the members of this special team?"

"I don't know. I was not told," Soucek repeated.

"And to get back to an earlier matter, what is Majestic Corporation's task in this operation and what is yours?"

"The same answer to both questions, Commander, and as I told you earlier: To run it."

Smith threw up her hands in dismay and frustration. "Dammit, I've fallen down the rabbit hole again!"

Corry looked at Smith. Even when she was angry, she was an attractive woman. "And your verbal orders, Commander, were that you were to command the team since this was a Navy operation?"

"Yes."

Corry took control of the situation again. "And, Doctor Lulalilo, you were told that your job was to establish communication with the underwater aliens?"

"Yes, Captain."

"Who told you this, Doctor?"

"I received a personal telephone call from the presidential science advisor."

"Do you know Doctor Frip?"

She shook her head. "No, but apparently he knows me."

"Are you sure you were speaking to the presidential science advisor, Doctor?" Smith asked her.

"No. But Doctor Frip has a Bostonian accent. The telephone voice sounded familiar. I didn't question it."

Corry knew she wouldn't think of doing a thing like that. Anyone could have called her and spoken as the presidential science advisor. It didn't make any difference now. She was in the *Shenandoah*. Corry knew that Dr. Evelyn Lulalilo didn't play the nasty little games of the intel people. She was pure scientist through and through. If she said something, Corry knew he could believe her. Evelyn Lulalilo was one of those persons with such a high level of personal integrity that she was incapable of lying, even to protect herself. So he directed his attention to the Navy surgeon. "Commander Zervas, what orders were you given and who gave them to you?"

"The presidential science advisor. And I know him because of my work with the alien corpse. I received no written orders, only verbal orders by scrambled telephone and travel orders by fax. I have the travel orders here if you wish to see them, Captain," Zervas offered openly. Corry sensed that the medical officer didn't want to make waves and wasn't really interested in the protocol of who could tell who what to do. He had already gotten his instructions from the highest possible level.

"And what are your orders, sir?"

"I was told to take charge of any EBE entities, corpses, or parts that were obtained during this operation. My superior officers seem to have gotten the word separately because they simply told me to have a good time in the south sea paradise. I don't think they were part of the loop because they never have been. The alien carcass has always been under the control of the White House. Bethesda has the facilities to keep it and maintain security. The hospital commander and the chief naval surgeon don't even know what it is. So I've enjoyed a certain level of autonomy in the naval medical service for the past several months. This has given me a wide latitude in doing research and requesting funds for it. I've been extremely careful not to jeopardize that for many reasons, not the least of which is the sensitive security nature of this matter."

Corry could see that LCDR Constantine G. Zervas was a medical politician. He had no bedside manner. He was a researcher, the type who runs a program and puts his name on the scientific papers and reports that emerge from it. From his earlier conversation with the Medical Officer of the U.S.S. *Shenandoah,* Corry realized that Zervas wanted to become the world's leading expert on the Awesomes and had discovered that CDR Laura Raye Moore was a formidable adversary because she knew almost as much about the Awesome corpse as he did.

So Corry queried the oceanographer next. "And you, Doctor Duval?"

"The National Science Advisor called me, too," Dr. Barry Duval admitted, then amplified upon his statement because he guessed that Corry would ask. "I've known Doctor Jonathan Frip for years. He married my aunt. And he's helped me with some grants from time to time. I have no written orders, Captain. We don't work with written orders in my part of NOAA, although some of the super-grade GS types wrestle a lot of program and project paperwork."

"Do you know why you were appointed a member of the special team, Doctor?"

"I think so. I've been studying the ocean floor of the Pacific rim and I've gotten some interesting information on sub-sea vulcanism. I wrote a paper on it for the last Woods Hole conference, and my hypotheses drew quite a bit of attention," Duval told him diffidently. That seemed to be the primary operational mode of the man. He seemed to be a snob. Corry had known professional snobs before.

"What did Doctor Frip tell you was your function on the team?"

"He wanted me to be the on-site expert on oceanography, particularly the sub-surface geological aspect. That's what he told me, period. He asked me to grab my data base, pack a bag, and get out to Hawaii ASAP. He arranged for airline tickets, and I picked them up at Providence airport. I have no written orders; I've never gotten written orders in my entire career. And, quite frankly, I don't really care who's in charge of the team, Captain. I hope you are."

"Until I receive written orders to the contrary, I am indeed," Corry said firmly. "The protocols of my profession are quite different from yours, Doctor. In matters such as this where people's lives are at risk and major capital equipment of the government is involved, we rely on written orders to eliminate ambiguity as much as we can."

Duval shrugged. "You're the Captain. I know enough about nautical protocol to realize what that means."

"How do you see yourself fitting into the operation of the special team, Doctor?" CDR Smith asked.

Again, Duval shrugged. "Doctor Frip told me nothing about underwater aliens. I've learned about that this morning. I don't know what my role on the team is. I suspect we'll work it out. If my expertise is useful and the team discovers something about this fascinating underwater alien species, maybe the knowledge that life exists peacefully on other worlds may bring us together a little better on this one."

"Well, Doctor, that's going to be your job for the next few days while we travel to the Solomons," Corry told him bluntly. He looked at each of the special team members. "No member of the team has written orders or instructions about what to do or who's in charge. Two of you believe that you're running the show but can show me no written documentation to back up the contention. I have not been relieved of command of this ship or the operation. Under naval regulations, I am in command. Any of you is free to lodge an official complaint later. However, this is what happens when lines of authority and responsibility are not clearly defined from the beginning. I hope you don't get yourselves into similar situations in the future. If any of you on the special team feels that the team itself needs a leader, I suggest you convene immediately afterward and work out your authority structure. I won't do it for you. In the absence of a team leader, I will treat each of you as a special expert. But, in the meantime, we are all in a ship on the high seas. Under it, actually, which makes the situation a little more critical. Therefore, our mission on this cruise is to capture—alive, if possible—one of the underwater alien creatures we encountered off Makasar and return it to Pearl Harbor."

He turned to Braxton. "XO, raise the boat from the bottom. Proceed at best cruising speed and depth to the original destination spelled out in the earlier CINCPAC order."

"Aye, aye, sir!" Braxton paused, then asked, "Captain, do you wish your detention order to stand?"

"No. In fact, I'd like Commander Smith and Mister

Soucek to have lunch with me later today once we're under way."

"Delighted to accept, Captain!" Smith responded.

"Captain, I didn't complete my briefing," Soucek pointed out.

"What do you have to add, Mister Soucek?"

"The reason why we're going to the Solomons."

"Very well, sir, please shed some light on that."

"The *Shenandoah* data from the Makasar cruise alerted Majestic Corporation to watch for activity between the ocean surface and space."

"Big weather balloons," Terri interjected.

"Eh?"

"We suspected that the Awesome starships had been detected, but that the radar and other tracks had been dismissed as glitches or as returns from ship-launched meteorological radiosonde balloons," the Commander of the Air Group explained.

"That's exactly right, Commander," Soucek said. "Once we were alerted to this, we began correlating the data points that fell off the curve, those 'weather balloon' anomalies, as you termed them."

"And I therefore presume that you've found a preponderance of these in the Solomons region."

"That's right."

"Any other active regions?"

"Several."

"Any commonality?" Terri's interrogation was definitely non-adversarial. Even a hidden man like Soucek would have trouble refusing the questions or requests of a woman as pretty as CDR Teresa B. Ellison.

But Soucek didn't seem to notice. He was preoccupied with the situation. "They seem to take place in relatively shallow coastal waters on continental shelves in proximity to known underwater volcanic activity."

"Why the hell would the Awesomes congregate around underwater volcanos?" she wondered aloud.

"Energy," the Engineer Officer spoke up. As the man in charge of the energy sources of the carrier submarine, CDR Ray Stocker would certainly think of this.

"For what, Ray?"

"That's a good question that shows a lot of insight. A

very important question. Do you have any other questions?"

"Thanks."

"Terri, I don't know."

"You just said that."

"Well, Captain, your Air Group commander and your Engineer Officer seem to understand why the Solomon region was chosen for this mission. I've told you all that I can right now," Soucek told Corry.

"Captain, I think your suggestion that the special team get together to organize themselves is a good one," CDR Matilda Harriet Smith spoke up. "Since we have several days to iron out our differences, we should have all problems resolved by the time you get the ship to the Solomon area."

She was an optimist.

8

"I didn't realize that being on a submarine would be so boring," CDR Constantine Zervas remarked.

"In the first place, Doctor, you're not *on* a submarine. You're *in* a submarine," CDR Laura Raye Moore corrected him.

For twenty-four hours, the U.S.S. *Shenandoah* had cruised at forty knots on a southwesterly heading toward the Solomon Islands. In such a high-speed cruise mode, the big vessel required only the services of the Ship Division, whose people stood regular watches. The Air Group was grounded, so the pilots flew sims while the aviation ratings carried out maintenance and repair on the F/A-48 Sea Devils, P-10 Ospreys, and C-26 Sea Dragons. The Marine batt exercised at quarters, drilled on the hangar deck, and otherwise practiced at being Marines.

And the special team argued and fretted over what they were supposed to do when the ship got to the Solomons. They had reached no consensus.

The only one in the boat who didn't seem concerned was Captain William M. Corry. The ship was still thirty-seven hours from the Solomons, so no urgent action was necessary. He was wise in the ways of interaction between people. He intended to allow matters to shake out on this second day.

The Medical Officer was concerned, however. She viewed the presence of the special team as something like a virus that had invaded the body and mind of the ship.

"I stand corrected, Doctor," Zervas replied. "But submarine duty isn't what I imagined it would be."

The two medical doctors had gotten together not be-

81

cause they especially liked one another—Laura Raye believed that Zervas was a medical politician and probably hadn't treated even so much as a cut finger since residency—but because they shared a common profession.

However, that's where the similarities ended between the two doctors.

Zervas was jealous of Moore's intimate experience with capturing the Awesome whose carcass he guarded at Bethesda. He believed the Medical Officer was merely another one of those pushy female doctors he encountered constantly at Bethesda, ones always angling for some advantage that would elevate them above the men around them. The United States Navy was technically a mixed-gender organization. However, some parts of it, such as the Medical Service, still suffered from the some of the ancient chauvinism of male doctors who tended to try to run the show. Zervas was a male chauvinist.

Moore knew it and therefore knew how to handle him. She also realized that Zervas was bent on maintaining his position as *the* expert on the physiology and biochemistry of the Awesomes. During most of the previous day, he'd queried her in depth. He wanted to learn everything that the Medical Officer knew as a result of her experience on the Makasar mission. Laura Raye Moore, on the other hand, was driven by professional curiosity to find out what Zervas had learned at Bethesda.

It was a professional alliance of mutual benefit, but Zervas didn't intend to let it go too far. Neither did Moore.

However, the two of them had exchanged information about the Awesome.

"What did you believe being in a carrier submarine would be like, Doctor?" Laura Raye wanted to know.

"I thought your work mostly would involve handling daily health problems—communicable diseases, digestive problems, the sort of afflictions that might be common in a large group of people."

Laura Raye smiled. "Not in a submarine. And not after the first forty-eight hours of getting under way."

"Well, I must say I'm impressed with your capability in sick bay. You and your team appear to be capable of handling a large number of different traumas. But what happens if you have an epidemic aboard?"

"Doctor, an epidemic requires a vector. While it's true that a crew member might pick up a local disease during a port call, we've all been immunized against a broad spectrum of bacterial and viral agents. Crew members have been trained to recognize when they're not well. They have no hesitation about coming to sick bay at any time. Being ill or in sick bay in a submarine is no fun; it means someone else has to do your work in addition to their own. We're all individuals in this boat, but we also know we have to live together in very tight quarters," the Medical Officer explained. "A healthy ship is a happy ship."

Zervas sighed and went on expansively, "Well, Doctor, I'm perfectly happy that you're in charge of the health of this crew. You certainly have the expertise and facilities for it. I'm basically a researcher. However, I'll need your cooperation when we catch a live EBE. I'd like to review the facilities available for keeping it alive if it's an underwater life-form."

"Frankly, I don't know how we'd do that, Doctor," Laura Raye told him bluntly. "We aren't equipped for that sort of thing. I guess we'll just have to improvise when the time comes."

"Improvise?" Zervas was surprised at this response. He never improvised. He planned and then managed what he'd planned. Like many people in Washington, he was procedures oriented. If it wasn't in the book, it couldn't happen. Or shouldn't.

Laura Raye nodded. "An Awesome is big, heavy, and strong. We may have to build a cage for it and flood a compartment with sea water. I'm not even sure what to feed it, what the dissolved oxygen content or temperature of the water should be, or how to handle its wastes." She paused for a moment, then added, "But I'll tell you what I'll do to prepare for this contingency. I'll check the ship's library data base. And I'll find someone in the *Shenandoah* whose hobby is tropical fish. Then we'll use that information and that person's expertise."

"Tropical fish? Doctor, we're dealing with an extraterrestrial species about which we know little at this point!"

"We have to start somewhere, Doctor. The first job is to get our hands on all the available information. Although this carrier submarine is a little world all in itself, we're surprisingly well equipped when it comes to informational sources. After all, we can't take the Metro down to the Library of Congress or access the NIH data base if we need some snippet of data or some reference. And if the information isn't in our library data base, we'll experiment. When in total ignorance, try anything and become less ignorant."

Obviously, this didn't sit well with Zervas. But he decided he'd have to play the hand as it was dealt. When he got off this ship later, he could go back to being the Big Man on EBEs in Washington. In the meantime, he decided he could use CDR Laura Raye Moore to his own ends.

That was a mistake. He didn't know her very well yet.

On the other hand, CDR Zeke Braxton was trying very hard to get to know CDR Matilda Harriet Smith, whose tall, statuesque appearance excited him. She had also revealed herself as a very smart person, and Zeke liked women who were both striking and intelligent. Besides, he told himself, Smith held the promise of offering some real competition to Terri Ellison, competition that would certainly break the Braxton-Ellison-Clinch triangle one way or another. In addition, Zeke found Smith to be mysterious.

Zeke didn't know what she thought of him. But CDR Smith went about her business as a professional after that first tension-filled wardroom meeting. She set her task as learning more about the ship and its people than Allan Soucek might have learned through his enigmatic Majestic Corporation. As an intelligence specialist, she'd been taught to amass as much solid data as possible as quickly as possible when it came to any operation in the spook community. Information was power. And she wasn't about to let Soucek get any power over her.

And she wanted to call the shots in the evolving mission. Control of this mission was, to her, essential to the future of her naval career. Because of the unfortunate confrontation with Soucek in the wardroom, she knew she had no ready access to Corry. Any approach to the

Commanding Officer would be viewed by him as an attempt on her part to elicit his help in gaining team control and, eventually, control of the mission. Besides, the Captain was an intimidating man and had shown he wasn't one who would easily or gracefully abrogate any of the power of his position and responsibility. So if Smith couldn't influence the Commanding Officer, she knew her next target should be the Captain's right-hand man, the XO.

But Zeke Braxton was more than a raging collection of male hormones. He was a naval officer who had learned to subdue his basic drives in favor of honor and duty. Which is why he surprised Smith when she visited his little office, intending to query him. Instead, Zeke began with, "Commander, the handwritten orders from CINCPAC said that you'd brief us on the international aspects of this mission from the standpoint of naval intelligence. Care to do so?"

"Only if the Captain is present, Commander," she told him as she sat down on the opposite side of the small terminal table that was Zeke's desk.

"Oh? He may not be available at the moment. But I'm his Number Two in the ship."

"Then I'll wait until I can see him. As his Executive Officer, you're responsible for looking inward into the ship while he looks outward," she reminded him.

Zeke shrugged. "I keep up with the real world. I won't be an XO forever. I intend to be on the promotion list and under consideration for command in a few years."

"So? How do you think this mission is going to affect your goal?" Smith got right to the heart of the matter.

"It may make it for me. Then again, it may destroy it," Zeke told her candidly. "I'll do my best to make it come out right. But sometimes external influences have a lot to do with the way an officer's career progresses. Especially when it involves activities as sensitive as this extraterrestrial matter seems to be."

"What do you think of this extraterrestrial activity?" Smith probed.

"It's too early yet for me to make a rational evaluation of it. I'm not sure if we're opening a new page of history for humanity or not. And some days I wonder why I got caught up in it. I joined the Navy to help defend my country. I certainly didn't do so with the idea of changing the course of history. I'm not sure why I'm sitting here involved in what may become both a planetary war and an interstellar war. Perhaps I was in the right place at the right time. Or the wrong place at the wrong time. Maybe I should have paid attention to what my grandmother said when she learned I wanted to be a naval officer.''

When Zeke paused, Smith urged him, "Well?"

He grinned, knowing that she had a sense of humor. He was trying to take some of the edge off her behavior that morning. "A parody on an old bit of folk wisdom. 'Go into the Navy if you wish, my son, but don't go near the water.' "

Smith laughed. "Ah, yes, a man of duty, honor, and perspective."

"I'm glad you can laugh, Commander. You were pretty tense when you walked in here a few minutes ago."

"And you're a perceptive judge of behavior. I may be forced to reevaluate my initial perception of you, too."

"I hope you decide to place me in the category of human intelligence, not animal."

"Ah, yes, you remembered my initial dart lofted in your direction! Commander, a lady must sometimes establish a protective wall against animal behavior while at the same time making it a facade that will accommodate human behavior."

"I have yet to encounter the facade, and I'm looking forward to it."

Smith smiled in a provocative way. "Anticipation is often more fun than achievement."

"Depends upon the achievement."

"You riposte and parry well, Commander."

"I was on the fencing team at the Naval Academy."

"Yes, and you still have a reputation for being somewhat of a swordsman."

"You noticed."

"No, like a good spy, I did my homework. Whether or not I decide to investigate the validity of your reputation may depend on just what I have to do to make you pliable."

Zeke snapped his fingers. "Now I've got it!"

"Got what?"

"Your name. Given your name, you fit perfectly into Naval Intelligence!"

She knew what he meant, but she continued to play with him. It wasn't often that she was away from somewhat stuffy superior officers who looked upon intel work as being super-serious without a human element involved. "Oh?"

"Matilda Harriet Smith. Mata Hari."

"It's my turn to say that you noticed."

"Do you ever operate in that mode?"

"Occasionally. After all, I'm a spy, you know. But I'm also a naval officer."

"And therefore subject to Regulation Twenty-twenty?"

She shook her head. "Spies are allowed to break the rules for good reasons."

"I guess I'll have to find a good reason."

"But you're not a spook, so that doesn't apply to you. Look, do you want that briefing or not?"

"Depends on whether or not that's why you came to my office."

"I came to learn more about you. After all, we'll be serving together in this boat for an unknown length of time. And a personnel file is a rather barren collection of documents."

"You checked?"

"Of course, as much as I had time to do. It was a long flight from Patuxent."

"Very well, time to become super-professional, Commander. What about the world situation with respect to our covert mission?" Zeke decided it was time to stop playing games because the relationship wasn't going anywhere at that moment. As XO, technically Zeke was always under Regulation 2020 when the *Shenandoah* was under way. He had fun when he could, however, providing the other party was amenable. And the Captain might decide to do a port call somewhere in the Solomons.

"It could make or break the present international situation."

"Because the Chinese know we've got an Awesome and they don't? Because they're worried that we may have some Awesome technology they didn't get?"

"More likely that they may prevent us from getting more of it."

Zeke growled in frustration. "I was afraid of that. Is that Op-thirty-two's latest and best evaluation?"

"It's one of many scenarios."

"Can they win if they start it?"

"No, but they may believe they can if they start it now versus starting it later when the United States may have more alien technology. The Chinese submarine captain saw the *Tuscarora* break the surface and climb into space. The Chinese are worried."

"Do they know anything about Majestic Corporation and the alien technology Soucek says we've gotten already?"

Smith shook her head. "No. That was a surprise to me, too. And it wasn't in my briefing from Admiral McCarthy. In this situation, if she didn't tell me, she doesn't know."

"So what you're telling me is that if the Chinese discover the *Shenandoah* is on her way to the Solomons instead of Cape Horn, they'll come after us."

She nodded. "A bit of maneuvering was required to deceive the People's Republic of China. And India, too."

"Do the Chinese know what's going on in the Solomons?"

"They may. It's not the only active area. Both China and India have space resources that can identify where the alien 'weather balloons' are coming and going."

"Maybe. The *Tuscarora* didn't have a lot of radar cross-section. Damned good radars would be required to discriminate that weak signal out of noise. Do they have that technology, Mata?"

She bristled. "Let's keep this professional, Commander. You'll know when I permit you to use my nickname."

In another part of the boat, the use of a nickname was encouraged and approved. "Eve, what can I do for you?" Corry asked once Dr. Evelyn Lulalilo was seated in his cabin.

He was pleased that she'd come but wary of her possible intentions. Her presence had uncovered some deep and almost forgotten memories of a time when a young ensign just out of the Naval Academy had courted another lovely young woman who once resembled the marine biologist in the way she acted and spoke. Those memories had long been buried out of necessity. In spite of twenty-first century mores, a naval officer's career isn't helped by a mid-life marital breakup. Corry lived in a special corner of hell when he was ashore. He still loved Cynthia very much, but she'd built a wall of ethanol between them. An enormous amount of personal energy had to be expended in keeping the situation discretely under control. It was known among the Navy wives and recognized by other officers. But no official notice would be taken, provided the Corrys behaved with discretion in public. After all, many other officers had similar problems.

"I'm frightened," Eve admitted, glancing around the little cabin.

"Do you suffer from claustrophobia, Eve?" That was one of the more common problems affecting people who hadn't gone through the submarine school at Groton and gotten used to always being inside.

She shook her head. "No. I've lived and worked in tanks and underwater habitats all of my professional life. That doesn't scare me."

"What does?"

"I don't know."

Corry knew then that he could and would step forward to fulfill the father role with this young woman. He didn't know her background yet, but he suspected she'd had a very strong father upon whom she'd relied in both childhood and adolescence.

Back in his Naval Academy days, the midshipmen had sung a raunchy bit of doggerel called "The Captain Is a Father to His Crew." While the title had several meanings, the song concentrated on the activities and proclivities of a captain and crew in the modern gender-balanced Navy during long submarine cruises. But Corry always knew that it had other ramifications of truth embedded in it. The Commanding Officer in a taut ship with a high-morale volunteer crew did indeed assume the father figure role if possible and if the crew permitted it. Corry had learned how to do it from a fortunate series of good commanding officers with whom he'd served and been trained.

Corry took a swing at the problem. "Eve, could it be the idea that you may encounter an underwater species with whom you can communicate and may be of superior intellect?"

She didn't answer for a moment, but her large eyes reflected her confusion. Finally she said, "No. I'd be excited about learning what they knew that I didn't. I think ... I guess ... Captain, I may be the crucial member of this team. If I make a mistake ... if I behave incorrectly with these aliens ... if it turns out I'm not smart enough to handle this ... well, I could do more than just blow away this mission. I could profoundly affect our whole future! *I don't know how to behave with these aliens in a way that won't alienate them!*"

Corry laughed. Then he held up his hand and told her, "I'm not laughing at you, Eve. I'm laughing at the way you just said that. Look at it this way: No matter how any of us behave with these extraterrestrials, it may be as alien to them as their behavior is to us. We're already alienated! A lovely play on words, by the way. And one that tells me why you're upset. You're not afraid of the Awesomes. You're afraid of yourself and afraid of making a mistake. Right?"

"I don't know."

"That's an honest answer. And one that a scientist should use more often, whether it applies personally to the scientist or to the scientist's approach, work, and conclusions," Corry observed. "You're a scientist who's suddenly been asked to become an explorer."

"There's no difference, Captain. A scientist is supposed to be an explorer."

"Some scientists are. But scientists are supposed to ask why. Explorers go looking for aspects of the universe about which they can ask why. Explorers search for the unknown. Scientists explain the unknown. The unknown is frightening, isn't it?"

"Yes."

"So is serving in a carrier submarine, Eve," Corry told her candidly. "Naval discipline is designed to help us overcome our fears. And we have many of those. Any dive could be our last. Any time we weigh anchor, it could be our last. Any encounter with an enemy could be our last. We never get used to it, but discipline and experience help." He paused, then admitted, "There are times when I'm scared."

"You?"

Corry nodded. "Except I'm not supposed to show it. You can."

"I'm not supposed to, either."

"Who told you that?"

"I . . . I don't remember. But the first time I went into the water with a professor to meet dolphins, I noticed that he wasn't scared. I was. There I was, operating in an environment that belonged to the dolphins. And they were *big*. I almost surfaced. But that would have meant the end of what I wanted to do."

"What did you want to do, Eve?"

"Learn how to communicate with another species. I thought—and I still believe—that we can learn things that will help all of us get along better with each other."

"One can hope," Corry remarked.

"And now I find myself faced with having to learn how to communicate with an extraterrestrial species that probably has the technology to wipe us out."

"You make too many assumptions. The Awesomes do indeed have some awesome technology, but they aren't super-beings. Talk to some of my officers who have met the Awesomes and won."

"I'll try." She got up. "Thank you, Captain. I apologize for taking up your time with my problems—"

"Who said you're taking up my time? Don't make so many unwarranted assumptions, my dear. Listening to and helping to solve people's problems are part of the job of any commanding officer." He suspected that Dr. Evelyn Lulalilo had always lived in the presence of a powerful personality in the form of a father, professors, or research organization managers. If he had to assume that powerful personage role during this mission, he would do so gladly for several reasons: It was his job, she was critical to the mission, and she reminded him so much of his wife in earlier days.

He also knew that she could do the job. Her visit that morning was an effort on her part to establish communications with the most powerful person in her life at the moment. And she'd done so.

If anyone could communicate with extraterrestrials, she could.

9

"Yesterday, each of you stated you were the leader of the special team," CAPT William M. Corry said to the two people seated in his cramped cabin office. "Did you work out your problem?"

CDR Matilda Harriet Smith shook her head. "No, sir." She'd adapted to submarine life quickly. Ship's Stores apparently had clothing in her size because the blue poopie suit fit her trim body well.

"Why not, Commander? You've had thirty-six hours to do it."

Smith and Soucek tossed quick and hostile glances at one another. Soucek remained silent, but Smith replied earnestly, "Captain, I've tried, sir. But I have no written authority to assume team command. Neither does anyone else. The team was assembled so quickly that no one seems to have thought about command structure. Some team members don't care because they're used to working in a very permissive manner. As for myself, I assumed this was a normal intel TDY and somewhere along the line I'd find written orders if they were needed. They were needed and they weren't there. With all due respects to my superiors, Captain, someone goofed."

Corry nodded. This didn't surprise him. Sometimes details got squashed in the rush to accomplish something. In this matter, he suspected either a situation in which everyone thought "George is doing that" or that something else had happened to throw the White House into total confusion. Corry didn't know and didn't care at this point. Naval procedures and protocols had been evolved to cover such contingencies. "Very well. I'll continue to consider that the special team is a group of expert consultants whose job is to help me carry out my written orders from CINCPAC," he stated flatly. Then he asked the next question. "Has the team organized itself yet?"

"Without a leader, how can it?" Soucek asked rhetorically. He didn't like Corry. The reason was simple. Soucek had no weapons with which to challenge the Captain's authority over him. In addition to his other fears, he was afraid of Corry.

Soucek wasn't accustomed to operating in such a situation. Normally, the mystique of the Majestic Corporation and an assignment from the White House had been enough. If he needed more, his Navy Reserve ID card tipped the scales. But the commanding officer of the U.S.S. *Shenandoah* was indeed a stickler for protocols and wanted to see hard proof. Soucek hadn't expected that. Most of his field activities had been with the United States Aerospace Force, whose officers usually had a far more lax concept of discipline and procedures. This was Soucek's first operation in a vessel of the United States Navy. He was learning that the USN is a different service than the USAF or the AUS.

"Certainly you've all gotten together as I requested," Corry said. He'd decided to allow the situation to play to endgame because he wasn't pressed for an immediate resolution to the team command problem. In the end, either the real leader would emerge or Corry would fall back on his foundation of authority as the master of the vessel. He had decided there would be no endgame. "Let me summarize what my written orders say. I've been told to capture a live Awesome. I've been told to use a special team that's a group of experts. I need to know how you've planned to work together and how you intend to interface with me and the crew."

"Captain Corry, the group is particularly sensitive to this problem," Smith admitted. "Only three of us knew anything about the Awesomes—much less extraterrestrial visitors—before coming aboard. Lulalilo and Duval know nothing about the Awesomes other than what they've been told since coming aboard. And none of the team members have ever been in a carrier submarine before." She'd picked up the subtle patois of the submariners. Corry didn't miss that. "I know what I'm supposed to do. So does Commander Zervas. Doctor Lulalilo can probably hack the task she was selected to perform once she gets a better grasp of it. As for Doctor Duval—well, I guess we need an expert on ocean bottoms, but I don't exactly understand why. And, frankly, I don't understand Mister Soucek's role at all. And he hasn't seen fit to explain it in detail to any of us yet."

"I see." Corry continued to sit with his arms on the table and his hands folded. The expression on his face didn't change. Insofar as he was concerned, this situation was far worse than the one on the previous cruise in which he'd been ordered to Makasar to investigate the disappearance of American citizens in Sulawesi. His crew had discovered the Awesomes. Corry knew some of what the Awesomes and their technology could do. He'd been astounded to learn from Soucek that the Awesomes were only one of more than seventy alien species that had been discovered on Earth.

As a commander who is also a leader, Corry had given the raw team members two full working days to get an act together and determine what role they would play on this cruise. He was irritated that they hadn't been able to do so. However, he had grown to know each of them enough to realize that they were *not* team players. They were rugged individualists. They had no concept of how to function as a team.

Corry knew he was going to have to merge them into the boat's crew and lead them.

"Mister Soucek, do you have any comment on Commander Smith's statement?"

"Captain, I've told all that I can tell. I've revealed more than I should have."

"I think you'd better reveal a lot more of it, Mister Soucek," Smith told him with both anger and frustration in her voice.

"Why don't you believe what I've told you?"

"Because you offered no data to back it up."

"You'll just have to take my word for it, Commander Smith. After all, I do come to this operation under specific orders from the White House."

"And I've seen no documentation to support that

other than the orders from CINCPAC," Smith explained.

"They should be adequate."

It was time to bring this bickering to a halt, Corry decided. "Commander Smith and Mister Soucek, I cannot have outside individualists operating within this boat without command oversight and accountability and without a recognized chain of command. And you've run out of time. Therefore, because of your failure to honor my request and organize yourselves, I must consider that you and the other three people who came aboard at Johnston Island are not a special team. You're a group of individuals with special expertise available to me upon my need and request. I shall treat you as special members of my operations staff."

Before either of them could voice an objection or a complaint about what he'd just said and the way he'd said it, he quickly went on, "Tomorrow at this time, the boat will be in the territorial waters of the Solomon Islands. We will also be in shallow water and within strike range of land-based aircraft. The world situation is such that we may encounter Chinese or Indian submarines on power projection missions probing the sea lanes between Japan and Australia in this region. The situation may have already deteriorated to one of the attempted sea control of this area by the navies of these two East World nations. I face the possibility of hostile action. Therefore, under these circumstances, my orders regarding the Awesomes notwithstanding, I will not take this ship and its crew blindly into those waters without a plan of operation."

He looked at the clock on his terminal panel. "Please find the other three members of your group and come to the main wardroom in fifteen minutes."

"Captain, I—" Smith began.

"Commander, time has run out. We're going to meet and formulate an action plan. And we're going to do it tonight even if it takes all night." He passed his hand over the intercom. "XO, this is the Captain."

"Braxton here, sir."

"Please ask the ship's division heads and the COB to

be in the main wardroom for a planning briefing in fifteen minutes. Have the chief steward clear the wardroom."

"Aye, aye, sir!"

He turned his attention again to Smith and Soucek. "Well, why are the two of you still sitting there? Commander, my orders often come in the form of requests. And as you should know because you're Naval Reserve, Mister Soucek, a commanding officer's request is the polite form of a direct order. If we don't have a plan and some alternatives for this operation in the Solomons region, I may not always have time to give polite orders." He rose to his feet. "Let's get busy. We have work to do."

"Captain, since you've decided to treat me as a civilian, I don't have to jump to your orders," Soucek pointed out, remaining seated.

"Don't be an ass, Soucek!" Smith snapped at him as she quickly got to her feet. "You're not inside the Beltway now! Whatever political clout you might have doesn't amount to a rat's ass in this present situation! So you'd better go with the flow. I'm sure Captain Corry would have no compunction about confining you to quarters. And he has the physical power to make it happen. Am I correct, Captain Corry?"

'You are quite correct, Commander Smith. And my patience is wearing quite thin."

"That would be a mistake. My presence and participation are critical to this mission," Soucek maintained.

"Mister Soucek, I can no longer abide such unsupported statements. Dismissed!"

Once the two of them were gone, Corry shaved and changed out of khakis, donning the dark blue shirt and trou of Submarine Officer's Class C Deck Uniform. He wanted the four gold stripes on each sleeve to be plainly visible. Apparently, the silver eagles on the collar tabs of his khaki shirt hadn't been intimidating enough for Soucek. Therefore, Corry intended to project his authority in a blatant, powerful manner. The Captain of the U.S.S. *Shenandoah* had grown tired of trying to be polite with the man from the enigmatic Majestic Corporation.

Precisely on time, Corry entered the wardroom. The

boat's division officers and the Chief of the Boat rose from their chairs.

"As you were," Corry told them and sat down. He noted that Soucek and Duval were missing.

The NOAA oceanographer dashed in. "Sorry, Captain," he apologized. His rumpled appearance with his unruly shock of blond hair falling over his forehead told everyone that he'd probably just rolled out of the rack in spite of the fact that it was 2030 hours, ship time. No one paid any attention to the fact that he'd been sleeping; in a carrier submarine, people kept the hours required to stand watch because there was no night or day inside the U.S.S. *Shenandoah*. But no one other than a civilian would dare show up at a high-level officer's meeting with the Captain if they were in such disheveled condition.

"This is a Papa briefing," Corry announced. "For the benefit of the special group, that means it's a planning meeting. We will leave this meeting with an action plan detailing what will be done, when it will be done, who will do it, and the purpose for doing it. We will develop several contingency plans or scenarios. Since the special group of experts hasn't been able to organize themselves or determine what role each of them is to play in the operation, I will assign them to my staff or to specific officers of the boat and give them specific tasks to be carried out in each scenario."

At this point, Allan Soucek came in, looked around, and saw that no chair was available at the head of the table near Corry. He was forced to sit far down the table and at the end of the row of chairs occupied by other special group members.

Corry didn't pause to give Soucek a chance to offer an excuse. He placed his forearms on the table before him so the four gold stripes on each sleeve were plainly visible.

Soucek noticed that and decided not to say anything about his late arrival.

The U.S.S. *Shenandoah* contained some highly classified equipment, and Corry knew the members of the special group couldn't be kept in the dark about it. Ignorance of the WSS-1 mass detector or masdet and the

SWC system might severely hamper the contribution of the special group members to this mission. And it would be difficult to keep the knowledge of this technology from them. So Corry queried the ship's Personnel and Legal Officer, LCDR Darlene H. Kerr, "Commander, do you have a record of the security clearances of the five members of the special group?" He had deliberately ceased referring to them as a special team.

Kerr shook her head. "No, sir, I do not. I have received no copies of DOD Form F-five-six-three-one-point-oh-two for any of the visitors."

Corry knew that, but he needed to ask for the record. "I see. Then I believe I have the authority to issue interim clearances, correct?"

"Yes, sir. United States Code Title eighteen, paragraph—"

"Thank you, Commander. Will you please take care of the details of granting interim clearance to the five people who boarded the ship near Johnston Island?"

"Yes, sir. Now or after the Papa Briefing?"

Kerr was a good personnel and legal officer. She left no form unfilled and no nit unpicked. Her obsessive thoroughness could, however, become a time-eater in certain circumstances. This was one of them. "Afterward, please," Corry told her, then addressed his Operations Officer. "Mister Lovette, what is the ship's present position?" This was a normal formality of a Papa Brief when the boat was under way. Its purpose was to let everyone know the pertinent details of *now* so that planning could proceed from that point.

"As of the last hourly fix made at oh-nine-hundred Zulu, the ship was eight-hundred-thirty-two nautical miles from Malaita Island on a heading of two-two-six true," Bob Lovette replied crisply.

"And when will we enter the territorial waters of the Solomon Islands?"

Lovette looked down at his palmtop display. "The boat will enter Solomon Islands territorial waters at eighteen hundred hours ship time tomorrow."

"What's our bottom now?"

"About two thousand fathoms, sir. We're coming up

on the Solomon Rise where it will come to a thousand fathoms. Plenty of additional dive room, sir."

"Any indication of targets resembling a *Tuscarora* or the Awesomes?"

"Negative, sir. If we spot something like that, you'll know right away."

"Any surface traffic around us at this time?"

"Other than merchant skunks identified by screw sounds and derived mass on passive sonar and masdet, negative, sir." Lovette paused. "Unless we count the whales fornicating and the dolphins flatulating in the vicinity, sir." The Operations Officer had bowdlerized his language in the presence of the two ladies of the special group.

"I presume that Mister Goff and Mister Ames are tracking those?"

"Yes, sir."

"Very well. Ladies and gentlemen, this mission has several phases that can be summarized as follows," Corry went on. "Phase One is search and, if possible, find Awesome activity. Phase Two is to close on this activity and arrange to capture an Awesome alive. Phase Three is to get out of here and back to Pearl with the live Awesome and without being attacked by one or more of the Awesomes' *Tuscarora* submersible spacecraft. An overriding factor is to prevent interference from any East World vessel. I am now entertaining suggestions on how we should go about making this happen."

When the Captain paused and looked at the other ten people seated around the green-covered table, he was greeted by silence for about ten seconds before Zeke Braxton asked, "Sir, what are the rules of engagement?"

Corry knew that Zeke would be the one to ask this. The man had learned a great deal as XO. He was ready for his own command now. In the meantime, while he served as XO of the U.S.S. *Shenandoah,* his insight and independent thinking, trained by Corry, were an important factor in operations. Corry knew what Zeke would do. And Corry also knew that Zeke was no bootlicker; the XO would look at a subject from one or more viewpoints different than the Captain's, then bring these forth as possible problems or different solutions.

Corry thought for a moment, phrasing his reply carefully in specifically chosen words. He had his breathing and his stuttering well under control at this point. "Rule Number One: I will not allow the boat to enter any waters where I have inadequate sea room to outmaneuver any hostile submersible, insufficient depth to dive for safety against orbital KE weapons, or the possibility of being bottled up in restricted waters by hostile vessels or aircraft. Rule Number Two: If shot at, I will attempt to escape without engaging. If I cannot disengage, I will assume the offensive. Rule Number Three: I will remain submerged, silent, and stealthy unless action to the contrary is required. Only three rules of engagement, ladies and gentlemen. We'll keep it simple."

CDR Terri Ellison spoke up boldly, knowing that this was the standard operating mode in a Papa Briefing. "Captain, these ROEs mean my chickens have to stay in the coop."

Corry nodded. "Yes, Commander, they do."

"Sir, the Air Group has a patrol squadron. The function of the Black Panthers is to look for specific targets."

"Commander, with the boat in an operational stealth mode, any enemy who sights an Osprey from your PatrolRon thereafter knows a carrier submarine must be in the vicinity," Corry pointed out.

"So we just sit and continue to fly the sims!"

"Fortunes of war, Commander. But be prepared. Those fortunes could change very quickly. You know that."

"Yes, sir. Air Group will be ready when you call on us."

"I expect nothing less, Commander."

"The Marines won't snivel," Major Bart Clinch put in. "We're trained. We're ready. Let us know what you want us to do."

"I'm not telling anyone what to do right now, Major. I'm entertaining input. Do you have some?"

"Not at this time, Captain."

"Very well. You've all heard the ROEs. Do you have any recommendation for the conduct of Phase One?"

"Mister Soucek, you told us earlier that Awesome activity was most probably going on in shallow waters near volcanic activity," Bob Lovette said to the man from Majestic Corporation. "You further stated that the Solomon Islands were one of the centers of known Awesome activity as derived from space-going *Tuscarora* activity. The Solomon Islands cover more than twenty-eight thousand square kilometers. That's a big area. So where in the Solomons is this activity taking place?"

Soucek replied with only two words: "The Slot."

"New Georgia Sound." Lovette gave the stretch of water its nautical atlas name.

"Yes. Captain, if you're really entertaining input, my suggestion is to enter New Georgia Sound," Soucek said.

"Is that a good idea?" Zeke wondered. "The first ROE would prevent that. We'd have no sea room."

"It is not a good idea," Corry put in. "It does indeed break the first ROE."

"Let's look," Zeke suggested and activated a control on the wall behind the Captain. A chart of the Solomon Islands came up in the holo tank mounted in the wall. When he saw the arrangement of the islands, he nodded. "I agree. It's not a good idea to go into the Slot. Two Chinese boats could bottle us up in there."

"Captain," Doctor Barry Duval spoke up, "I've had the opportunity to study the bottom charts and currents with your Navigator earlier today. New Georgia Sound has indeed become volcanically active in the past fifty years. A lot of trenches in this region. For example, Savo and Kolombangara are active volcanoes—"

"Doctor Duval, underwater geology and oceanography are your specialties. I intend to listen to you in detail when I need information about those things. Do you have some specific suggestion regarding where I should position the boat?" Corry asked him. He knew that academics often got wound up and carried on for at least fifty minutes, which is the usual length of a class period.

Duval brought himself up short but didn't otherwise react to Corry's interruption. Instead, he said, "Yes, sir. If you want to surveil the New Georgia Sound and not be in it, you could do it quite well by positioning the ship about a hundred kilometers due west of Guadalcanal and south of New Georgia Island. You could look northward into the Sound and you'd have at least a thousand-fathom bottom there."

"We need to be in the Sound," Soucek insisted.

Corry ignored him. "I don't favor a transit of the passage between Malaita and Santa Isabel. The soundings there aren't recent."

"Sir, we can take up a southerly heading now and pass around the southern end of San Cristóbal Island; then we'll have a straight deep-water shot to the patrol location suggested by Doctor Duval," Bob Lovette pointed out on the chart.

"Any objections to that? No? Very well. Make it so, Mister Lovette," Corry told him. "When we reach Doctor Duval's position, we'll continue passive sonar and masdet scans. We shall see what we can see. What then? Suggestions?"

"Captain, I recommend we table discussions about detailed plans beyond this initial Phase One activity," Zeke suggested. "This has turned into an exploratory mission. I don't see how we can make specific plans beyond what we've just done."

"Contingencies, XO?" Corry asked.

"We have two. We stand our ground and handle whatever action, if any, is mounted against us. Or we get under way in the direction of Brisbane or Port Moresby. We've got open sea in all directions from southeastly through westerly headings. And we've got depth to the west of us," Zeke observed. "We can get the hell out of there if we have to."

"Captain, you must get in closer to New Georgia Sound," Soucek insisted.

Corry decided to find out why the man was riding that horse. "Why?"

"We're supposed to make contact, not engage in probing and patrolling. Alien action has been reported in the Sound."

Corry didn't ask what sort of action. He should have, but he was irked at Soucek for continuing to be so enigmatic. "And we're going to find what the action is before we plunge into it. I'm not taking unwarranted risks with this ship and its crew."

10

The U.S.S. *Shenandoah* was rounding the southern cape of San Cristóbal Island, the watch routine was normal, and no IX or skunks were showing on passive sonar or masdet. Everyone was on edge, however, because no one knew what to expect. This wasn't "nominal" procedure in a carrier submarine because Execute Orders were always more precise than the one Captain William M. Corry and the crew were operating under on this cruise.

Command is lonely. And there are times when command and leadership aren't required on a minute-to-minute basis. This is true in a carrier submarine in cruise mode. Therefore, Captain William M. Corry didn't object when Doctor Evelyn Lulalilo asked to see him.

Corry knew why she wanted to be with him, and he felt the instincts of a father within himself. However, he also knew he had to be very careful about his relationship with the marine biologist.

Therefore, he didn't close the door after she came in.

"Captain Corry, I've listened and listened to the recordings you made when the Marines fought the Awesomes near Makasar," she began in explanation. "I really don't know if I can do what's expected of me."

"Eve, you're an expert in communications with aquatic mammals," Corry reminded her. "Do you 'speak' dolphin?"

"I can understand the meaning behind some of the sounds dolphins make," she admitted. She had a worried look on her face. "But anyone who has a dog or cat can understand animal sounds when they try to communicate with us. Communication isn't all auditory. It's visual as well."

"Body language. Quite so." From her own body language, Corry could tell she was very unsure of herself and somewhat hesitant to try controlling her surroundings.

"Yes. The way a dog, cat, or dolphin looks and moves conveys information." She paused, then confided in him, "Captain, with respect to the Awesomes I've heard in the recordings, I might make a wild guess at the meaning of some of their sounds. But I don't know what they were *doing* when they made them. You have no video records. So I can't make any sense out of their sounds alone."

"Eve, no one expects you to come up with a textbook on the structure, grammar, syntax, and meaning of Awesome sounds," he told her, trying to ease her apprehension. "Not in a few days, in any event. I think that Doctor Frip sent you on this mission not because dolphin language might be similar to Awesome language. I believe you were chosen for other reasons. First, you were available and your absence wouldn't provoke speculation about where you went or why. However, the most important reason is probably because you've been trying to accomplish communication with the closest thing we've had to an alien species thus far."

"I haven't been very successful at it, Captain. But I was making progress. Learning dolphin language poses some real problems that I haven't fully solved yet. It's not like learning how to speak another human language."

"How many human languages do you speak, Eve?"

"Uh, English, of course. And French, Greek, and Japanese, although none of them with great fluency," she admitted.

"That's unusual. Most Americans don't speak any language very well, including English," Corry said with a smile. "I speak Spanish and Russian, and I can read several others. Have you been to Europe?"

She nodded. "And to Japan."

"Did you learn your second languages in an academic setting or in the country of the language?"

"I took French as my undergraduate language because of the French predominance in marine biology," she told him. "I learned Greek and Japanese when I was studying in the Aegean and Japan."

"How did you learn those two tongues?"

She paused, then answered, "By immersion."

"Yes. As I learned the few I speak. By being in the culture. By hearing the language spoken all around me every day. By being forced to communicate using the language."

"That's the way we all learned our 'milk tongues,' by the way."

"Yes. And it takes me several days of immersion before I can begin to think in another language. So why did you believe I'd expect you to learn the Awesome language by listening to some confusing and distorted audiotapes?"

Lulalilo didn't say anything for several seconds. "You didn't, did you? And you don't. Thank you, Captain. I know what my job is now. When we find Awesomes, I'm going to immerse myself in their universe just as I try to do with the dolphins."

"It's going to be an alien universe, Eve."

"So is the universe of a dolphin. And our universe is just as alien to the Awesomes."

Allan Soucek appeared in the open doorway. He seemed less imperious today. "I'm sorry, Captain. If I'm interrupting something, I'll come back later. But your cabin door was open."

"Figuratively, my door is always open to anyone, Mister Soucek. I often have to close that physical door when I require privacy or discuss certain activities with my lead officers." Corry wasn't sure what Soucek had on his mind. The enigmatic man seemed to be avoiding him since the Papa briefing yesterday. "Doctor Lulalilo had a professional problem she needed to discuss with me. I believe we've resolved it. Helping people resolve problems is one of my duties as Commanding Officer. Do you have a problem, sir?"

"I need to speak with you, Captain," Soucek told him. Then the little man added, "Alone."

It was apparent from Eve's body language and tone of voice that she didn't like Soucek. "I'll leave, Captain." She arose and moved out of the cabin and through the door in a way that kept the maximum distance between her and Soucek. "Thank you, sir."

"Eve, you solved your own problem," Corry reminded her.

"Not without your help, sir." And she was gone.

Soucek came in and carefully closed the door behind him. When Corry motioned for him to sit where Lulalilo had been, he did so while looking carefully around the cabin.

"You seem suspicious, Mister Soucek," Corry observed.

"I am, Captain."

"May I ask why?"

"You don't like me very well, do you, Captain Corry?" This sudden question came out as a statement of belief.

"I do not dislike you, Mister Soucek. But you've given me few reasons to trust you, and a feeling of trustworthiness is one of the first attributes of liking someone," Corry told him frankly, because Soucek's remark had also been frank. The Captain of the U.S.S. *Shenandoah* didn't have major problems with the ship or crew demanding his attention right then. On the other hand, Corry didn't want to waste time talking to someone who didn't seem to want to cooperate with him and continued to act in a furtive and frightened manner. "Did you wish to see me in order to bury the hatchet, so to speak? Or is something else on your mind?"

"Captain, I need to convince you of my sincerity and make you aware of the fact that I have a lifetime of experience in the matter of extraterrestrials."

Corry didn't respond at once. Finally he said, "Mister Soucek, I know nothing of you. You come with no credentials. You came aboard my ship assuming I would relinquish command authority to you without suitable proof that I should do so. I do not doubt your sincerity. I am not aware of your expertise. Therefore, I must act as an agnostic. I reserve judgment pending further proof, sir."

Soucek almost sighed in frustration. "I was afraid of that. What would you accept as proof of who I am and my role on this mission?"

"Written confirmation from my superiors, sir."

"You know the reason why I cannot provide that."

"No, sir, I don't. You've made some astounding claims and maintained that they come from information so highly classified that I'm not allowed to be privy to it."

"That's true. There's much you don't know. You don't have the level of clearance required. And you don't have a need to know."

"If I'm being asked to risk the lives of seven hundred fifty people in a multibillion-dollar capital ship of the United States Navy, I do indeed have a need to know, Mister Soucek."

"I assure you that they will not dock your pay if something happens to this ship on this mission."

"Pay be damned, sir! I mentioned more than seven hundred people! What price the human life?" Corry was more than weary of playing head games with this man.

"Of those seven hundred fifty people, how many of them do you know well?"

"Most of them, sir."

"That I doubt. Are you willing to vouch for the fact that some of them may not be human beings?"

Corry didn't reply to that for a moment. He was now angry beyond the point where he could naturally continue behaving as a gentleman. But he forced himself to do so. "What do you mean by that, sir?"

"Captain Corry, I mentioned before that we know of at least seventy extraterrestrial species. Not all of them are monsters. Many of them are humanoids who are *slightly* different in appearance but could otherwise pass as human, given the wide variety of physical attributes of the human race."

"Are you trying to tell me that I have aliens in my crew?"

"You very well may. They've shown up elsewhere in critical places where mingling with humans helps them attain what they want. I'm suggesting that you perhaps take a careful look at your crew. I need to warn you that, as this mission progresses and unfolds, some of them may turn out to be other than what you believe. A great deal of competition and jealousy exists between some of those seventy alien species, Captain. Alien agents are among us to keep our activities from affecting their interests on this planet. And, of course, that's just what we're doing on this mission."

Corry was now firmly convinced that Allan Soucek was insane. Or, if not certifiably nuts, at least badly paranoid. However, given the fact that Soucek had come aboard as part of the special group, Corry was reluctant to take action against him. So he chose his words carefully. "Mister Soucek, you've just made another unsubstantiated charge. If you want my trust and cooperation, you're going to have to reveal many things to me and my officers. Furthermore, you will have to provide some documentation in the form of orders or other bona fides."

"I can do that, Captain, if I may be allowed to communicate with Washington."

"I'll arrange for that," Corry promised. He didn't tell Soucek that he would communicate first by SWC once the ship had reached its sentry position west of Guadalcanal. "When we're in a situation where I can break communications silence without disobeying my orders to maintain stealth, I'll invite you to contact whomever you please in Washington to provide me with the documentation I need."

"Thank you. I'll do that. In the meantime, I caution you to beware. There's much you don't know."

"And much I damned well had better be made aware of!"

"I can't reveal it to you at this time, Captain."

"Then we have nothing further to talk about." Corry rose to his feet. He couldn't dismiss Soucek. Instead, he said, "I request that you remain in your quarters until I'm able to establish communications. In the meantime, please excuse me, as I have work in hand and responsibilities to attend to."

"You're placing me under arrest, Captain?"

"No. I'm asking you to remain in quarters."

"I don't have to comply with that request, Captain."

Corry touched the intercom panel. "Chief Master-at-arms to the Captain's quarters on the double with a visitor escort detail!"

There was an immediate knock on the door. When

Corry called for entry, his Chief Staff Petty Officer was already there. Two men were with him.

"Just happened to be nearby, Captain. I saw Mister Soucek come in earlier," Chief Warren remarked in an offhand manner. He'd served with Corry for years. He could read his Commanding Officer very well.

"Please escort Mister Soucek to his quarters and see to it that he remains there and is brought meals."

"Aye, aye, sir!" The way Warren said it conveyed additional meaning. He was telling his CO, *It's about time, sir!*

Corry decided he'd better find out what Soucek had been up to since he'd come aboard.

So he called Zeke Braxton to his cabin and inquired.

"I anticipated you'd ask, Captain," Zeke replied. "I had Chief Armstrong put a couple of his rates to watching Mister Soucek's activities in the boat."

"And?"

"The man is a recluse, Captain," the XO observed with some distaste. He wasn't used to having a recluse in a submarine. Because of the nature of the Silent Service, its personnel were rarely silent among themselves. Submariners were, in general, a gregarious lot. They lived so close together that they had to like one another reasonably well, at least enough to keep from fighting and engaging in other non-social behavior. All naval personnel were bound by a tight but specific general code of conduct. It was enforced differently in different departments and among different teams in the boat. The chiefs kept close watch on their rates for signs of trouble in the social interaction sphere. The officers were bound by stricter but more psychological behavior codes. When a person suddenly became reclusive and stayed that way for several days—everyone had their bad days, of course, but a string of them was something considered unacceptable—it was time for the superior to ask that person to report to sick bay for an evaluation and some counseling because such behavior presaged trouble.

"Mister Soucek met with the special group several times yesterday in the main wardroom while they were trying to sort out their structure. He's visited the bridge twice and just watched for about thirty minutes each time. Other than that, he's kept to his quarters," Braxton went on to report.

"Please ask the Chief to continue his surveillance. I had to confine Mister Soucek to quarters a few minutes ago," Corry told his Number Two.

"Yes, sir. I know. And I'll make sure Chief Warren maintains vigilance. I don't know exactly what happened here today, but whatever caused you to confine him to quarters was undoubtedly justified. This guy Soucek is a loose cannon and he doesn't want to acknowledge that he isn't running the show. A Commanding Officer can't allow that."

"What do you believe his problem is, Zeke?" Corry asked.

"He's got something bottled up inside that scares the hell out of him. To add to it, he's been so indoctrinated by security procedures that he's scared to tell anyone anything for fear of telling someone who shouldn't be told," Zeke surmised, calling upon his experience as both a squadron commander and an XO. "I think he desperately wants to tell someone, but he can't. Or he's scared shitless because he knows something that we don't, and he's afraid to tell us."

Corry nodded. "I agree. What do you think we should do about it?"

Zeke thought about this for a moment. Then he replied, "Nothing, sir."

"Nothing?"

"Yes, sir. Nothing. Neither of us can solve his personal problem for him. But something might happen that's going to cause him to explode. I don't know what that something will be. However, we could very well get into a situation with the Awesomes that could trigger it." Zeke paused, then added, "I think you made a very wise move confining Soucek to quarters, Captain. If he's going to go over the edge, it's better that he do it in his cabin than out in the ship somewhere. I don't know how much he knows about submarines, so I don't know if he'd try to do something deadly or not."

"I don't think he knows much about submarines, but I believe he does know a lot about extraterrestrials, Number Two," Corry pointed out. "I don't want to bottle him up. He probably has some extremely valuable and important information that could tip the scales in this operation."

"Tough call, sir."

"What would you do, Number Two? How would you handle it?" Corry knew what he intended to do. He wanted to see if Braxton had a better idea.

"I'd keep him informed. If we go to General Quarters, I'd have him on the bridge—with a couple of big security people standing by in an unobtrusive way." Zeke thought for a moment, then added, "I'd also allow him to come to the wardroom for meals. And I'd encourage the members of the special team to visit him at least daily. Contact with other people might help."

"I hadn't considered that last, but you're right. Thank you, Zeke. Inform Chief Warren that I'll allow Soucek out of Coventry at mealtimes. And during Papa and Oscar briefs as well."

After Braxton left, Corry took care of several administrative chores and got his yeoman out of his hair. He continually monitored several N-fone channels, as usual, but it wasn't until the press of immediate tasks was relieved that he noticed it was very quiet in the boat.

It was 1100 hours boat time, enough time for him to make a casual walkaround before lunch.

In the door mirror, he checked the knot in his black tie before he stepped out of his cabin. In Corry's book, the Commanding Officer was always on parade, always on duty, always there as an example to others in the boat. Therefore, he was specifically aware of his personal appearance every time he stepped out of his cabin.

The bridge was quiet. The deck watch was on duty. Everyone was at their posts.

"Captain on the bridge!" called out LT Donald G. Morse, the OOD, when he saw Corry.

"Carry on, Mister Morse," Corry told him, checking the digital display of the ship's position and looking at the chart on the main screen. The U.S.S. *Shenandoah* was shown to be eight-seven nautical miles southeast of its planned sentry point in the Solomon Sea west of Guadalcanal.

Over at the navigation consoles, LCDR Natalie Chase was studying a screen with Dr. Barry Duval.

Corry hadn't noticed before, but Duval was certainly a tall, ectomorphic, blond-haired individual who towered over the petite Navigator. Duval looked aside at Corry as the CO stepped up to the console.

"Good morning, Captain," Chase greeted him.

"Good morning, Commander. And good morning, Doctor."

Duval returned the greeting in a rather surprised manner. Apparently he wasn't used to such commonplace protocols. Corry decided that scientists lived and worked in a world all their own that was often far removed from the reality of the submarine service.

Then he brought himself up short because of that thought. The world in a submarine was part of a larger world beyond the hull in which Duval and others lived. Corry had briefly fallen into the fantasy that often plagues submariners, the feeling that everything outside the boat was somehow another world.

"Doctor Duval and I were going over the data concerning the bottom in the New Georgia Sound, Captain," Chase explained. "He seems to have more recent information than that on my charts."

"Doctor, did you bring more recent charts with you?" Corry asked the tall oceanographer. The CO was somewhat concerned about an outsider messing around with the official and anointed naval charts upon which the undersea navigation of the boat depended.

Duval nodded. "Before I grabbed my bag and ran for the airplane from Woods Hole, I managed to upload a cube with the latest data obtained by seasats. The Defense Mapping Agency and the Geological Survey have been revising the charts for this part of the world on their regular update schedule," Duval explained.

Corry was relieved. The last thing he wanted was for some science johnnie like Duval to come booming in to change the data in the ship's navigational data base. However, Duval had apparently brought a machine-readable memory cube with the latest information. Chase was as cautious as the CO, and he knew she wouldn't accept anything she didn't believe was the genuine article.

However, cautious as CAPT William M. Corry and LCDR Natalie Chase were, they had no control of something outside the boat—a meeting of Soucek's superiors half a world away in distance and worlds away in terms of its participants.

11

Summertime was pleasant in Appalachia. The air was clear and cool, but the sunlight was warm.

But none of the twelve men sat in the sunlight. Their skins wouldn't withstand it.

"Miserable weather!" Stanfield Inteus growled. "I can't wait until I get back to Nun. One more year...."

"I agree. Too cold here. No wonder women refuse to come." This was said by Dr. Karl Songan, another tall, light-haired man who wore a heavy parka. "I'm just glad I managed to get that dean's position in southern California. Even Colorado had terrible weather most of the year."

General Hoyt Beva wasn't happy, either, but he interrupted the corporate CEO and the university dean by reminding them, "You have it easy, both of you! The military track requires thirty years here."

"Well, it's not as easy to rig the military records. You knew that before you accepted the assignment, Hoyt," Admiral Stephen Tyonek reminded him.

"Yes, but the perks were better."

The language of the conversation on the enclosed porch was spoken nowhere else on Earth except among these twelve people.

"You do get a better choice of subsequent assignments," Dr. Enos Delsin pointed out.

"There had to be some compensation for this long duty watch," Tyonek observed.

"Well, the Country Club is comfortable enough because we can keep it warm," Beva remarked. The accommodations at this mountain resort known only as "the Country Club" weren't lush. The place was a bit rundown. However, it was adequate. And it was very private. Unlike many other Appalachian resorts, it wasn't open to the public. It had been purchased only for these special meetings. But few meetings had taken place over the past several decades.

Lyle Muraco shook his head in frustration. "I'm having trouble re-learning how to speak Dumuzi. Can't we shift back to English?"

"Yes, it would allay any suspicions," Dr. Armand Grust agreed. "Most of the staff is new, but they won't wonder why we don't speak Dumuzi."

"I presume they've been screened."

"Don't worry. They're fine. We can shift back to English if you want, but I need the practice."

"English, please," was the request from General Danforth Chesmu.

"That's what happens when we don't meet often enough," Dr. Bourke Renap remarked. "This is only the second conference since I've been here. No wonder we're all going native."

Dr. Armand Grust rapped the knuckles of his long, bony hand on the table. "And it will be our last conference unless we get down to business and figure out what we're going to do. The Majestic Twelve will please come to order."

The other eleven men fell silent and gave Grust their attention.

"We haven't met recently because we had everything well under control. Ergo, there was no reason to meet," the man with the thinning yellow-gray hair and long face went on in English. "Too many meetings could draw attention to us. It took us a long time to maneuver all the locals off Majestic Twelve so we had exclusive control. We grew complacent and interested only in serving out our assignments. Then the Makasar incident hit us."

"I did the best I could," General Chesmu put in.

"I know you did. And on short notice, too. I'm not saying we dropped the ball, gentlemen," Grust pointed out. "I *am* telling you that the powers that be won't be very happy about this."

"That damned cutter captain should be court-martialed!" Tyonek muttered. "After he cleaned up the renegade Sama base and killed their Dagda workers north of Makasar, he should have gotten out of there as he did after he failed to ram the Chinese submarine and discovered the *Shenandoah* lurking in stealth."

"How the hell did the *Shenandoah* know where he was? The cutter was stealthed, wasn't he?" Fergus Antol asked. As the CEO of a major defense contractor, he knew almost as much about military and naval affairs, doctrines, and tactics as the general and flag officers of Majestic Twelve. "Or he should have been unless he broke the rules of engagement."

"He was pinging sonar, so the *Shenandoah* saw him," Tyonek recalled. "The *Shenandoah* was rigged for stealth, too. Those big Rivers-class carrier submarines are surprisingly hard to detect."

"Then how did the *Shenandoah* follow him when he went quiet and ran during the earlier encounter?" Antol wondered.

Tyonek shrugged. "I don't know." And he didn't. As the chief of the Naval Reconnaissance Office, he had no "need to know" about the White Oak Laboratory mass detector mounted in the SSCV-26, nor of the new submarine tactics permitted by the masdet.

"Be that as it may, the cutter captain was recalled to Nun and reassigned," Grust told them. "That's not our worry. What *is* our worry amounts to this: We knew the Samas were running our blockade. We knew they'd enlisted the help of the Dagdas. We couldn't stop them because no defense is perfect. However, as long as the Samas kept their human-hunting at a low level, their activities were lost in the noise. And we could handle the patrolling duties. Our patrol activities to keep the Samas from wholesale slaughter of humans for their black-market operations have been a small price to pay in preventing an interstellar war."

General Danforth Chesmu nodded. "Yeah, I may not like this place, but the people are pretty decent in spite of having a vicious streak in them. I wouldn't want to see them thrown back ten million years by letting the Samas hunt them to near extinction."

"Oh, come on, Chesmu!" Dr. Jonathan Frip objected. "Humans breed faster than ermins. The Samas would have to mount a huge operation to actually commit genocide. And long before they could do that, humans would find out and fight back. You have no idea how violent this species can be! They have one of the highest ferocity indexes known!"

"I came up the ranks in the United States Army, so I'm well aware of that," Chesmu replied. "Which is another reason I'm glad we concluded the agreement with them in the last century. Getting our crash debris back before they figured it out and erupted into this sector of the galaxy with the technology was small price to pay for agreeing to keep the Samas out of here."

"Be that as it may, no one believed the arrangement would work for more than a century or so," Fergus Antol put in. "These are smart people. Before the Dulce blow-up, the campaign to get them to accept the Samas was working. You know very well that any intelligent being will figure out how to do something once it knows others have done it. These people do that very well. Now most of them accept the reality of galactic life and know it's only a matter of time before they develop their own starships. They're a typical Level Two culture; their science and technology are progressing on a cubic curve with no sign of inflecting yet. If the Makasar data ever leaks—and it will—they'll have an even greater incentive. Remember: Their submarine technology is almost to the level of starship technology."

"Don't worry. The Makasar data won't get out," Admiral Tyonek assured the group.

"Well, it has," Dr. Armand Grust pointed out.

"It *has*?" Tyonek responded with disbelief.

"Yes, and through Naval Intelligence, too. That's your bailiwick, Tyonek."

"I missed it."

"I'll say you did."

"That woman they have in there is very good at what she does."

"And that's why we had to convene this meeting. We got so smugly complacent that we let the White House send the *Shenandoah* down to the Solomons before we could act."

"Well, the *Shenandoah* got some awfully good data,"

Dr. Karl Songan admitted. "Best I've seen. Better than some Star Patrol recruiting video in terms of quality."

Grust sighed. It was one of the few emotions he revealed during this meeting. Dumuzis weren't renown for wearing their emotions in the open because they preferred to let their competitors guess what was going through their minds. Dumuzi traders had good business sense, a factor that had permitted them to build one of the most extensive interstellar trading cultures. Their human colleagues, not knowing what they were, merely considered each of them to be somewhat cold and calculating in personal and business relationships.

"Yes, they're very good at communications and documentation," Grust admitted. "We've learned a lot from them. We're still learning. But that's a side issue here this morning, Songan. The *Shenandoah* is in the Solomon Islands region right now. That's a prime area of Sama exploitation. Those beasts are not only harvesting humans but also lots of carbon and nitrogen. The waters there are so warm that life is prolific."

"The Sama can't make a dent in the ecology there," Dr. Jonathan Frip pointed out. "Not at their present level of exploitation, at any rate."

"Can we get a full brief on the exact situation and what led to it?" Fergus Antol asked. "Not all of us have the deep sources of some of you. Obviously, we're going to have to take some action. It may not be benign. If I'm going to have a part in such a recommendation, I want to know as much as everyone else."

"Fair request," Grust admitted. "Let me give it a try. If any of you have additional information, don't hesitate to interrupt."

"Don't worry. We won't hesitate to make additional inputs. That's the Dumuzi way of reaching consensus," Lyle Muraco reminded them.

Dr. Armand Grust, the de facto leader of the Majestic 12 because of both longevity of his Earth tour and his nominal rank in the Star Patrol, began, "We knew the Samas were using the Dagdas to hunt humans in the warm and shallow tropical waters of the Earth. They don't have the biotechnology to replicate the endocrines and other biochemicals they need to counter the mutations caused by the blow-up of Bisanabi. They were the closest to that supernova and caught the worst of the radiation. Being members of the Amalgamate, they received the early discovery data about Earth."

"It was a mistake to let the Samas into the Amalgamate," Frip opined. It was obvious he didn't like the Samas, but neither did any of the others on the enclosed porch that day.

"Better to have them in the Amalgamate and know what they're doing," General Hoyt Beva pointed out. "Underground operations are always more difficult to police."

"Well, the Samas are underground now!" Stanfield Inteus reminded him.

"True, but we know what they're doing. And it's at such a low level of activity that it isn't worth enforcing the canons against them," Beva explained.

"The Samas are deceitful anyway," Dr. Enos Delsin said. "They got here fast and discovered that the biological components of life here were compatible with their own. You know the Samas; they have little respect for any life-form other than their own, and we've had to correct their approach on several occasions."

"Tell me. I still bear the scars of the Pakavi Incident," Dr. Bourke Renap muttered. "What a beastly species they are!"

"Beastly or not, they're a self-aware species that qualifies them for treatment according to the Canons of Metalaw," Grust said, reminding them of the overall philosophy of metalaw that governed the behavior of galactic species. "However, like all of us, they follow the law of least effort and made a deal with humans to provide them with biological products. The only group on this planet with the wherewithal to do that was the United States because of its leading role in the world economy. Its companies were multi-national. The deal fell through, of course, because of the continually increasing demands of the Samas for biochemicals they simply didn't have the capability of understanding or producing. That's when Star Patrol had to step in and arrange to keep the Samas off this planet in exchange for getting our ship debris and dead crews back."

"That was no deal, Grust!" Songan snapped. "The humans could have done nothing with our technology in the last century!"

"Agreed. But they knew of it. No matter the species of an engineer, once it's known that another engineer can do something, the first hurdle of disbelief is cleared and the other engineer can make it happen," Stanfield Inteus said, recalling his own experiences with several aerospace companies, including his present firm, General Aerospace West. "Besides, speaking as one who has concluded several contract deals in my mundane persona, humans don't consider a deal to be a deal unless an exchange takes place. Otherwise, they look for the hidden agenda or the kicker, as they call it. They can't figure out that Star Patrol can't charge them anything for doing what the Amalgamate says we must do and what the canons require anyway. So we took back a worthless pile of non-working junk. Never mind; they'd gone over it carefully at Wright-Pat and Site Fifty-one. And we never did get back the ship that was so big they could do nothing but bury it. But I don't believe anyone now remembers where it was buried."

"Well, things quieted down and have stayed quiet for the last thirty or forty years," Grust went on. "That caused us to get complacent. And that's why we weren't immediately on top of the data that the U.S.S. *Shenandoah* got near Makasar. We bobbled the whole affair, gentlemen. We've forgotten how to handle the consequences of the close encounter scenario."

"My fault. Mea culpa," was the remark from Newell Carew, who spoke up for the first time. As President of the Majestic Corporation, he'd been on vacation on Nun when the *Shenandoah* affair had occurred. "I got back here as quickly as I could. But by that time, Dolores McCarthy and Alan Dekker had set the wheels in motion to send the *Shenandoah* back to capture a live Dagda. It took a lot of work, but Frip and I finally got the right people into the *Shenandoah* as a special team."

Carew sighed. "I had to give a full Star Patrol brief to Soucek. Otherwise, he would have started asking embarrassing questions, especially around the White House. And that could have blown our cover and revealed that

Majestic Twelve and Majestic Corporation were controlled by other than humans. I really hope I didn't screw up by briefing Soucek."

"How did he take it?" Grust wanted to know. Some humans came unbonded when they were told because the revelation demolished some of their most deeply held and strongly cherished personal beliefs.

"I believe he'll do all right. He was frightened. And he was shaken. We've seen that before. But the man is also a zealot; he *likes* the sort of work he has to do at Majestic Corporation because he's followed the phenomenon all his life and wants answers."

"Did he like the ones he got?"

"No. They weren't the ones he'd hoped for. But I put him in charge of the team on the submarine. He's got the full story, so he's in the best position to make the mission work, if that's possible."

"He will," Dr. Johnathan Frip stated. "I arranged for one of our covert Earth investigators to get on the team. Soucek will have someone to remind him of the importance of the mission and the need to keep the Majestic lid on tight."

"Good thinking, Frip," Grust complimented him.

"Tyonek, I'm wondering," General Beva put in, "why the *Shenandoah* was sent to the Solomons. Yes, the Samas have a fishing operation going there. But why that one?"

"Beva, you know the world situation as well as I do right now. Ordering the *Shenandoah* to Cape Horn was the obvious thing to do. But it fools no one. The Chinese and the Indians expect a covert change in orders. Sending the ship to the Solomons is expected by the East World powers. They don't suspect that the ship is also on a fishing expedition to get more of what they know the Americans found near Makasar. They'll consider it a countermove in the southeast Asia game, and they'll make their own countermove with both submarines and aircraft. On the other hand, if they *do* know of the fishing expedition, they'll move to get a piece of that action. Remember, they *know* about the Dagda and are upset that the Dagda carcasses they were given on Sulawesi decomposed before they could do anything about it."

Majestic Corporation CEO Newell Carew sat back and folded his hands across his chest. "The *Shenandoah* will have to deal with the East World naval forces. We war-gamed it at Majestic Corporation yesterday. Several outcomes have equal probabilities of taking place. Briefly, here are the high probability war gaming outcomes: The *Shenandoah* may be able to maintain stealth and carry out the Navy's intel mission to capture a live Dagda; if that happens, we'll have to meet again to deal with the consequences. On the other hand, the carrier submarine may be found by the East World naval forces even now on their way to the area. They may cooperate with the *Shenandoah* if they know of the Sama-Dagda base or find out about it. If a confrontation takes place between the *Shenandoah* and the East World forces there, an entirely new set of possibilities is created. The *Shenandoah* may prevail, in which case East World may use the incident as an excuse to initiate an armed conflict of broader scope. On the other hand, the United States may provoke such a conflict if the *Shenandoah* is sunk."

"Carew, what is the probability of that last?" Tyonek asked. His mundane assignment was in the United States Navy. He knew the consequences of losing a major capital ship and its crew.

"Better than point-five."

The members of Majestic 12 were stunned by that statement. No one said anything for a moment. Then Dr. Enos Delsin blurted out in the Dumuzi language, "We can't allow that to happen!"

"Why?" General Hoyt Beva replied in English.

"Because of our laxity, we could be held responsible by Star Patrol Judge Advocate General for violation of the Fourth Canon of Metalaw!"

"Let's see ... as I recall it, 'An intelligent being must not affect the freedom of choice or the survival of another intelligent being and must not, by inaction, permit the destruction of another intelligent being,' " Grust replied pensively.

"The JAG would be stretching the Fourth Canon to indict us, Delsin," Chesmu pointed out.

"That's how metalawyers stay busy," Delsin said. "Be that as it may, I can't condone the Majestic Twelve standing by and allowing one of our employees and one of our coverts to be killed!"

"I agree with Delsin," was Dr. Jonathan Frip's assessment. "We can't wash our hands of it. We must interject ourselves into this situation to a greater extent than we've already done by putting our people on the ship."

Eight others either nodded or muttered agreement.

"Very well," Grust said, noting the general agreement, "so now what is Majestic Twelve going to do about it?"

12

CO, this is Special Sensors. We have contacts! came the call from LT Charles B. Ames. *Multiple signals indicating Awesomes in the Slot, sir! We've counted at least thirty, and the count keeps rising.*

CAPT William B. Corry decided he didn't want to sit on the bridge and just watch the masdet display. He wanted to see the first-generation displays themselves. The boat was at Condition Two. Passive sonar showed no IX or even skunks. He felt he could leave the bridge at this time. Besides, it had been a long time since he'd visited Special Sensors. He got to his feet and told Zeke, "XO, you have the con. Maintain Condition Two. Maintain stealth and station. I'll be in the masdet compartment."

Braxton was studying the masdet display repeater screen. He knew the situation and understood the Captain's desire for a nearly hands-on experience at this point. Even Zeke was discovering that command somehow separated the commander from the skull sweat of the commanded. "Aye, aye, sir! I have the con. Maintain Condition Two. Maintain stealth and station. Looks like good hunting in the Slot!" He checked the position readout log again. The SSCV-26 U.S.S. *Shenandoah* was stationary at fifty meters depth positioned 100 kilometers due west of Guadalcanal. Her bow was pointed north by northeast to give the bow-mounted masdet "antenna" elements a clear "view" of New Georgia Sound. And the boat was very, very quiet.

LCDR Natalie Chase was also studying the masdet repeater at the Navigation station with Dr. Barry Duval. "Your new charts tally very close with what the sensors are showing, Doctor Duval," she told him.

"This new mass detector is going to revolutionize oceanography, Natalie," the tall, ectomorphic, blond-haired man replied in a distracted fashion as he marked up his charts on the basis of what he was seeing on the display. He seemed to be unaware of the masdet display pips that Natalie had tagged as Awesomes swimming in the New Georgia Sound. Nor had he paid the slightest attention to Natalie. He was engrossed in the new mass detector technology that had been revealed to him on this cruise. "Sonar was good, but this is better! Mass detectors will do much the same for oceanography as radar did for meteorology. With some practice, I'm going to be able to read the density of the subsea geological forms."

Natalie Chase was rated as several millihelens by other members of the crew—one millihelen being the amount of feminine beauty required to launch one ship. On duty, she never tried to get a reaction from men. She normally didn't have to work at it anyway, but she was right then. On the basis of Duval's behavior, she'd decided he was a total sci-nerd. She could tell when a man noticed her as someone more than just another naval officer. And Duval seemed totally disinterested.

But she also admitted to herself that Duval was bright and intelligent. He certainly knew and understood the scientific ways of the sea, at least from an academic standpoint and, to a certain extent, from his experience in small boats and on oceanographic ships. However, Chase got the impression that he didn't understand women. It bothered her a little bit but she didn't allow it to distract her from her job. Duval had an interesting if nonconformist way of looking at the sea. She wanted to use that to help her get the U.S.S. *Shenandoah* wherever the Captain decided to go without running aground. In these waters, Duval's insights were valuable. When the boat had come around the south end of Makiira, he'd shared the navigational work load. He understood sea bottom charts and acted as if he'd been to the Solomons area before. Natalie decided the man had a natural feel for converting undersea topographical data from charts to reality.

In the masdet compartment, Corry slipped into an

empty seat next to Ames at one of the main masdet display consoles. He was beginning to get the same feel for the masdet displays, as he had with those of sonar. But sonar was a mature technology and its displays had evolved over the years to present data with the optimum human-machine interface. On the other hand, the masdet was too new. Just getting it to work was a technical miracle. Keeping it working was a full-time job. Therefore, little effort had yet been put into displaying masdet information in a way that the human mind could rapidly assimilate. It was basically blobs of contrast on one or more screens accompanied by measurements on tape or dial meters. An understanding of mass detection technology was required for Ames and his specialist ratings to decipher the data and then interpret it. Corry was getting used to it but hadn't become an expert yet. He depended upon Ames and his people for that.

And Corry paid no attention to the jargon. He asked Ames verbally, "What have you got, Charlie?"

Ames pointed to a blob on the screen. "There's the density discontinuity line that's the southwest coast of Santa Isabel Island. Here's Guadalcanal. This group of signals to the left shows the presence of Nggatokae, Vangunu, Tetpare, Rendova, and New Georgia. The discontinuities are more prevalent because of the sharp rise of those land forms off the sea bottom around here."

Corry noticed a feature that didn't appear as strongly on the bridge repeaters. He pointed to it and asked what it was.

"Gentle gradations in the sea bottom. But the blips here . . . and here . . . and here are undersea volcanoes. Judging from the signals, they're dense and therefore probably new in comparison to the soft responses from the sea bottom in the vicinity," Ames explained in his detached and informal manner. Although he was a line officer, he'd come out of NROTC at MIT, gone straight to White Oak Laboratories, and thence been assigned to mother-hen the masdet installation in the U.S.S. *Shenandoah*. This was his first blue-water posting.

Corry didn't reprimand him for lack of disciplinary protocol. The CO knew that the scientific/technical career path in the Navy produced officers less inclined to snap and pop than line officers. They were even more informal than the "brown-shoe Navy" in the Air Group. Ames was good, and Corry was happy to have the man in the boat. The masdet brought a whole new element of sensing technology to submarine operations. And as a result of the *Shanna* being one of the first ships to mount a masdet, her officers and crew had the opportunity to write the new book on submarine operational doctrine and tactics. The Captain and the crew of the U.S.S. *Shenandoah* had "eyes" that other submarines didn't. They could "see" objects that other boats had to sense by sonar.

"And these mobile indications are the Awesomes," Ames went on. He indicated a bank of vertical tape instruments. "Assuming that the mass of an individual Awesome is one-fifty kilograms—which was that of the one we captured and took back to Pearl—my computer can calculate a likely distance based on signal strength degradation through sea water."

"I'm glad you can make sense out of it all," Corry admitted to him. "It's taken me a long time just to get used to the difference between the masdet data display and what we get from sonar, radar, and lidar. I'll be happy when the human factors people get a shot at this."

Ames hesitated a moment, then admitted, "Captain, you may chew me out for this, but I've got something here that may help make better sense out of the masdet outputs. . . ."

"I won't chew your butt for showing initiative and creativity, Mister Ames," Corry promised him, "unless you've destroyed a lot of expensive government hardware in the process."

"I haven't, sir." The masdet expert performed a ritual with a keypad and ball. The display on the screen changed. "Hey, it's working this time! Great!" Then he realized he was speaking to his CO and went on to explain, "Sir, on the cruise from Pearl this time, I didn't have a lot to do. So I hacked a megamacro that would display a lot of the masdet data in a presentation something like a PPI radar screen. It's still not very good, sir, as you can see. It sort of gives only a horizontal slice, like looking out through a horizontal slit. I haven't figured out how to display it in a holo tank to get the additional dimensional data up. I'm just glad the mega-macro is working right now. Uh, it still has some worms and germs in it, sir. Sometimes it just paints abstract art on the screen. It's nothing that I'd want to submit for naval qual certification . . . yet."

The new generation of naval officers was turning out to be completely at home with the new technology that kept pouring over the Navy, Corry decided. Of course, he realized this had always been the case for the last hundred years or so. Furthermore, they embraced it with a type of pragmatism different from that of the systems managers of the Aerospace Force or the Army rank and file. The warriors of those two services had a greater tendency to take what they were given, use it, and break it if they could. The Navy depended upon working technology to help its people remain alive in a violent, hostile, and deadly environment: the sea. The Aerospace Force and the Army had never had to worry about having an airport or a battlefield sink.

Navy people had a tendency to take technology, modify it to get it to working better if they could, and make it do its job.

"Mister Ames, your megamacro masdet presentation is an order of magnitude improvement over what we've had to date," Corry complimented him. "Please arrange to display it on the repeater on the bridge."

"I will if I can keep it working, Captain."

"I'm sure you'll figure out how to do it. Now, what are we seeing here?"

"Awesomes here and there, these signals that are moving. Something I haven't identified yet here and here."

"Awesome underwater bases perhaps?"

Ames shrugged. "I don't know, sir. I have no referent. I don't know what an Awesome base would look like or consist of. Or how it might be different from its surroundings when it comes to mass."

"Plot their positions and make sure the Navigator gets the data. We may want to have a closer look at those places."

"Yes, sir. Now these signals are islands I mentioned

earlier. And reefs. We're seeing only those portions below water level, sir."

"Too bad the masdet won't work across the water-air interface," Corry mused.

Ames paused again, then admitted, "Oh, but it will, sir."

This surprised Corry again. "Eh? White Oak told me it wouldn't."

"Oh, they were just covering their anatomies, Captain. They didn't want to jeopardize the chance to get the masdet in a ship so it could be tested under real-world conditions. So they didn't want to claim anything for it that they weren't absolutely sure it would do," Ames explained. "I, uh, don't much care for Navy politics, Captain. I've got enough trouble trying to make the universe do what I want. I haven't got the time or the talent to try to make people do what I want."

"So you can make the masdet see upward?"

Ames nodded. "The air-water interface is a major density discontinuity, and it isn't a smooth one. But I saw the computer programs that Barbara Brewer uses to take the air-water interface out of airborne radar and video signals coming from the Ospreys. Like when the *Tuscarora* was coming southward in the Makasar Straits during our last encounter with one there. So I tried modifying it to process masdet signals ..."

"And?" Corry prompted when Ames paused.

"It works, sir, but I'm not real happy with the results."

Corry knew that Ames would be happy only with perfection. What the Special Sensors Officer had accomplished thus far might be perfectly adequate for basic use. It could be perfected later. So he asked, "Can you detect airborne aircraft?"

"Yes, sir, but I can't identify size and type yet. And I can't give an altitude with an accuracy of more than a thousand meters or so."

"Good heavens, man, if you can do that, it's more than what we have now!" Corry exploded, but with delight and not rage. "When we're running submerged, we have no eyes above the water! And the *Tuscarora* alien ships we've encountered thus far operate on both sides of the air-sea interface. Being able to remain submerged and track them is a damned valuable capability. How far along are you with your mod?"

"It isn't a modification. Just a manipulation of the output data stream. I can put it up on a display, sir. But I can't guarantee the accuracy of the information," Ames admitted sheepishly.

"Why haven't you told me these things, Mister Ames?"

"Sir, I'm not authorized to experiment with the masdet. So I'm not supposed to be doing this," Ames told his CO with some reluctance. Then he added, "I, uh, just got a wild idea while staring at the bulkheads on the way out from Pearl. So I thought I'd give it a try. Idle hands and all that. But I wasn't sure I wouldn't be reprimanded for fooling around with the data. My duty is to get operational sea experience with the masdet."

Corry sighed. Sometimes Navy procedures were more hindrance than help. "Charlie," he told his Special Sensors Officer in a gentle tone, "as far as I'm concerned, processing and manipulating the data stream from the masdet *isn't* experimenting with it. And I'll tell that to the White Oaks people if necessary. Or anyone else with a need to know. So don't worry. Now, I want to have that data on a bridge display, too."

"Uh, Captain, we don't have a spare display available on the bridge."

Corry just looked at him and pointed out, "Charlie, you weren't daunted by a formidable problem involving getting more data out of the masdet. I'm sure you can scrounge a display and install it in CIC."

"Sir, I didn't think scrounging was encouraged."

"This is your first blue-water assignment, isn't it?"

"Yes, sir."

"You'll quickly learn, Mister Ames, that no United States Navy vessel could possibly operate successfully if naval personnel weren't experts in scrounging. I would like to have that new display on the bridge. Make it so."

"But it will upset the integrity of the human factors design of the bridge displays, sir!" Ames was a perfectionist.

"A pretty bridge is a poor excuse for jeopardizing this ship, Mister Ames. As I said, please make it so."

"Aye, aye, sir. When?"

"ASAP. Unless otherwise specified, the requests of the CO are always ASAP, Mister Ames." He paused and looked at the new PPI masdet display. It was a huge improvement. It jerked and jumped and went out of focus occasionally, but it gave Corry a much better picture of the outside world. "And I'm not displeased with you, Charlie. In fact, well done!"

Ames suddenly smiled. "Thank you, sir."

Corry returned his attention to the data on the new display before him. "This is a three-sixty presentation?"

"Yes, sir. We can see all around the ship except for a few segments where the masdet sensing 'antennas' have no overlap."

"I want you to come up with an illustration showing where those are. I want to know where we're masdet-blind."

Ames began to wonder if it had been a good thing to confide in his CO. He was being given a lot of work to do as a result. He told himself that the orders covered aspects that he hadn't considered and that he should have looked upon as part of his experimentation. "Not real easy because the blind spots are also a function of vertical scan. It will be a complex presentation. But can do, sir."

"Good. In the meantime, watch and record the activities of the Awesomes in the Slot. I want to see if a pattern emerges. Then we may have a close look at those unidentified targets you believe may be their bases."

As he arose to go back to the bridge, the N-fone mounted behind his right ear chimed and Zeke's voice echoed in his head, *CO, this is XO. Comm reports an SWC message for you coming in from CINCPAC.*

Thank you, XO. I'll step over to Communications for it, Corry told him.

Old terminology dies hard, and the communications compartment in the U.S.S. *Shenandoah* was still referred to familiarly as "the radio shack." That harked back to the days early in the preceding century when radio was so new on board that no compartment was available for it. The equipment had also been so large and required such a close proximity to the long wire antennas strung between the masts that a literal shack was constructed topside for the new technical miracle. The radio shack in the *Shenandoah* was a far cry from the primitive enclosures of old.

The radios had also evolved from something capable of being lifted only by ten men and a boy to elements that could easily be held between two fingers of one hand.

The scalar wave communications equipment was an exception to that. The SWC was still so new that it hadn't been super-miniaturized. It had the same "laboratory look" as the masdet. It wasn't neatly packaged with pristine wire harnesses and carefully integrated mechanical components. If the *Shenandoah*'s bridge looked like something out of a science fiction television series, then the SWC gear in the radio shack would have seemed perfectly in place on the set of the castle laboratory of a movie's mad scientist. The BRC-98 SWC equipment hummed and clicked and chattered as it printed out the hard copy of the incoming message.

Corry waited quietly until the signalman pulled the copy from the slot, hit it with the time-date stamp, and handed it to him.

SWC transmission 27–04–44 from CINCPAC to CO SSCV-26. Operational advisory. Surveillance satellites, HR-82 overflights, and other national technical means indicate 6 East World submarines in your vicinity or headed toward your area. Proceeding southeast north of Papua in Bismarck Sea are S.46 Maoi fung, S.30 Cheng du, and S.42 Jilin of PRC navy. In Arafura Sea approaching Torres Strait are Rajput K51, Kavaratti K42, and Talwar K44 of Indian navy. All running submerged. Intents unknown. No open armed conflict in other areas at this time. Situation now DEFCON 3. Kane CINCPAC. End message. End Message. End message.

Carefully, Corry folded the sheet of paper, unfastened the flap on his shirt pocket, deposited the message therein, and resealed the flap. Then he touched the

N-fone behind his right ear. *XO, this is CO. Please meet me in my cabin ASAP.*

Aye, aye, sir!

What's our bottom now?

Four hundred meters, Captain.

Do we have a deep scattering layer under us?

Unknown, sir. I'll have Sonar drop a probe.

Please do so. We have potential enemy submarines coming in from the north and west. We may have to go deep to remain stealthed. Prepare the boat to do that.

Aye, aye, sir! Is Condition One warranted, sir?

Negative, Number Two. But stay at Condition Two until we can learn what these boats intend to do. We are at a severe disadvantage if they know we're here. Six to one odds are not the sort of favorable ones I like to work with.

13

This is the Captain speaking. The voice of CAPT William M. Corry sounded softly throughout the U.S.S. *Shenandoah.* Everyone heard it through their local intercoms or N-fone receivers. But because the boat was operating in silent stealth, it wasn't broadcast on the loudspeaker system for fear that the oncoming Chinese and Indian submarines might pick it up in their passive sonars.

I have received information that three Chinese and three Indian submarines are proceeding toward our vicinity. The Chinese boats are presently located north of Papua in the Bismarck Sea. The Indian boats are west of the Torres Strait. I do not know the precise locations of these boats, nor do I have information relating to their intentions. However, given the present world situation and the fact that the United States defense establishment is now at DEFCON Three, I must presume we may encounter hostile action from these boats. We will not interdict them. They have every right under the law of the sea to cruise with peaceful intent in international waters and may make innocent passage within territorial waters.

We will remain submerged in our present mode. We will look for sensor indications of the Chinese and Indian boats. We will continue our passive watch over the Awesomes we've sighted in large numbers in New Georgia Sound. If we detect active sonar from any source, I may take the boat deeper to gain the additional advantage of a deep scattering layer that underlies the warm northwesterly Solomons Current at this location. The boat will remain at Condition Two. We will monitor the movements of these six boats when our sensors detect them. We will take no overt action at this time.

As usual, be prepared for several optional actions. We

135

may surface and launch patrol or ASW aircraft. Or we may be forced to elude attack and launch fish. We may move to make a peaceful port call at Honiara. Or we may withdraw to Brisbane. The Air Group has potential actions it can now plan for. The Marine batt should stand by to service deck guns if we must surface. We may even have to seek safe harbor and put both the Air Group and the Marine batt ashore. Although these are standard contingency plans that are already part of our SOP, I wanted to remind everyone that we face a wide array of action options.

We knew we might become engaged with East World forces in this area. The possibility of hostile action was secondary to our major mission goal of capturing an Awesome. However, circumstances may force us to reassign priorities. Again, the ROEs are clear. We shall not initiate offensive action. However, if attacked or if it appears that the boat may be endangered, I will certainly not hesitate to initiate offensive action.

Carry on.

Speaking from his command post on the bridge, Corry had deliberately used formal, stilted, wordy language in his message. It was expected of him. It signified that he was very much in command of the situation. He could have phrased it in simpler and more direct terms. However, that might have projected the image that he was unsure and not fully aware of the entire situation.

He *was* somewhat unsure. Zeke knew it. "Nice pep talk, Captain," he remarked from his console position alongside the CO.

"I hope it brought everyone up to the same level of ignorance and confusion that I enjoy at this moment," Corry grumbled. Zeke saw that the man's sense of humor hadn't deserted him. If that ever happened, it meant that William M. Corry was indeed under a lot of stress.

"Well, we certainly don't have enough information yet to do anything except what you outlined," Zeke observed.

"Yes. So we'll play the old waiting game, Number Two," Corry said, sitting back in his chair and studying the array of displays on the bridge.

Three of Charlie Ames' ratings were setting up a spare display panel, clamping it to another display with ordinary C-clamps and stringing cables back into the Special Sensors compartment. Corry was pleased to see that Ames could respond quickly and create a lash-up when necessary. Functionality came first. Prettiness could be arranged when time was available for it.

"I've decided not to take the boat deeper right now, Zeke. We're well stealthed. The East World boats will have to ping to find us, and we'll hear that at a longer range than they can receive a firm return. I'm not going to do anything for the moment but wait. First of all, I want to see where the six boats go," Corry confided to his Executive Officer. "I hope they'll split their forces. If they don't, maybe I can cause them to do so. If their intention is to close and attack, I don't want to be caught in the position of having to deal with six targets at once, especially when they might be shooting at us in the process. I'd rather deal with those boats one at a time. Two at a time in the worst scenario."

"Two simultaneous threats is all that we're expected to handle in War College sims," Zeke recalled.

"That's because no CO should allow himself to get into any situation with more than two simultaneous threats," Corry explained. They were in a waiting mode now, watching for the reported incoming boats and continuing to track the Awesome activity in New Georgia Sound. No action was immediately required. But Corry didn't want to leave the bridge. With the Captain there, Zeke's job was at his CO's side unless Corry ordered him to be somewhere else. So it was the usual situation that engendered professional banter between the two men.

Zeke sighed. "Well, we faced multiple threats off Sulawesi, Captain. And it wasn't your fault that several of them materialized at once."

"It could happen to us again in the Solomon Sea," Corry replied. "And no matter what the circumstances, it's indeed my fault if we get into a situation with more than two threats. Thanks to everyone aboard, we pulled a rabbit out of a hat off Sulawesi. And, XO, in order to pull a rabbit out of a hat, one must first put a rabbit *into* the hat! That's why I'm going to try to do here by getting on the problem early."

"I'm glad that CINCPAC notified you."

"Admiral Kane had the big picture, data that we don't have because we're submerged."

"I suspect he was worried about losing a multibillion-dollar capital ship."

Corry shook his head and gently reprimanded his XO. "Zeke, that's not a fair appraisal. It's always possible to apologize to Congress for the loss of a ship. It's a hell of a lot tougher to deal with the families of seven hundred fifty people."

"You're right, sir. I'm sorry, sir! My apologies."

"No apologies necessary, Number Two." Command was always a learning process. Learning how to command was, too.

The watch changed, but Corry didn't leave the bridge. Neither did Zeke. Above the surface, the sun set and the stars began to come out. The submariners wouldn't have known it except by checking the clocks, now set to local time, Zulu + 11. Or by noticing on the masdet displays that the activities of the Awesomes dropped to zero.

As in Makasar Straits, the Awesomes appeared to operate only in daylight. LCDR Laura Raye Moore's brief studies of the frozen Awesome carcass they'd taken back to Pearl Harbor revealed that the Awesomes didn't have good distance vision. Such a trait wasn't required for underwater living if it could be supplemented by dolphinlike active sonar. The Medical Officer hadn't been able to determine the characteristics of Awesome sonar from the dead alien. And Zervas hadn't told her he'd discovered anything new in that regard as a result of his examinations at Bethesda.

The diurnal aspect of the Awesome life-style made sense, but Corry and the other people in the *Shenandoah* knew they could be dead wrong in making such an assumption. It was too closely tied to human behavior. And even human behavior could be highly modified. Life in the U.S.S. *Shenandoah* was proof of that. The officers and crew of a submarine know no day-night cycle.

The chief steward brought hot tray dinners to Corry and Braxton. Food tested good. Food was always good in a submarine. It had a high morale factor.

"I don't know why," Corry admitted as he finished the tray, "I'm sitting here watching unchanging displays. I must be on edge."

Braxton knew that was the case, but he put it diplomatically to the Captain. "Well, sir, this could evolve quickly into a situation with very high pucker factor. As for myself, I want to see any new data as quickly as it comes in. I don't like the idea of sitting around waiting for someone else to do something."

"We often have no other choice, Zeke. But I won't wait forever," Corry promised. He paused, got his breathing and stuttering under control, then went on "We need to use this time to carry out some good contingency planning."

"Yes, sir. Better to do it now than under the gun."

"Yes. Quite so," Corry replied. Then he asked his Executive Officer one of his famous Embarrassing Questions. "In our present situation, knowing what we do, what would you recommend in the way of action, Number Two?"

Zeke had been expecting that for several hours. He'd been turning over in his mind some of the options and possible actions. "Right now, I wouldn't do anything except what we're doing, Captain."

"Why?"

Zeke also expected the second question. "We don't have enough data, sir. We have nothing to lose by sitting here with our sensors out. No one knows we're here ... I hope."

"Can we safely assume that's true, XO?"

"No, sir, but we have no solid data that indicates otherwise. We know that East World submarines are heading into this region, but we don't know their missions. We can't know their intents. They may not know we're here. In any event, we shouldn't allow the fear of potential enemy submarines to scrub our primary mission."

"How long should we sit here, Zeke?"

Braxton thought about that for a moment. Then he replied, "Sir, we don't want to get bottled up in New

Georgia Sound by those six boats, if that is indeed their intention. On the other hand, coordinating the movement of six boats from two different naval forces is an incredibly complex operation. It would require extensive tactical communications to carry it off. So I don't believe they're coming after us, sir."

"What do you think their missions are, Zeke?" Corry could be relentless when he was conducting his infamous question-and-answer session.

"My estimate is that those boats are being positioned for sea control purposes preliminary to armed conflict in Asia itself. They're probably tasked with controlling sea lanes and thus reducing the threat on East World's southeastern flank. Australia was an important staging base in the Pacific operations of World War Two. The Japanese realized that and mounted an aggressive campaign in this area to cut the American-Australian link. This is a neglected strategic area in any Pacific war." The Executive Officer of the U.S.S. *Shenandoah* paused, then added, "Captain, that's wardroom speculation on my part. We'll likely know more tomorrow. In the meantime, since you've taught me not to make an irrevocable decision on the basis of incomplete data, I'd sit here quietly and see what develops, sir. We've sure as hell worked hard enough to get where we are without drawing attention to ourselves."

"What sort of additional data would you require before making an action decision?"

Again, it was a loaded question. Zeke knew that Corry had probably thought through the options. The CO was doing two things at the moment. First, he was seeking input from another officer he trusted. Second, he was using the luxury of time to help train a potential CO in the thinking processes that a commander must develop. "Two items, sir. I'd like to know the actual positions and courses of the Chinese and Indian boats so we can evaluate the threat potential. And I'd like to have another day to watch the Awesomes because we may have been seeing their equivalent of having Sunday off. If we get no sensor indications of the Chinese or Indian boats in the next twenty-four hours, and if we continue to get the same sort of data on the Awesomes from New Geor-

gia Sound tomorrow, it may be time to move into the
Slot and do what we're supposed to. However, I'd move
in there at night because the Awesomes are inactive then
and we don't need daylight to operate."

"What would you do once the boat was in there?"

Zeke had an immediate answer to that. "Exactly what
we did off the beach near Makasar, Captain, with a few
additions. I'd have the machinists in Engineering build
a stout baited trap first. I'd like to design that tonight.
Once we got in there near an Awesome concentration,
I'd first put Brookstone's underwater special team out
with explosives to do some selective mining of the Awesome positions. Then I'd put two companies from the
Marine batt in the water to round up an Awesome and
get it into the trap. This is a general plan. Details would
depend on the underwater topography and Awesome activity patterns."

"Any Air Group involvement?"

"Of course, sir! I'd have Sea Dragons over the Marines for insertion and extraction. And to haul the Awesome and trap back to the ship. I'd use the patrol
squadron in an ASW mode to keep other Awesomes
away from our operation. If required, I'd arm the Sea
Devils in ASW mode, too, to provide faster response
than the Ospreys could give."

"Are you recommending that we take these actions in
the territorial waters of the Solomon Islands, XO?
Would that be in violation of international law?"

That was one hot question from the CO. "Yes, sir, it
is. But because we're here under an Execute Order, I
have to assume that the President and the Department
of State are prepared to deal with the consequences of
their order. Frankly, I don't think the Solomon Islands
government is going to do much of anything about it,
even if they find out. Not that we ought to play the role
of the insolent bully, but we certainly don't have to go
into New Georgia Sound broadcasting apologies to Honiara. If something happens, you'll have to work through
our embassy in Honiara because you're the CO of this
boat. But otherwise, we should get in, do a fast and
surgical job, and get out."

Corry didn't answer for a moment. When he spoke,

he asked another question. "Suppose I told you that you've basically outlined exactly the operational plan I'd formulated?"

Zeke grinned. "Captain, I'd feel both happy and concerned. I'd be glad that my CO had trained me so I could anticipate his actions. And I'd be worried that both of us might have missed something."

Corry sighed and said to no one in particular, "I've trained a pessimist!"

"No, sir, I think you've trained a realist. I now look on the glass as being half empty."

"As I said, I've trained a pessimist." Corry put both hands on his console ledge and positioned himself as though he were going to push his chair back and stand. "I can only hope that I have not trained out of you the willingness to take warranted risks. The only way to find out is to give you a chance to take risk. We'll move tomorrow night unless conditions change. So I'd like you to have an ops plan ready for me at an Oscar briefing no later than fourteen hundred hours tomorrow."

"Can do, sir!"

At that moment, CDR Matilda Harriet Smith walked onto the bridge. She caught Zeke's attention immediately. He was never one to ignore attractive women, and Smith was certainly attractive. With the other women in the boat wearing poopie suits or Air Group flight suits, she stood out in her tropical whites. Zeke didn't know whether that was deliberate on her part or not. However, he didn't complain. He only wished he had more time to develop a relationship. Right then, it didn't look like he was going to have time for sleeping, much less socializing.

Smith came up on the other side of Corry's console desk and spoke. "Good evening, Captain. I have a request, sir."

"Good evening, Commander. What may I do for you?"

"The special group would like to have a meeting with you, sir."

Corry drew back to his console and put his arms on it, folding his hands. "What would the members of the group want to talk about, Commander?"

"Sir, we've worked out our problems. We'd like to discuss this operation with you, especially in light of the recent information concerning the Chinese and Indian submarines." She paused, then added, "Sir, I have some intel data on that. I've already shared it with the group. We believe the integration of this data and other information in possession of the team members would be of interest to you, sir."

"I assume the group asked you to come to the bridge and represent them to me?"

"Yes, sir."

"Including Mister Soucek?"

"Yes, sir. I understand you don't like him, Captain, but—"

"The man tried to usurp my command, then challenged it more than once, Commander."

She nodded. "Yes, sir. I think you'll find him cooperative now."

"How did you arrange that?" Zeke wondered.

"My nickname is Mata Hari," Smith said with a provocative smile. "However, I can be intellectually persuasive, Commander Braxton. And I was. The group met in Soucek's quarters so your orders wouldn't be disobeyed, Captain."

"You got *five* people into an officer's cabin?" Zeke asked in amazement.

Smith smiled again. "Yes, Commander. It was, shall we say, cozy. But it was also important that we get together. If that's the only discomfort we encounter on this mission, we'll be lucky."

"When would you like to meet with me, Commander?" Corry asked and indicated the quiet bridge around them. "At the moment, we're in a watch and wait mode. I'm not needed on the bridge unless something happens. This would be a good time."

" ' 'Twere well it were done quickly,' as the Bard once wrote."

Corry was as well read as she. "Yes, Commander, but not in the same context as Shakespeare wrote it. I have no intention of permitting an assassination. And a Lady Macbeth you'd better not be."

Not to be outdone, Zeke added, "Act One, Scene Seven."

"My, you do read a lot, Commander," Smith observed.

"Sometimes there's not much else to do in a submarine, Commander," Zeke told her.

"With a mixed-gender crew, I didn't realize you would be socially deprived, Commander," she shot back with a smile.

"I'm not," Zeke stated.

Corry broke into the witty repartee. "Commander Smith, please bring the special group to my cabin in fifteen minutes. Seven of us will fit. It will also be cozy, but I don't want to commandeer the wardroom when my officers will need it for off-duty relaxation and a sandwich or cup of coffee." He turned to where the COB was sitting. "Chief, please inform the police petty officers that Mister Soucek is permitted to leave his quarters for a meeting in my cabin."

"Aye, aye, sir."

"Number Two, please join me. Officer of the Deck, you have the con."

14

The other four members of the special team were subdued as they crowded into Corry's cabin office. Dr. Evelyn Lulalilo looked somewhat confused and scared. LCDR Zervas appeared to be a bit angry but otherwise very determined. Dr. Duval seemed to be nonchalant. But Allan Soucek was white and trembling; something was seriously wrong with the man, Corry decided.

The CO didn't have to ask who was the leader of the special group. He could see that Smith had assumed that position. None of the other group members seemed upset with that.

Zeke and Duval remained standing because the cabin office had no room for additional chairs to seat them.

Corry nodded toward Smith. "Commander, you requested this meeting. Proceed."

"Thank you for giving us time, Captain," Smith replied. "Several members of the group have information they've been reluctant to share for reasons I won't go into here. However, we've worked out a division of turf, so to speak. The external situation has demanded that we begin to work more closely as your special mission staff. That's the way you told us you wanted to use us. In the process of briefing one another, we've gotten to know each other better. We've given other group members a full and frank briefing of what we know. So now we'd like to share with you what each of us knows so you can conduct this operation with more knowledge than you presently have. Doctor Zervas, please tell the Captain what you told us earlier."

The naval surgeon hadn't given up turf. He was still the expert on the physiology of the Awesomes, provided the ship's Medical Officer was kept out of the game.

He'd decided that the best way to ensure that she remained in a secondary role was to gain more direct access to the CO. This would effectively bypass CDR Laura Raye Moore. Instead of fighting to establish turf, he fell back on one of his well-proven techniques: He would take turf and then force contenders to assault a well-prepared position. If he'd read Clausewitz—which he hadn't; he could barely keep up with the interoffice memos that told him who was doing what to whom and who was paying for it—he would have recognized the principle of warfare that maintained "defense is the stronger form of combat." However, he'd neglected the fact that a successful defense also requires depth and reserves. He had neither in the *Shenandoah* but he didn't realize it.

CDR Constantine Zervas therefore simply stated, "When I autopsied the brain of the alien you recovered near Makasar, I found a nervous system that wasn't highly developed. In fact, it was primitive, somewhere between that of a shark and a seal. I found no brain portions that I could recognize as being able to support cognitive thought processes. No cerebrum, for example. Although the brain structure was different from terrestrial animals, we do know enough about neurophysiology that I could tell the brain was not developed to the point I consider to be the minimum for self-directed action."

"What do you mean by that, Doctor?" Zeke asked. He'd fought the Awesomes at Makasar. He thought he knew what Zervas was saying, but he wanted to make sure. Zeke had always suspected that the Awesomes weren't very bright. They'd certainly revealed no cunning. Nor had they fought in an organized fashion.

"I think they may be worker animals. They probably can take direction well but don't have the capability for creative or self-directed thought processes. I can't speculate beyond that until I have a live Awesome to work with."

"So your assessment of their mental prowess leads you to believe the Awesomes are stupid?" Corry asked.

Zervas nodded.

"Doctor, they're smart enough to set traps and hunt

for humans. And they've done it for God knows how long without being discovered," Zeke reminded him.

"They could be following orders," Zervas pointed out. "However, I believe my hypothesis has some support from Doctor Lulalilo. I yield the floor to her because I don't want to intrude upon her turf." The naval surgeon's remark told Corry and Zeke that the group members hadn't resolved *all* their differences yet. Corry's assessment of Zervas told him the man was almost obsessed with his "turf" because of his position inside the Navy's Medical Service in Washington. However, Eve apparently had used her own talents in the politics of Big Science to build some bridges of trust with the man.

So Corry turned his head to look at the marine biologist seated next to him. "Doctor Lulalilo?

Dr. Evelyn Lulalilo wasn't hesitant about speaking up. "I have no turf to protect, Captain. And I'll freely share my information. I spent a lot of time today with Lieutenant Goff in the sonar room. I listened to the sounds your hydrophones picked up. The Navy has much better hydrophone technology than I've ever had access to. I was able to listen to the Awesomes communicating under what were probably normal circumstances. I may be wrong because I don't fully understand the subsea culture of the Awesomes, their day-to-day life-style, survival problems, and interactive needs. I don't know what they're saying to each other. And I don't understand what I heard. Therefore, I can't hand you a lesson tape so you can learn to speak to the Awesomes. But I can report that I don't believe the Awesome 'language' is as complex or varied as that of the dolphins. Therefore, my findings would support the physiological observations of Doctor Zervas. These Awesome creatures probably aren't very intelligent. Or certainly not as intelligent as dolphins, judging from the complexity of their sounds, which I must assume to be a combination of sensing and communicating. Therefore, we can probably catch one or more of them alive."

She paused for a moment, apparently considering what she was going to say next. "I could be very wrong, Captain. Their communication seemed terse. On the other hand, what I've heard on the bridge of this ship is also very terse language. We tend to streamline our communications when social and work conditions require it. I suspect the Awesomes might do the same. I was probably listening to their work communications. It certainly seemed that way because they were operating to and from those bases Doctor Duval and Lieutenant Ames think they've spotted."

"Doctor Lulalilo, I didn't claim to have discovered operating bases," Dr. Barry Duval interrupted.

"Apparently you've discovered something that led Doctor Lulalilo to that conclusion," Corry observed.

"Perhaps. I'd like to withhold comment until I can be more certain."

Smith looked at him and said, "Doctor, I understand the reticence of a scientist to speculate on professional time. But you were pretty enthusiastic about what you learned today and reported to the group earlier. I think the Captain and the Executive Officer need to know this. Label it speculation if you wish. However, in situations like this, we often have to operate on intelligent guesses. I know I'm forced to do so in naval intelligence work. I realize that's different from scientific inquiry, but it could provide an important piece in the puzzle. So please do what you agreed to do and tell the Captain what you told us earlier today."

Dr. Barry Duval seemed mildly offended and answered in a diffident tone, "Very well. While I was working with the Navigator comparing the latest subsea volcanic bottom information with the charts, the Navigator pointed out that the aliens appeared to be operating to and from nodes that coincided with four of the volcanic upwelling hot spots in New Georgia Sound. Many such subsea volcanic sites exist in this region of the planet, of course. However, the aliens seem to be concentrating their activities around the newest ones, the ones that wouldn't necessarily be on the latest charts. By the way, your charts are about ten years old. This isn't surprising. Since the United States doesn't seem to have economic interests in the Solomons, the charts aren't in great demand. The updating and revision activity on the part of NOAA and Defense Mapping Agency is therefore directed elsewhere."

"What do you make of this data, Doctor?" Corry asked, aware that he was dealing with an academic and wishing to get to the real data.

"Geologically—"

Corry shook his head. "No, from the standpoint of finding the Awesomes colocated with these hot spots. What are the Awesomes doing that requires them to seek out volcanic sites?"

"I'm not qualified to answer that, Captain. I'm just an oceanographer."

"Captain, one of our scenarios developed by Naval Intelligence in the last few weeks presumes that the Awesomes have established a fishing industry on Earth," Smith added quickly before Duval could launch into a fifty-minute academic lecture on undersea vulcanism as he'd tried to do in the earlier group meeting. "It doesn't take a commissioned study from the Naval Postgraduate School in Monterey to point out that any industry needs energy sources. Therefore, I'll take responsibility for the speculation Doctor Duval now appears reluctant to discuss again. My training in intel work leads me to the postulate that the Awesome bases we spotted today in the Slot are processing factories of some sort. Mister Soucek volunteered some additional information on this from his extensive background on the subject of extraterrestrial species. Allan?"

Soucek wasn't hesitant to unburden his fears. "First of all, let me state that I didn't expect this mission would involve becoming engaged in a war with East World," he admitted. "I'm not sure that it isn't an armed conflict being provoked by the Mantids, who are using the aliens you call the Awesomes as their fishers."

"Are you telling us, Mister Soucek, that the Awesomes aren't working alone?" Zeke pressed him.

Soucek nodded. "I am. That seems to be confirmed by the speculations of Doctors Lulalilo and Zervas. And it ties in with what I know about this other stellar race we've tagged as the Mantids because of their appearance. This is all highly classified, of course. We couldn't let the public know that an extraterrestrial race was hunting us for our endocrines, some intestinal tissue, reproductive organs, and blood chemicals. They don't have the biotechnology to synthesize the items. The Mantids discovered Earth to be a bountiful source. In the last century, they abducted human beings and mutilated them—usually without killing them first.''

Zeke snorted. "The UFO people used to go nuts over those reports. I can't understand why the United States government knew about it and apparently condoned it. Hell, most of the American public was armed. They would have killed those Mantids! Unless you're telling me that the Mantids had superior weapons technology. If they did, and if they still do, we'd better know about it right now!"

"They don't, but they had incredibly advanced space technology. The federal government believed that would be useful in the Cold War. That's why they cut the swap deal with the Mantids. My predecessors tried working with the Mantids for several decades. That's why we have a lot of data about them. But the Mantids had no intention of giving us any technology that would threaten them. They won't give us star flight or create their own competition."

"Competition? For whom? With what?" Braxton asked.

"Some of their product they used themselves, but most of it went into an interstellar black market. That was very lucrative for the Mantids. They'd monopolized the source."

"They overdid it," Duval said pensively.

Soucek looked strangely at him. "They did. Apparently, other interstellar species stepped in and deemed the Mantids' activities here to be contrary to some manner of loosely enforced interstellar law that governs those seventy species I told you about."

"So these Mantids aren't supposed to be operating here?" Zeke continued to press the man. It was a fantastic story. Zeke still didn't know whether or not he believed it.

"No. At Majestic Corporation, I had no idea the Mantids were continuing to carry on under the oceans until you brought in the Awesome specimen from Makasar. Then the situation became clear to those of us in Majestic Corporation. Because the Mantids aren't aquatic, they're using a less intelligent species of aquatic aliens you call Awesomes to do the work for them. The Awesomes will someday learn the folly of dealing with the Mantids."

"Mister Soucek, as I told you before, I find your assertions extremely difficult to believe," Corry put in. This sounded like more of the seemingly demented ravings Soucek had vented before.

"Captain, I'm now inclined to believe Mister Soucek," CDR Smith interjected. This surprised Corry. "For years, we've had a lot of disconnected data that Soucek's stories seem to flesh out. I can't vouch for their accuracy. However, we have a lot of open files in Naval Intelligence we've never been able to close. I'm going to be able to close some of them when I get back."

"Didn't you know of Mister Soucek and the Majestic Corporation, Commander?" Corry asked.

She shook her head. "No, sir."

"I find that surprising."

"Captain, there are a *lot* of intelligence operations in the Washington area," she advised him. "That's why I'm not surprised. And Admiral McCarthy won't be surprised, either."

Corry turned his attention back to the man from the enigmatic Majestic Corporation. "Mister Soucek, unless these Mantid creatures have some very advanced weapons technologies, we can handle them on the basis of what you've told us thus far. Don't worry. The U.S.S. *Shenandoah* is capable of handling not only the East World submarines but probably the Mantids as well. Their underwater vessel ran from us once and showed itself to be friendly on the second contact."

Soucek shook his head. "Your reports didn't describe a Mantid vehicle."

"Now that you mention it, it probably wasn't. We suspected we were seeing the game warden at work."

"You probably were. They're a different species. I just learned about them before departing Washington for this mission," Soucek admitted. "Captain, I'm deeply concerned about two things. If any of us happen to be captured by Mantids during this mission, they'll process us. Not only are these beasts the most vile creatures you've ever seen, but they have no scruples at all."

"What's your second concern, Mister Soucek?" Corry was beginning to understand this man's deathly fears, provided his assertions were correct. As more information came in, Corry found himself believing the man.

"That this new game warden species I don't know anything about might destroy the *Shenandoah*."

"Why would they do that? They had the chance to do it before and didn't."

"They could do it to cover up *their* mistakes, Captain. They were given the job of keeping the Mantids under control here on Earth. They didn't. Instead, you and the crew of the *Shenandoah* uncovered the whole thing and actually managed to get a dead carcass to study. Furthermore, it wasn't just an American discovery. It was seen and documented by people from two other countries. They can't plant stories that will cause the incident to be laughed away. They can't easily destroy the data because it's in several independent hands. So the easiest way to cover up their mistake is to have it destroyed in a human war. Archives and records rarely survive wars."

"How in the world could they plant stories? Or destroy data?" Zeke was trying to punch holes in this man's preposterous story.

"I'm told they can pass as humans. A lot of strange-looking people walk the streets of any city in the world. That's why I expressed concern about your crew, Captain. They could have been planted aboard this submarine to destroy it. Sending the *Shenandoah* to the bottom with both the crew and our special team aboard would eliminate a prime source of further trouble for them."

"Mister Soucek, they could not have known that we would encounter them in the Makasar Straits. No new people joined the crew when we returned to Pearl," Corry pointed out. He didn't like Soucek, but he now realized that the man was bedeviled by fear and the terror of facing the unknown. It had probably driven Soucek to the edge of insanity to be assigned to the *Shenandoah*'s mission fearing for his life as a result. Some people can't handle that. A submariner faces the unknown every time the boat is dived.

Corry was basically a compassionate man. Some naval officers rise to blue-water command and flag rank without that trait. But the best commanders and admirals in the Navy have an empathy for their subordinates. He realized that a great gulf existed between him and Soucek. The man's fear plus his paranoic deep intelligence background were at the root of his behavior. Corry decided that he might be able to help Soucek. "I believe your fears are unfounded, sir. But I will heed your concerns. And I suspect you may be suffering from acute anxiety. My Medical Officer can certainly help you. I won't confine you to sick bay, but if you'll let Doctor Moore check you over, perhaps I can lift the quarters restriction. Do you have any objections to my suggestion?"

Soucek shrugged. "No. I guess not, if you and your ship's doctor realize that I'm not allowed to take certain drugs and others will have no effect on me."

"Good heavens, Soucek!" CDR Constantine Zervas exploded. "I've been in the Navy for eighteen years, the last ten of them at Bethesda. I've been involved with some highly placed people and dealt with highly classified material! If you're Naval Reserve, you ought to know that we're not monsters capable of shooting you full of anti-inhibitory drugs. Or even doping you to the point of docility! For God's sake, man, I'm a medical doctor and so is Commander Moore! Both of us will place medical ethics ahead of any orders! Doctor Moore is certainly authorized to disobey any orders intended to bring harm to anyone by her actions! In my opinion, you are suffering from acute anxiety. Get some help, man!"

Before Soucek could reply, the intercom unit on the wall of the cabin chimed. "CO, this is Special Sensors Officer."

"This is the Captain. Go ahead, Mister Ames!"

"Sir, the special sensor reports a target."

When Ames paused, Corry prompted him, "Where, Mister?"

"Over us, sir."

"Over us?"

"Yes, sir. I haven't been able to calibrate the air-water interface program, so I can't give you a size. But it came out of the zenith and is sitting directly over us on the surface at the moment."

15

"The Mantids! They've found us!" Soucek gasped.

"Don't be so sure of that, Allan," CDR Smith told him.

CAPT William M. Corry ignored them. His adrenaline level and heart rate had jumped, but he maintained an outward appearance of calm professionalism. Turning in his chair, he toggled his wall intercom to VOX mode and brought up the masdet display from the main data bus.

An unusual masdet return showed itself at the same position as the U.S.S. *Shenandoah*.

"Mister Ames, this is the Captain. Is the target in the air or on the surface?"

"I can't tell yet, sir. If it's on the water-air interface, its displacement is approximately fifteen tons."

Soucek stood up and leaned over the table toward Corry. With utmost earnestness in his voice instead of imperial arrogance, he said, "Captain, believe me when I tell you it's a Mantid beam ship! We have an operational one in storage at Site Fifty-one. Code name Corona. Diameter sixteen-point-seven meters. Weight fifteen thousand six hundred kilograms. Carries four Mantids."

"He's right, Captain," was the comment from CDR Matilda Smith. "And don't ask me how I know, Soucek. Naval Intelligence has its ways, too."

"Mister Soucek, can this Corona vehicle see us submerged?" Zeke wanted to know.

"Yes. Where do you think the United States got the basic technology for the mass detector? It was part of the Mantid swap agreement back in the last century," Soucek explained.

"How good is their masdet?" Corry asked.

"I don't know."

Corry stood up. "Well, we'll find out, then. I've got to adjourn this meeting, ladies and gentlemen. We face a possible threat. I would like to have this special group present at the bridge to advise me and give me any input you believe is important. Commander Zervas, if you'll kindly lead the way, none of us can move out of there while you're blocking the door."

Zervas also stood. "Sorry, Captain."

"No apologies needed, Commander. It's crowded in here." The use of the doctor's naval rank broadcast the fact that Corry intended to treat the members of the special group as part of his naval staff.

The Captain's calm behavior impressed CDR Smith. Some of her superiors would have gone hyperbolic in similar circumstances. But this man not only accepted bizarre data without getting hysterical about it but also maintained a very level head in what was obviously a crisis. Furthermore, now he didn't seem to hold any sort of a grudge against Soucek. Smith understood why the officers and crew of the U.S.S. *Shenandoah* trusted their CO and why CNO had chosen his ship for this mission.

What she couldn't see, of course, was Corry's heightened alarm level. Anyone who wouldn't become a little frightened in a situation like this was an idiot. Corry was no idiot.

And on the bridge of the U.S.S. *Shenandoah,* everyone was all business, too.

Captain on the bridge, announced the OOD, LTJG Olivia P. Kilmer.

Carry on. I have the con, Lieutenant, Corry told her, indicating that he hadn't relieved her as OOD.

You have the con, sir, she repeated.

Corry saw that the boat was at fifty meters. *Make heading one-eight-zero.*

Coming to heading one-eight-zero.

Engineman, all ahead. Make five knots.

All ahead. Make five knots.

"XO, issue N-fones to the special group and explain to them how the system works."

"Aye, aye, sir!" Zeke motioned for the Quartermaster, LTJG Fred Berger, to come over and then spoke to him.

"I'm commanding via N-fone, but I'll speak verbally until you get your receive-only units," Corry explained to the special group, touching the little pink box behind his right ear. "Special Sensors, this is the CO. Report what the IX does as the ship moves slowly south. Tag it as a Corona-type vehicle. Assume its weight is fifteen thousand six hundred kilograms and diameter sixteen-point-seven meters. Please report range when you have it computed."

Aye, aye, sir!

"Mister Braxton, sound General Quarters."

Aye, aye, sir! Sound General Quarters!

A hushed feminine voice spoke quietly in N-fone receivers and through intercom speakers throughout the ship, *All hands hear this. General Quarters. General Quarters. Battle Stations.* Long ago, psychologists discovered that both men and women will immediately pay attention and listen to a female voice. The overtones not only penetrated noise better but triggered memories in the subconscious mind because everyone began life listening to what mother wanted them to do. And, because the U.S.S. *Shenandoah* was operating in silent stealth mode, the voice was quiet and subdued.

The boat came alive with the movement of people.

CO, this is Special Sensors. The Corona is reacting to our movement. It's trying to stay over us.

"Navigator, what is our bottom?"

Navigator here. Our bottom is presently four-zero-zero meters, sir. We're on the edge of the Solomon Deep. Our present heading is taking us to a deeper bottom.

"Steady as she goes," Corry told the bridge crew in verbose mode as well as by N-fone. He was watching the masdet target smudge that was the Corona.

It moved to follow the ship, then stopped, then moved again.

"Mister Ames, assume that the Corona has a masdet and can see us," Corry called to his Special Sensors officer. "What is it doing?"

Sir, if the Corona has a masdet, it's not a very damned

good one. Resolution must be terrible. We move about a hundred meters before it begins correcting to follow us.

"Is that because of our size, Mister Ames?"

Negative, sir. When tracking a large target, a masdet seeks the center of mass. So the Corona masdet resolution must be about a hundred meters and its recomputational response must be on the order of a second or so. Very slow.

"Is our masdet's resolution and response significantly better than theirs?"

Oh, yes, sir! If you drive a golf ball off our bow when surfaced, I can track the ball on a millisecond basis if I know its mass beforehand.

"Captain, the White Oak people must have made significant improvements over the primitive masdet the Mantids once showed us," Soucek advised. He seemed to be calmer now. Maybe it was the fact he was at the center of action and had some input concerning what was happening, Corry thought fleetingly. He didn't have time to consider that further because he had his hands full of threat crisis at the moment. Until he could resolve the magnitude of the threat, everything else was secondary.

Soucek's observation combined with Ames' explanation told Corry that he might be able to sneak around the shortcomings of the Corona's masdet and learn what the vessel's intentions were.

"Diving officer, come to periscope depth and up periscope."

Aye, aye, sir. Coming to periscope depth. Periscope Number Three is extended.

"View astern," Corry snapped.

The image from the tiny video camera on the slender periscope boom showed nothing but greenish blue water. As the U.S.S. *Shenandoah* slowly rose from the depths, the image on the screen began to show a mirrorlike surface that was the air-water interface.

Suddenly the videocamera lens on its stalk of fiber-optical fibers broke the surface. The view steadied as the motion correction circuitry steadied the image.

The screen filled with a view of a silvery object shaped like an upside down dinner plate with a coffee cup inverted atop it. It appeared to be floating on the surface of the Solomon Sea. The image grew larger on the screen as the Corona vehicle approached.

Corry had learned what he wanted to find out. Soucek was right.

But before Corry could do anything, something that seemed to be a long, skinny, shimmering golden rod snapped forth from the cup-top of the Corona and speared directly at the periscope camera.

The screen suddenly went black and a message appeared, *"VIDEO SIGNAL TERMINATED."*

"They hit the periscope with a force beam!" Soucek reported. "A new type! That golden shimmering hasn't been reported before!"

"You didn't tell me the Corona ships were armed," Correy reprimanded him.

"I didn't know whether it was or not, Captain. Most of them aren't. This one was. It's not a reconnaissance ship. It's the attack version."

"Dive! Dive! Dive! Make depth four hundred meters and level the bubble," Corry called out. This was no time to dawdle near the surface with a hostile vessle out there.

Aye, aye, sir. Dive! Dive! Dive! Come to four-zero-zero meters and level the bubble, LCDR Mark Walton responded from his position on the bridge.

The deck pitched as the *Shenandoah* started her dive.

"That periscope stalk was very small. So much for the theory that their sensor resolution is coarse," Zeke muttered.

"Their radar is very good and has high resolution, Commander Braxton," Soucek told him. "That's how they saw the periscope head."

"Does their force beam work through water, Soucek?" Correy asked.

"I don't think so. Otherwise, they would have used it against us when they saw the ship come to periscope depth."

CDR Terri Ellison staggered into the bridge, here steps carefully made as she held handrails. The deck was tilted at about five degrees because of the dive. "What the hell is happening, Captain?"

"Sit down before you fall down," Zeke advised her, swinging her chair toward her. "A flying saucer just shot at us and blew away one of the periscopes."

"Yeah, and I'm Jacqueline Cochran reborn! Dammit, Zeke, this is no time for jokes! What's going on?" Terri shot back as she slid into the chair before the console tagged "Commander Air Group."

"I wasn't joking. Let me roll the tape replay for you. I'd like to see that again myself," Zeke told her, punching up the replay on her screen.

Major Bart Clinch was right behind her. He did a little jig across the deck of the bridge to keep his balance and slid into the chair at his CIC position. "Marine batt is ready for whatever, Captain. Jesus Christ, Terri, that's a damned flying saucer on your screen there!"

"Yeah, it just wiped out Periscope Number Three," Terri told him.

"Captain, do you want me to stand by to board that thing?"

"Come to a readiness status where you might have to, Major," Corry told him in a distracted fashion, then asked, "Soucek, does that Corona have underwater capability?"

"Some of them do and some of them don't."

"Please give me a straight answer. Our lives could depend on it."

If Soucek was scared, he didn't show it now. He was engrossed in the operation. He was seeing things he'd only studied about. "If it did, it would have come after us submerged, Captain. However, we suspect one version is being used to service the undersea processing factories. Or for that job they may have another vehicle that can operate across the air-water interface."

The special staff group has their N-fones now, Captain, Berger advised him. *They're rigged receive-only because none of the group has had thought suppression training.*

An untrained neophyte wearing an N-fone always had trouble keeping background thoughts suppressed so they didn't clutter up the channel with stream of consciousness garbage.

"I'm qualified for N-fone operation," Harriet Smith said.

Okay, Commander, let me toggle the transmit capability on your unit, Berger told her.

Special Sensors, CO here. What's the Corona doing? The image on Corry's screen was behaving in a way he hadn't seen before.

Ames here, sir. It's entered a search pattern. At least, it's the sort of search pattern we'd use if we'd lost a target lock, sir.

CO, this is Sonar. The IX has started pinging. That's what it sounds like. But it's no sort of pinging I've ever heard before.

Can you confuse it, Mister Goff? Countermeasures?

CO, this is Radar. Sir, the Corona is sweeping with something that looks like very powerful u-v lidar. And we're seeing some very strong electromagnetic pulsing fields emanating from the Corona but being damped by the seawater.

CO, this is Communications. We're receiving something that appears to be scalar wave pulses.

Soucek leaned over between Corry and Braxton. "Whatever you did, Captain, I think the Corona lost us on their masdet. They're searching with other sensors. They'll have trouble finding the *Shenandoah* because of the composite hull and other stealth features I assume are carried."

Quiet on the command net, please! Corry snapped. *Mister Soucek, say again, please.*

"Captain, the Mantids apparently have made no improvements over the mass detector they showed us decades ago. It lost mass lock at the slightest sudden change of density in the medium between the mass detector and the target. White Oak has apparently solved that problem. My guess is that the Corona lost mass detector contact and it's trying to reacquire while also searching with some of the other sensor systems the Mantids never explained to us."

Captain, the efflux from our aquajets must have done that when we dived, Zeke surmised. *Our thermal trail due to jet exhaust is only a few degrees warmer than ambient for about ten meters behind the slots. Apparently that's enough of a density change to upset their masdet.*

Stop dive! Level the bubble. Come ninety degrees left and go to ten knots forward, Corry suddenly ordered.

Aye, aye, sir. Stop dive! Stop dive! Stop dive! Come zero-niner-zero on the heading and ten knots forward. The boat is at one five zero meters.

Verbally, Corry asked his Executive Officer for input. "Zeke, give me your thoughts on the intentions of the Corona."

Braxton also replied verbally, keeping his thoughts out of the N-fone circuitry. This was a common practice for Corry and one reason the CO and XO were seated next to one another on the bridge. It permitted private conferencing. "Sir, it was probably tasked with keeping us under surveillance."

"How did it know we were here?" CDR Smith asked. "The entire mission has been conducted in the highest secrecy. How did these Mantid creatures learn of it?"

"They found us the same way we found them: by masdet," Zeke surmised.

"Oh! Of course! They'd certainly post sentries and pickets to protect their processing factories in New Georgia Sound," Smith added.

"What are their intentions now? Speculate. Best guesses welcome."

"They shot at us, trying to keep us from seeing more. They also hoped to blind us. Standard Mantid tactics," Soucek remarked.

"Agreed. It resembles what they've done in some past air and land contacts where they seemed to be protecting something," the woman from Naval Intelligence put in.

"That's what they did at Dulce and Pietown," Soucek agreed. "Captain, they'll either call for reinforcements or try to sink us."

"How can they sink us if their force beam doesn't work underwater?" Zeke asked.

"They'll get us to surface out of curiosity. They believe we'll do it because of past behavior patterns. They know that if humans don't run scared, they get curious. The Mantids are counting on us being curious."

Corry thought about this for a moment. Then he said verbally to all of them, "Well, this time we're going to do something different. We can see them on masdet, and they don't know it. They're operating in our environment where we have equal if not better capabilities. I don't know that they've ever tangled with a submarine before." He paused, got his breathing under control so he wouldn't stutter in this high-tension situation, then went on sternly, "They shot at us. I can't disengage. So I'm going to shoot back. They've got to realize we're not a pushover."

"Captain, you'll escalate this!" Dr. Barry Duval objected. "Can't we try to communicate with them and establish a dialogue?"

"Duval, you don't understand the Mantids!" Soucek told him vigorously.

"Well, maybe so, but—"

"The Mantids have a history of talking only when it's to their advantage or when they're forced onto a level playing field. Captain Corry is doing the right thing, Duval," Soucek told him.

Corry thought for an instant that perhaps Soucek was thinking straight again under the pressure of the crisis. Sometimes this happened when hysterical-anxious people were suddenly confronted with a "fish or cut bait" situation. Certainly, the man could never have been promoted to the rank of Captain without having some capability for straight thinking, nor would he have been able to function as an executive of a spook tank in Washington without that.

"What other weapons do the Mantids have aboard those Corona vehicles, Soucek?" he asked.

"Nothing that I know about other than the repulsor beam we saw. They have a tractor beam that operates in reverse, but it has no destructive powers."

"Depends on how it's used, Mister Soucek. Anything can be turned into a weapon," Zeke reminded him.

Corry had made up his mind what he was going to do. "Ladies and gentlemen, I'm going back to N-fone comm. We're going to shake the hell out of that Corona ship and its occupants." He turned back to his console.

Weapons Officer, this is CO. Stand by to launch three fish with HE blast warheads. Program them to run out one kilometer in different directions, then turn and close on the Corona from three directions using passive sonar terminal guidance. Program detonation of warheads one meter from the Corona hull at intervals of two hundred milliseconds, Corry gave the order to CWO Joe "Guns" Weaver. *Inform me when you have a TDC solution and are ready to launch.*

An overhead target, sir? That wasn't a normal shot.

Do you have a problem with that, Guns?

No, sir. Fifteen seconds to program the fish.

"Captain, are you sure you're doing the right thing?" Duval continued to press. "There's much to be said for the philosophy of 'turn the other cheek.'"

"Doctor, we have another philosophy in the Navy that says, 'Turn the other cheek, get another Purple Heart,'" Terri Ellison informed him.

"Been in any barroom fights, Doctor?" Clinch asked rhetorically. When Duval shook his head, the Marine went on, "When someone pops you in the chops, you'd better pop him back or he'll use you for a rug. You may get bloody in the brawl, but win or lose you can look your bloody self in the eye the next morning."

CO, this is Guns. Ready to launch fish.

Corry didn't hesitate. *Fire three fish.*

The U.S.S. *Shenandoah* was so large and heavy that the ejection of three underwater guided missiles—submariners still thought of them as torpedoes and called them 'fish'—from their launching tubes wasn't felt or heard at all.

All hands, this is the Captain. We've launched three fish against the IX on the surface. The fish will detonate underneath it. Batten down and hang on. We've got a hundred fifty meters of water between the boat and the explosions, and the Shanna *has more than fifty thousand tons of mass. We'll fell the shock waves, but they shouldn't cause any damage.*

The three missiles sped away from the boat, their guidance systems waiting for a sonar return that would identify the target and cause them to turn to intercept with it.

Corry watched the masdet tracks of the fish. *Go to active sonar.*

Again, because of the size of the *Shenandoah*, no one heard the sonar signals. Each pulse carried within it a code that each missile would identify and tell the guidance system to home on the pulse echo. Homing on the Corona's active pinging couldn't be done; the Corona sonar signals were too unusual.

Missiles have acquired target, Guns reported. *Missiles have turned to intercept courses. Fifteen seconds to intercept. Shifting to high pulse rate on sonar. Ten seconds to intercept. The target has not initiated evasive tactics.*

This is Sonar. Corona has stopped its sonar pinging. Now we see something that looks like countermeasures but doesn't have the pulse codes in it.

Three . . . two . . . one . . . intercept! Warhead activation!

Three sharp sounds like hammer blows were heard on the bridge. The 58,700-ton U.S.S. *Shenandoah* shuddered and shook momentarily.

Stop active sonar pinging. Corry had broken stealth by going to pinging. He wanted to stop it now that the counterattack was over. Had any of the six inbound submarines been listening, they would have heard strange sonar sounds from the Corona and a brief spate of guidance sonar pulses from the U.S.S. *Shenandoah.* Then the underwater explosions. They would know that an undersea submarine battle was taking place off the Solomon Islands.

But Corry didn't intend to stay there very long.

It turned out that he had to.

16

All stop. Come dead in the water, Corry passed the order to Mark Walton.

Aye, aye, sir. All stop.

Special sensors, this is the CO. Report the status of the Corona.

Special Sensors here. We're still massaging the data. The Corona appeared to leave the air-water interface and then return to it. LT Charles Ames paused for a moment, then added, *Sir, it looked like the three warhead explosions under the Corona blew it vertically out of the water. Then it returned and splashed. We'll have confirmation of that shortly. Good shooting, Guns!*

Piece of cake, sir. Captain, Weapons Officer has reloaded tubes.

Thank you, Guns. Stand by.

"I think we did indeed shake up the Corona crew, Captain," Zeke observed verbally.

"Captain, you may have killed the Mantids inside," Soucek told Corry. "They come from a planet with about half the gravity field of Earth. Three shocks like that would overcome the inertial dampers in the Corona—if indeed they were turned on. Commander Braxton is right. I suspect the four crew members got knocked around."

"Let me board it, sir," Clinch said.

"Stay cool, Bart. Let's wait a moment and see what happens," Corry responded. He was taking the cautious approach to this situation. He wanted to see what the Mantids' next move would be.

Two minutes later, they hadn't made one.

Special Sensors, this is the CO. I see on the repeater that the Corona isn't moving. Please confirm.

CO, this is Special Sensors. The Corona is on the water but not moving.

Sonar, do you still read the active Corona pinging?

This is Sonar, LT Roger Goff reported. *Negative, Captain.*

Radar, any output from the Corona in the e-m spectrum?

This is Radar. Negative, sir. The strong e-m fields have also disappeared. The scalar wave emanations have stopped.

Communications, this is CO. Any attempt to communicate from the Corona?

This is Comm. Negative, Captain.

Mister Walton, what's the lighting situation on the surface?

Local time is oh-one-hundred. We have a full moon overhead. First light of dawn in four hours, sir.

Make for a sea point one kilometer south of the Corona.

Aye, aye, sir. One kilometer from the Corona, position one-eight-zero true from target.

"Their drives are out and their shields are inoperative," Soucek reported.

"Zeke, Terri, Bart," Corry addressed his division chiefs, "if the Corona doesn't act during the time we're moving to the one klick distance, I'm going to surface. Zeke, I want all deck guns ready and all tubes loaded with warshots."

"Aye, aye, sir! If the Corona is playing dead and opens fire on us with that ray gun, they won't be able to target every weapon on this ship simultaneously," Zeke observed. "We're a big ship with lots of secondary targets on it. The Corona is small, and we can concentrate fire on her."

Corry told his CAG, "Terri, when we break water, I want a CAP in the air ASAP. Put one flight over the Corona's position and armed with attack weapons and another over the *Shenandoah* with a third standing by on the cats."

"Roger, you'll have it, sir!" Terri snapped back. She was all gung ho and ready for action. The long days of sitting around in the *Shenandoah* doing nothing were over. "I presume we'll surface with the bow toward the Corona. That will keep the aft lower flight deck out of any line of fire. I'll have flight of Sea Devils airborne off the aft lower flight deck within two minutes. In fact, I can get the whole Tigers squadron airborne in about four minutes."

"Stand by to do that, Terri. And be ready to launch a couple of Ospreys configured for ASW."

"Captain, if that flying saucer is indeed out of commission and full of aliens, let me board it," Bart Clinch growled, sensing that he might be left out of the action unless he put his oar in the water. He saw this operation as an opportunity for his Marine batt to shine. "We can make this mission one thousand percent successful by capturing an alien ship and its occupants."

"Approved, Major. But shoot to kill only as a last resort. Set your assault rifles to riot control stun. I want live aliens."

"Yessir! One boarding team in assault boats, another in the water. Rifles set to stun. I'll lead it, sir!"

"Very well; do so." Corry decided he wouldn't begrudge the man the opportunity to lead the boarding party. Clinch needed it. He hadn't played a significant role in this mission yet.

"Captain, I'm not trained like your people, but let me go with Major Clinch," Soucek put in. The request surprised Corry. "A long time ago, I saw the Corona in storage at Site Fifty-one. I know something about it."

Corry made a quick decision. He didn't want to put this civilian at risk. And he wasn't convinced that Soucek had gotten over his acute anxiety. So he shook his head. "No, Mister Soucek. As you said, you're not trained. But I have people who are. You can give them instructions and directions from here."

Then Corry added, "Major, coordinate with Stocker and Walton. I want a volunteer boarding team from Engineering and the deck department to go along. You three pick the team, but make it volunteers and do it fast. If the alien occupants don't want to lay off the aggressive action and talk, perhaps we can take the Corona as a prize," Corry decided. It was a long shot and depended on a lot of luck. The warhead explosions might have knocked out the alien Mantid crew if they hadn't killed them. He didn't know how long the aliens would stay unconscious if this had happened. And he didn't know the condition of the Corona. But unless he and his people risked something here, they wouldn't make the most of this incredible opportunity.

"Yessir! We'll get a line on it so we can tow it back to Pearl," Clinch announced.

"Come on, Bart! Have you been taking stupid pills today?" Terri snapped at him.

Only Terri could have spoken that way to Clinch and gotten away with it. "Have you got a better idea, Commander?" he asked formally, stressing the use of her rank.

Terri outranked Bart, and both knew it. "Damned right! A Sea Dragon is bigger than that Corona. We can handle that flying saucer on the flight decks, on the lifts, and in the hangar deck. We can put it inside and trundle it home to Pearl all snug and dry," Terri told him.

"And we'll have the thousand percent mission success that Major Clinch just spoke of," Harriet Smith pointed out. She was pleased at this development. Decades ago, the Air Force had kept their captured and crashed alien ships to themselves. Now Naval Intelligence would have one. Admiral McCarthy would be pleased. For the moment, CDR Harriett Smith's plans hadn't gone much beyond that.

"If we can get out of here without the East World boats finding us," Braxton pointed out.

"Or another Mantid Corona ship coming along," Soucek said in warning. He was very much aware of the fact that his stock had risen greatly in the eyes of the Captain. Much of his defensive aggressiveness had disappeared. "Unless the Mantids already know about our attack on their surveillance ship, they'll likely wonder where it went after a few hours."

"We'll work fast, Mister Soucek," Zeke promised him. Indeed, the crew would. A carrier submarine on the surface has lost its stealth. It may be a difficult radar target because of its RAM surface materials, but it's a visual target. If East World was indeed making a power projection push into the region, they could quickly call down from orbit a cheap anti-ship kinetic kill weapon. No ship could carry enough armor to withstand the impact of a thirty-meter steel telephone pole impacting at twelve kilometers per second.

"Commander Braxton, I fervently hope so. I fully understand the need for quick action. However, Captain, you're assuming that the Corona is dead in the water," Soucek went on. "It might well be. But the Mantids are known to be devious. I should warn you that you may be walking into a trap when you surface."

"I'm aware of that, Mister Soucek. But I'm not going to sail away into the sunrise and leave that Corona and its occupants sitting there on the water. If they're out of action, I don't want one of the East World boats to find them. And if we did damage them, the rules require that we stand by and offer assistance. Don't worry. I'm going to cover my anatomy." He directed his thoughts into the N-fone and continued to verbalize. "Communications, this is the CO. Stand by to take a message."

Go ahead, Captain.

"Take and hold this message for possible emergency SWC transmission on my specific coded command. 'To CINCPAC from Corry, CO, SSCV-two-six. I have encountered a strange vessel on the surface of the Solomon Sea.' Mister Atwater, get our coordinates from the Navigator and insert them here. 'Vessel is circular in shape, diameter about sixteen meters. Vessel attacked us. We have engaged and are boarding it. Outcome in doubt. Request immediate—repeat, immediate—support from orbital kinetic kill weapon aimed at adversary target. We are diving immediately.' Sign that for me and put it on emergency hold. Upon receiving my transmit order in the form of the code word 'magic,' transmit immediately via SWC."

Aye, aye, sir. Confirmation hard copy coming up on your screen now. Request verification of draft wording, sir.

Corry looked over the text as it marched across one of his screens. "Affirmative, Mister Atwood. You're clear to send the message on receipt of the code word from me."

"Captain, anyone could trigger that transmission by

using the code word!" Harriet Smith objected. She wasn't used to the operational protocols of a carrier submarine in an action situation, but she was aware of security matters. "You said the code word in the clear for anyone on the N-fone net to hear."

Corry shook his head and smiled. "Commander, with all due respects to the expertise of Naval Intelligence, we do have a few security tricks of our own. You could yell the password for hours and Atwood's computers wouldn't respond to your voice. My voice print is on file for such occasions as this. The computers will match it before it transmits that message."

"I should have known that," Smith said with chagrin.

"We get a lot of practice at this," Zeke reminded her.

"But I appreciate your input, Commander," Corry added.

Captain, this is the Navigator. We have arrived at the sea point one kilometer due south of the Corona, Natalie Chase reported.

Mister Ames, what's the Corona doing? Report.

The Corona hasn't moved, Captain.

Mister Goff, anything to report from the hydrophones?

Negative, Captain. The Corona is silent.

Lieutenant Brewer, any electromagnetic emission from the Corona?

Negative, Captain.

Mister Atwood, any attempt by the Corona to communicate?

The Corona is silent, Captain.

Very well. Number Two, come to periscope depth and up periscope.

Any preference to which periscope you may want to lose, Captain?

No. Let's have a look at our flying saucer.

Aye, aye, sir. Coming to periscope depth. Periscope Number Two extended. Recorders on. Periscope view over the stern on screen.

Again, the people on the bridge watched the greenish image from the periscope videocamera suddenly change as it broke the surface. As before, the image intensifier circuitry kicked in and made the view as bright as if the surroundings on the surface were lit by daylight. The motion dampers went into action and steadied the image of the Corona.

The strange vehicle was riding the quiet swells of the Solomon Sea. No lights were visible. And no activity was in evidence.

Captain, the Corona is lower in the water this time, Zeke observed and reported. *The warshots may have split the hull. It could be taking on water.*

Come about one-hundred-eighty degrees in yaw. Point the bow toward the Corona. Then surface. XO, man the guns. Air Group stand by to launch. Marine batt, prepare to board.

XO, aye, aye, sir.

CAG, roger, sir.

Marines, semper fi, sir.

Corry momentarily took his eyes away from the Corona's image on the screen and noticed that both Terri and Bart were no longer on the bridge. They were people who liked to lead from the front. He could never keep them in the CIC when action was imminent, and he'd quit trying. They were competent people. They would do what was required of them. He could count on them even though they weren't at his side.

As the 390-meter length of the U.S.S. *Shenandoah* broke the surface of the Solomon Sea, he decided he wasn't going to stay below in the bridge. This could be a historic action. He wanted to be able to say to flag officers, a board of inquiry, and other interrogators that he'd seen it happen with his own eyes, not through the electronic gadgetry of sensors and screens. Being on the bridge of a carrier submarine was something like participating in a simulator with the latest virtual reality technology in use. In fact, the land-based sims were so realistic that Corry often had trouble disengaging himself after an exercise and returning to the real world of the naval bases at Pearl Harbor, San Diego, or New London.

Zeke, I'm going topside. Extend the dodger bridge. Transfer command to the dodger bridge upon my arrival there. Chief Armstrong, I want you and Chief Thomas to join me. Bring night vision equipment.

Aye, aye, sir. Extending dodger bridge. I will transfer command there upon your arrival.

COB here. Aye, aye, sir. Right with you, sir.

"Commander Smith, I want you and Mister Soucek to come with me topside."

"Aye, aye, sir." It was the first time Harriet Smith had responded that way. She had quickly slipped into the action procedures and responses.

On the dodger bridge, the night was warm. The full moon illuminated a glassy sea. Directly over the bow, Corry could see the Corona. Its silvery surface reflected the moonlight as it bobbed on the slight swell.

It was so small!

He realized he'd been looking at it through the periscope's long lenses.

A quick look upward showed the damaged Periscope Number Three still erected. Its top looked like it had been cleanly sheared. The fist-sized streamlined enclosure for the videocamera was gone. Apparently, so was the videocamera body.

Captain on the dodger bridge! Chief Thomas announced.

Mister Braxton, I have the con, Corry told his Executive Officer, who was still at his post on the main bridge below.

Aye, aye, sir. You have the con, Captain.

The air was full of F/A-48 Sky Devils from the Tigers squadron. Three hovered over the *Shenandoah* at three hundred meters altitude. Another three were almost over the Corona. A P-10 Osprey catapulted from the port side of the aft lower flight deck, followed within seconds by another one off the starboard catapult.

The seventy-five-millimeter Mark Four zip gun mounted forward of the dodger bridge had erected its pedestal so its zone of fire cleared the upper flight deck, permitting it a complete 360-degree sweep in azimuth. It was pointed toward the Corona.

Black Bart reporting! Boarders away!

Six small boats containing men in battle gear could be seen on the water as they pulled away from the U.S.S. *Shenandoah* and headed toward the Corona.

Prize crew shoving off. Stormin' Norman in command, came the voice of the Assistant Engineer Officer, LCDR Norman E. Merrill. *We'll bring home the bacon!*

What's this Stormin' Norman crap? came the unmistakable "voice" of Major Bart Clinch. Even over the N-fone, his thought patterns seemed to have a verbal growl to them.

Black Bart, everyone gets a call name when operating away from the boat, don't they?

Yeah, but—

I volunteered for this mission. So mine is Stormin' Norman.

This is the Captain. Good luck, Stormin' Norman, Corry put in quickly. He'd placed his stamp of approval on the call code by doing so. Merrill was right, and Corry wasn't going to allow Clinch to rain on Merrill's parade. It took guts to go out in the middle of the night and board a potential enemy vessel. It took more than that to board an alien flying saucer.

The Marines were expected to do things like that. They didn't give a damn whether it was a Chinese armed junk or a space ship. It was all the same to them. But for the Assistant Engineer Officer to do so voluntarily was above and beyond the call of duty.

Corry made a mental note to recommend Merrill for at least the Navy Cross when this was over. The man had shown his courage before in the Makasar mission by being one of the first to do battle with the underwater Awesomes.

It took only a few minutes for the Marine detachment to cross the kilometer of water between the carrier submarine and the Corona. Chief Armstrong had handed Corry a set of night vision binoculars and given others to Chief Thomas, Commander Smith, and Allan Soucek. Together, they stood on the dodger bridge and watched the operation unfold.

Nearly everyone else in the U.S.S. *Shenandoah* watched as well if they didn't have some duty that prevented them from witnessing the scene picked up by the long lenses and image enhancers on two periscopes and switched to every display screen in the boat.

Major Bart Clinch was the first to clamber out of the boarding boat and up onto the shiny surface of the pie-plate section of the Corona. He was followed by six men of the Alpha Company.

It's wallowing, Bart reported. *Acts like it's taken on some water. But I can't find any hatches. This surface is as smooth as a baby's butt. I'll see if I can find the asshole that will let us go in.*

Stormin' Norman's aboard with the prize crew on the other side of the inverted coffee cup superstructure, Black Bart. So don't let your gun apes shoot at us. We're friendlies, but we can get nasty. Just keep us covered. We'll look for openings.

How come you know so much about it?

You mentioned babies' butts, Black Bart. I used to change my baby brother when Mom was at work and I had the duty.

Well, if anyone can find an asshole, you can.

Thanks a whale. I prefer the other side. I thought Marines did, too.

The members of the special group in the *Shenandoah* were amazed at this raunchy conversation between two men facing unknown danger. None of the scientists and intelligence specialists had ever been in combat, nor had they been in life-and-death situations. Few people can understand the sort of black humor that whips back and forth between people in danger. Actually, it's a partial release of the incredible tension that comes from an operation with the aptly termed description of a "high pucker factor."

"Mister Soucek, you said you'd seen one of these before. Is there a hatch on it anywhere topside?" Corry asked the man standing beside him.

"It's been years since I saw it, Captain. I hope this Corona is the same type. As I remember, there's a small circular door on the rear side of the superstructure."

Corry passed that information along to Merrill.

Captain, this thing is literally as smooth as a baby's butt, the Assistant Engineer Officer responded. *I can't find a handle or control switch anywhere.*

"Have him look for a marking that's a circle with a horizontal double-ended arrow inside it," Soucek instructed as he heard Merrill's report in his receive-only N-fone.

Here's a circle about ten centimeters in diameter with a lozenge inside it.

"Have him put his fist against it. It should be a door latch that's triggered by a Mantid's body heat that's about the same temperature as ours."

The technology must be neat, but it's kind of a dumb way to make a doorknob.

"The Mantids aren't the most brilliant species in the universe," Soucek told them. "But when they get something that works, they stick with it for a very long time."

Okay! Yeah! It worked! A circular hatch about a meter in diameter just opened outward! Damned near knocked me into the water! Norm Merrill's excited voice came to them. *I'm going in.*

The hell you say, Merrill! We're the boarding party, and we're the ones who are armed! Bart Clinch snapped. *Stand aside. Pres, you and Carmick cover me. Wren, you and Henderson follow me. Ugh. Not the easiest thing in the world to get through that hatch. And not much room in here, either. Hey, the walls are perfectly transparent! Outside, they looked like solid metal.*

Soucek nodded. "No one was able to figure out that one-way glasslike metal. Same for a lot of other material and equipment aboard. They gave up and put the ship in storage. Our technology still isn't up to it."

Captain, get a medical team over here ASAP! Bart's voice had taken on a new tenor. The Marine officer was still excited, but a timbre of revulsion had crept in. *We've got four ... uh ... monsters here. One of them is pretty messed up. The other three were apparently strapped in and didn't get tossed around. They look unconscious, but I don't want to touch these things!*

17

"Mantids," was Allan Soucek's comment. "Coming from a half-g world, they couldn't take the shock of the warhead explosions."

CO, this is Stormin' Norman. Yeah, I agree with Black Bart about the occupants. But I'm inside now and heading down from the upper deck under the inverted coffee cup. I'm in the saucer part now. Lots of water. Okay, I see where the lower hull is split. Funny-looking split. Almost like it was torn. The ship is taking water. Maybe we could stop it if we could put one of Brookstone's men outside so he could lay a patch over the split.

I've got to get a line on this thing somewhere. That's the next job. Even if it sinks, we won't lose it with a line on it. We can tow it to shallow water and salvage it. I don't know how we could put a tow line on that outside hull, Clinch went on. *It was perfectly smooth. No place to secure a line.*

It won't help much to get this under tow, Black Bart. That won't stop it from taking water through that split unless we patch it.

"Captain, you could take the Corona aboard if you could lift it out of the water," Soucek suggested.

"Mister Soucek, even if we could get a flight deck crane topside in time, we'd have to make a sling to go under the saucer to lift it," Chief Thomas pointed out. "Rigging a large sling capable of hoisting fifteen tons isn't done real fast."

Corry knew what could be done. Time was short, and he didn't have time for his usual practice of running the idea past his senior officers and CPOs. So he gave a series of orders verbally and via N-fone.

"CAG, CO. Terri, keep your chickens aloft and

launch the birds on the upper flight deck. Clear the upper flight deck. Close fore and aft doors and secure the lower flight deck."

Roger from CAG.

"XO, clear the guns and tubes. Then stand by to dive the ship and level at ten meters depth. Disable the dodger bridge retraction circuits because we're going to stay up here."

Aye, aye, sir. Stand by to dive and level at ten meters. Dodger bridge retraction interlock disabled. You still have the con.

"Chief Thomas, I'll need your eyes to help me drive the boat under the Corona. Then we'll surface to pick it up on the upper flight deck."

"Tough job in the dark, sir, but we'll do it," Chief Thomas replied, then suggested, "If we can have the deck edge and centerline lighting, that will help. And we'll need some lights on the Corona, sir."

I'll station five of my Marines topside with their helmet lights on, Clinch offered. *Show me the truck light over the dodger bridge or on the periscopes, and I can talk you right under us.*

Captain, this is CAG, Terri Ellison's voice sounded in Corry's head. *We land our chickens right on the lift a lot of times. Let me put an approach light system on the forward lift.*

Can you do it without losing the trolley? Clinch wanted to know. Approach light systems were mounted on mobile platforms so they could be positioned at various deck locations for night landing operations. They were battery-powered for mobility. *Seawater might not mix well with the trolley's electrical system.*

Bart, if our flight deck equipment wasn't hardened against seawater, it would go tits-up constantly. In case you don't know, a flight deck is wet most of the time, even with nothing more than spray, Terri reminded him. The Marine officer wouldn't necessarily know that, of course. He and his gun apes had all they could do countering the seawater effects on their equipment in spite of the fact that most of it was stainless steel or non-corroding composites. *This will work, Captain. Give me another two minutes to get the third Devil flight off the*

*upper deck. I'll report when the lower deck doors are
closed and sealed.*

"Very well. CAG and XO, report when ready to submerge. I'm going to move in on the Corona," Corry
stated to everyone. "Black Bart, I see your lights. XO,
ahead slow on the bow thrusters."

Aye, aye, sir. Ahead slow on the bow thrusters.

"Medical Officer, this is the Captain."

"Medical Officer here. Go ahead, CO."

"Doctor, I want an emergency medical team ready on
the upper flight deck once we pick up the Corona and
surface again," Corry told her. "Go aboard the Corona
and do what you can to save the living aliens. I suggest
you get Doctor Zervas to accompany you."

"Aye, aye, sir. But I can handle it."

"Doctor, you're likely to need all the help you can
get."

"Zervas hasn't seen one of these Mantids, either."

"I know, Doctor. But I don't want to shut Bethesda
out of this. You are in charge of the team. Doctor Zervas will serve as your assistant," Corry explained to her
and added that last remark more to establish a command
structure than to appease her. Corry suspected that Zervas could become somewhat overbearing and cause trouble on the team otherwise. The arrangement wasn't
going to sit well with Zervas anyway. However, Corry
decided that was just tango sierra. He'd made his decision based on his evaluation of the situation. Laura Raye
Moore was current in trauma medicine; Zervas probably
wasn't. Furthermore, Laura Raye knew her people and
Zervas didn't.

"I just hope the Mantids' biology is close enough to
ours that I can get a handle on what to do."

"Captain," Soucek interrupted, "I'm no xenobiologist,
but I've seen a Mantid before. I've studied a little bit
about what we know of their physiology. I'd like to accompany your Medical Officer into the Corona when
you get it aboard."

"Do it," Corry said without hesitation. "Chief Armstrong, help Mister Soucek find his way to where the
medical team will assemble. Commander Zervas is on

the bridge. Pick him up and take him with you. Then report back."

"Aye, aye, sir. Come along, Mister Soucek. We'll get Commander Zervas and I'll show you where to go."

Chief Thomas had unlimbered the pelorus and was now sighting on the center of three visible helmet lights of the Marine detail on the Corona. "Target bearing three-five-four off the bow."

"XO, CO; come six degrees to port, make heading three-five-zero true."

Aye, aye, sir. Heading three-five-zero. We have excellent masdet bearings to confirm your visuals.

CO, CAG; Upper flight deck is clear and secured. Approach light trolley is in position and dogged down over the forward lift. Lower deck doors closed and seal integrity confirmed. Air group is ready for the dive, sir.

"Thank you, CAG. Stand by. Steady as she goes."

Slowly, the 390-meter hulk of the U.S.S. *Shenandoah* approached the Corona. When the bow was about 200 meters from the foundering vehicle, Corry called, "All thrusters stop. Submerge by flooding forward and midships. Stand by to flood aft. Come to depth of ten meters."

All thrusters stop. Flooding forward and midships. Ready to flood aft. Steady the bubble at ten meters, Braxton reported back from the bridge below.

Corry and Thomas had to estimate the situation very closely. Without the assistance of their night vision equipment, it would have been difficult. The momentum of the fifty-one-thousand-ton carrier submarine caused it to continue to move forward slowly through the water as its bow began to submerge. Killing the forward momentum would have required too much time and maneuvering sea room. Corry didn't want to remain on the surface carrying out this operation any longer than necessary. The *Shenandoah* was vulnerable in these waters, six potentially hostile submarines were coming into the region, and Corry didn't know the overhead pass times of East World surveillance satellites. Working in such a data vacuum, the speed of the operation was essential to survival. The quicker it was completed, the better.

Major Bart Clinch continued to provide a stream of

piloting data. *I see the lower forward deck edge lights under me now. I have the approach lights in sight. Come to starboard about a degree. That's good! Gently. Slowly. Flight deck is under us. You can surface at any time and have us on board. First time I've ever landed a flying saucer on a carrier!*

Zeke's voice came back, *What do you mean, Black Bart? I'm the maneuverable one. This is like putting a floating drydock under a floating wreck.*

I see the approach trolley lights passing below us now.

"Captain, I see the Corona over the forward lift," Thomas reported.

"Surface! Surface! Surface!"

Surface! Surface! Surface! Zeke repeated on the call back.

The deck of the dodger bridge pitched up beneath them. The flight deck broke the surface and seawater ran off it through the scuppers.

The Corona was positioned in the center of the forward aircraft lift.

"Nice piloting, Chief," Corry remarked.

"No problem, Captain. We could see it with our head-mounted calibrated eyeballs all the way. Not like when we're totally submerged and have to rely on techie sensors." The Chief knew what he was doing. He'd served an exchange tour in a Russian Typhoon boat that had been converted, not with total success, to a primitive carrier submarine. He had served as boatswain of the watch to bring the *Behleey Shtohrm* into Polyarnyy in the arctic night after it had accidentally rammed the ice breaker *Purga*. Between Corry and Thomas, there weren't two more experienced carrier submarine drivers in the United States Navy.

As the Corona was lifted out of the water, it tipped sideways on its rounded bottom. If it had landing gear or jacks, they weren't in the down position. Merrill didn't know how to extend any landing gear, and he wasn't about to fiddle with strange controls on the upper deck of the Corona.

The medical team erupted immediately out of a flight deck hatch.

Water was pouring out of the split in the Corona's

bottom and running off through the flight deck scuppers. The opening was too small for a person to get through it.

Get us a ladder! We can't get up on the top to go through the hatch, Laura Raye Moore called.

Terri Ellison had her deck rescue squad primed for this. The firemen were in position, just in case; she wasn't going to take chances that the Corona might catch fire because of some unknown type of fuel aboard. Her monitors were also around the Corona, checking their counters for any possible radiation. A cockpit rescue unit came up to the side of the Corona and unlimbered a folding composite ladder that they laid against the lip of the vehicle.

CDR Laura Raye Moore had no idea what to expect after she'd clambered up the ladder and ducked through the round open hatch into the vehicle. Zervas was right behind her, unwilling to be left out of the activity by even as much as a few seconds. He wanted to be there to see what the ship's Medical Officer saw.

Both of them were therefore unprepared.

Three apparently unconscious *things* were strapped into something resembling seats before some sort of control console or board that stretched around the inner surface of the inverted saucer. As Merrill had reported, the external solid-seeming metallic material of the Corona was as transparent as good glass when looking out of the vehicle. The only lights available were those on the three Marines' helmets plus the flashlights carried by both Merrill's prize crew and the medical team.

Laura Raye didn't really like what she saw. But few humans really enjoy the magnified images of insects.

These creatures looked like big humanoid bugs. When Laura Raye began checking one of them strapped at a control seat, she saw that the main body was fleshy but covered with something resembling clothing.

Six appendages were attached to this main body that appeared to have an internal skeleton or structure consisting of a series of stacked plates. The front pair of appendages were multi-jointed and terminated in what could be described as hands—four multi-jointed extensions that could apparently grasp. The rear two pairs of appendages seemed to be legs terminating in foot pads. This main body had several orifices in it at the top and bottom.

The head was a long skin-covered exoskeletal part very much like a skull in structure. It was mounted atop the upper end of the main body at an angle so that the beast had a fore and aft aspect to it. Two eyes capable of stereoscopic vision were on the front. What appeared to be a vestigial eye was atop the skull. All three eyes were covered by clear nictitating membranes but had no humanlike eyelids. Other openings and spots were located on this head.

Laura Raye felt a momentary surge of distaste and loathing go through her. As a doctor who ministered to humans, she could be highly emotional and empathetic. But she was also a surgeon, and a surgeon can't get emotional when cutting open a patient. So she retreated into her surgeon persona, burying her emotions.

She started thinking of the creature as an animal that had to be treated. She'd grown up on a farm in Nebraska. During her childhood and adolescence, she'd helped treat injured and diseased farm animals. It was different from treating a pet or a human. This thing was an animal to her right then.

"A Mantid," Allan Soucek identified it. "I've seen the dead ones preserved at Wright Patterson."

"This thing is totally different from the alien that was sent to Bethesda!" Zervas exclaimed. He'd had no qualms doing autopsies on the whalelike Awesome with its strange anatomy. This was something else. He didn't even like the smell of it. "We should have brought an entomologist! This is an insect!"

Laura Raye was looking it over carefully. "It's still a living being, Doctor. It's got to breathe, eat, and defecate. Mister Soucek, what do you know about it?"

"The Mantids are oxygen breathers. They have a circulatory system and their blood is ... just blood. It's yellow."

"I've got to manage to stabilize it and get it to sick bay," she went on, running her hands over it and checking the first three items in trauma management. "Got to find its airway. Then check its breathing. Then find its pulse to check its circulation. I can't make a diagnosis until I do. None of these openings on its head have air going in or out of them. God, it's been a long time since I took zoology! Does it have spiracles?"

"No," Soucek told her. "The pictures I've seen show those two orifices on the upper part of the body as a breathing tube and feeding tube, respectively."

Laura Raye checked these. "Okay, we have breathing, such as it is. In and out, anyway. It's breathing and it has an airway. The other opening must be its mouth." She put her stethoscope on it. "Sounds, but no heartbeat."

Zervas also had his stethoscope on it. "Rushing sounds. Multiple pulse. As I recall, an insect has a tube like a major vein containing valves that runs along the back. It has no heart. Blood is pumped forward to the brain by muscles, by peristalsis."

"Quiet, please. . . . Okay, Doctor Zervas, you're right. I can hear valve sounds. No muscle sounds. Maybe I can hear a pulse if I can get my stethoscope on its back," Laura Raye reported. "Any open wounds anywhere?"

"Not that I can see," Zervas told her.

Laura Raye took a penlight out of her pocket and flashed it in the creature's three eyes. "The eyes have something like irises, and they do respond. But the eyes don't track my light. My scratch diagnosis is that it's been knocked out like a prizefighter. We need to get it out of here and down to sick bay. Get a couple of HMs over here."

Zervas had stepped over to where another motionless Mantid was strapped in a seat. He reported, "Also unconscious here. Be careful moving this one. It looks like one of the arms has been broken. Perhaps a leg, too."

Laura Raye moved aside as two corpsmen unstrapped the Mantid and gently lifted it over to a bundle stretcher, where it could be secured for transport inside the soft, pliant foam carapace. When she saw that was proceeding well, she moved to the third Mantid.

This one caused her to shake her head. "No breathing. No circulatory sounds. No pupillary response. This one's dead."

"Get it in deep freeze right away!" Zervas urged. He

was again the researcher, the observer, dissector, reporter, and report author. He'd never liked trauma medicine, and he detested surgery. In fact, he didn't like people very much, either. He was interested in what made people work and how to control them. "We'll need an intact cadaver to study. The other one here has been pretty well broken up. Apparently it wasn't strapped in when the warhead exploded under this vehicle. Yes, their blood is yellow, isn't it? But their muscles look gray."

"Looks just like what happens when you squash a big cockroach," Laura Raye observed as she looked at the Mantid debris on the floor and bulkhead. "Okay, I'll get a team up here to scrape it off the deck, bottle it, and label it. Let's go, Doctor. We have work to do in sick bay. Sooner or later, one of our two unconscious Mantids is going to wake up. I want to be there when it happens."

"And you'll want to get them restrained while you can do it," Allan Soucek reminded her.

Laura Raye turned and looked at him. She saw a man who was frightened but no longer suffering from acute anxiety. Someone was listening to what he had to say. "You don't like these Mantids very much, do you, Mister Soucek?"

"No, Doctor, I do not."

"Why? If you've never met or dealt with them, why do you pre-judge them?"

"Because of the reports I've read and the studies of a lifetime, Doctor. Extraterrestrial life-forms have been my work. I'm perhaps the first exobiologist. It's a rather lonely specialty. We've had to keep it very quiet. Knowledge of the Mantids and some of the other seventy stellar species would set this world upside down. Now that you've seen a Mantid, do you understand why?"

"They just look like big insects. I haven't met any of them socially yet. I've seen worse 'aliens' in science fiction movies and TV shows. They're scary at first sight, but so are a lot of purely terrestrial animals. Even some people," the Medical Officer told him.

"That's a problem, Doctor. Wait until these two wake up. You'll discover what I've learned in studying the data. The Mantids aren't friendly, cooperative, or even docile. After all, they have a long history of capturing humans and mutilating them while still alive. They're cruel. When we have more time, I'll tell you my hypothesis of why this is so."

"If they're as nasty as you say, Mister Soucek, how should I handle them in sick bay?"

"I suggest you keep them in secure rooms and restrain them when they're out of them. These are not friendly aliens, Doctor, but they're not very strong, either. Two of them can take down a human, however, so don't give them that chance."

Med Officer, this is XO, Laura Raye's N-fone spoke in her head.

Med officer here. Go ahead, Zeke.

You got two of them?

Yes. One of the four aboard has assumed ambient temperature. Another one will have to be scraped off the deck and bulkheads. But we got two live and unconscious ones on their way to sick bay.

Okay, stay aboard the Corona for a few minutes. We're striking it below to the hangar deck on the lift. Ride it down. We've detected two of the East World boats. They either heard the battle or we were spotted by one of their surveillance satellites. So we're diving deep. I'll let you know when we have a steady bubble.

18

Captain, I'm trapping my chickens as fast as I can, Terri complained via non-verbal N-fone. She wasn't hassled or panicky, just pushed. She pushed on others, and she expected the CO to push on her.

I know you are, Terri, CAPT William M. Corry replied as he settled back into his chair on the bridge. The Air Group had a whole squadron of F/A-48 Sky Devils up, plus two P-10 Ospreys. He couldn't and wouldn't dive the boat until they were safely back aboard.

The Corona is fouling the forward lift, she reported. *We've got it down on the hangar deck, but we can't move it off the lift platform unless we can figure out how to get its landing gear down . . . providing it has landing gear. I can't tell. That outer hull is absolutely smooth, and I can't see any landing gear doors.*

CAG, this is Engineer, came the voice of CDR Ray Stocker from his post in the engineering compartment midships and aft. *I'm sending Bob Benedetti to the hangar deck with some of his carpenter's mates and repairmen. We'll build a cradle for that saucer so you can put it on a low-boy tug.*

Engineer, CAG here. My aviation types can handle it. We'll modify some ordnance lift trucks. All we have to do is to move it off the lift platform and clear the elevator. We'll push it with tugs if we have to. May scrape its hull, but I've got to free that lift. Three operable lifts will slow down striking the aircraft below for diving. I need that fourth lift.

CAG, accept the Engineer Officer's help, Corry advised her. He was aware that Terri Ellison didn't like to think she was dependent upon anyone, and she was like a mother hen with her Air Group. Occasionally—and this was one of those occasions—Terri had to be gently reminded that the Air Group was part of a team. *The Corona already has a hole torn in its belly. I don't know how the tear has compromised or weakened the structural integrity of its hull. We've got it aboard and it's pretty valuable. I don't want to damage it in handling. Please concentrate on getting your chickens trapped and struck below, even if you can't use that lift. Every minute we sit here on the surface is another minute we're vulnerable.*

Terri didn't voice an objection. There were times when she might argue with the Captain. She often did so during Papa briefings when she detected a problem in the operational planning. But she knew better than to do it on the N-fone command net during a crisis. Corry was more than just her Commanding Officer. He also wore the gold wings of a naval aviator alongside the twin dolphins of his submariner's badge. Getting both those took a lot of work and dedication. Terri had her golden wings; that's all she ever wanted. She knew she would never wear the twin dolphins because she really didn't want them. Flying was her life, and she had no desire to operate a submarine. Corry was also a pilot and understood the pilots in the Air Group. So Terri replied a bit easier, *Roger that, Captain. I'll report when Air Group is ready to dive.*

Corry turned his attention again to the submarine threat. If he orchestrated this situation properly, he'd have to handle only one threat at a time in sequence. *Special Sensors, CO here. Have you identified that masdet contact in the Saint George Channel yet?*

Captain, at that range, getting a mass reading is problematical. We see it in the channel. We know the range, so we can guess at the target's mass. But it's just a guess.

Speculate, Corry told him. LT Charles Ames didn't like to do that. Even in response to a direct order, he was hesitant to make any estimate he couldn't back up with hard data.

Uh, aye, aye, sir, but please don't hold me to it. Uh, give or take ten percent, I'd guess it masses at about twenty-five thousand tons.

Tag it as a Chinese Winds class submarine, Mister Ames, Corry told him. The Winds class submarines were the only PRC boats that big. Chinese copies of the old Soviet/Russian Typhoon boats minus the submarine-launched ballistic missiles, the Winds class used the volume inside the huge hull to house large nuclear units that gave the big boats outstanding underwater sprint speed. Corry knew he could outrun the Winds class. The Typhoon hydrodynamic design technology was more than fifty years old and didn't come close to the sophisticated modern know-how that had gone into the United States Navy's Rivers class boats such as the *Shenandoah*.

"Maybe it's our old friend Captain Qian and the *Bei fung*," Zeke said in a verbal aside.

"In a way, I hope so, Zeke," Corry admitted. "We know each other, but he knows how I can fight this boat. On the other hand, a new Chinese skipper will only know what Qian has told him in a briefing. It makes no difference to me; Chinese submarine operational doctrine is pretty much set in concrete. They follow the book, the Russians wrote the book, and the book suffered in translation to Chinese."

"Yeah, the Chinese copied the Typhoon class *and* the manuals that went with it. It's not what the Chinese have got. It's how they use it that counts."

"Yes." Corry gave his usual terse one-word statement as he checked again on the threat status. The PRC Winds class submarine was the only one on the displays at the time. Terri was recovering her aircraft rapidly. He could do nothing for the moment but wait and watch.

So he turned to where Dr. Evelyn Lulalilo was seated in the observer's gallery behind him on the bridge. "Eve, Doctor Moore will have the two unconscious aliens in sick bay shortly. I would like to have you there as a translator."

Lulalilo looked surprised. "Captain, I'm not a linguist."

"You're the closest thing I've got to an alien linguist," Corry pointed out.

She got to her feet and smiled wanly. "I'll try," she promised as she left the bridge.

Corry knew she would.

CDR Laura Raye Moore was also trying, but the most

trying aspect of her existence right then was CDR Constantine Zervas.

"Let's get sterile here, Doctor. We don't know what their biochemistry is, and we shouldn't expose them to our benign protozoa," Laura Raye insisted. She told one of her corpsmen, "Gown and gloves, please. And the same for everyone here."

The two unconscious Mantids had just been brought into sick bay together with the dead one. The corpsmen and nurses were securing them to examination tables. The tables were designed for humans and didn't have enough restraints to handle four legs and two arms. The Mantids were taller than humans, also. One was slightly smaller than the other, but still it was almost two meters long. This was more than the 95th percentile human that sick bay equipment was designed to handle.

"Doctor, I want full protection—cap, gown, gloves, and mask," Zervas replied. He didn't want to take *any* chances. Moore knew he hadn't worked in a trauma center for more than a year, if ever.

"I have total isolation suits if you want one," the Medical Officer told him.

"Not necessary. I just want some protection against unknown viral agents. I want to do a biopsy on this specimen as quickly as I can."

"No, sir, I cannot permit you to do that," Laura Raye told him adamantly.

"Doctor, I—" Zervas started to complain.

"Sorry, Doctor, but this is my sick bay. I'm responsible to the Commanding Officer for the welfare of these creatures. Perhaps taking a biopsy might be indicated if we were dealing with a known terrestrial organism. But we don't know *anything* about these creatures. Until we find out, applying the Golden Rule of doing unto them as we would have them do unto us could kill them."

"Very well, Doctor," Zervas replied stiffly. "I'll begin the autopsy on the dead monster." He decided not to try pulling rank—which technically he couldn't anyway because Laura Raye was a three-striper as against his two and a half. His position on the staff of Bethesda Naval Hospital didn't make him special here. Zervas was in Moore's sick bay with her people. And he knew she wasn't going to turn the ship's Medical Department over to him. He decided to fall back on professional protocols. That wouldn't cost him anything and was a good excuse. He could even cover it over later in his report he'd write back at Bethesda. And it would look and sound good on the audio-video record the ship's Medical Officer was making as the examination continued.

"I'd like another pair of professional eyes and hands here," Moore told him. "I'm working in a near vacuum. This thing looks like a big insect, but it isn't. And it's been a long time since I took Zoology One-oh-one."

"I'd be happy to help you," Zervas told her, but he wasn't happy.

Laura Raye Moore continued to talk as she checked the Mantid. She was talking not only to verbalize her findings for the audio portion of the video record being made, but also to keep her sanity in this bizarre situation. "Now that I've got diagnostic equipment available, I've got to find out about them. I've got to find out what *they* need. Okay, here's a report for the record. I'm having a hard time getting vital signs data or making any sense of it. I don't know if this thing's breathing rate is normal or not. I can't get a pulse, only the peristaltic sounds of its linear heart, if that's what it has. I can't get a blood pressure reading because I can't find a vein. The creature seems to be full of fluid, sort of a soft bag with skeletal supporting structure to contain the body fluids. In a way, this is sort of like doing a workup on a big beetle except it has no exoskeleton. Okay, if I can't do anything else, I can try to get a mass spectrometry on its exhaled breath. It's got a real bad case of morning breath. The mass spectroscopy will give me an indication of its metabolic processes...."

"Yes, that will help," Zervas agreed. "I would also check its blood composition and chemistry."

"If we can find a place to draw a blood sample without killing it," Laura Raye muttered as she brought the breathing tube from the mass spectrometer over to cover the mouth of the Mantid. "Our first job is to make sure their conditions are stabilized. Then we've got to bring both of these creatures back to consciousness. After that, maybe we can communicate with them. It always helps if the patient can tell the doctor where it hurts."

"I'd think it extremely important that we find out something about their biochemistry," Zervas remarked as he pulled on a clean gown and held his hands up to be gloved. He wasn't about to expose himself to any unknown organism the Mantids might be carrying.

Allan Soucek had accompanied them to sick bay, but he stood back and stayed out of the way. Part of this seemed to be a reluctance on his part to get too close to the Mantids. "According to the reports I've read about the Mantids and everything we know about the seventy extraterrestrial species, the Mantids are biologically compatible with us. DNA is DNA," he said. "Hemoglobin is hemoglobin. The biochemistry is basically pretty much the same for all life-forms we know about thus far. Small variations exist from species to species as they do on Earth, of course."

"Those small variations could have large consequences," Moore remarked as she held the mass spectrometer's input tube over the Mantid's breathing orifice.

"Doctor Moore, I've stopped the bleeding around the other monster's broken leg. Or arm. I don't know what it is," reported LT Bill Molders, one of the nurses. "I managed to collect enough of this yellow blood for lab analysis and a CBC."

"Good job, Moldy! Posty, get on it, stat!" she told her Chief Pharmacist Mate as she watched the mass spectrometer begin to analyze the exhaled breath of the Mantid on the table.

"Yellow blood?" CPO Nat Post observed as he took the sample from Molders. "How can that involve the same biochemistry as ours?"

"Many insects have yellow blood," Molders pointed out. "Ever step on a cockroach?"

"It won't surprise me if their biochemistry is basically similar to ours. If Mister Soucek is right—and I don't challenge your veracity, sir—it's got to be close if they want our body chemicals and parts," Moore remarked absently as she watched the output readings. "The probabilities of DNA or hemoglobin being formed as a result of random chance in the universe are just too great. The universe hasn't existed long enough for all the molecular combinations to have randomly come together. Or maybe it was planned."

"Perhaps life was spread by Arrhenius' panspermia hypothesis," Soucek put in.

"I don't know. But I'll tell you one thing: If I were God, I would have made it simpler. And I wouldn't have created this thing!" Laura Raye Moore remarked absently, chatting just to break the silence as many doctors and nurses do in an operating room.

"I'm sorry, I don't know this Doctor Arrhenius. Has he published recently in the journals?" Zervas asked.

Laura Raye said a silent prayer to be delivered from the Philistines. "Not recently. Anyway, that's a moot point right now. I've got to work with available materials. Come on, come *on*! Damn, this spectrometer is slow! Okay, there we go. Carbon dioxide. Expected. But look at all these aldehydes! Permanent case of bad breath."

"Mantids are not known for smelling good," Soucek put in.

"Mister Soucek, any data on the atmospheric composition of the Mantid home world?" Laura Raye wanted to know.

"No, but they tolerate Earth's atmosphere well."

"Okay, I'm going to give it a little oxygen to see what that does. I'm sure as hell not going to try any drugs at this point."

"Be careful. Too much oxygen could kill it," Zervas warned. "If it came from a world with half the gravity of Earth, the oxygen partial pressure could be less there."

"Doctor, I'm being as careful as I can with my ignorant approach," she admitted. "And not necessarily lower oxygen partial pressure, sir. We don't know what the atmospheric composition of their home world is. I can only watch carefully here and hope that additional oxygen has the same effect on this Mantid as it does on a human. . . ."

The supplemental oxygen did indeed have an effect.

The clear nictitating eyelid of the Mantid single head-mounted center eye snapped up and back. Then the nictitating eyelids of both forward-looking stereoscopic eyes retracted. The eyes tracked back and forth, studying the Mantid's surroundings.

Moore withdrew the supplementary oxygen hose and her hands. She also took one step back from the examining table. She wasn't sure that the restraints would withstand any efforts of the Mantid to free itself.

The two arms twitched and came up against the restraints. One leg moved but stopped when the leg straps held it. The Mantid made no further move.

But from its breathing orifice in the upper part of its thorax came sounds.

"Mifala wea? Wea?" The words came out as modulated hisses, more like a loud whisper than a true voice. The sounds were uninflected, flat, without timbre. And hesitant. The Mantid was either groggy or not used to speaking as it did. It paused, then looked at Laura Raye. "Iufala mere."

Laura Raye shook her head. "I don't understand you. Do you speak English?" This may have been a stupid question to ask an extraterrestrial, but it was the first thing that came into her mind.

"Iufala toktok langwis waetimani. Mifala toktok an save lelebit."

At that point, Doctor Evelyn Lulalilo came into sick bay. "Doctor, the Captain asked me to come and be here. He thinks I might be able to help translate if necessary. But I don't know what language these things speak." She looked at the Mantid, recoiled momentarily, then decided that it didn't look any more revolting than some of the marine life she'd encountered. So she reassumed her scientific persona. The Mantid became something to be examined, studied, and understood.

"It just started talking, but I don't know its language. It sounds like English, but it isn't," Laura Raye explained, relieved that Lulalilo was here. Maybe the marine biologist who talked to dolphins might be able to make something of the strange sounds coming from the Mantid's breathing orifice.

Lulalilo went over to the table and looked down at the restrained Mantid. It looked back at her.

She held up her hand, palm out, in a gesture of greeting. Some cultures might mistake this as a threat to strike. So she waved it back and forth. "Hello. What is your name?"

The group was surprised when the Mantid answered, "Elo. Nem blong mifala drek. Hu nao nem blong iufala."

"Nem blong mifala Evelyn," she spoke back to it with a smile on her face. "Warem nao?"

"Mi laek somting fo dring."

Lulalilo turned to Laura Raye. "Its name is Drek, and don't laugh," she announced seriously. "Drek wants a drink of water."

"Doctor, I must compliment you as a linguist. How did you decipher an extraterrestrial language so fast? I know it sounds like English, but . . ." Zervas observed. He was surprised. So was everyone else.

There was a twinkle in Lulalilo's eye. "It *is* English, Doctor. And it's spoken on nearly every Pacific island. Including the Hawaiian Islands. Not much anymore around Hawaii. I haven't heard or spoken Pidjin English since I was a little girl."

"Pidjin English?" Soucek didn't believe what he was hearing. "That's an old bastardized version of English from colonial days! It's not a language! It was a colonial dialect!"

"But it's what the people of the Solomon Islands still speak. So that's what this Mantid learned so it could communicate with them," Lulalilo pointed out. "I can speak with it. What I've forgotten about Pidjin, I'll relearn. I wish it was as easy for me to learn to speak dolphin. . . ."

"Why does it know Pidjin English?" Zervas wondered.

"It must be based here, so it learned to talk to the natives who were caught," Laura Raye guessed.

"Mantids were known to speak English," Soucek recalled. "They learned it from Americans. Apparently they learned it in order to negotiate with us. I don't know why this one speaks the local language."

"We'll find out," Laura Raye promised.

"It sounds funny. Hard to follow it. No sound. No inflection," Soucek said.

"There's a reason for that," Lulalilo explained. "Drek

apparently has no vocal cords like ours. That's why its words come out as a rasp or whisper. That's the only sound it can make. I'm not sure how it forms some of the sounds it's making because it has no tongue. But I can indeed talk with Drek here." She felt very confident. Furthermore, in spite of the fact that circumstances were forcing her to operate outside of her field of marine biology, she was happy that she would be able to make a solid contribution to this mission at last.

She looked back at the Mantid called Drek and began to speak with it, albeit somewhat slowly and haltingly as she recalled an English dialect she'd known as a child.

If Doctor Evelyn Lulalilo had a shortcoming, it was here tendency because of her education and field experience to become too empathetic with different life-forms. For years, she'd worked hard to communicate with dolphins. She hadn't been successful doing that. It almost seemed like the dolphins weren't interested in communicating with humans. She wanted desperately to communicate with a different species. As a result, she was overeager when she saw an opportunity to do what she wanted to do, but with an extraterrestrial species instead of the dolphins.

She let down her guard.

That moment in sick bay when she'd reached out and communicated with a strange being, a Mantid, was a crucial one in her life.

And for the lives of other people as well.

19

Captain, the bubble is level at three-five-zero meters. The bottom is seven-zero meters, reported LCDR Mark Walton.

Thank you, Mister Walton. CAPT William Corry was watching the displays and readouts. He swiveled in his chair to face Doctor Barry Duval behind him. "Doctor, please get with Commander Chase. Help us find a massive seamount or volcano nearby. I may need to hide next to a large, high-density covering mass. It may confuse the masdet readings of the next Mantid Corona ship that comes looking for the one in the hangar deck."

"I can do that," Duval told the Captain as he got to his feet. He rarely used honorifics. This neglect to use a term of respect for the Captain caused some members of the bridge crew to bristle. "My current data shows some subsea massifs that your charts don't."

If Duval was going to be informal, Corry wasn't. "That was my thought, Doctor. If the Mantid masdet is as poor as Mister Soucek believes, we ought to be able to spoof it."

"I think we can position the ship to confuse it, Captain."

Corry turned his attention back to the ship. He saw that the U.S.S. *Shenandoah* was level at 350 meters depth, everything was shipshape, and all sensors were passively working. But he could sense the high level of tension in the ship. *All propulsion stop.*

Aye, aye, sir. All stop.

Rig for quiet.

Aye, aye, sir. Rig for quiet.

Come to Condition Three and set the watch, Mister Walton. OOD has the con, was Corry's final order.

Condition Three. Setting the watch. Mister Brookstone is OOD, and he's on his way to the bridge.

Corry leaned back in his seat. Without taking his eyes off the displays and monitors, he told his Executive Officer, "Zeke, make sure everyone gets a good, hot meal. And at least four hours' rest if they're not on watch. We aren't out of this yet, but we're in a good position to watch and wait for the next development."

Zeke nodded. He'd been on duty for something more than twenty-four hours. So had the rest of the ship's complement. "Aye, aye, sir. I don't think anyone will need any encouragement for that. It's been a busy night."

"And the day before that, too."

"High pucker factor."

"Yes. But we're secure for the time being. We're sitting under an excellent deep scattering layer. Chinese sonar is going to have a hard time finding us."

"And when they start to ping, we can confirm the masdet data."

"Yes." He went to the N-fone channel. *Medical Officer, this is CO.*

The reply didn't come for about twenty seconds. Zeke was ready to have some Marines or police petty officers get down to the sick bay when Laura Raye's voice replied, *Medical Officer here. GA.* Although the N-fone tended to pick up thoughts and transmit them without emotional content, this wasn't always the case. The Medical Officer sounded hassled.

Are you all right, Doctor?

Everything is nominal, Captain. I was very busy with the wounded Mantid, the Doctor replied.

Can you report any progress with the Mantids?

Yes, sir. Doctor Lulalilo is in communication with the Mantid that regained consciousness a few minutes ago.

She's talking to it already? That was an astounding piece of news. Corry suspected that Evelyn Lulalilo was good, but this was an outstanding development.

Yes, sir. It speaks Pidgin. Probably learned it from contact with the Solomon Islanders. She paused, then went on, *The second Mantid apparently has a broken—uh, appendage is the best word I can think of. One of its four legs coming out of the large body segment has a broken bone. The Mantid looks like a big insect, but it doesn't have an exoskeleton. It's more like the endoskeleton we have, but smaller and more fragile. The muscles seem to bear most of its weight. At least, that would be my guess based on the X rays I'm looking at right now. I may be able to splint this leg and treat it like I'd treat any broken bone in a human. I think both of our two alien guests will be up and around in six to twelve hours.*

I'm going to have Major Clinch put a Marine guard on them.

They're all right here in sick bay, Captain. We have both of them in restraints.

You can't keep them in restraints forever, Doctor. As you pointed out just now, they'll probably both be mobile soon. I want them secured in quarters with a Marine guard on them.

Do you really think that's necessary, Captain? Eve tells me that Drek, the first Mantid, seems quite friendly.

Yes, Doctor, I do, based on what Allan Soucek tells us about Mantids.

Do you believe Soucek, Captain?

I do now. Everything he's told us thus far has been correct.

So you believe the rest of his story is true?

What's your assessment of Mister Soucek's mental condition, Doctor?

Laura Raye paused before she answered. *Apparently you've changed your mind about him, sir. Reluctantly, I'll have to admit that I've changed my assessment of him, too. He's scared of these Mantids. I probably would be, too, if I wasn't looking at them from a professional medical viewpoint. Ugly beasts.*

Doctor, we're more than three hundred meters down and several East World submarines are coming our way. I expect another Corona will come looking for the one we have on the hangar deck. Therefore, I'm going to be cautious, regardless of what Doctor Lulalilo believes. The Marine guard is on its way.

Yes, sir. We'll leave the Mantids in restraints until they get here, Captain.

How about the other Mantids that were in the Corona?

One of them became interior decoration for the vehicle. Messy. Some of my people are in the Corona collecting whatever they can scrape off the bulkheads and decks. Another one had assumed ambient temperature by the time we got to it. Doctor Zervas is doing an autopsy on that one now. That will keep him busy and out of the way for a day or so.

Corry knew that his Medical Officer didn't like the Bethesda doctor. He didn't know that Zervas had been so inept helping her with trauma procedures that she'd told him to go ahead and start cutting up the dead Mantid. But Corry suspected something like that had happened. CDR Laura Raye Moore brooked no nonsense, even from her Commanding Officer. But she didn't argue with him in non-medical matters.

Very well, Doctor. Carry on. Call me if you learn something I should know.

That's SOP, Captain!

Zeke studied his CO for a moment, then suggested, "Captain, let's get some breakfast."

Corry nodded his head. "Sounds like a winner. However, I must do something first." He shifted to N-fone. *Communications, this is the CO.*

This is Communications, Lieutenant Atwater speaking. Go ahead, sir.

Stand by to transcribe and transmit a message to CINC-PAC on the SWC.

Thirty minutes later, VADM Richard H. Kane tore the hard copy from his fax. The SWC station at Pearl Harbor had just received the message via the highly classified, top-secret scalar wave communications system that allowed submarines and shore installations to communicate without fear of message interception. Scalar wave physics didn't make sense to Kane. SWC apparently didn't obey the inverse-square law of ordinary electromagnetic spectrum communications technology. Distance degraded the signal-to-noise ratio, reducing the usable bandwidth. That required messages to be transmitted in digitized code form over long distances. The techies would soon find a way to solve that one, Kane decided. In the meantime, SWC provided a way to communicate in a clandestine manner. He could live with the terse nature of the messages.

Kane read the hard copy with mixed emotions.

SWC Transmission 26–10–44 from CO SSCV-26 to CINCPAC. Status report. 1. SSCV-26 has aboard two live subjects, one dead subject, one dismembered subject, and one intact but damaged vehicle. 2. Vehicle occupied by subjects attacked SSCV-26 and was subsequently damaged by SSCV-26 in encounter. 3. Other mission type targets have been detected and tracked in New Georgia Sound. Because of possible threat situation from East World vessels, SSCV-26 has not entered Sound to investigate this further. 4. SSCV-26 is presently submerged in stealth watching East World vessel movements and New Georgia Sound activities. Intention is to watch and wait for developments before taking any action or returning Pearl. 5. SSCV-26 is tracking East World vessel proceeding submerged heading roughly one eight zero true and 60 km south of Saint George Channel. Intentions unknown. On basis of world situation, SSCV-26 assumes probably hostile intent but will not initiate action. 6. No other East World vessels detected. Would appreciate latest data. Corry CO SSCV-26. End message. End message. End message.

Kane ran it quickly through the copier and handed the duplicate to RADM Dolores T. McCarthy who was sitting in his office trying to get her circadian rhythm adjusted to a five-hour time difference from the American East Coast. The fractional orbit ship had delivered her from Andrews Air Force Base to Barber's Point NAS in less than an hour.

McCarthy read the SWC message without comment. She nodded as she read. When she finished, she placed it on Kane's desk. "I never saw this here, Admiral. Combust it, please. You should have no additional copies in your files."

Kane looked askance at her. He knew intelligence activities were absolutely necessary in a world that was full of deceit, lying, obfuscation, confusion, and self-aggrandizement. The intelligence people on his staff, the N-2 group, had saved his butt many times in the past by coming forth with some tidbit of information that caused him to re-evaluate his actions. He knew all intel people were somewhat paranoid, but a good spook was invaluable. Furthermore, giving these people something legitimate to do kept them busy at what they liked, therefore keeping them out of highly classified internal CINCPAC activities. He could trust his N-2 people, although he really didn't like them very much.

But when it came to Naval Intelligence, he tried to operate at arm's length. Who knew what these people had in their files? They weren't supposed to look inward into the service for which they worked. But Kane was never sure about that. So he treated RADM McCarthy with great respect. He didn't know much about her as a person, but he did know she wasn't an Academy graduate. In these days of a naval service greatly reduced in terms of ships and personnel, it was unusual for anyone to rise to flag rank without having graduated from the Naval Academy.

So he took the extra copy of the SWC message, walked over to little oven used for total destruction of classified documents, slipped it inside, closed the door, and pushed the DESTRUCT button. "Done," he told her as he returned to his desk and sat down.

"Do you intend to forward the original to George?" she asked.

"Eventually."

"Good. No hurry. It will create a flap," she advised.

"How so?"

"The Aerospace Force has been sitting on a Corona vehicle for decades," she admitted. "Several, I think. But they haven't been able to do much with those artifacts. They were powered by energy storage units—I'll call them 'super batteries' for want of a better term. These went dead a long time ago. Their techies never figured out how to re-activate them. I suspect some of our energy storage techies could have helped, but we'll never know."

"So now the Navy has a fresh Corona with batteries that may have some life left in them," Kane guessed.

"Plus it can be inferred from Corry's message that they have a couple of live aliens aboard," McCarthy went on. "The Aerospace Force will want them, too. In fact, General Lundberg raised hell when he found out the Navy had the alien corpse from Makasar and his medicos couldn't get it." She paused, then added, "Actually, he wanted to hide it with the other alien cadavers that have been stored away for decades."

Kane thought about that for a moment. "You know, Dolores, I've heard scuttlebutt about that ever since I was a kid. Now I hear you confirming it—"

"Not really," McCarthy replied cautiously. "You never heard it from me, Dick."

"Why do they continue to sit on this?"

Dolores McCarthy had a sense of humor that she allowed to show on rare occasions. One had to have a sense of humor to stay sane in the sort of work she did. So her eyes twinkled momentarily as she replied, "Because when the Aerospace Force first got handed this hot potato back in the last century, they screwed the ewe, if I can use an expression you naval aviators have. And they kept right on doing it because they were scared."

"Scared of aliens?"

"Not really." McCarthy thought for a moment before going on. "Scared that the ineptitude of their people would reflect upon them as commanders. And scared that the 'flying saucers' and 'unidentified flying objects' would knock them off their high pedestal."

"I'm sorry, but I don't follow you. Maybe I need another cup of coffee."

"I could use one of those myself. I'm still running on D.C. time."

After Kane refilled her mug, she added creamer to the hot, black Navy coffee. Kane got another piece of hard data about her. She had to have come originally from the east coast. And she'd come into the Navy through the NROTC door. Only easterners creamed their coffee. Even real Navy types from the east coast drank it as black as they could get it.

"When the Aerospace Force was formed back in the last century," she went on, "they were the darlings of the services. Supermen who operated the most advanced and dangerous machines in the world. White scarves whipping in the slipstream. Wild blue yonder. 'Live in fame or go down in flame.' They knew very well that air power alone never won a war. And never has since. They continue to write books and papers that claim otherwise. But in their hearts, they know what we know: Sea power protects our nation, the poor bloody infantry has to go in and occupy ground, and air power amounts to a combination of long-range artillery and transportation where loads are small and the destination can't be reached by sea." McCarthy was voicing standard Navy policy, position, and doctrine.

"Hell, I know they hate our stealthy submersible airfields," Kane agreed. "They still claim their hypersonics can do everything an SSCV can."

McCarthy nodded. "They were on fragile ground when they became the Air Force and they still are. How could they admit that someone or something had flying machines they didn't understand? That they couldn't even catch? That they couldn't offer a defense against? The only thing they could do to protect themselves was to be tasked as the service to investigate these phenomena, then cover it up if they could. They covered, they blew it, but they kept on covering it. They got to the point where they couldn't admit it. So they've done their best to make the whole thing forgettable."

Kane nodded in understanding. "And the Navy is bringing it into the limelight again."

"Yes. And, Dick, we must be very careful." She paused. "When do you intend to forward Corry's SWC message to George?"

"I don't see anything in it at this point that would warrant my forwarding endorsement to CNO," Kane said carefully. "I want more information before I report to Washington. Forwarding that message to George Street in its present form would trigger a lot of baseless speculation in the E Ring and across the river."

"Mostly in the E Ring." RADM Dolores McCarthy was a circumspect person. One does not climb the greasy pole of promotion to become a flag officer in charge of Naval Intelligence by using normal Navy political protocol. She knew things she couldn't even tell CINCPAC. He didn't need to know ... yet. If he did need to know, she'd tell him then.

As it was, she was at Pearl Harbor not because CNO had put her on TDY there. She had written her own orders; she could do that, and no one would question them right away. She really wanted to be aboard the U.S.S. *Shenandoah*. But since she couldn't, she had to depend upon a trusted subordinate.

When she went on, she prefaced her statement by using Kane's rank, which told the CINCPAC that what she was saying was official business and should not go beyond his office. "Admiral, the Aerospace Force isn't going to stand by idly and let the Navy investigate whatever it is that Corry has in the *Shenandoah*. I managed to get Commander Smith on the ship as part of that special team, but it wasn't easy. She has orders to do whatever is necessary to take control of the situation and keep control of it. She'll do it, too. She's one of the best operatives we've got."

"I didn't notice that the Aerospace Force had any personnel on the special team we ferried out to Johnston Atoll," Kane recalled.

"But they did. That team was put together by the presidential science advisor."

"He's not Aerospace Force."

"Yes, but the Aerospace Force has some hidden operations and organizations within it. They've penetrated deeply into national security and scientific affairs." She didn't reveal that the United States Navy did, too. Survival in Washington often depended upon such things as well as the Old Boy Network, the Old Salts Club, and other unofficial cabals. In fact, she didn't need to tell Kane that. He knew about such groups. He was a member of several himself.

"We discovered a new one in this operation. It's called the Majestic Corporation, one of the beltway bandit operations. When their vice president in charge of operations was placed on the special team, their existence was revealed. That's why I had to get Smith on board."

"Hell, Dolores, the Washington area crawls with such think tanks," Kane observed.

"Yes, but no one knew about this one. My people are checking into it now. I'll have more information when they dig it out. I'm interested in Majestic Corporation because it's done a lot of UFO work. For whom, I don't know."

What the Chief of Naval Intelligence did *not* reveal to CINCPAC at that time was that the discovery of Majestic Corporation had in turn uncovered yet another covert committee, something called Majestic Twelve. Admiral McCarthy didn't have a clue about that group yet, but her people were searching.

Unfortunately, they were looking in the wrong places.

20

"Didja see the big cockroaches they've got inside?" The young Marine lance corporal shuddered as he spoke to his compatriot standing on the other side of the door to the sick bay.

"Naw. Big Al boarded that flying saucer with Sergeant Luke. He told me all about them," the other lance corporal replied distastefully. He shifted his stance and moved his M33 assault carbine to the crook of his left arm. "I seen all the big bugs I wanna see. Or didn't you go through Basic at Lejune?"

"I survived it. But I ain't never seen any bug as big as those monsters!"

"Stuff it! The Captain!" the Marine hissed as Corry came down the companionway and headed toward them.

The two of them snapped to attention, trying to look good. The best they could do was to look like Marines. CAPT Corry was glad to see them on duty.

"Good afternoon, Captain," one of them said formally.

Corry nodded and replied, "Good afternoon. Stand at ease. Everything okay inside?"

"As far as we know, sir," the second Marine replied. "No one has hollered for us yet."

"Good! But I want you inside keeping an eye on those aliens." Corry stepped into sick bay. In the contagion ward, the two Mantids were sitting on the deck. Laura Raye Moore and Evelyn Lulalilo were with them.

Corry understood why the Mantids were sitting on the floor. Human chairs weren't designed for them.

Corry had wanted to see the aliens in the flesh, so to speak. He couldn't decide whether or not that had been a wise decision. He did decide they were indeed among the ugliest beings he'd ever seen. He was glad he'd gotten a few hours sleep first. Otherwise, they could have been part of his worst nightmares. He was also glad he hadn't just eaten.

His Medical Officer didn't seem fazed by the Mantids. However, he surmised that Laura Raye Moore was treating these organisms as interesting medical specimens. Certainly she must have seen much worse in microscopes.

As for Eve Lulalilo, she was chatting away with both Mantids in a strange mixture of English and Pidjin. Like Moore, she was engrossed in the scientific excitement of the situation and had obviously repressed any emotions she might have experienced on the basis of their appearance.

Allan Soucek was also in sick bay, but he was standing warily at a distance and watching everything with an air of detached interest and disgust. "Here you have it, Captain. Garden variety Mantids. Right out of the old photos," he told Corry.

"Is this the species for which the underground labs at Dulce and Pietown were set up?" Corry asked him.

Soucek nodded. "The same ones we fought against during the first interstellar war in 1979."

"I should like to apologize," Corry told him. "You told me such a fantastic story that I couldn't believe it."

"Apologies accepted, Captain. I can understand why it sounded fantastic," Soucek said. "I had trouble believing all the documents and photos when I first came to work for Majestic Corporation twenty years ago." He didn't speak of the shock of learning what *really* had gone on when he was briefed by Newell Carew, his boss, before leaving Washington for this mission. His first reaction had also been disbelief. However, the briefing had tied together so many of the unanswered questions he'd formulated during twenty years at Majestic Corporation.

"Where were you before you joined Majestic?"

"At Cornell. I was an astronomy major in the Sagan Scientific School. I was recruited directly into Majestic Corporation when I graduated."

"I see." The man's scholastic credentials were impeccable, although Corry had had little contact with people from those liberal eastern college science programs.

Their graduates tended to be on the other side of the ideological fence from graduates of the service academies. Except in the higher circles of the armed services, where some administrations attracted such people as civilian advisors, Corry hadn't worked with them. He guessed Soucek had been with Majestic and embroiled in the Washington scene for so many years that the man's approach to the military had mellowed. However, Soucek's reserve commission might have come about as part of a requirement to serve under military jurisdiction because of the potency of the security laws. "Have you any suggestions on what I should do with them?"

"Lock them up, throw meat in to them twice a day, and don't let them out until we get to Hawaii."

"Somewhat drastic," Corry observed. "I certainly wouldn't want to be treated that way."

"The Mantids have treated humans far worse," Soucek pointed out. "Captain, these beasts are cruel and deceitful. I'm glad you have a Marine guard posted here now. Both Doctor Moore and Doctor Lulalilo are being far too friendly with them."

Corry looked around. "Where's Commander Smith?"

"On the hangar deck with the Corona. I've seen one before. I haven't seen live Mantids. On the other hand, she'd never seen the Corona kept in storage by the Aerospace Force."

"Commander Smith knew about the Aerospace Force having one of those machines?"

Soucek nodded.

Corry was annoyed at this revelation. He didn't like people keeping information from him, especially when it affected what he and the crew did. He realized he might have taken a very large risk during the encounter with the Corona on the surface. He'd done it because he'd been ignorant. Maybe he would have done things differently if he'd known. Then he realized it wouldn't have made any difference. And that indeed he had known. Soucek had told him about the Corona while the engagement was in process.

He realized he needed to have a chat with Commander Matilda Harriet Smith.

However, his current visit to sick bay was to see the

Mantids. So he went over to where Moore and Lulalilo were with the beasts.

"Captain, here are our alien guests," Moore said in greeting.

Lulalilo said something to the Mantids that sounded ike, "Drek an Merhad, hem i wanfala bigman Captain Corry."

Six eyes focused on Corry. They didn't blink as human eyes did, but the nictitating membrane over each eye flipped down several times.

One of the Mantids extended what appeared to be a hand toward him. "Hello, Captain Corry. Mifala happy duim meet iu. Mifala blong nem Drek."

Without hesitation, Corry extended his own hand and clasped it around that of the Mantid.

It was a warm hand, but the skin was dry.

Corry's palm was a bit damp.

The two Marine guards came to a higher level of alert, raising their assault carbines slightly. Neither of them had the slightest compunction about blowing either Mantid away if they threatened to hurt the Captain.

The Mantid called Drek then said, "Hemfala blong nem Merhad."

The other Mantid extended its clawlike hand. Corry shook hands with it, noting that the alien hands had four multi-jointed fingers, each of which was apparently capable of opposing any of the other three in the same manner that the human thumb can touch each of the other four digits.

"Hemfala savvy toktok langwis blong iufala fastaem," Drek added. "Lulalilo teech toktok langwis blong iufala."

Corry could barely follow Pidjin. Seeing the querulous look on Corry's face, Eve quickly translated, "Both Drek and Merhad say they're learning how to speak our form of Pidjin very quickly, thanks to my teaching. Captain, they learn fast. They're very bright and quick."

"Their species also has a history of mutilating us, Doctor," Corry reminded her. "And they're the big bosses of the Awesomes who are hunting humans right now. Let them know that we don't like this. And please don't get too friendly with either of them."

"What are you going to do with them?" Eve was suddenly concerned.

"I don't know what the Department of State will decide to do. We'll certainly try to make them as comfortable as we can while they're aboard. In a sense, they're our guests in this boat," Corry told her, hoping that the Mantids could follow English better than he could understand their Pidjin. "However, I understand from Mister Soucek that they also engaged in armed conflict with humans in the last century. So I will treat them as de facto prisoners of war. They'll be kept under guard and not allowed to leave their quarters. That may be changed when I receive any orders about them. I've reported to CINCPAC that they're aboard."

Corry wondered whether the Department of State would have jurisdiction or if the Bureau of Immigration and Naturalization would take over at Pearl. He could see a turf battle raging because both had some jurisdiction over "aliens," and they'd probably argue endlessly about the real meaning of that word.

He also knew that wouldn't be the only battle that would rage inside and outside the government.

"Doctor Lulalilo, please continue your work learning the language of these beings," Corry told her.

"Captain, I don't know what their native language is," the marine biologist replied. "They've spoken only Pidjin."

"Do the best you can, then."

"Yes, sir, I will," she promised.

"Doctor Moore, may I speak with you please?" Corry asked his Medical Officer.

She nodded and led him into an adjoining compartment that apparently served as her office. It was small but its walls were covered with displays and screens.

"Doctor," Corry told her when they were alone, "I want you to maintain constant video surveillance of both Mantids."

"No, problem, sir. We've got pickups throughout sick bay so nurses and HMs can monitor patients if necessary," she told him, indicating the screens around the office. She passed her hand over a series of switches.

Several scenes showing the Mantids and Doctor Lulalilo appeared. On another screen was Allan Soucek.

"I presume you have recording capability?"

Again, Laura Raye nodded. "My medical computer has only enough memory to handle a twenty-four-hour sequence. Then it starts dumping old memory data into the bit bucket and recording new data. Normally, a day is long enough to keep a constant record of a patient. If I need to keep a spot long-term record over several days to check patient improvement, I can edit the real-time storage and put about ten channel-days in erasable cubes."

Corry thought about this for a moment. "I want a constant record of these aliens while they're on this ship. And I want the primary record backed up. Would you be willing to network with Holland for additional storage?" Holland was the name given by the crew to the *Shenandoah*'s megacomputer.

"No problem, Captain, as long as I can select the networked data and preserve medical confidentiality if we get any human patients."

"That's always your prerogative, Doctor, and I shall not interfere with medical ethics," Corry assured her and touched his N-fone behind his ear to activate it. *Operations, this is the CO.*

Operations here. Commander Lovette speaking. GA, sir.

Corry explained to him what he wanted done with the sick bay video data. *Any problem?*

None that I can see, sir. I'll check with Mister Atwater. Uh, I assume this has the approval of Doctor Moore. She's usually very prissy about the confidentiality of her sick bay data.

I assure you that it's been cleared through the Medical Officer, Commander. He toggled off the N-fone transmit mode.

"I have no problem with this, Captain," Laura Raye explained, perhaps unnecessarily, "because I remember all too well the effect of our wall-to-wall data about the Awesomes and the *Tuscarora* from Makasar. No one could argue the quality and quantity of our data. And this is going to be even more important."

"Yes. Please make sure that Doctor Zervas doesn't try to sequester his autopsy data."

Laura Raye pursed her lips. "That may be more difficult, sir. I can't be with him constantly."

"You do have surveillance cameras in the compartment where he's working, don't you?"

The Medical Officer smiled. "I think we've been submerged too long. I shouldn't have overlooked it. Thank you, Captain."

"That's what a team is for, Doctor. None of us is omniscient, omnipresent, or omnipotent. It's my job to catch your oversights and your job to catch mine."

Leaving the sick bay, he went to the hangar deck. He wanted to see the Corona up close.

Part of the hangar deck was closed off with welder's curtains. Another armed Marine stood near the opening flap. Corry paid no attention to the Marine and was brought up short when the burly gun ape stepped in front of him as he tried to enter the curtained area.

"Sorry, sir, but direct orders from Commander Smith. No one, but no one, goes behind the curtain without her specific permission." The Marine seemed very uncomfortable. "Uh, a direct order, sir. I can't disobey a direct order."

Corry kept his cool. He touched his N-fone. *XO, this is the CO. Get Major Clinch and meet me in the forward hangar deck ASAP.*

Aye, aye, sir. Problem?

Yes. And you might bring Chief Armstrong with you, please.

On our way, sir.

The Marine knew that Corry was communicating by N-fone on another channel. This made the Marine very edgy. He knew he probably shouldn't deny entry to the Captain. Yet he'd been told by his first sergeant to do what Commander Smith wanted. She in turn had given him a direct and unambiguous order. The Captain's silent communication with someone else told him that he'd probably stepped in it very deeply. He'd never been in the brig. He started wondering what it was like.

But Corry made no additional moves and didn't converse with the Marine. In a few minutes, the Marine's heart sank. The XO, Major Clinch, and the Chief of the Boat showed up on the hangar deck.

"What's the problem, sir?" Zeke asked.

"We seem to have a conflict of command taking place here, XO. I didn't want to take action without you and Major Clinch being involved," Corry told him.

"So what's the problem, sir?" Zeke repeated.

Corry waved his hand toward the opening in the welder's curtain. "Please go in, XO. After you."

The Marine really didn't know what to do, but he followed orders. He stepped in front of the Executive Officer. "Sorry, sir. Commander Smith has denied access to anyone who doesn't have her okay."

Zeke looked at Corry, then back at the Marine. "Did you deny access to the commanding officer, soldier?"

"Had to, sir. Commander Smith hasn't told me it's okay."

Major Bart Clinch blew his stack. "You dumb-ass gun ape! The Captain *always* has the authority to go *anywhere* he wants on his ship! Dammit, didn't those fucking drill instructors manage to pound anything into your head except how to fight and fuck?"

"No, sir. They didn't."

"Let the Captain and the Exec pass," Clinch snapped the order.

"Sorry, sir, but Commander Smith outranks you, and she told me—"

Corry thought that Clinch was going to deck the poor lance corporal.

But the commotion had brought Commander Matilda Smith to the opening. "Do you have a problem, Corporal? Oh! Yes, I see that you do! Please come in, Captain. You, too, Commander. And you, Major."

Corry didn't move. "Commander Smith, who gave you permission to cordon off part of the hangar deck?"

Smith seemed surprised. "This is an intelligence matter, Captain. I didn't think I needed permission to protect sensitive material."

"From whom are you protecting it, Commander?" was Corry's next question.

This confused Smith. "Why, this is normal security

procedure, Captain. This flying saucer is going to be classified at least Cosmic—"

"It isn't yet," Corry reminded her. "And I won't classify it."

"Captain, this is an important piece of information that need to be protected because it affects national security—" Smith started to complain.

"Please don't speak of protecting national security to anyone serving in this boat, Commander. That is exactly why we're here." Corry was working very hard to control his anger and his stuttering. "Everyone in the U.S.S. *Shenandoah* took part in the encounter with this vehicle. They watched while brave people from the Marine batt and the Engineering Department boarded it at great risk to their lives. And everyone was involved in getting it onto the flight deck and down here into the hangar. I will not try to hide it from them for whatever reason. My people fully understand the security regulations under which they serve. So I intend to allow them to see it and to touch it. It is important that they do so."

"Captain, it's important that the information this vehicle contains be restricted to those who have a need to know," Smith tried to argue. She should have known better.

"We *all* need to know about this vehicle and its occupants, Commander. It's going to profoundly affect our lives." He paused. When Smith didn't speak, he went on, "I want as many of our technically trained people as possible to see it. They may spot something that would otherwise be missed."

"Captain, as a Naval Intelligence officer, I cannot permit this intelligence data to be compromised," Smith tried again.

"It hasn't been. And it won't be," Corry promised her. "The time for you to start worrying about security is when we reach Pearl Harbor. Right now, the vehicle is in the most secure of all possible environments. No one except CINCPAC knows we have it. And only the Navigator knows exactly where we are."

The Captain looked around. The Corona's highly reflective surface shone in the hangar desk lights. It was a strange craft, but not too different in shape from the

F/A-48 Sky Devils densely parked on the rest of the hangar deck. "XO, please have these curtains removed," he told his Number Two.

"Aye, aye, Captain!"

"Major Clinch, your Marines are needed to guard the Mantids. They are the only things aboard right now that prudence suggests we guard for our own safety. Withdraw the Marine guard from the hangar deck."

"Yessir! Sorry this happened, Captain. I wasn't expecting it when Commander Smith asked for some security," Clinch explained.

"A modicum of security will be needed," Corry pointed out. "Commander Smith, I'll ask Commander Ellison to station some of her air group petty officers here to make sure no one decides to take a souvenir. That will give the aviation technical types a chance to look this thing over."

"Captain, I don't want anyone playing touch-feely with this vehicle," Smith said.

"No one will, Commander. On a carrier submarine, the crew doesn't't play touchy-feely with any part of the ship. Any knob-twisters or button-pushers got weeded out in submarine school. Or they died, hopefully without taking any of their shipmates with them," Corry said, reminding her of a verity of submarine living. Turning his head, he told the Chief of the Boat, "Chief Armstrong, inform the crew they may visit the Corona at will on a hands-off basis. And have them make any notes and sketches they wish, said items to be turned over to their superior officers, who will in turn transmit them through the XO and me to Commander Smith here."

"Aye, aye, sir."

"Commander Smith, you'll receive the most thorough technical inspection and analysis you've ever seen," Zeke promised her. "Relax. We've just saved you a lot of work. And you'll end up at Pearl with everything you need to make a fast and complete report to Washington."

Smith liked that idea, but she wasn't exactly happy about the rest of it. However, she couldn't do anything about it. And she didn't want to try at this point. She remembered when Soucek had challenged the Captain's authority. She had no intention of being that stupid. She had other, more sophisticated techniques to get her way.

Corry's N-fone sounded in his head. *Captain, this is the Officer of the Deck, Lieutenant Morse speaking.*

This is the Captain. Go ahead, Mister Morse.

Special Sensors just reported that a target of Corona size just materialized on the surface directly above us.

21

CAPT William M. Corry entered the bridge with CDR Zeke Braxton right behind him. As usual, the place was quiet except for the muted noise of purposeful activity. Everyone was on station. The displays and readouts presented their information in a user-friendly manner. As Corry had often observed, the bridge and CIC of the U.S.S. *Shenandoah* was a better starship bridge than anything he'd seen on television, even on the kiddy-viddy shows. Furthermore, it was more than a collection of impressive visual effects; everything on the bridge had a purpose and everything really worked.

Captain on the bridge! LT Morse announced.

Mister Morse, I have the con, Corry told the OOD.

Aye, aye, sir. You have the con, the Steering and Damage Control Officer repeated and got out of the command chair. He didn't leave the bridge, however.

Corry then ordered, *XO, come to Condition Two.*

Aye, aye, sir. Coming to Condition Two.

Throughout the ship, intercoms and N-fones came alive with a recorded female voice quietly announcing, *Hear this, hear this, hear this! Come to Condition Two! Condition Two!*

The tactical situation was displayed on several screens showing passive sonar and masdet data.

Special Sensors, CO here. Say latest information on the IX positioned above us.

Special Sensors here. The masdet target over us has an estimated mass of fifteen tons. It is located on the surface a hundred meters north of our position.

"It's another Corona," Zeke surmised. "It's looking for the first Corona. It's found us."

"Perhaps not for long, XO," Corry told him as he

recalled his contingency plan and the groundwork he'd already put in place. *Back slow on the aft thrusters,* he ordered.

Aft thrusters, back slow, was the repeat from LCDR Mark Walton, who was now at his post on the bridge. Reversing the aft thrusters would spread the sheath of condensed steam along the hull of the U.S.S. *Shenandoah* and further cool and mask it from any additional detectors the Corona might be using.

Special Sensors, track the Corona target. Tell me if it follows us. Give me an update on the estimated resolution of the Corona's masdet on the basis of what you find. Mister Ames, I want the same sort of first-class guesstimate that you gave me during the first Corona encounter.

Yes, sir! Ames was still a techie and often neglected standard on-board command response protocol when he was deeply engrossed in the operation of his "baby," the WSS-1 Mass Detector.

Navigator, CO.

Navigator here. Lieutenant Zar on duty. Commander Chase is on her way.

Report the location of the nearest sea floor mass anomaly.

Wait one, please, sir. That's a new and special data base not on the main bus. I'm accessing it now. Coordinates when I have them, sir.

"XO, find Duval," Corry spoke to his Executive Officer. "I want to snuggle up to the closest mass anomaly he helped Chase locate in this vicinity."

"Aye, aye, sir."

LCDR Natalie Chase dashed onto the bridge. Zeke knew from her appearance she'd been rousted out of the rack by the Condition Two call. She slid into the seat that Marcella Zar automatically vacated upon seeing her.

But Duval wasn't with her. Zeke thought this was strange. He'd caught all the subliminal signals that indicated Chase and Duval had been taking advantage of the Dolphin Club. Or at least Natalie Chase radiated all the data indicating she wanted to make that visit with him. Zeke didn't know about Duval. The man was an odd duck who seemed to keep his emotions to himself.

Zeke suspected that Duval, like many scientists he'd known, was somewhat afraid of women. However, if anyone could get Duval to overcome that quirk, it was Natalie Chase.

Chase ran a tight group, and she was obviously briefed on the situation very quickly by Marcella Zar. *CO, this is the Navigator. Commander Chase speaking. With Doctor Duval's latest charts, we located a mass anomaly that is presently eleven kilometers west-southwest of our position. That is the closest one at this time.*

Compute a course to it, Navigator.

Aye, aye, sir. Coming up on the display now.

Commander, where is Doctor Duval?

I don't know, Captain. I don't keep track of him.

Her remark told Zeke that Natalie had been frustrated in her attempts to grow closer to Duval, to put it mildly. Chase sounded like a lady spurned. Only her professionalism kept her from being bitchy about it. Like everyone aboard, Zeke had learned the same sort of professionalism and gentleperson behavior so he wouldn't become a brass-plated bastard when spurned by a lady officer. Duty came first, and personal emotions had to be repressed. It wasn't an easy thing to do, but the modern Navy with its mixed-gender crews wouldn't exist without such personal discipline. It would have been considered impossible by naval officers and bluejackets a hundred years before. A culture in which women greatly outnumbered men—the situation in the United States in the mid-twenty-first century—had molded people's thinking.

The text came up on Corry's navigation display, *Course 262 degrees true. Distance 10.8 kilometers or 5.72 nautical miles.*

XO, come to a heading of two-six-two true. All ahead, make twenty knots silent.

Aye, aye, sir. Come to two-six-two. Make twenty knots silent.

Slowly, the U.S.S. *Shenandoah* swung in yaw until her bow was pointed along the new course.

Captain, Special Sensors reporting.

GA, Special Sensors.

The change in heading has degraded the signal from

*the Chinese boat proceeding from Saint George Channel.
We're still reading it well enough to provide tactical data.
And we're still reading the Corona overhead. However, a
new masdet target has appeared where I had degraded
signal capability before. The range of the new target is
unknown at this time.*

I see the new target, Mister Ames. It was west of them.

"Another East World submarine," Zeke surmised.

"Yes. Six were reported," Corry recalled, refreshing
his memory by back-checking the tactical data bank. He
found the time period he wanted to look at and studied
the record for a moment before going on. "We've seen
one coming down the west side of the Solomon chain.
Others have been reported in the Torres Strait and Vitae
Strait. One should be coming down the east side of the
Solomons if our reading of the Chinese submarine doctrine is correct. What do you think this new IX is, Number Two?"

"Another East World submarine, Captain," Zeke repeated. "But that's just a guess. I'd like to watch the
new target and see where it goes before making any
additional WAGs."

Corry nodded.

Captain, Operations.

GA, Mister Lovette.

Sir, we've lost the scattering layer above us.

*Thank you, Mister Lovette. Continue to look for a new
one.* Corry was experienced enough to know that he had
acquired new stealth conditions at the expense of losing
the old one. In his career, he'd also learned never to
count on getting something without having to give up
something else.

Yes, sir. We're looking for a new scattering layer now.

Carry on.

CO, Sonar.

GA, Sonar.

*The Chinese masdet target heading south from Saint
George Channel is now pinging, sir. Its sonar signature
indicates it's the Chinese 'Wind Song' sonar system
mounted in the Winds class submarines. Doppler analysis
indicates that the target is cruising submerged at forty*

*knots. We haven't tracked it long enough to get a first
integration to provide course data.*

*CO, Special Sensors. Captain, we see a change of
course for the Winds target. Early approximation indicates it is now on an intercept course to our position. Uh,
wait one! Stand by, please. New target data. . . .*

Corry and Braxton together saw the new target appear
on the masdet display repeater. It was south of their
present position.

*CO, Special Sensors again. A new target just appeared,
bearing one-seven-zero true. No fade-in that would indicate it was an IX just coming into masdet range. It was
a quick pick-up. It suddenly appeared on the surface or
submerged. I can't tell yet if it's on or under.*

*Keep giving me new data and personal analysis as you
get it, all of you,* Corry instructed them. He turned his
head to look at Zeke. "Now what do you think, Zeke?"

Braxton didn't come back with a fast answer. He
thought about everything for a moment. Then he replied, "One: The Chinese Winds class target has seen
the Corona on active sonar. He changed course to intercept. He may believe the Corona to be the *Shenandoah*
or another West World naval vessel. He's coming to
have a look. Two: The target to the west of us is another
East World submarine. My evaluation of that threat
hasn't changed, sir. Third: I haven't the foggiest goddamned notion what that new south target is. It acts in
a way that makes me want to believe it's a *Tuscarora.*"

"What would you do, Number Two?"

"Exactly what you're doing, Captain. The deep-sea
gravity anomaly will confuse the masdet on the Corona,
and we'll be over that in nine minutes. The presence of
the Corona over us will mask the fact that we're beneath
it until the Winds target gets close enough to see two
returns. But our return will be muddy because of our
anti-sonar coatings. I hope the Winds sonar operator
may decide we're a glitch in the bottom return because
this bottom is still littered with a lot of sunken ships
from World War Two." Zeke paused and thought about
what he would say next, because he did indeed have
something to say. "Sir, the situation isn't getting any
better. We've got to stay out of an undesirable multi-

threat position. With this in mind, and if I were the commanding officer, I'd go to General Quarters now, sir."

Corry nodded. He'd trained this man well. Someday very soon, Zeke Braxton would make an excellent commanding officer in an SSCV of his own. And this wasn't just because Zeke thought as Corry did. Sometimes the man didn't. But he'd learned the rudiments of strategy and tactics he'd need to run an SSCV. "I agree. XO, come to General Quarters."

"Aye, aye, sir! Come to General Quarters. And I'll brief the crew on the situation." With one hand, he raised the security cover on the GQ switch and passed his other hand over it. The *Shenandoah* was running silent, so the squawking GQ alarm didn't sound. The red lights began to flash, however, and Holland put out the Battle Stations call in a female voice on muted intercoms and all N-fone channels.

Submariners drilled for this and hoped it would never happen. But when it did, they knew exactly what to do. And they did it fast.

The boat was already at Condition Two, so it took only two minutes and thirty-four seconds for Zeke to report to the Captain, *Sir, the boat is at General Quarters.*

Brief the crew, Corry told him.

Ellison and Clinch slipped into their seats at the CIC console, neither commenting to Corry because they were listening to their N-fones. As Zeke was giving a briefing on the situation to the department heads on one N-fone channel, Corry tuned to the chatter on the tactical net where Sonar, Special Sensors, Radar/Lidar, and other groups were in contact with one another.

Special Sensors, Intel. That southern target sure has the data bank characteristics of the Tuscarora *we tangled with off Makasar. Especially the way it suddenly appeared out of nowhere.*

That's my guess, Ralph. But the bridge doesn't like guesses.

Well, maybe you can eliminate one guess. On my repeater, it looked like the target went behind Bellona Island.

It did.

Can you get a mass reading on it, given the range to Bellona Island?

Yeah. Just finished the computer guesswork. Fifty thousand tons. It's the Tuscarora again for sure. Unless someone raised the wreck of the New Jersey and refitted it.

Come on! That went down in a hundred fathoms of water off Eniwetok during the orbital kinetic kill weapon tests. It's a pile of rust by now.

Knock it off! Pause. *The western target has initiated long-range pinging.*

And it's changed course. Another pause, then, *CO, this is Special Sensors.*

GA, Mister Ames, Corry replied.

I have a fifty-thousand-ton mass estimate on the southern target. Analysis indicates a point-nine similarity to the Tuscarora encountered off Makasar. Western target has changed course and is now on an intercept course with the Chinese Winds boat.

CO, this is Sonar. Western target has commenced long-range active sonar pinging.

Thank you, Mister Ames and Mister Goff. Carry on.

Corry didn't like the way the situation was developing. It felt like another Makasar Straits encounter, where he found himself facing four simultaneous external threats. He put down the urge to do something, anything, because that was the wrong thing to do. He had to wait. Waiting was the tough part. The only rational move right then was to make no move at all.

"Captain, the AttackRon is manned on the lifts and the PatrolRon is standing by on the lower cats," Terri Ellison reported. "We can launch when the water clears the decks after surfacing. And when you have a moment, I can give you a preliminary report on some of the things my techies and mechanics have learned about the Corona in the hangar deck."

"Thank you, Terri. Stand by on the report. Things are coming to a head above us. I have no intention of surfacing right now. No one except the Corona knows we're here. Or maybe it doesn't. And I don't want to get into a fracas on the surface when we don't have to," Corry explained, trying to get her to leaven her normally aggressive approach. Terri didn't like a cruise during which the boat spent nearly all its time submerged. It didn't give her a chance to fly, and she worried that her pilots and deck crews would lose their sharp operational edge.

Major Bart Clinch worried about being submerged for long periods, too. His Marine batt trained constantly for boarding and amphibious land operations. But any combat outfit can be worn out by constant training and no opportunity to put that training to use. "The Marine batt is ready and at Battle Stations, sir. This would be a good time to surface and let us take that second Corona. Then we'd have two of them," the Marine Major observed.

"I don't want to be greedy, Major. We've got one Corona already. Which is more than anyone except the Aerospace Force has. However, ours is newer and probably operational. So I want to get out of here with it. That's the first priority at the moment," Corry explained in short, clipped sentences as he fought to overcome his stuttering under the tension.

CO, this is the Navigator. We are over the position of the sea floor mass anomaly, Chase reported.

All thrusters stop. Maintain position. Navigator, report our bottom.

Presently we have twenty-seven meters beneath the keel, sir. We're right on top of a subsea volcanic neck. The water temperature has risen six degrees Celsius and is upwelling. Mister Walton will need to maintain a down vector on the thrusters if we are to hold our present depth.

Mister Walton, hold present depth by active thrusting.

Aye, aye, sir. Holding present depth by thrusters.

Sonar, this is the CO. Did you hear that report from Navigator?

Yes, sir. I heard it.

What effect will that have on active sonar from any of the targets closing on us?

The upwelling should appear as a vertical scattering layer, sir. On the basis of my knowledge of East World sonar systems, this vertical column of warm water will confuse them. It's almost as good as a scattering layer.

CO, Special Sensors here. The Corona is behaving like it lost us on its masdet. It appears to have initiated a search pattern on the surface. It seems unaware of the

Winds boat bearing down on it. Range to Winds boat is now two-seven kilometers and closing at forty knots.

"Twenty-one minutes to intercept," Terri said. She was used to making fast mental calculations, especially ones involving intercepts.

"Let's watch what happens, Terri," Corry advised.

CDR Matilda Smith and Allan Soucek came onto the bridge together. Corry noticed their arrival and returned his attention to the tactical situation. They had no assigned battle stations and normally would have been required to return to quarters during Condition One. However, the specific knowledge possessed by each of them might come in handy, Corry decided. So he made no move to send them to quarters.

Smith leaned over Terri's shoulder and asked in a quiet voice, "What's going on?"

"Another Corona on the surface," Terri told her. "And a Chinese submarine closing fast on it. But it's looking for us. I don't think it's detected the Chinese sub yet."

"I had Mister Ames take a look at the Corona's masdet a few hours ago," Smith revealed. "He says it looks primitive, although he doesn't recognize some of its components. Something about having a limited number of superconducting inertial field coils or something. He thinks it may be target-limited."

Corry heard that and immediately called, *Special Sensors, this is the CO. Mister Ames, please.*

This is Lieutenant Ames, sir.

I understand from Commander Smith that you've had a look at the Corona's masdet on the hangar deck.

Yes, sir.

Smith reports you believe it may be target-limited. Can you confirm this? Any other information or conjectures?

Corry knew Ames didn't like guesswork. It was difficult to get him to speculate. But it was critical that Corry have *any* information about the alien mass detector's capabilities.

Uh, sir, even basic mass detector technology is highly classified. I'm sorry, but I can't talk about the specific technical details of a mass detector, not even what I saw of the Corona's.

Mister Ames, I don't want a technical description. I do want your best guess concerning its performance capabilities. I need to know if you believe it can detect multiple targets.

Uh, sir, all I can say is that it's like a spotlight, not a floodlight.

Thank you, Mister Ames. That's all I needed to know.

"No wonder they're having trouble reacquiring us after we slipped out of their resolution circle," Zeke remarked. "Captain, it looks like the Corona is engrossed in finding us. I don't think they see the Chinese boat coming up on them."

Corry nodded slowly.

"And I don't believe the Chinese boat has detected us, either," Smith added. "What Naval Intelligence knows about Chinese submarine technology and doctrine tells me that the Chinese captain had concentrated his limited sensor and computer capability on the single Corona target."

"Yes, Commander, thank you for your input. I'm well aware of Chinese operational doctrine," Corry said quietly.

CO, this is Sonar. Sounds indicate the Chinese boat has launched a fish. It's a noisy fish. We can follow its track.

"Ten kilometers," Zeke noted from the displays. "He's shooting at extreme range on his sonar data."

"The missile is probably a Chinese Mark Sixty UGM," Smith added, drawing on Naval Intelligence data. "Long range, peroxide steam jets, passive sonar guidance, no terminal guidance, contact fuze, runs at five meters constant depth. If the Corona's on the surface, the Mark Sixty will probably go underneath it."

"We'll see, Commander. It's not headed for us. We're too deep for it. It sounds like the Chinese captain fired a trial shot. He apparently wants to engage at extreme range because he fears counterattack. Steady as she goes," Corry muttered. He was watching a naval engagement develop. The U.S.S. *Shenandoah* was in the enviable position of being an unseen witness to it. The Chinese captain apparently thought that his sonar contact was the U.S.S. *Shenandoah* conducting air operations on the surface. The position and identification information could have come from an East World surveillance satellite that had caught the *Shenandoah* on the surface during the Corona recovery operation.

Chinese fish has passed under the Corona without detonating its warhead, came the report from Sonar. *Chinese boat has slowed to ten knots. Distance has closed to six kilometers.*

"I'll bet he's coming to periscope depth to see what he shot at and missed," Braxton speculated. All data pointed to that conclusion. Slowing would reduce the periscope wake, and the range had closed to the point where the target was well within the horizon distance.

Special Sensors reporting. The Corona target has disappeared.

"It saw the periscope head and went airborne," Zeke continued to speculate.

"Yes. Let's see what the Chinese boat does," Corry replied, continuing his strategy of watching and waiting.

Sonar here. The Chinese boat is surfacing.

Suddenly the waiting was over. Even through the thick composite pressure hull of the U.S.S. *Shenandoah* was heard a series of explosions.

Sonar here! The Chinese boat is under attack! Damned strange sounds, Captain! Like a heavy blow to a hull followed by a decompression explosion, perhaps a ballast tank. Like something punched a hole in the boat followed by outrushing air. Several repeated blows, some accompanied by decompression explosions . . . I'm hearing sounds like the Chinese boat is taking on water . . . The Chinese boat is in trouble—

CO, this is Communications. We have just intercepted a mayday call in Chinese on TBS. . . . Now we're getting it in English.

This is the CO. Let me hear it, Mister Atwater.

It came through Corry's N-fone somewhat garbled, as between-ships communication usually was received when the *Shenandoah* was submerged and intercepted such messages. *Mayday! Mayday! Mayday! This is Chinese People's Navy submarine SS-forty-six Maoi fung! Position zero-niner-slash-three-five-slash-one-seven south, one-five-eight-slash-two-seven-slash-one-three east. Cheng-du, if you hear us, we need help! We are*

*under attack from unknown ship and we are taking water
and sinking! Mayday! Mayday! Mayday!*

Corry made an immediate decision and snapped orders. *Surface! Surface! Surface! Emergency surface!
Make course toward the Chinese boat! Guns, be prepared
to open fire on an airborne Corona immediately upon
surfacing! Air Group, stand by to launch CAP and engage a Corona!*

22

Surface! Surface! Surface! CDR Zeke Braxton repeated.

Throughout the boat, intercoms and N-fones repeated this command in order to alert all hands of a change in deck angle. The deck suddenly pitched up steeply as the diving officer commanded full power and full up on all thrusters. As he did so, he blew tanks to assist driving the *Shenandoah* to the surface as quickly as possible.

I'll have four Devils in the air as fast as the water clears the upper flight deck! CDR Terri Ellison promised. *Captain, do we have permission to attack the Corona?*

If your aircraft or this ship are attacked by the Corona or the Maoi fung, *affirmative! Please put as many Devils in the air as you can,* CAPT William Corry told her.

Roger that, sir! I know how to handle that Corona. We'll use saturation attacks with Fox Four, missiles, all quadrants. Do you want us to bring it down or drive it off?

Divert its attention from the Maoi fung, Corry instructed. *We're on a rescue mission in response to a distress signal. Stand by with Sea Dragons for possible rescue of the* Maoi fung *crew. Major Clinch, stand by to board the* Maoi fung *to place a line on it. Number Two, stand by to take the* Maoi fung *under tow to shallow water. And I want the zip guns unlimbered and targeted on the Corona as quickly as possible after breaking the surface.*

Black Bart is ready with the Marine batt. Two platoons will be ready to hit the upper flight deck with inflatable boats when we surface!

Standing by to take the Maoi fung *in tow when we get a line on her. Guns Weaver says zip guns are at standby and ready when we clear water,* Zeke responded.

No officer or crew member raised a question at Corry's order to surface. They knew the international rules of the sea. Other submariners—albeit Chinese—were in trouble.

But CDR Matilda Harriet Smith of Naval Intelligence didn't understand. She wasn't a submariner. "Captain, this isn't our fight. Neither the Chinese or the Mantids know we're here. Are you sure you want to break stealth at this time?"

"Yes, Commander," Corry replied without looking at her.

"Why?"

Smith shouldn't have asked that question because it caused Corry to turn and snap at her, "B-B-B-B-Because I'm answering a mayday call, Commander Smith! Under international law, I'm required to respond! I could be court-martialed if I didn't!"

"But that's a Chinese submarine, and you know the international situation—"

"Yes, Commander. However, the United States of America is not at war with the People's Republic of China."

"Someone's fighting up there!"

"Yes, Commander," Corry repeated. "The Chinese submarine is under attack and probably sinking. I'm responding to its mayday call. If the Corona attacks me in the process of conducting a rescue mission, I'm within my rights under international law to defend myself."

Smith realized that CAPT Corry was using the first-person pronoun to refer to himself and the SSCV-26 U.S.S. *Shenandoah*. The Captain, the crew, and the ship were as one at that moment. She was only a passenger. So she shut up, watched, listened, and tried to remember everything. If Corry screwed up and she had to appear as a witness in a court-martial, she wanted to be aware of what happened in this encounter. It could mean her career. More important at the moment, however, was the fact that she was scared—really scared—for the first time in her life. And she had no one to lean on, no one with which to share it. She was just a passenger in this carrier submarine about to go into action against a formidable foe.

Smith knew something about that foe from the many encounter and contact reports she'd read. Coronas had shot down the world's best fighter planes in every confrontation where individual pilots had attempted to close. The alien weaponry was impressive, and she knew of no defense against the Mantids' force beam.

But no Corona had ever before taken on twenty-first-century Earth's most sophisticated and powerful weapon, a U.S. Navy carrier submarine.

Not everyone in the ship had been prepared for the quick change in deck angle.

In the sick bay, Dr. Evelyn Lulalilo was sitting on the deck conversing with Drek and Merhad, the two Mantids. CDR Laura Raye Moore had just gotten to her feet to get another medical diagnostic tool so she could continue her examination of Merhad, the injured Mantid. As Moore did so, she was thrown momentarily off balance.

The sudden change in deck angle caused her to stumble and fall against one of the Marine lance corporals standing guard over the group.

The Marine was likewise caught off guard by the sudden deck angle change. When Moore fell against him, he dropped his M33 assault carbine.

The rifle slid across the smooth, polished deck.

Drek grabbed it as it went past him.

The alien knew what human guns were. And its physiology was such that it could grasp the rifle like a human and point it. The Mantid aimed it at the other Marine.

"Drop gun!" Drek hissed.

The young Marine was a fresh lance corporal on his first SSCV posting. He was caught totally by surprise. In basic training at Camp Lejune, the drill sergeants had turned the young civilian into a Marine. They'd taught him to do what he was told and follow orders without questioning them. He was conditioned to respond quickly to an order. He'd never been in an armed conflict situation before. So he dropped his gun to the floor.

The second rifle slid across the deck to where Merhad could grab it.

Now both Mantids were armed.

It had happened in less than five seconds.

No one on the bridge knew about it.

I want most accurate possible radar and lidar ranging on both the Maoi fung *and the* Corona *as quickly as we reach the surface,* Corry said as he tried to get a mental picture of the situation, the "situational awareness" that's so important for anyone involved in a fight.

"Captain, everyone's set to move instantaneously when we surface," Zeke told him personally. "We don't know how quickly the Mantids in that Corona will react. Or how much the Chinese are keeping them busy."

"I'm counting on the element of surprise, Number Two," Corry admitted, not taking his eyes off the displays on the bridge that had now become the CIC. *Display view from Periscope Two. Display view from dodger bridge camera. Do not deploy the dodger bridge upon surfacing,* he ordered as he saw the ship rise through fifty meters in its emergency climb to the surface. He didn't want the dodger bridge and its retractable sail to be wiped off the ship by a possible Corona force beam attack.

The angle of the deck, exaggerated in the minds of the crew because it was usually level, had caused unshipped objects to roll toward the rear of the bridge. Now the angle lessened as the steersman and divingman eased off on their controls, swinging the thrusters to bring the ship level when the flight deck broke through the surface of the water into the air. Surfacing level was critical in the task of getting the Sea Devils up and launched quickly as well as getting the zip gun tubs clear of water rapidly.

The screens showing the periscope and dodger bridge views no longer displayed varying shades of green. The blue sky dotted with fair-weather cumulus clouds appeared. The horizon came into view.

The periscope camera rapidly swept in azimuth until the *Maoi fung* came into view. The dodger bridge camera showed the *Shenandoah*'s upper flight deck with the water draining quickly through the scuppers back to the sea.

Display wide angle view from Periscope One, Corry called on the N-fone command channel.

Another display screen flashed to life with the fish-eye view from a second periscope camera.

The Corona was hovering in the sky near the *Maoi fung.*

Four F/A-48 Sea Devils took off from the deck lifts as quickly as the lift platforms rose high enough to let them do it. Normally, no liftoff was authorized until the lift platforms were even with the flight deck. But Terri and LCDR Pat "Bells" Bellinger didn't want to waste a second. Bells was the first Devil off the deck. As its landing pads cleared the lift, the platform started down again to pick up another Sea Devil.

Tigers are airborne! Terri reported.

Boarding party away! Clinch called out. The flight deck camera showed a Marine platoon departing the *Shenandoah* in their inflatable rafts.

CO, Medical Officer. Emergency! We've got a big problem! Laura Raye Moore's "voice" came over the N-fone.

Corry knew right away from the "tone" of it that something had gone wrong. An N-fone isn't supposed to transmit the emotional inflections that are common in verbal speech. But the pacing, timing, and emphasis of subvocalized language can be transmitted by the nervous system through the skin to an N-fone. *CO here, Doctor! Report!*

It's a long story. I'll fill you in later, if we survive. Both Mantids are now armed with rifles taken from the Marine guards. They're herding Doctor Lulalilo, both Marine guards, and me up to the hangar deck. They say they'll shoot us and anyone who gets in our way. They want their ship, they want us as insurance, and they want to leave. They can't hear me talking to you on the N-fone channel, of course.

It was Major Bart Clinch who responded. *Captain, I'll handle this. Those are my Marine guards. They were duped somehow. Captain O'Bannon can handle the boarding party from our batt CIC.* He started to get to his feet.

So did Terri Ellison. *I'm with you.*

Clinch pushed her back into her chair. Terri was strong, but she was smaller than Clinch. And Clinch had a powerful physique. "You've got an air battle to run ... maybe," he told her verbally.

"Dammit, it's my hangar deck! And I want to be there if you start shooting holes in my chickens!"

Clinch grinned. He pulled his 9mm M7 Astra from its holster and slapped the loading and chambering cam. "Don't worry," he told her.

Corry almost hesitated. A commanding officer often has to delegate. This was one time he didn't want to, but he already had his hands full.

CDR Laura Raye Moore and Dr. Evelyn Lulalilo were captives of those alien monsters. For all of the gender equality in the twenty-first century Navy, Corry still operated with the basic philosophy of "women and children first." He repressed an emotional surge of protectiveness over Eve Lulalilo, who looked and acted so much like his wife. Corry knew he'd unconsciously created this perception of her. However, this wasn't the time for fantasies on the part of the Commanding Officer.

Do it, Major! Try not to cause casualties. I want our people to come out okay, and we need those two aliens alive.

Clinch had a strange grin on his face. *Captain, some of my Marines may be dumb gun apes, but fighting doesn't have to involve shooting. If we do this right, we may not have to fire a shot! Casualties aren't the better part of valor!*

And with that cryptic remark, he rushed off the bridge, communicating silently with his Marine batt officers on their assigned N-fone channel.

Another flight of four Sea Devils took to the air.

Corry, the others in CIC, and the Sea Devil pilots quickly learned an important fact about the Mantids.

The aliens were easily surprised.

Bells, Heater. That thing on stupid pills or something?
Don't bet the farm on it. CAP One, Bells here. Heater, get on top of it. Sharky, take minus-x. CAP Two, when airborne and formatted, cover us and stay between the Corona and the Shanna.
Roger from Sharky!
Roger from Heater!
Roger from CAP Two! We're ranged and ready!
Bells, Pecks. Is it too focused on the Chinese boat?

The Mantids in the Corona certainly weren't slow to react once they became aware.

A scintillating golden beam full of sparkling lights reached out from the Corona and touched the F/A-18 piloted by Bells, LCDR Pat Bellinger, who commanded VA-65 AttackRon.

The Sea Devil literally came apart as if it had been hit by a huge hammer.

As the pieces began to fall toward the surface of the Solomon Sea, a parachute blossomed. Bells hadn't ejected; his aircraft had come apart around him.

Tigers all, this is Pecks! Saturation attacks! Fox Five! No radar return from it, so program your Snakes for lidar homing, proximity detonation! Squadron vice commander LT Mike Burns picked up the thread of command as his squadron commander descended by parachute. Bellinger was out of the fight. That didn't stop it; that started it.

Guns, CO! Corry gave the order to CWO Weaver. *Target is the Corona! No missiles! Zip guns only! Commence firing!*

Target Corona with zip guns only. Commence firing. Aye, aye, sir! Guns Weaver knew the drill. With aircraft in the air around the target, shipboard SAMs had a good chance to hit the Sea Devils by mistake, their artificial intelligence homing circuits notwithstanding. The range was 1,650 meters, almost point-blank for the 50mm high-rate guns mounted in four barbettes around the *Shenandoah*. The zip guns didn't miss.

But the penetrator rounds from the zip guns apparently didn't penetrate, although they got to the Corona before the first air-launched missiles arrived. No sparks flew. Whatever the material of the Corona's saucer-shaped hull, the tungsten-uranium penetrator rounds merely bounced off if they happened to strike at an angle. When the shells struck parts of the Corona normal to the skin, the kinetic energy was apparently absorbed by the Corona. Even if it had some sort of force shield around it, the Corona was having trouble handling the shocks of many three-kilogram rounds hitting it at over a thousand meters per second.

The Corona didn't fire its force beam again. It was

simultaneously attacked by seven Sea Devils dispersed in the sky around it and firing more than a dozen missiles at it.

As it was being battered by the shock of hundreds of 50mm penetrator rounds hitting its silver disk, sixteen missile warheads began to detonate around it. It wobbled in the air.

Clone, this is Lizard! Get out of there!

Roger that! A zip gun ricochet just took off my number three missile pylon! I've got to trap! But lemme give it the other two Snakes before I bug out.

Alley Cat, Pecks! Someone gonna get Bells out of the water?

He's okay. We'll recover him when the furball is finished.

Hell, he could be hurt, Alley Cat.

Pecks, fight your fight! Alley Cat will worry about Bells!

If it hadn't been for the high-speed nanocomputers directing the fire of the four zip guns at a target flying in a sky full of other aircraft that weren't targets, Sea Devils would have gone in the water. The 50mm shells couldn't been seen, so no Sea Devil driver really knew how close these rounds had come to some of the aircraft.

And Terri Ellison couldn't worry about it, either. She had to maintain faith in Guns Weaver not to shoot her chickens out of the sky in this multi-pronged saturation attack.

Weaver succeeded. Or the computers on his guns did.

Another series of fourteen missile warheads detonated around the Corona.

And the zip gun shells continued to batter it.

The force of the explosions or the impacts of the shells apparently breached its saucer hull. Something that looked like dark smoke puffed from it.

We got it! We got it!

We ain't got nothing until it splashes. What did I teach you?

When the targets starts to smoke, that's the signal to blast it all to hell!

Right! So what are you waiting for? I've got two more Snakes. So should everyone else. Keep it up, Tigers!

But before the six Sea Devil pilots could fire their remaining missiles, the occupants of the Corona apparently decided they'd had enough.

Like a bear harassed by bees, it got out of there.

It went straight up with a suddenness that surprised the Sea Devil pilots.

Jesus, I wish I could climb like that!

What the hell, I'm trying anyway.

Clone! Lizard! Knock it off! Fight's over! It couldn't pick us off when we swarmed it, but it could sure as hell swat you individually! Get back here! That's an order!

Dammit, Pecks, you take the fun out of it!

Fun, my ass. I don't want to send you home in pieces. I'd rather have you around to whup my ass at pinochle.

Corry had watched and listened to the fracas from his position in the bridge CIC. As an old attack pilot himself, he hated the idea of being stuck inside a big composite bottle while the fight was going on.

But he'd controlled himself better than Terri Ellison, who had sat at her position and bounced around like a manager trying to coach a boxer at ringside. Now she was ecstatic. "Yeah! Yeah! Way to go, Tigers!" Then she suddenly realized where she was and what she had to do. She slipped back into her persona as CAG. *Duke, Alley Cat. Launch Victor Alpha Charlie and Delta. Launch a Dragon as a Sucker to get Bells out of the water. Trap Victor Alpha Alpha and Bravo. Reload tubes, top them, and get them ready to go again.*

Roger, Alley Cat. Launching Victor Alpha Charlie and Delta flights. Shadow is ready with a Dragon for pickup.

CO, this is Lidar. The Corona is out of sight and out of lidar ranging. It went straight up. We never had it on radar at all.

Flight Deck Officer still has it visually, climbing vertically, almost out of sight overhead.

"Captain, I'm keeping a CAP over us in case the Corona comes back," Terri informed her commanding officer. "And I don't trust the Chinese, so I'm keeping an airborne cover over us and over them."

"Very well, but clear the lift closest to the Corona we have on the hangar deck," Corry advised her.

"You aren't thinking of letting the Mantids take it

back, are you?" Terri asked incredulously. It wasn't like her Captain to appear to be passive in a situation like this.

"They have hostages," he reminded her. "I may have to bargain for their release and allow the Mantids to leave with their ship."

"But, Captain—" Terri began.

Corry shook his head. "I won't gamble the lives of my Medical Officer and Doctor Lulalilo."

"But, Captain—"

"No arguments, Terri. Now that we've eliminated one threat temporarily, let's see what Bart's doing." He went back to N-fone, *Black Bart, CO. Report!*

No response.

23

Black Bart, answer CO! Corry thought into the voiceless and soundless N-fone.

When no reply came after a long five seconds, Zeke got quickly to his feet. *I'll check it out, Captain,* his "voice" sounded in Corry's head.

A new voice sounded in the N-fones of both of them. *Black Bart here! If that's the XO, stay put on the bridge. I've got the situation under control.*

Even with this report from Bart, Zeke was hesitant to resume his seat. With a wave of his hand, Corry motioned him to sit down and then replied, *Black Bart, CO. Report!* The Captain of the U.S.S. *Shenandoah* didn't waste words, even on the ultra-fast N-fone circuit that allowed silent communication at least five times faster than by vocal means.

Sorry about the delay, sir. I was talking to Laura Raye on the medical N-fone channel. She can't switch without revealing she's got her N-fone on.

We'll take care of that here. Number Two, have Atwater patch the med channel over to command channel, Corry told his Exec.

Aye, aye, sir!

Black Bart, do you have the hostage party in sight? Corry said, pushing for a report on the situation so he could gain situational awareness. The resources available to him in the U.S.S. *Shenandoah* were extensive, but he didn't want to place Moore, Lulalilo, and the two Marine guards in jeopardy.

Negatory on visual contact. But I know precisely where they are. Moore has been told by the bugs to lead the party to the Corona on the hangar deck. So she's leading them along Passageway Two Papa. She'll bring them up

Ladder Six Papa to the hangar deck. I've cleared their way. Nobody's in Two Papa. I'm giving them a clear shot at the hangar deck.

Corry began to get a picture of where everyone was. Like most commanding officers, he carried a rough mental map of the ship in his head. When he needed details, he could always ask Holland for a display. However, he didn't depend on the ship's megacomputer for everything. It could go in-op. His own head-mounted jellyware wouldn't unless he suffered a personal power outage, which was unlikely in view of his excellent physical condition. But he needed more information to complete his awareness image. *Where are you, Black Bart?*

Hangar deck, sir. Just aft of the Corona.

You seem to have the situation scoped out.

Yes, sir. That's why I like to command from the front. I think we can't take care of this little matter without anyone getting hurt too bad. Except maybe the bugs if they act stupid.

Care to let me in on your secret?

Yes, sir. Sorry about that. You were busy with the Corona battle overhead and the Chinese boat, and I sort of got wrapped up in this internal security matter. I don't want to give a Naval Undergraduate School lecture here, but we've got all the elements in hand to win.

Tell me.

We outnumber them. We out-gun them. We're on our own playing field. And we've got communications. The bugs don't know I'm in N-fone communication with Moore. I've cleared a path for them to the hangar deck, and Laura Raye is leading them along it because they don't know the layout of the boat. So I'm controlling the situation. I want to get the hostage party up on the hangar deck before I take any action.

What action do you intend to take, Black Bart?

Sir, I don't want a confrontation in the passageways. That's too damned confined, and I can't move my men around. When the hostage party gets to the hangar deck, we'll be able to surround them.

Goddammit, Bart, I don't want your gun apes to start shooting holes in my chickens! Terri Ellison objected.

We won't. We—

Zeke broke in, *Bart, here's something we learned during the air fight just now. The bugs apparently have trouble handling multiple targets or doing simultaneous tasks. They tend to concentrate their attention.*

Good! I'll keep that in mind.

Black Bart, this is Alley Cat. The Tigers drove off the other Corona by using saturation tactics, Terri advised him. *The bugs don't check six. So you can probably catch them in their minus-x.*

I'd considered that tactic. I'll use it because we have tactical security. We can communicate by N-fone and the bugs can't hear us doing it.

Don't assume that, Corry warned. *We don't yet know all their sensing organs.*

Captain, this is Medical Officer. Apparently I'm patched in to your net now.

Med, this is CO! Report your condition and that of Doctor Lulalilo!

We're all right, Captain. No one hurt thus far. Eve is scared but she hasn't panicked. The two Marines are pissed off because they blew their duty. I've told them verbally to shut up and follow my orders because they haven't got N-fones, Laura Raye Moore responded. *As for the bugs knowing about our N-fone communications, they've given no indication thus far that they even suspect it. I've even made a test N-fone broadcast that was 'look out behind us for an armed Marine.' The bugs never twitched.*

Those damned things must be slow and stupid! Terri put in.

I won't count on it. Bart obviously wasn't going to take chances.

Laura Raye added, *They're not slow and they're not stupid, Terri. They're smart and sharp. But like you pointed out, they focus too much. They compensate for their shortcomings in this regard by using deceit and deception. But they don't look around much. Their eyes and other sensors are mounted on the upper of their three body elements, sort of like our heads except their mouths and breathing orifices are down on the middle body element. Apparently because of their anatomical structure, they can't swivel those heads a lot.*

Can you catch them when they're not looking? Zeke asked. *Maybe you can get those rifles away from them.*

I'm not going to try that, Zeke. It's Bart's job to rescue us, so I'm going to do what he says. Besides, this passageway is far too crowded. Merhad is in front and leading because one of his four legs is broken and he has to move with three. Drek is bringing up the rear.

We'll take care of this situation once you get up on the hangar deck and we have some maneuvering room, Bart promised.

Okay, Bart, Merhad has started up the ladder to the hangar deck. He's having trouble with only three legs. Apparently they're not used to stair steps.

We're ready for you. Steer the bugs toward the Corona when you get up here. It will be behind you, Clinch instructed her.

"Captain, try not to kill those Mantids," Allan Soucek said earnestly. "They're the first live ones we've seen in decades!"

"Mister Soucek, if it comes down to a choice between the safety of human beings and killing a Mantid, there is no choice," Corry reminded him. "Major Clinch will do his best. His Marines are well trained. And the Major isn't one of those types who would kill everything and let God sort it all out."

"Allan, don't worry about something like that now!" Matilda Smith told him. "We have a dead one anyway. And we'll eventually have to return the live Mantids to—well, whatever authority has jurisdiction over interstellar repatriation."

"But we have so much to learn from them!" Soucek complained.

"If they'll let us learn," the Naval Intelligence officer pointed out.

Zeke interrupted, *Captain, the Marine boarding party has a line on the* Maoi fung *now. The Chinese captain isn't happy about it. He's refusing the tow to shallower waters.*

As the internal situation grew more tense, the external situation and threats continued to increase. Corry tore his attention away from the hostage situation long enough to evaluate what was happening outside the

U.S.S. *Shenandoah*. He didn't want to become fixated like the Mantids. *Communications, get me a TBS channel to the* Maoi fung. *I'll use the verbose handset here.*

Aye, aye, sir! I have Captain Jianghu on the TBS, sir. Go ahead when ready.

"Captain Jianghu, this is Captain William Corry of the U.S.S. *Shenandoah*."

"Captain William Corry, why have you boarded us?"

"Captain Jianghu, you transmitted a distress call. I responded. I drove off the aircraft that was attacking you," Corry pointed out. "Your message stated that you're taking water and sinking. I believe I can help you save your boat by towing it to Guadalcanal where you may beach and repair. Or wait for one of your submarine tenders to arrive."

"My plans for my boat are of no concern of yours!"

"Captain Jianghu, you transmitted a distress message. Are you withdrawing that message now that I've arrived and signaled that I'm willing to assist you? If so, I hope you're prepared to justify that action before the Admiralty Board of the World Court. I will certainly urge that the United States bring such a matter before the Board. Responding to your distress message and driving off your unknown assailant caused me to place my boat and people in jeopardy. I lost an aircraft in the process."

"I regret your loss. However, now that the attacker is gone, I no longer need your help. Remove your boarding party and tow line!"

"If you wish, Captain. However, you're still taking water. You'll sink without a tow to shallow water. If you abandon your ship, I'll board and claim it as a prize. If you then attempt to repel my boarding party by force and violence, I will sink you." Corry paused, then added in what he hoped was a reasonable tone of voice that would be recognized as such by the Chinese commander, "For heaven's sake, Captain, don't be stubborn. Our countries are not at war with one another. You have every right to be here in international waters just as I do. And I responded to your distress call in a sincere manner because we're both submarine officers."

The Chinese captain didn't answer immediately. Corry knew the man was checking with his political officer.

Like airmen and spacemen, submariners have a silent bond of camaraderie because the first enemy is always the universe. Submariners of different nations could be wary of one another, but they were always willing to buy each other a drink at the bar. It was a matter of mutual respect between people who continually put their lives at risk in dealing with the universe. Corry hoped that factor would tip the scales here.

It did. Finally the response came, "I will gratefully accept your offer of aid, Captain William Corry. I am indeed in distress and sinking. Be advised that I do not intend to abandon my ship. If necessary, I will go down with it. However, I would rather save it instead. Thanks to your help, I may be able to do that. My crew will assist your boarding party in the task of attaching a tow line."

"Thank you, Captain. We will therefore proceed," Corry told him. "I will stand by on this frequency if you wish to communicate."

Then he quickly turned his attention back to the pending action on the hangar deck.

Before he could, his N-fone sounded in his head, *CO, this is Special Sensors. The* Tuscarora *target to the south has ceased to close and is stationary.*

Report on the western target!

The inbound target from the west has continued its course. No range data, even assuming the target is a twenty-five-thousand-ton Cheng du class Chinese submarine.

Too many things were happening at once. Corry had to sort them out and assign priorities to them. However, at that moment, it seemed that all the threats were of equal intensity. Therefore, time was the critical factor. He needed to find out when he would be forced to bump each up to the immediate action category.

Thank you, Special Sensor. Radar, is the incoming western target on the surface? Can you read a blip from it?

CO, Radar. Negative contact on western target, sir.

Sonar, this is the CO. Go to active pinging. I want range and closing rate on the western target ASAP.

"Captain, do you intend to break sonar stealth?" CDR Matilda Smith asked, using a respectful question to remind Corry that the western target may not have spotted the *Shenandoah* yet, although it probably picked up the *Maoi fung*'s pinging during the second Corona encounter.

"We've already broken sonar stealth, Commander," Corry pointed out. "If it's an East World boat, we can use their help. Let them tow the *Maoi fung* so I can dive and get out of here. With the world situation as it is, I'm uncomfortable staying on the surface as long as I have."

Smith shook her head. "Captain, don't worry about orbital attack. East World won't target a kinetic kill weapon on us. We're sitting alongside one of their attack boats that's in trouble. Another one is on its way. Our latest intelligence data says that multiple surfaced targets in close proximity will confuse the terminal guidance system East World puts in their flying flagpoles. They could sink their own boat instead of us."

"The multiple target scanning and discrimination problem also has a fairly simple solution, Commander," Zeke told her. "Our space rods have had it for the last four years. At the rate technology is moving, it means East World got it through leaks or graduate students. With all due respects to Naval Intelligence, ma'am, I'd rather be where the weapon isn't than have to hold a final post-engagement briefing on the bottom."

The Captain of the U.S.S. *Shenandoah* didn't say anything to CDR Smith but told his Executive Officer, "Number Two, please keep radar scan up in case." The SPY-48 phased array radar mounted on the hull could detect the plasma sheath around an entering KE kill weapon. Drills had shown it was possible to dive quickly and deeply enough for the KE weapon to lose final target lock. It had never been tested in a real encounter. Corry didn't want to be the guinea pig.

"Aye, aye, sir."

Medical Officer and Black Bart, this is the CO. Report. CDR Laura Raye Moore emerged from the top of the ladder onto the hangar deck behind Evelyn Lulalilo. Merhad, the injured Mantid, was standing at the head of the ladder, keeping the M33 assault rifle trained on his human hostages and turning his body back and forth to scan the lighted expanse. The hangar deck was nearly empty because all F/A-48 Sea Devils were either airborne or refueling on the upper flight deck. Six P-10 Ospreys huddled on the far end of the hangar while eight C-26 Sea Dragons were tucked in among them.

None of the Air Group pilots or rates were to be seen. The deck seemed to be empty.

When Laura Raye turned, she saw the captured Corona sitting alone on its belly atop a makeshift pallet of wood and composite beams. Its silvery surfaces gleamed in the overhead lights. A slender ladder rested against it for access. The hatch on the upper inverted cup portion was open.

Standing next to the ladder was Major Bart Clinch and Marine Battalion Sergeant Major Joe McIvers.

Bart's 9mm Astra pistol was holstered. McIver's M33 assault rifle was slung over his right shoulder.

When Drek stepped onto the hangar deck, he waved the rifle and hissed to his hostages in the whispery voice that was the best that the Mantid mouth could make, "Iufala walkabout long skibot. Olketa go fastem. Iufala go bifor. Iufala duim. Not dium, mifala kilim finis."

"Drek wants us to walk ahead of the two of them," Eve translated primarily for the Marine hostages. She and Laura Raye had quickly figured out the tortured English of Pidjin, which sounded like a thick dialect. Her voice broke as she added, "Drek says he'll kill us if we don't."

"So we do what he tells us," Laura Raye told her. "You, too, Marines. Walk with us ahead of the two bugs."

One of the young Marines acted scared but the other apparently had gotten a little time to think. Some bravado had come back to him. "Commander, let us take these bugs right here. We can do it—"

Laura Raye shook her head. "Major Clinch apparently has something planned out already. Walk!" She also projected the same words into her N-fone.

Keep coming, Doctor, Clinch told her. *Get out in the middle of the hangar deck there about halfway to the Corona. And follow my instructions. You won't get hurt.*

I wish I could believe you.

Believe me. I'd tell you, but your reaction might give it away.

You pull this off, Bart, and I've got something for heroes, she told him.

Promises, promises. Shut up and do as I tell you. Even through the N-fone, Bart sounded sublimely self-confident.

Laura Raye couldn't understand why. She was walking across the deck with an M33 pointed directly at her. She'd served in submarines for ten years and had gotten used to the queasy feeling of being underwater and occasionally, as in Makasar Straits, under fire. But she'd never had a firearm pointed at her, nor had she been threatened by a person with a firearm. It was an experience she decided she could do without for the rest of her life, provided her life didn't end here on the flight deck with a bullet through her brains. She was the only doctor aboard. She didn't know if Zervas could handle trauma surgery. She didn't think he could. He wasn't that sort of a doctor.

When the hostages and the Mantids were about four meters from where Bart and McIvers stood at the base of the ladder against the Corona, the Marine officer broadcast the thought command to the Medical Officer, *Stop right there!*

He should have given it as a verbal command.

Laura Raye stopped in her tracks.

The other three humans kept walking, taking perhaps one more step before seeing that she had halted.

Merhad ran into the Medical Officer. It threw the injured three-legged Mantid off balance.

The Marine whose confidence had returned took that opportunity to throw his body weight against Merhad. He reached out in an attempt to grab the M33 at the same time.

Drek saw this and reacted. He pulled the trigger on the M33 pointed directly at CDR Laura Raye Moore's head.

24

When Dr. Evelyn Lulalilo saw the Mantid called Drek point the M33 assault rifle at Dr. Laura Raye Moore's head and pull the trigger with one of its four multi-jointed fingers, she screamed.

But that was the only sound that echoed through the hangar deck.

The M33 didn't fire.

Laura Raye didn't know what had happened or why Eve had screamed. So she whirled, bringing up her arm as she did so. She hit Drek's M33 and knocked it out of the unprepared alien's hands.

But not before Merhad, the other Mantid, recovered from being body-blocked by the young Marine. Merhad flailed about, trying to keep from falling because of the bad fourth leg. The injured Mantid didn't succeed in regaining its balance. It didn't let go of the M33, but it swung the gun around like a club and caught Laura Raye on the side of the head. It was a powerful blow delivered by a strong, dense, three-kilogram object. Moore wasn't expecting it.

The Medical Officer was knocked completely off her feet and fell to the deck without a sound.

Major Bart Clinch walked quickly and purposefully toward the confused group.

Merhad looked down at the M33, then pointed it at Clinch and pulled the trigger several times.

Bart didn't waiver and he didn't flinch. When the M33 didn't fire, he simply walked up to the Mantid, grasped the assault rifle by the muzzle of its protruding barrel, and pulled it out of the Mantid's grip.

Drek, now without an M33, lunged at Clinch.

The sound of a single muffled shot echoed off the

bulkheads. Drek went down, yellow goo flowing from a hole in the side of the third body element.

Battalion Sergeant Major McIvers slowly swung the muzzle of his M33 to cover Merhad. "Don't move, bug," the poker-faced master sergeant said in a low voice. "Even at riot-control stun setting, the slug from this Thirty-three will hurt like hell. Worse, it could go right through you. Look what it did to your buddy!" His words were so intense that they slopped over into the N-fone in his helmet and were heard on the command net.

Dr. Evelyn Lulalilo unfroze. After a fraction of a second, during which confusion played across her attractive features, she dropped to the floor beside Laura Raye Moore.

The entire action had consumed less than ten seconds.

It seemed that armed Marines suddenly appeared everywhere on the hangar deck.

Clinch looked over the M33 he'd taken from Merhad. "Goddammit, just as I thought!" he growled verbally and into the N-fone circuitry. He looked at the two young Marines who'd been taken hostage. "Who the hell put you on guard duty in sick bay without telling you to load and lock?"

The aggressive Marine swallowed hard and replied stiffly in a scared voice, "Sir, I was told never to carry a loaded weapon inside a submarine, sir. We never do, sir. We've been told over and over again, sir, that even an accidental discharge could damage something real critical, sir."

The other Marine stood stiffly at attention and added, "No one told us to load and lock, sir. When the bugs grabbed our rifles, I was so goddammed scared shitless that I forgot it didn't have a round in the chamber, sir! In fact, sir, I didn't even have a clip in it."

"Well, it's a damned good thing you followed orders, or this could have been bloody as hell!" Clinch growled and handed the M33 back to the young Marine. "But if you had the brains to blow your nose, you should have remembered that the only thing the bug had was a high-tech club! You should have done something right away down in sick bay, Corporal!"

"Sorry, sir!"

"Sorry don't feed the bulldog, Private."

"Yes, sir!"

"Major," came the plaintive cry from Eve, who was kneeling on the deck alongside Laura Raye, "the doctor is hurt! She's unconscious. Shallow breathing. Rapid heartbeat. And her hands are cold and clammy. Get a medical team up here right away! She either has a concussion or is going into shock. Or both!"

As if on cue, a sick bay team erupted from the ladder hatch to the lower deck. *We're right here,* came the N-fone and verbal message from the man leading them, Chief Pharmacist Mate Nat Post. *Followed quietly the whole way. Wanted to be ready for anything. Move aside, Doctor Lulalilo. We can take over from here.*

CO, this is Black Bart reporting.

We saw the action on the hangar deck surveillance cameras, Black Bart, Corry replied. *Why didn't you tell me that those rifles weren't loaded?*

I figured you knew the standing order to the Marine batt about loaded weapons inside the pressure hull, Captain, Clinch admitted. *When it became obvious you'd either forgotten or hadn't been told, I tried twice to tell you. Got interrupted both times. You were busy, so I just went ahead and did what had to be done.*

On the bridge, Corry sighed. Both Zeke and Terri heard it. It was a signal of frustration and relief combined. "I should have known about the standing order, Captain. My fault," Zeke admitted.

Corry just looked at him and said, "This boat is just too big for everyone to know everything, Number Two. Sometimes, in spite of the best communications and data base technology we've ever had in the Navy, the word doesn't get passed."

Zeke nodded. "It reconfirms the truth of the saying that there's always someone who doesn't get the word."

Terri fidgeted as if she wanted to say something in addition. But Zeke noticed that she kept quiet. That was unusual.

Corry had to turn his attention to the external situation again. So he passed the order, *Black Bart, make sure those two aliens are securely locked up this time.*

Captain, one of them is lying on the deck leaking yel-low goo. The other one has an injured leg it can't walk on, Clinch reminded them.

Get them to sick bay, then, Corry told his Marine com-mander. *But put a guard on them this time with orders to shoot them to stop them. I thought that's why the Navy spent so much money to perfect the variable muzzle ve-locity technology of those assault rifles of yours.*

Yes, sir. But we haven't got a Medical Officer now. She's unconscious.

We've got another medical doctor aboard, the CO of the ship reminded them all. *Time to put him to work for a change. Get Doctor Zervas to sick bay.*

Captain, this is Chief Post. Doctor Zervas isn't current in surgery, sir. And he isn't trained in trauma medicine.

Are you, Chief?

Uh, yes, sir. As much as a Pharmacist Mate can be, sir.

In submarines and destroyers in the last century, phar-macist mates were the only medical personnel aboard. So you're now the Acting Medical Officer until Doctor Moore is fit to resume her duties. In the meantime, use Doctor Zervas as an assistant. If he won't take medical orders from you, let me know at once. Corry wasn't going to take any more nonsense from any of the members of the special group, least of all the pompous naval surgeon from Bethesda who would have to be a real doctor for a change. Then he asked, perhaps unnecessarily, *Major Clinch, Chief Post, do you understand those orders?*

Yes, sir!

Aye, aye, sir!

Corry had to turn his attention to other matters. *Terri, keep your CAG over us in shifts. I want you to launch three Ospreys and find out what that incoming western target is.*

Roger, sir! She decided that she'd also put another two P-10s out to the south to see if they could spot the apparent *Tuscarora* target reported on masdet.

Before she got engrossed in getting the Air Group busy at their new tasks, Zeke leaned over and said qui-etly to her, "Did you have something you wanted to report to the Captain, Terri?"

"Yes, but it can wait. It's not important right now."

Zeke shrugged. "Okay." He turned back to his tasks.

CO, this is Deck. We have the tow secured to the Chinese submarine. We're ready to tow, was the report from LCDR Mark Walton, the ship's First Lieutenant in charge of the Deck Department.

Navigator, this is the CO. Give helm a course for Honiara, Guadalcanal.

Navigator here. Come to heading zero-eight-seven true. Distance to Honiara is one-zero-four kilometers.

Mister Walton, stand by to get under way towing, Corry thought his orders into his N-fone. *Any estimate from our boarding party concerning the best tow speed to help keep the* Maoi fung *afloat?*

Negative on the best tow speed, Captain. The Chinese crew won't allow our party below to help assess the damage.

Mister Atwater, put me on TBS to Captain Jianghu.

You have a circuit, Captain. Go ahead.

"Captain Jianghu, this is Captain Corry. We are ready to tow. What is the tow speed you would like us to maintain?"

"Captain Corry, can you make twenty-five knots with my ship in tow?"

Corry knew that the Chinese captain was probably requesting a high tow speed to see if the *Shenandoah* could do it. It would give the Chinese some idea of the propulsion capabilities of the American carrier submarine. Corry knew the *Shenandoah* could do more than twenty-five knots towing a twenty-five-thousand-ton submarine on the surface. But he also guessed that the sea pounding that would result from a tow speed that high might further damage the *Maoi fung*'s hull. So he replied, "Captain Jianghu, I believe fifteen knots might be a safer speed, especially if your hull is damaged and you're taking on water."

"We have evacuated and sealed the compartments near the hull damage, Captain Corry. I can handle twenty-five knots. I have some leaks that will be critical in a few hours. I will lose positive buoyancy in four hours. Therefore, it is necessary that we reach shallow water as quickly as possible. If we can reach Honiara harbor in the next three hours, we will be able to ground my boat on a shoal, stop the leaks, and await the arrival of help.

"I presume the *Cheng du* is on its way."

"I am not at liberty to discuss the position of other Chinese vessels, Captain Corry."

"I'm sure you aren't. But you may like to know that I have a likely sonar target to the west that is headed this way. And, as I recall, part of your distress call mentioned the *Cheng du*."

"We also see and hear the target to the west, Captain Corry. Please rest assured that it is not a Chinese submarine. We presume it is another American vessel."

"Not so, sir. As you saw, I just launched patrol aircraft to fly out and attempt to identify it." Corry didn't mention the identified *Tuscarora* target that was still stationary to the south of them. "Very well, sir, I am ready to tow. I will maneuver handsomely until we take slack."

Corry released the talk switch on the verbal handset and passed the order via N-fone, *Come stern to with the Chinese boat. Take tow slack handsomely.*

Towing another submarine is not something that a U.S. Navy carrier submarine is expected to do. But it had the propulsion power. However, its crew hadn't drilled on towing.

As a result, the first attempt to take slack in the line caused it to part. It took another hour to get a new line on the *Maoi fung.* At that point, Corry opted for a twenty-five-knot towing speed.

And he transferred command to the dodger bridge. He needed to see the activity, and he began to understand why Bart Clinch liked to command from the front line. All the high-tech sensors and information-handling gadgets in the world can only supplement the outstanding sensor suite possessed by a human being.

The reasons a retractable dodger bridge had been incorporated into the construction of the *Shenandoah* became clear to Corry. However, he and Zeke surmised that the boat's designers had no idea that it would be used to help conn the ship in a towing operation.

While the *Shenandoah* was trying to tow the *Maoi fung,* other problems occurred in sick bay.

"I must try to save this Mantid your Marines shot!" Zervas insisted.

"Commander Zervas, I'm not a doctor," Chief Post explained, "but I am the Acting Medical Officer under orders from the Captain. Doctor Moore appears to have suffered a concussion and threatens to go into shock. She has priority. I need your help!"

Zervas was faced with several difficult situations at once. He didn't want to stoop to taking orders from a CPO. He hadn't actually practiced medicine in the twelve years since his residency. He knew he could make a very bad mistake in Laura Raye Moore's case and thus be subject to additional ridicule and perhaps even censure and discharge "for the good of the service." If the word of this situation got out—as it most certainly would in the reports of the ship's officers and perhaps even that of CDR Smith—his career was finished.

He came to a fast decision. Somewhere deep in his personality, he realized he was a doctor first and a naval officer after that. He could be bilged for refusing to assist a medical emergency in a ship under way. However, if he pitched in and did his best as a doctor, no matter the circumstances, he would also have a report to write. The consequences of trying and failing as a doctor weren't as bad as refusing to assist as the CO had ordered.

Zervas had also had a few hours to study the dead Mantid. Like a terrestrial insect, the Mantid had a linear heart that lay along its back. It pumped its yellow blood forward into the brain case, where it was simply dumped into the Mantid's body cavities to be forced back into its third body element. He noted that the wound from the M33 round had merely ruptured the Mantid's skin and not lodged within the alien's body. He could stop the bleeding quickly and help Chief Post without the Mantid's life being left at stake.

"Very well, Chief. Give me one minute to close the wound in this Mantid. Then I'll be right with you."

Post took a deep breath. He hadn't enjoyed coming head to head with a two-and-a-half-striper. But he'd prevailed. Now all he had to do was to keep his Medical Officer from going into deep shock. Once that was accomplished, he could start work on discovering the nature and extent of her concussion.

Evelyn Lulalilo stayed with them in sick bay. Not only was she fluent enough in Pidgin to converse with Merhad, the Mantid with the broken leg, but she was also reasonably well grounded in anatomy. She could try to help the Chief Post and the other medical personnel, even if only as a gofer if necessary. She wanted desperately at this point to be needed and wanted.

An hour later, they'd succeeded in preventing Laura Raye from going into shock. The Medical Officer was still unconscious and had suffered only a mild concussion. With the medical technology available on the *Shenandoah*, Post and Zervas believed Moore would recover in a day or so.

So they began work under Zervas treating the injured Drek.

Zervas later had to admit to himself that he learned more Mantid anatomy and physiology during that intense period of work than he had in the previous hours dissecting the dead third Mantid. Part of it was due to the crash brush-up course he got in human medicine treating the ship's Medical Officer.

As the *Shenandoah* entered Iron Bottom Sound with the *Maoi fung* in tow, the report came from Air Group, *CO, this is Alley Cat. Meryl Delano's Osprey has a make on the incoming western target. In fact, Flak is talking right now to the captain through the sonobuoy. I can have the link patched through to your position.*

Please do so, Alley Cat. And have it put on verbal, please.

Zeke looked askance at Corry and the Captain looked back at his Executive Officer. "I wish Terri would run her show from the CIC," Corry remarked.

"Captain, she likes to do it from PRIFLY," Zeke reminded him, then speculated, "I think being in PRIFLY gives her the feeling that she's really part of the air action. Being CAG means she doesn't fly many real dangerous missions anymore."

Corry sighed. He'd been a naval aviator before learning to command carrier submarines. "I know about that, too, Zeke. Being always on the bridge tends to give one the idea that the ship is the only real world."

Zeke smiled. "That's why we have the dodger bridge, Captain."

The handset beeped, signaling that the link to the western target through Tikki's sonobuoy had been routed up to the dodger bridge. Corry picked it up. "Captain William Corry speaking."

"G'day, Captain Corry! This is Captain Algys Swan, Australian Navy submarine *Derwent*. Welcome to the bottom of the world!" came the reply. "I understand you've bagged a big Chinese fish."

"Your intelligence sources impress me, Captain Swan."

"We do share ANZUS intelligence information, including satellite imagery, Captain."

"Of course. Very well, our situation is this. We have the Chinese submarine *Maoi fung* in tow. She suffered an accident in the Solomon Sea."

"Yes, we picked up her distress signal. That's why we're on our way to help. Apparently you were closer. Do you need my help now?"

Zeke nodded and Corry agreed. "Yes, sir, your presence would be appreciated. We are towing the *Maoi fung* to Honiara, where her captain will probably beach her and wait for Chinese help. Except for our aircraft, this towing operation puts us at a tactical disadvantage because we can't dive. We understand that several East World boats are operating in this vicinity. Having your command alongside might deter some rash action."

"Right-oh! Agreed! We'll meet you at Honiara in a few hours. Perhaps we can have dinner together tonight."

"Captain Swan, with all due respects and thanks, I have urgent orders to proceed elsewhere because of the international situation at the moment," Corry explained obliquely.

"Oh, you must mean the five other East World boats proceeding this way so they could possibly cut the ANZUS sea lanes. Don't worry about them, Captain. Our latest intel data shows that they turned and proceeded north after your patrol plane bagged the *Maoi fung*. You did a good job of breaking up their southeasterly push. My compliments, sir. Well done. I'll see you in Honiara harbor."

Corry looked at Zeke and decided not to correct the Australian captain's impression of what had occurred.

"If Captain Swan got that from ANZUS intel data," Zeke said, "then I'll bet CINCPAC is sweating bullets. But why haven't we gotten an SWC message about it?"

"I suspect, Number Two, that Admiral Kane may be waiting to hear from us," Corry surmised. "I told him I'd keep him advised. And I haven't had time to do so until now. Let's get the *Maoi fung* out of danger; then I'd better give my boss a call. . . ."

25

"You've got *what* aboard?" VADM Richard Kane, CINCPAC, had trouble believing what CAPT William Corry just told him.

With the U.S.S. *Shenandoah* surfaced off Honiara in the lee of Point Cruz, Corry could use the lasercom satellite link. It was wide-band, thus permitting sharp two-way holographic transmission between the carrier submarine and Pearl Harbor. SWC transmission might be more secure because East World didn't have it yet, but encrypted satellite lasercom gave Corry the opportunity to see Kane and vice versa. Corry believed this was absolutely necessary because his report to CINCPAC was somewhat bizarre.

"Admiral, as I reported in my last SWC message, we were attacked by a flying saucer in the Solomon Sea. We disabled it and took it aboard along with its inhabitants," Corry repeated. "We have outstanding records and data to confirm this. If you wish, I can transmit some of this to you. However, because of the sensitive nature of the information, perhaps it might be better to deliver it personally upon our return to Pearl."

"Sensitive? Why?" The Admiral was a conservative old-line Navy officer. The whole idea of the United States Navy becoming involved in discovering a race of fishing aliens at Makasar had been bad enough. Now his top carrier submarine commander was confirming the disturbing SWC message received earlier.

UFO matters had been the exclusive province of the United States Aerospace Force for about a hundred years. Kane had been happy to let the wild blue/black yonder types have the job. The Navy had its own tasks that didn't include such chimerical activities. Now the

Navy not only had delivered one alien carcass to Washington, but Corry reported he had an operable flying saucer aboard the U.S.S. *Shenandoah* along with two live insectlike aliens, one dead one, and pieces of another.

"Admiral, in the course of this cruise, the experts of the special team we took aboard at Johnston Atoll revealed to me information that I didn't believe at first," Corry explained. "I'm now inclined to believe what Allan Soucek of Majestic Corporation has told me, fantastic as his story may be. Some of his data has been confirmed by Commander Smith of Naval Intelligence. And we've learned firsthand the truth about some of the rest of the fantastic stories. We've encountered one extraterrestrial species fishing for humans off Makasar. More of them are operating in New Georgia Sound. And we've discovered a second species that Soucek calls the Mantids. If we thought the Awesomes were strange, the Mantids are outright weird. And ugly. I'm going to transmit a portion of our videotape data so you can see what the Mantids look like." He reached over and activated the video player.

When the one-minute tape segment finished, Corry went on, "Soucek maintains that people in Washington know of seventy extraterrestrial species that have been or are now on Earth. Some of them apparently look like us and can mingle with us without being detected. If this is the case, I submit that the interests of some of these species may not be amicable to us. Witness the Awesomes, who work for the Mantids and fish for human beings. Apparently some of these extraterrestrials hunt us on land as well. Our reproductive organs, certain tissues, and a number of our biochemicals are traded on an interstellar black market by these Mantids. Commander Smith has shown me the extensive Naval Intelligence data base of missing and mutilated people in the United States. Therefore, Admiral, this is indeed a national security issue. In fact, if human beings are considered to be livestock by extraterrestrials, it's a *world* security issue!"

Kane broke in, "Bill, if the White House knew, we would have been told."

"Admiral, I know you weren't told or you would have told me in the final classified briefing before the *Shenan-*

doah departed Pearl. As it was, I learned about it only after the mission was under way. The man who tried to inform me was unprepared, ill equipped, and incapable of doing so. Allan Soucek was scared stiff because he'd been briefed just before leaving Washington. He believed he hadn't been given the full story because of all the questions his boss couldn't or wouldn't answer. He only knew that he was going into an unknown situation full of danger. Some people aren't equipped to handle that," Corry said bitterly.

He paused, hesitant to say what he believed he had to say to his immediate superior. "Admiral, either the President knows or is being kept in the dark by others who aren't telling him, for some reason. But *somebody* at the White House knows! Otherwise, a covert group known as Majestic Twelve wouldn't exist, nor would its operational arm, Majestic Corporation. I don't know why it's been a top-level secret so long, sir. But I suspect either a cover-up of high-level incompetence or covert internal government activities that aren't in the best interests of the citizens of our country."

Admiral Kane's expression grew stern and serious at this point. One of the hallmarks of the armed services of the United States is its apolitical stance and its subservience to civilian control. Questions arose in his mind about suddenly dumping this on CNO without doing a little investigation of his own first. CNO's furtive and often conflicting actions following the Makasar incident hadn't been normal. Kane had been disturbed about the way ADM George Street's staff had behaved. Now he was even more disturbed because of Bill Corry's discoveries and his old comrade's uncharacteristic and highly improper open criticism of higher command, naval and civilian.

However, he felt he had to raise a storm signal. "Bill, it isn't our duty to speculate about high-level national affairs beyond the defense of the country. Nor is it within our civil rights to criticize the actions of our civilian superiors."

"I agree, Admiral," Corry replied with equal seriousness and concern in his voice and expression. "But as an officer of the United States Navy who has taken an oath to defend the Constitution of the United States of America, not its political leaders, it *is* my duty to be concerned about the security of my country. The Constitution requires the government to provide for the common defense. I am deeply concerned, Admiral, that the common defense of the United States and its citizens is *not* being considered in this matter. If, as Mister Soucek claims, government personnel have known about seventy extraterrestrial species visiting this planet for over a hundred years, I have a legitimate concern that perhaps some government personnel have been co-opted by one or more of these species. Or that one of these species capable of passing among us unnoticed has assumed control of some critical government functions for its own purposes, some of which may not be friendly."

VADM Richard Kane pursed his lips and looked away from the holovideo pickup momentarily. Corry was treading on the fine edge of propriety as a naval officer. Kane had known the man for a long time. Bill Corry had been one of his plebes. Kane considered that Corry still had promotion and flag command potential. He didn't want such a fine officer and leader to blow it away. The Navy always needed good people like William Corry. But it also needed people who were willing to do more than blindly follow orders, who would lay their careers on the line when necessary. Kane now knew that Corry would do that if necessary. But it wasn't necessary right then. Kane understood that he himself might have to do so. CINCPAC was in a better position to do it than the captain of a carrier submarine who had flag potential.

Kane decided he'd do his best to protect Corry up to the point where his own career might be jeopardized. So he went on in a formal manner, "Captain, I consider your remarks to be ones of legitimate concern that are part of your verbal report to me. They're duly noted. I'd like to remind you that a formal report and official logs should not include speculative or critical claims."

"It will be difficult to draw conclusions or make recommendations without doing so, Admiral," Corry replied honestly.

"Then I suggest that you don't draw conclusions or

make recommendations. Let others draw what conclusions they wish from your reports. Let them make recommendations on the basis of your hard data," the Commander in Chief of Pacific naval forces told him. "They may be in a better position to take risk and accomplish something."

Corry knew a direct order when he heard it, even though it was voiced as a suggestion. "Aye, aye, sir," he replied, tight-lipped. Then he went on, "Sir, I believe I have accomplished my mission, although I haven't captured a live Awesome. I've acquired other live aliens and their artifacts. Therefore, I would like to return to Pearl soonest with the Corona vehicle and its occupants. I don't believe this valuable material should be risked by remaining in the Solomons region, even though you're the only one who knows we have this material aboard."

"I agree," Kane said without hesitation, "that your mission has been accomplished. Please return to Pearl immediately."

"Thank you, sir."

When the connection had been cut, Kane turned to the other person in the office, who had remained silently out of the pickup's field of view. "Dolores," he said to the Chief of Naval Intelligence, "I'm not attuned to the latest wrinkle in the rat race around Playland on the Potomac. So I'm wondering how and when I should pass along this hot skinny to George."

RADM Dolores T. McCarthy had been thinking about it, too. She was inwardly upset that information about the Majestic 12 and Majestic Corporation had been kept from Naval Intelligence for all these years. What bothered her the most, however, was that she hadn't been briefed when the Navy had become involved by accident. She'd had to find out for herself, and the officers and crew of the U.S.S. *Shenandoah* had learned about it the hard way. It wasn't a matter of turf. Her job was to see to it that Naval Intelligence knew what might affect the people who served in the United States Navy and placed their lives on the line for their country by going down to and under the sea. This vital information had been withheld and was still being withheld.

She shared CAPT William Corry's concerns. But she didn't say so.

"Don't," she said curtly.

"Don't what?"

"Don't pass it up the line to George Street right away."

"I should, you know. In fact, I must."

She shook her head and put out her hand. "No, you don't. Not now. Naval Intelligence is assuming authority and responsibility at this point. Please give me the memory cube containing the record of your conversation with Bill Corry just now. I'm officially classifying it Cosmic Top Secret with INTEL and ORCON caveats and SCI compartmentation. I'll brief George myself in person and covertly." She paused. "Those long-secret outfits in Washington are going to have to deal with *me* from now on, Dick."

Kane hesitated momentarily. McCarthy extended her hand even farther, indicating she wanted that memory cube *now*. So Kane extracted it from the phone and handed it to her. "They may cut you to ribbons, Dolores."

She shook her head and smiled. "Dick, I may be only a two-star going up against four-star types and even more. But I *do* know where bodies are buried and what skeletons are in whose closets. No intel organization can survive without that sort of information."

Kane sighed. "Okay, it's your problem, Admiral. Now, how do you want me to handle the U.S.S. *Shenandoah* when she arrives at Pearl?"

"Just provide me and my people with all the armed Marines and SPs I need. No one is going to take anything off that boat or go on or off that boat that I don't know about. Or for any reason that I don't approve. If I'm over-ruled by George, SECDEF, or the White House, it will be a matter of record. This super-secrecy that jeopardizes the lives of naval personnel has got to stop unless we're given very good reasons otherwise! And they will have to be *very* good reasons indeed!"

She paused, then added, "And please don't be alarmed by the retinue that's going to accompany me from now on, Dick. They're my bodyguards. Now, may

I please use your lasercom system? I need to pass some orders to my subordinate in the *Shenandoah*. We have to prepare for that onslaught from Washington."

That was being mounted there even as she spoke.

It started in an office on a floor that didn't exist in a high-rise commercial building within sight of the White House. The secret offices could be reached only by a special elevator activated by a special key. That portion of the building was also encased in electromagnetic protection far more effective then the old TEMPEST technology. It had been there a long time. The contractor and workers who'd built it were long dead. The building's plans didn't even show the phantom 13th floor. No one expected that a building would have a 13th floor, anyway.

It was the *real* Washington office of the Majestic Corporation. Allan Soucek had never been there.

The executive committee of Majestic 12 had convened.

Newell Carew presided. ADM Stephen Tyonek sat pensively across the table from him. Dr. Enos Delsin had come in from Bethesda. Lyle Muraco had managed to postpone his meetings and get over from Crystal City.

"Things have happened too fast to call the entire Twelve together," Carew began. "And calling another meeting this soon after the last one could possibly attract attention from our non-member colleagues."

"I agree," Tyonek put in. "Any attention at all is too much right now."

"Why did this happen?" Delsin wondered.

The conversation then slipped into the Dumuzi language that was as much body language as verbal communication.

"Soucek was the wrong one to send."

"Knowing what we know now, one of the Majestic Twelve should have gone instead."

"That would have been too risky."

"Agreed. But that's done. We can't go back and do it over."

"We may be in trouble."

"Yes. There will be questions. It may appear that we were slack."

"We're going to be asked why we weren't aware of the capabilities of the Rivers class carrier submarines."

"We can't follow all human science and technology like we used to. Progress is accelerating too fast."

"We may need more staff at Majestic Corporation."

"Probably. Soucek was overloaded. He'd been working too hard. He was almost on the edge of a nervous breakdown when we sent him."

"His position as a Naval Reserve aviator was helpful in keeping track of what we considered to be the most advanced human technology, aerospace."

"But he didn't know that submarine technology had outstripped aerospace."

"He didn't know much about carrier submarines."

"He should have. We pay him well to stay abreast of terrestrial technology."

"It's not the technology that we should watch, my friends. Technology provides only tools. Those who use the tools are the important factors."

"The humans have gotten very good at using the tools they've developed."

"Yes. Better than we believed possible. They are indeed versatile."

"Why didn't we spot it?"

"We've concentrated our attention too long only in national capitals."

"What's that got to do with it? Humans are humans and always have been."

"No, they evolve. Otherwise, we wouldn't be here."

"Well, it's apparent now that government people try to manage technology, if they do anything at all. Often, that's all they do because they can't use that technology. As a result of paying attention only to them, our evaluation of human capabilities as tool users is skewed badly."

"And our psychological and social evaluations are probably also terribly distorted. People in national capitals think differently. I now believe they may be retarded in comparison to other humans."

"The recent happenings would tend to confirm that. I certainly couldn't rank Washington people very highly when it comes to their development toward species adulthood. They haven't the foggiest notion of how to behave according to the Canons of Metalaw."

"Save the lectures for the students. We have a problem. Soucek failed. What do we do?"

"We aren't without recourse. We have another representative aboard. And a ship standing by in the vicinity. Let us not take hasty action here."

"Agreed. Hasty action got us into this mess. We must watch carefully."

"We need more data. Then we must use this data to think this through. Our solution must be workable."

"Yes. I certainly don't want to return to Nun without having a success here. This assignment is a ticket to better things if we don't fail."

"Agreed. So we will arrange things in a manner that we can't fail."

"But always within the limits imposed by the Canons of Metalaw. Don't revert to human behavior. We all face the possibility of going native if we stay here long enough."

"That's why I want to bring this to a successful conclusion. I want to get out of here and back to the home world."

CAPT William Corry only wanted to get back to home port. The sun was setting at Honiara. The Australian submarine SS-7 *Derwent* had just surfaced off Point Cruz and the Chinese boat S.46 *Maoi fung* was grounded on a bar with her deck and sail well above water at high tide. It was time to leave suddenly and without fanfare.

He made quick farewell calls on the TBS to Captains Jianghu and Swan. Without leaving the dodger bridge—he wanted to relish the sea breeze and the sight of clouds and sky for a few minutes longer—he and Chief Thomas conned the U.S.S. *Shenandoah* out into Iron Bottom Sound. Finally he went below to the bridge.

Amid the purposeful but ordered activity of a carrier submarine, Corry sat quietly in the command position and watched the displays as the boat slowly moved out into water deep enough to permit diving.

Zeke sat beside him, noting that the U.S.S. *Shenandoah* was ready to dive. With the flight deck hatches closed and sealed, Air Group reverted to submerged cruise mode.

Corry was tired. No, he decided he was exhausted. And he could tell from the way the bridge crew behaved that they were tired, too.

"There are more tired commanders than there are tired commands," he muttered.

"Sir?" Zeke asked.

"N-N-N-Nothing, Number Two." He caught himself. He was so tired that he hadn't remembered to control his breathing to eliminate stuttering. Zeke recognized the deficiency as a sign of fatigue on Corry's part. So he said nothing.

"Zeke, once we've dived and set course for Pearl, go to cruise mode. And let's have an informal midrats immediately thereafter. We all need to unwind," Corry told his Executive Officer.

"Aye, aye, sir, that we do." He checked the depth gauge and the position plot display. "Captain, the boat is ready to dive and we have enough bottom to do so."

"Good! Let's do it." Corry toggled his N-fone. *All hands, this is the Captain. Dive! Dive! Dive!*

26

Midrats is a midnight meal served to those who missed dinner because they were standing the second dog watch or would miss breakfast because of standing morning watch. It's always informal.

That evening, it was very informal.

It was the first time in days that the officers and crew of the U.S.S. *Shenandoah* had been able to kick back and relax a little.

It was impossible to relax totally at any time in a submarine, of course. The only true relaxation came during liberty or leave.

Because midrats was informal, the mess rule against talking shop wasn't in effect.

"We've cleared Cape Astrolabe on the northern tip of Malaita Island," LCDR Natalie Chase remarked to her midrats companion, Doctor Barry Duval.

"Well, you've got deep water ahead between here and Pearl Harbor," the oceanographer remarked. "I hope I was helpful in the last few days."

"You knew things about the bottom in the Solomons area that saved our buns, Barry," Natalie told him.

"Well, if that's the case, fine. I still don't really know why I was asked to join the team."

"You mean no one ever briefed you?"

"No. But it's been interesting. I didn't realize you could do so much with that new mass detector. That's really going to make a big impact in my field of work," he admitted. Duval didn't seem to be quite as intimidated by Chase now. But Natalie still considered him to be a strange guy. "I guess it really helps to see things on the masdet that other submarines can't."

"Yes, including other submarines."

"What happened to the *Tuscarora* signal, Charlie?" LTJG Barbara Brewer turned to ask the Special Sensor officer.

LT Charles Ames was slowly evolving from a persona as the ultimate techie nerd into a sociable member of the U.S.S. *Shenandoah*'s crew. He was still frightened of women. But he'd discovered that the women technical officers in the ship were easy to talk to if he overlooked the fact they were female. This disturbed some of the women who tried to look as female as possible in spite of the standard submariner's blue poopie suit that was the everyday uniform of the watch. But some, like Barbara Brewer, who saw Ames as a challenge, recognized the problem and adapted to it. As a result, Brewer— along with LTJG Olivia Kilmer and LT Paula Ives— found Ames to be an interesting personality beneath his carapace of gender terror.

"We lost it when we went north of Guadalcanal," he told her. "It was moving east when it disappeared from the display."

"Mister Ames, I want you to look for it to the south of us when we clear the Solomons in a few hours," LCDR Bob Lovette told him.

"Sir, the masdet watch has been ordered to report anything and everything," Ames replied.

Major Bart Clinch showed up late for midrats. CDR Matilda Smith was with him. He thumped into a chair at the table with Corry, Zeke, and Terri. Smith took a seat next to him.

Terri was the first to ask the question, "How's Laura Raye?"

Bart tried to look surprised as he shook out his napkin and started to attack his meal. "Why should I know that?"

"Because you've hovered around sick bay like a worried friend for hours," Zeke pointed out.

"Look, I'm responsible for her getting clobbered. I'm damned well going to hover around until I know she's okay," Bart snapped back. He was tired and stressed out, too.

"Take slack, Bart," Zeke advised him. The Executive Officer knew that Bart, like the other men aboard, couldn't shake his basic American cultural conditioning that women were special. And, in spite of being a Marine officer, Major Bart Clinch was also a gentleman. "So I repeat Terri's question: How's Laura Raye?"

"She's back in the world of the living," Bart reported.

"She wants to sign herself back to duty status, but Connie Zervas won't let her," the naval intelligence officer added. "He wants her to get a good night's sleep. Right now, she's got a slashed scalp and a real bad headache. I would, too, if I'd been hit with an assault rifle."

"Better that than an assault rifle's bullet," Terri observed. Then she began to tease the Marine officer. "Bart, for a few minutes there today, I thought you were taking stupid pills again."

"I quit years ago. No withdrawal symptoms, either. So how and where did I fool you this time?"

"This time? Have there been other times?" Terri goaded him.

"Many. And I'll let you worry about them yourself. So when did you think I wasn't a smart Marine this time?"

"When you walked up to that bug and took the gun from him," she admitted, then added, "But you blew it when you admitted you knew it was unloaded all along. What other little secrets do you Marines have that you haven't told the rest of us?"

"I'll never tell," Bart quipped. "Besides, you enjoy cajoling them out of me."

"Speaking of secrets," Zeke put in, "what is it that you were reluctant to talk about earlier when the bugs threatened to take the Corona?"

"Nothing important," Terri replied diffidently, tossing her blond curls out of her face. "You could have let them get aboard the Corona, Bart. They couldn't go anywhere even if we'd lifted the Corona to the flight deck."

"What the hell are you talking about?" Zeke wanted to know. "What do you know about the Corona that you haven't told us?"

"Only that it won't fly very well with its energy source disconnected."

"Huh?"

Terri explained, "My aircraft chiefs and techs went

over the Corona carefully. We don't know yet why it flies. But we thought it might be a good idea to safe any systems we could find. We couldn't figure out the controls or read the placards. But we could see that the propulsion system is electromagnetic, so it had to have energy storage. Chief Phillips found it. It's some sort of liquid chemical that's catalytically converted into a plasma for energy. We'll let the science johnnies figure it out."

"Not without approval from Naval Intelligence at this point," Matilda Smith put in. "Captain, I need to meet with you perhaps first thing tomorrow morning to discuss the orders I received from Admiral McCarthy before we left Honiara."

"Yes, I understand that your shop has assumed responsibility now," Corry remarked. "I don't know whether I like that idea or not. But an order is an order. And I don't have to ask why Naval Intelligence took over."

"I'll tell you anyway. It's for your protection."

"Really? Well, perhaps we should discuss that in the morning, Commander, after we've all gotten a good night's sleep."

"My intelligence sources indicate that some people won't," Smith replied cryptically, looking at Bart. "So, Terri, how did you and your techs figure out how to disconnect the propulsion system on the Corona?"

"Well, in the Air Group we've always had to deal with alien technology."

"Oh? How's that?"

"Aerospace engineers who design our ships don't have to strap their pink bods into them," Terri pointed out. "So we have to go in and figure out the latest strange technology they've conjured up and then make it really work. One of the first things we discovered about the Corona's energy source was that the Mantids know what we know: One of the most effective ways to carry a portable energy source is in liquid form. Then it can be pumped around where you want it and metered as you need it. Ergo, The Corona has piping. And piping has disconnects. The ones in the Corona aren't threaded, though. They're male-female connectors."

"Explain," Zeke urged her.

"Commander Braxton, you're the last person I ever thought I'd have to explain a male-female connector to!"

Clinch thought that was hilarious and broke out in loud guffaws, almost choking on his food in the process. Smith whopped him on the back several times until he stopped choking.

"So show me," Zeke coaxed her.

Terri rolled her left hand into a fist and pushed her right index finger into her rolled left fingers. "Like that."

"I think I can give you a better demonstration," Bart remarked.

"Probably. Undoubtedly."

"That must mean that the Mantids have two sexes," Zeke guessed.

"Zervas says they do," Matilda Smith reported. "He patched the one Sergeant McIvers shot and says it's male. The other one is female, and so is the dead one he's engrossed in cutting up right now. He says it's easy to recognize their reproductive organs."

"Guess how they got the idea for their male-female connector." Zeke grinned.

"Why, obviously the same way we did, of course," Terri said. "And wipe that grin off your face ... sir! Or I will be forced to demonstrate how the connector disconnects."

As CAPT William Corry finished his tuna salad sandwich, his standard snack, he told himself that his officers and crew did indeed need this unwinding midrats. They were letting off steam. He'd told Zeke that the Dolphin Club would be open until eight hours of out of Pearl. He'd never take advantage himself of a suspension of Naval Regulation 2020, but he was glad that the tension release would be available to those who wanted it. It helped ensure a crew healthy in mind and body.

He was bone tired. And his presence really wasn't needed in the wardroom any longer. So he rose, excused himself, and went to his cabin. He was looking forward to a few hours of rack time.

He was therefore both surprised and somewhat dismayed to find Dr. Evelyn Lulalilo waiting for him. She hadn't asked to see him. She'd let herself in and was sitting at his little conference table.

"Well, good evening, Eve," he told her.

"Good evening, Captain." Her voice wavered.

He saw she'd been crying.

She appeared to be in extreme emotional distress. Weary as he was, he couldn't just ask her to leave and come back in the morning. So he sat down on the opposite side of the little table. "Is something wrong, Eve?" he asked.

"This expedition is a lot more than I expected," she managed to say.

She reminded him so much of his eldest daughter! And she looked so much like his wife, Cynthia, at the time they got married. "What did you expect?" he asked her in kindly tones.

"A scientific expedition," she replied, wiping her eyes.

"And what was different than you expected?" Corry knew that somehow and for some reason she was frightened right down to her basic belief level. The best way to work her through her problem was to get her to talk about it.

Even so, he had been under extreme tension himself during the past several days. He knew he'd been able to control his emotions and drives during his career in a mixed-gender Navy because he'd had a lovely and lovable wife to come home to when a cruise was over. But now middle age vanity and alcohol had replaced him in Cynthia's life.

He really wanted to do more to help Eve than just talk with her. Like many others in the boat that night, he wanted the warm, intimate touch of another human being. He wanted to hold her. But he didn't. He'd taken a chair with the table between them to serve as a reminder that he should not, he *must* not. It was more than a feeling of marital loyalty to his wife. He was the commanding officer of a major ship of the United States Navy, and his behavior had to be beyond reproach, even in private.

"I've always wanted to communicate with another species because human beings are so vicious and cruel. I believed I could find some answers to this problem in the behavior and lives of other species," she admitted to him. Her words began to tumble out now. She was saying things that she would never talk about in her professional life with those she worked with in marine biology. Corry knew what was going on. It was a tension release mechanism for her. But it was more than that, too.

"I loved cats, but cats are violent hunters. So I tried dogs. I loved my dogs because they were so warm and friendly ... until one of them bit me when I tried to keep it from mating. So I tried dolphins. But I couldn't communicate with them because their world is so different. Then my two favorite dolphin friends got into a fight over another dolphin. When I stopped to think about that, I realized *everything* fights—for food, for mates, and even for friendship." She paused and breathed deeply, flipping her dark hair out of her face with a finger. "My work came to a halt, Captain. That's why I jumped at the chance to come on this expedition. I thought perhaps the aliens you found at Makasar might have been misunderstood by your people. After all, you do operate a warship. I hoped maybe I'd find a species that was benign."

Corry let her talk, but suddenly she stopped, put her face in her hands, and began to cry. He wanted badly to hold her. How many times had he held his daughter close when she wept?

She looked up at the wall with tear-filled eyes. She didn't look at him. "The Mantids are even more violent and vicious and nasty and cruel and deceitful than human beings! I could accustom myself to their monstrous appearance; I've seen more horrible creatures in the sea. But I can't accept their behavior! Why do they have to be so violent? Why do *we* have to be so violent?"

She stopped talking.

"This is a violent universe, Eve," he finally managed to say.

"It doesn't have to be."

"Maybe it does. I don't know the role aggressive behavior plays in the overall scheme of things. I only know that it's here," Corry told her. With some reluctance because he'd once had trouble dealing with his own aggressive nature as a young man, he went on, "Do you perceive me as a violent person, Eve?"

"Oh, no, no! You're one of the kindest persons I've ever met! I could love you easily!"

"I don't think you'd find it easy, Eve. I'm a very violent person inside."

"But I do anyway because you control it!"

"And you probably have little appreciation of what it takes. Four years at the Naval Academy. Years at Pensacola, the Naval Postgraduate School, the National War College, and continual study, evaluation, testing. I've been trained as a professional warrior, and that requires the most difficult sort of self-control." William Corry sighed. "My job, my duty, my responsibility is the controlled application of force and violence, acting only on someone's authorized orders, also given under strict controls. This is necessary because each of us in the *Shenandoah* has the capability to kill hundreds, maybe even millions of people. We've learned to control ourselves because we're accountable for our actions. *It's not easy to be accountable*! It's ... not easy...."

"You ... must be very lonely."

"We all are. Including you. I was ... born alone, and I'll ... die alone. My loneliness is a consequence of learning to be a civilized adult capable of accepting total responsibility for myself. I believe that's why I have command." He stopped, then apologized. "Sorry. I don't mean to lecture you about my morality."

"Did you ever love anyone?"

"Oh, yes! Very much! My wife. My daughter, and my son. And I'll never do anything, Eve, to be anything but responsible to them."

"Then ... can we be friends?"

"We are. And you don't have to fight for my friendship."

Evelyn Lulalilo smiled. It was now a pretty smile. Corry kept steely control over himself.

"Eve, you have a worldview that's naive but refreshing," he admitted. "Maybe the universe is indeed full of hate and violence. But keep your outlook. Not all of us have it. And we sometimes need it around us.

Why? I don't know. I don't know who or what we are or where we're going. Or why. But we're going somewhere as a species. And it's interesting to be along to find out, don't you think?"

She nodded. "Yes."

"So do you agree now that this has indeed been a scientific mission of exploration?"

She nodded again. "Yes, but not as I expected. However, now I can live with what it is."

"Good. Because it isn't over yet," CAPT William Corry told her.

APPENDIX I

SSCV-26 U.S.S. *SHENANDOAH*
Crew Roster

Commanding Officer: CAPT William M. Corry

Ship Staff
Executive Officer: CDR Arthur E. "Zeke" Braxton
Personnel & Legal Officer: LCDR Darlene H. Kerr
Quartermaster & Ship's Secretary: LTJG Frederick G. Berger
Chaplain: LT Thomas H. Chapman
Chief of the Boat: SCPO Carl G. Armstrong
Chief Staff Petty Officer: CPO Alfred K. Warren

Ship Division
Operations Department
Operations Officer: LCDR Robert A. Lovette
Communications Officer: LT Edward B. Atwater
Sonar Officer: LT Roger M. Goff
Special Sensor Officer: LT Charles B. Ames
Radar/Lidar Officer: LTJG Barbara S. Brewer
Intelligence Officer: LTJG Ralph M. Strader

Deck Department
First Lieutenant: LCDR Mark W. Walton
Gunnery Officer: CWO Joseph Z. Weaver
Cargo Officer: LTJG Olivia P. Kilmer
Steering & Damage Control Officer: LT Donald G. Morse
Underwater Special Team: LT Richard S. Brookstone
Chief Boatswain's Mate: CPO Clancy Thomas

Navigation Department
Navigator: LCDR Natalie B. Chase
Assistant Navigator: LT Bruce G. Leighton

Assistant Navigator: LT Marcella A. Zar

Engineering Department
Engineer Officer: CDR Raymond M. Stocker
Assistant Engineer Officer: LCDR Norman E. Merrill
Main Propulsion Officer: LT Paula F. Ives
Damage Control Officer: LTJG Robert P. Benedetti
Electrical Officer: LT Richard Fitzsimmons
Electronic Repair Officer: LTJG Myra A. Hofer

Supply Department
Supply Officer: LT Frances G. Allen
Disbursing Officer: LTJG Harriett B. Gordon
Stores Officer: LT Kenneth P. Keyes
Mess Officer: LTJG Calvin S. Baker

Medical Department
Medical Officer: CDR Laura Raye Moore, M.D.
Dental Officer: LT Fred S. Rue, D.D.S.
Chief Pharmacist Mate: CPO Nathan C. Post, P.N.
Chief Nurse: LT Bill Molders, P.N.

Air Group
Commander Air Group: CDR Teresa B. Ellison (Alley Cat)
Flight Deck Officer: LT Paul J. Peyton (Duke)
Aircraft Maintenance Officer: LT Willard L. Ireland
Squadron Commanders:
 VA-65 "Tigers" AttackRon: LCDR Patrick N. Bellinger (Bells)
 VP-35 "Black Panthers" PatrolRon: LCDR Meryl P. Delano (Flak)
 VC-50 TransportRon: LCDR Virginia S. Geiger (Tikki)

Marine Battalion
Marine Officers: Major Bartholomew C. Clinch
                     Battalion Sergeant Major Joseph McIvers
Marine Company A: Captain Presley N. O'Bannon
                     First Sergeant Solomon Wren

First Lieutenant Daniel Carmick
First Lieutenant Archibald
Henderson
Marine Company B: Captain John M. Gamble
First Sergeant Luke Quinn
First Lieutenant George H. Terrett
Second Lieutenant Anthony Gale
Marine Company C: Captain Samuel Miller
First Sergeant Jeff Mackie
First Lieutenant Alvin Edson
Second Lieutenant Chester G.
McCawley

OTHER CHARACTERS
Contact Two Team:

CDR M. H. Smith, Naval Intelligence.
LCDR Constantine G. Zervas, M.D., Bethesda Naval
Hospital.
Dr. Evelyn Lulalilo, National Science Foundation.
Dr. Barry W. Duval, National Oceanic and Atmospheric
Administration.
Allan H. Soucek, Majestic Corporation.

Majestic 12

Dr. Armand Grust
Dr. Johnathan Frip, Presidential Science Advisor
Dr. Bourke Renap
ADM Stephen Tyonek, USN, National Reconnaissance
Office
General Hoyt Beva, USAF Space Command
General Danforth Chesmu, AUS, Defense Mapping
Agency
Dr. Karl Songan
Dr. Enos Delsin
Newell Carew, President, Majestic Corporation
Stanfield Inteus
Lyle Muraco
Fergus Antol

Others:

ADM George L. Street, USN, Chief of Naval
Operations.

RADM Dolores T. McCarthy, USN, Chief of Naval Intelligence.

VADM Admiral Richard H. Kane, USN, CINCPAC, Pearl Harbor, Hawaii.

Alan M. Dekker, Director, CIA, Langley, Virginia

General Tony R. Lumdberg, USAF, Chairman, Joint Chiefs of Staff

Captain Wei Shi Jianhgo, Commanding Officer, Submarine 5.46 *Maoi fung,* Navy of the Peoples' Republic of China.

APPENDIX II

Majestic 12 Origin Documents

The following documents were obtained in 1989 under a Freedom of Information action. The poor quality of their reproduction is typical of the copying technology of the time and, in addition to the ancient typewriter printing, tends to authenticate them.

TOP SECRET
EYES ONLY
THE WHITE HOUSE
WASHINGTON

September 24, 1947.

MEMORANDUM FOR THE SECRETARY OF DEFENSE

Dear Secretary Forrestal:

As per our recent conversation on this matter, you are hereby authorized to proceed with all due speed and caution upon your undertaking. Hereafter this matter shall be referred to only as Operation Majestic Twelve.

It continues to be my feeling that any future considerations relative to the ultimate disposition of this matter should rest solely with the Office of the President following appropriate discussions with yourself, Dr. Bush and the Director of Central Intelligence.

NATIONAL SECURITY INFORMATION
TOP SECRET

EYES ONLY   COPY <u>ONE</u> OF <u>ONE</u>.

BRIEFING DOCUMENTS: OPERATION
MAJESTIC-12
PREPARED FOR PRESIDENT-ELECT DWIGHT D.
EISENHOWER; (EYES ONLY)
18 NOVEMBER, 1952

<u>WARNING</u>! This is a TOP SECRET—EYES ONLY
document containing compartmentalized information essential to the national security of
the United States. EYES ONLY ACCESS to the
material herein is strictly limited to those pos-
sessing Majestic-12 clearance level. Reproduction in any form or the taking of written or
mechanically transcribed notes is strictly
forbidden.

                    TOP SECRET
<u>EYES ONLY</u>   T52-EXEMPT (E)

SUBJECT: OPERATION MAJESTIC-12 PRELIMI-
NARY BRIEFING FOR PRESIDENT-ELECT
EISENHOWER.

DOCUMENT PREPARED 18 NOVEMBER, 1952.

BRIEFING OFFICER: ADM. ROSCOE H.
HILLENKOETTER (MJ-1)

NOTE: This document has been prepared as a
preliminary briefing only. It should be re-
garded as introductory to a full operations
briefing intended to follow.

* * * * * *

OPERATION MAJESTIC-12 is a TOP SECRET Research and Development/Intelligence operation responsible directly and only to the
President of the United States. Operations of
the project are carried out under control of the
Majestic-12 (Majic-12) Group which was established by special classified executive order
of President Truman on 24 September,
1947, upon recommendation by Dr. Vannevar
Bush and Secretary James Forrestal. (See
Attachment "A") Members of the Majestic-12
Group were designated as follows:

> Adm. Roscoe H.
> Hillenkoetter
> Dr. Vannevar Bush
> Secy. James V. Forrestal*
> Gen. Nathan F. Twining
> Gen. Hoyt S. Vandenberg
> Dr. Detlev Bronk
> Dr. Jerome Hunsaker
> Mr. Sidney W. Souers
> Mr. Gordon Gray

Dr. Donald Menzel
Gen. Robert M. Montague
Dr. Lloyd V. Berkner

The death of Secretary Forrestal on 22 May, 1949, created a vacancy which remained unfilled until 01 August, 1950, upon which date Gen. Walter B. Smith was designated as permanent replacement.

                    TOP SECRET
EYES ONLY   T52-EXEMPT (E)

APPENDIX III

METALAW
DEFINITIONS AND RULES (CANONS)

Definitions

Law: A system of rules of conduct and action governing the relationships between intelligent beings. These precepts are classified, reduced to order, put in the shape of rules, and mutually agreed upon.

Metalaw: A system of law dealing with all frames of existence and with intelligent beings of all kinds.

Intelligent being: An organized system having all of the following characteristics:

    a. Self-awareness.

    b. Time-binding sense—able to consider the future, conceive optional future action, and act upon the results thereof.

    c. Creative—able to make bi-sociative syntheses of random matrices to produce new concepts.

    d. Behaviorly adaptive—capable of overriding the pre-programmed behavior of instinct with behavior adapted to perceived present or imagined future circumstances.

    e. Empathetic—capable of imaginative identification with another intelligent being.

    f. Communicative—able to transmit information to another intelligent being in a meaningful manner.

Zone of Sensitivity: A spherical region about an intelligent being that extends out to the threshold of sensory detection, physio-bio-psycho-socio effects, or some arbitrary boundary within those limits that is announced by the being.

The Canons of Metalaw

First Canon (Haley's Rule): Do unto others as they would have you do unto them.

Second Canon: The First Canon of Metalaw must not be applied if it might result in the destruction of an intelligent being.

Third Canon: Any intelligent being may suspend adherence to the first two Canons of Metalaw in its own self-defense to prevent other intelligent beings from restricting its freedom of choice or destroying it.

Fourth Canon: Any intelligent being must not affect the freedom of choice of the survival of another intelligent being and must not, by inaction, permit the destruction of another intelligent being.

Fifth Canon: Any intelligent being has the right of freedom of choice in life-style, living location, and socio-economic cultural system consistent with the preceding Canons of Metalaw.

Sixth Canon: Sustained communication among intelligent beings must always be established and maintained with bilateral consent.

Seventh Canon: Any intelligent being may move about at will in a fashion unrestricted by other intelligent beings provided that the Zone of sensitivity of another intelligent being is not thereby violated without permission.

Eighth Canon: In the event of canonical conflict in any relationship among intelligent beings, the involved beings shall settle said conflict by non-violent concordance.

APPENDIX IV

GLOSSARY OF TERMS AND ACRONYMS

(*Note:*) A = Air Group term
M = Marine unit term
S = Ship term
G = General military/naval term

ALO: (G) Active Level of Operation readiness. Every unit has one. Usually it varies according to the whims of the high brass and how badly CNO and JCS want to assign a tough mission to an exhausted, depleted ship or outfit.

Anchor watch: (S) Personnel available for night work. When not standing watch, eating, sleeping, or recreating, naval personnel work on professional advancement, maintenance, repairs, sweepdown, and other tasks that must get done because no one else is available to do them. Some personnel standing day watches thus become available for night work.

AOG: (A) Aircraft on the ground. A grounded aircraft that is damaged or needs unavailable parts. An expensive naval aircraft is worthless unless it is either flying or flight-capable. "AOG" therefore is a super-emergency get-it-fixed-quick term applied equally to aircraft or any other air division equipment.

AP: (M) Anti-personnel. Applied to ammo, bombs, mines, or the first sergeant's latest set of work detail assignments.

APV: (M) Armored Personnel Vehicle. A small, lightly armored, fast vanlike vehicle intended to give Marines the false sense of security that they're safe from incoming while inside.

ARD: (S) A floating dry dock. Sometimes an SSCV or SSF must undergo hull repairs. The Navy maintains a few floating dry dock ships that can go to a damaged SS and repair it.

ARS: (S) A submarine salvage vessel. The sort of ship submariners greatly dislike. They hope they never have to call for one.

Artificial Intelligence or AI: (G) Very fast computer modules with large memories which can simulate some functions of human thought and decision-making processes by bringing together many apparently disconnected pieces of data, making simple evaluations of the priority of each, and making simple decisions concerning what to do, how to do it, when to do it, and what to report to the human being in control.

ASAP: (G) As soon as possible.

ASW: (G) Anti-submarine warfare. Engaged in between submarines and sometimes between surface vessels and submarines. Often undeclared. Submariners believe in only two types of ships: submarines and targets.

AT: (M) Anti-tank. Refers to ammo, guns, missiles, or mines. Few main battle tanks are left in the twenty-first century world because of the effectiveness of shoulder-launched and air-launched AT weapons.

Bag: (A) Flight suit. So named because the standard-issue full-length coverall-type flight suit is extremely baggy. Naval aviators, both male and female, have to be in outstanding physical condition and therefore arrange for smartly and tautly tailored bags. Some have opted for the tight-fitting combination flight suits and g-suits. A non-flying naval type can always be spotted on the flight deck by the baggy, non-tailored issue flight suit.

Bingo: (A) Minimum fuel for a comfortable and safe return. When you hit bingo fuel, you'd better either have the carrier in sight or have picked out a suitable "bingo field" to land on because you will shortly descend.

Binnacle: (S) The stand or enclosure for a compass. Not often used in SSCVs because of sophisticated space-borne and other electronic navigational systems. A magnetic compass is still carried "just in case" the electronics suffer a nervous breakdown, something the earth's magnetic field has never been known to do.

Blue U: (G) The United States Aerospace Force

Academy at Colorado Springs, Colorado. A term usually spoken with varying degrees of derision because the Aerospace Force stole blue as a service uniform color back in the days of the "wild blue yonder." The Navy, whose uniforms have been blue for much longer, has never really forgiven the Aerospace Force for stealing the Navy's color.

Blue water ops: (G) SSCV operations beyond the reach of land bases that can be reached by CAG aircraft or Marine unit boats. This is what the SSCVs were designed for. A submarine in a harbor or coastal waters is like a gazelle in a pen.

Bohemian Brigade: (G) War correspondents or a news media television crew. Highly disciplined military and naval personnel often dislike the sloppy appearance, sloppy dress, and sloppy discipline of news media people. The Navy assigns officers to cater to the news media in hopes that the media people will leave the rest of the real Navy types alone to do what they're paid for.

Bolter: (A) An aircraft landing attempt aboard a carrier that is aborted, forcing the pilot to take the aircraft around again, thus screwing up the whole recovery flight pattern. Once was more common when the Navy pilots landed jets on CVs and CVNs, an operation that involved crashing onto the deck under full military jet power. With VSTOL aircraft on SSCVs, a bolter usually occurs because of a screw-up in approach control, a damaged aircraft, an injured pilot, or bad weather.

Boomer: (G) A nuclear-powered ballistic missile submarine. Some of these are still in commission in the United States Navy, more in the navies of other nations. In a world where it doesn't pay to use thermonuclear area weapons, the dominant role of the SSBN diminished in favor of SSCVs and other sea control ships capable of dealing more effectively with brush fire and regional conflicts.

Braceland: (G) Naval slang referring to the United States Military Academy at West Point, New York. The Naval Academy operates with a far more sophisticated plebe disciplinary system involving more psychological pressure than physical abuse.

Briefback: (A) (M) (S) A highly detailed discussion of

the intended mission in which all commanders participating take part. Some of the plan is in the computers, but not all of it because technology has been known to fail when most urgently needed. Therefore, the operational plan is always presented and then briefed-back to ensure that it has been committed to human memory as well as computer memory.

Bug juice: (S) Fruit punch available from the galley at any time. The Navy still runs on coffee day and night, but fruit juices contain roughage and vitamins that coffee doesn't.

Burdened vessel: (S) The vessel required to take action to avoid collision. The burden of maneuver is on the vessel that must alter its course. In twenty-first century submarine jargon, a burdened vessel is the one that makes contact first and upon which the burden of initiating attack rests. The submarine captain is the one who actually bears the burden of decision making under these conditions.

CAG: Commander Air Group, the SSCV's chief pilot. Or "carrier air group," the SSCV's aircraft complement.

CAP: (A) Combat Air Patrol, one or more flights of fighter or fighter-attack aircraft put aloft over a carrier submarine to protect the ship against attack from the air.

Cat's paw: (S) A puff of wind.

CP: (G) Command Post.

Channel fever: (S) A predictable behavior pattern of the crew after a long submerged patrol as the ship approaches its base or a tender.

Check minus-x: (G) Look behind you. In terms of coordinates, plus-x is ahead, minus-x is behind, plus-y is to the right, minus-y is left, plus-z is up, and minus-z is down.

CIC: (G) Combat Information Center. May be different from a command post. On an SSCV, it is usually located in the control room which is the brainlike nerve center of the ship.

CINC: (G) Commander In Chief.

CJSC: (G) Chairman of the Joint Chief of Staff.

Class 6 supplies: (G) Alcoholic beverages of high ethanol content procured through nonregulation channels; officially, only five classes of supplies exist.

CNO: (G) Chief of Naval Operations.

CO: (G) Commanding Officer.

COD: (A) Carrier Onboard Delivery aircraft used to transfer personnel and cargo to and from the SSCV.

Column of ducks: (M) A convoy proceeding through terrain where it is likely to draw fire. Has also been applied by submarine officers to the juicy torpedo target of a convoy proceeding in line astern.

Comber: (S) A deep-water wave.

Confused sea: (S) A rough sea without a pattern.

Conshelf: (S) The continental shelf.

Crabtown: The city of Annapolis, Maryland, so-called by U.S. Naval Academy midshipmen because of the famed seafood of the area.

CRAF: (G) Civil Reserve Air Fleet. Nonmilitary commercial aircraft of all designations and sizes that the government has paid to have militarized or navalized. All or part of the CRAF can be called up in an emergency to provide airlift support for the Department of Defense at taxpayers' expense. However, the concept of the CRAF means that the government doesn't have to buy large numbers of aircraft and maintain them for use only in emergencies.

Creamed: (G) Greased, beaten, conquered, overwhelmed.

Crush depth: (S) The depth at which the water pressure causes the pressure hull of a submarine to implode. The "never exceed" depth of a ship, numbers that are deeply engraved in the memories of the ship's officers and operating crew.

CTAF: (A) Common Traffic Advisory Frequency. A radio communications frequency set aside for use by all aircraft where ground control frequencies and facilities such as airport control towers don't exist. These are normally in the VHF frequency spectrum and can be monitored and used by any radio-equipped aircraft.

CYA: (G) Cover Your Ass. In polite company, Cover Your Anatomy.

Dead reckoning: (S) (A) A method of navigation using direction and amount of progress from the last well-determined position to a new position. Not a widely used or desirable navigational method in the twenty-first century, but a method still taught for use in an emergency. Most officers reckon that if they have to use it, there's a high probability they'll be dead soon after. Actually, derived from the term "deduced reckoning."

Dead water: (S) A thin layer of fresher water over a deeper layer of more saline water. Dead water causes problems with sonar if you're looking for a target. On the other hand, dead water can be turned to an advantage if you're trying to avoid contact.

Deep scattering layer: (S) An ocean layer that scatters sounds of echoes vertically. Some submarines can dive deep enough to make use of this phenomenon. If you can get into a deep scattering layer, enemy sonar can be confused and even lose track of you. When the enemy uses this ploy, it becomes more than frustrating.

Degaussing: (S) Reducing the magnetic field of a ship to protect against magnetic mines. With the twenty-first century naval vessels using titanium and composite hulls, degaussing has become less of a requirement. Modern SSCVs and SSFs cause practically zero magnetic anomaly.

Density layer: (S) A layer of water in which density changes sufficiently to increase buoyancy. This can raise hell with a commanding officer's planned operation by causing the ship to inadvertently change its running depth. A density layer can also cause sonar anomalies. Apparently the new masdets aren't immune to this, either.

Dodger: (S) Once a term applied to a canvas windshield on an exposed bridge. Since the topside surface bridge on an SSCV is on the retractable tower, this term has been applied to it.

Dog: (S) A metal fitting used to close ports and hatches.

Dolphin Club: (S) That portion of a naval vessel unofficially set aside exclusively for privacy between male and female crew members. Like the U.S.S. *Tuscarora*, it doesn't officially exist. However, no captain who is concerned about the physical and mental health of his mixed crew prohibits the establishment of the Dolphin

Club on his ship. It is closed temporarily only during Condition Two and General Quarters—or for longer periods of time if members of the crew abuse the privilege.

Double nuts or coconuts: (A) The CAG's aircraft usually has a ship's operational or squadron number ending in 00. This has been corrupted, in the usual bad taste of hot pilots, in the term "double nuts" if the CAG is male or "coconuts" if the CAG is female. However, the ladies who fly and otherwise occupy combat positions look upon such tasteless slang as indicating that they are "one of the boys," that they have been accepted. Some personal pilot call names are even more tasteless.

ECM: (G) Electronic countermeasures.

ELINT: (G) Electronic intelligence gathering.

FCC: (G) Federal Communications Commission.

FEBA: (M) Forward Edge of the Battle Area.

FIDO: (A) (M) Acronym for "Fuck it, drive on!" Overcome your obstacle or problem and get on with the operation.

FIG: (G) Foreign Internal Guardian mission, the sort of assignment American military units draw to protect American interests in selected locations around the world. Also known as "saving the free world for greed and lechery."

Following sea: (S) Waves moving in the same general direction as the ship. Therefore, they break over the ship with less force.

Fort Fumble: (M) Any headquarters, but especially the Pentagon when not otherwise specified. Some naval officers call the Pentagon the "Potomac Interim Training Station." More often, they use the acronym for that.

Fox One (Two, Three, or Four): (A) A radio call signifying that a specific type of attack is about to be or has been initiated. The meanings have changed over the years as new weapons have entered service. Fox One is the simplest sort of attack, usually with guns. Fox Four is an attack with complex weapons such as missiles.

Fracture zone: (S) An area of breaks in underwater rocks such as sea mounts, ridges, and troughs. Nice places to hide if you're pinned down and want to become invisible to sonar.

Freshet: (S) An area of fresh water at the mouth of a

stream flowing into the sea. Can change the water density, which in turn changes the buoyancy of a submarine. Something that navigators try to warn submarine commanders about well in advance.

Frogmen: (S) Underwater demolition personnel, crazy people who don scuba and flippers and then go out to play with high explosives having a high probability of going bang while they're working with them.

Furball: (G) A complex, confused fight, battle, or operation.

GA: (G) "Go ahead!"

Galley yarn: (G) A shipboard rumor. Much the same as "scuttlebutt." Usually clears through the nebulous Rumor Control Department.

Gig: (S) The ship's boat for the use of the commanding officer.

Glory hole: (G) The chief petty officer's quarters aboard ship.

Golden BB: (A) (M) A small-caliber bullet that hits where least expected and most damaging, thus creating large problems.

Greased: (A) (M) Beaten, conquered, overwhelmed, creamed.

Hangfire: (G) The delayed detonation of an explosive charge.

Horsewhip: (S) The ship's commissioning pennant, rarely flown from a submarine. Refers to English Admiral William Blake's gesture of hoisting a horsewhip to his masthead to indicate his intention to chastise the enemy.

Hull down: (S) A ship slightly visible on the horizon.

Humper: (G) Any device whose actual name can't be recalled at the moment. Also "hummer" or "puppy."

ID or i-d: (G) Identification.

IFR: (A) Instrument flight rules, permitting relatively safe operation in conditions of limited visibility. Usually conducted through clouds that contain rocks ("cumulo granite").

Intelligence: (G) Generally considered to exist in four categories—animal, human, machine, and military.

Internal wave: (S) A wave that occurs within a fluid whose density changes with depth.

"I've lost the bubble": (S) "I'm confused and in trouble."

IX: (S) Designation for an unclassified miscellaneous vessel or target.

JCS: (G) Joint Chiefs of Staff.

JIC: (G) Just In Case.

KE: (G) Kinetic energy as applied to KE kill weapons. Missiles that kill or destroy by virtue of their impact energy.

Kedge: (S) To move a ship by means of a line attached to a small anchor—also called a kedge—dropped at the desired position.

"Keep the bubble": (S) Maintain exactly the angle of incline or decline called for. Also maintain a level head, a cool stool, and a hot pot at General Quarters.

Klick: (G) A kilometer, a measure of distance.

Lighter: (S) A bargelike vessel used to load or unload a ship. Usually welcomed by SSCV and SSF crews who have been on long patrols and are beginning to run out of such essentials as ice cream and toilet paper.

Log bird: (A) A logistics or supply aircraft. For an SSCV, as welcome as a lighter. (See LIGHTER.)

Mad minute: (G) The first intense, chaotic, wild, frenzied period of a firefight when it seems every gun in the world is being shot at you.

"The Man": (G) Term used to designate the President of the United States, the Commander in Chief.

Masdet: (S) The highly classified mass detector sensor system used on a submarine. Has replaced passive sonar (which is nevertheless still carried). A trained masdet operator (masdetter) can determine bearing, depth, and (if the displacement of the target is known) range of an underwater object. Masdet will not work across the sea surface interface.

Midrats: (S) The fourth daily meal served in a submarine, usually at midnight, ship's time.

Mike-mike: (M) Marine shorthand for "millimeter."

MRE: (M) Officially, Meal Ready to Eat; Marines claim it means "Meal Rarely Edible."

NCO: (M) Noncommissioned officer.

No joy: (A) (M) Failure to make visual or other contact.

Non-qual: (S) A person fresh from submarine school who is being taught firsthand how a submarine operates by on-the-job training, usually under the watchful eye of a petty officer.

NSC: (G) National Security Council.

OOD: (S) The Officer of the Deck, the officer in charge who represents the Captain.

Order of battle: (S) The disposition of ships as they ready for combat. Or the personnel roster of a Marine or Army unit.

Oscar briefing: (G) An orders briefing, a meeting where commanders give final orders to their subordinates.

Our chickens: (S) Term originating from the World War II submarine service, where it referred to friendly aircraft detailed to escort submarines engaged in rescuing downed pilots. Has been appropriated by SSCV crews to describe the aircraft based aboard their ships.

Papa briefing: (G) A planning briefing, a meeting during which operational plans are developed.

Phantom bottom: (S) A false sea bottom registered by electronic depth finders.

Playland on the Severn: (G) Derogatory term applied to the United States Naval Academy by those who never attended same. Not used in the presence of an Academy graduate without suffering the consequences.

Poopie suit: (S) Navy blue coveralls worn in a submarine.

PRIFLY: (A) The primary flight control bridge of a carrier submarine where the CAG and others can direct air operations.

Pucker factor: (G) The detrimental effect on the human body that results from an extremely hazardous situation, such as being shot at.

Q-ship: (S) A disguised man-of-war used to decoy enemy submarines. Submariners don't give any quarter to such deception on the part of the enemy, the only good Q-ship being one that's permanently on the bottom.

Rack: (S) A submariner's bed or bunk.

Red jacket: *(S)* A steward in the officer's wardroom/mess.

Reg Twenty-twenty: (A) (M) (S) Slang reference to Naval Regulation 2020, which prohibits physical contact between male and female personnel when on duty except for that required in the conduct of official business.

Rigged for red: (S) The control room lighting set for night operations. Was once deep red lighting. Term remains in use meaning ready to operate under Condition One or General Quarters.

Rips: (S) A turbulent agitation of water, generally caused by interaction of currents and winds. If this occurs deep, it can tear a submarine hull apart by stressing it in many directions at once. A large submarine hull that will handle rips above a certain level of turbulent activity cannot be designed and built.

Rough log: (S) The original draft version of a log. the rough log is later loaded into the ship's computer memory, where it becomes the final log. The rough log can be corrected before becoming the final log.

Rules of Engagement or ROE: (G) Official restrictions on the freedom of action of a commander or soldier in his confrontation with an opponent that act to increase the probability that said commander or soldier will lose the combat, all other things being equal.

SADARM: (M) Search-and-destroy armor, a kind of warhead. Navy types do not like this warhead because it can wreak havoc against the exposed portion of a ship on the surface.

Salinity: (S) The quantity of dissolved salts in seawater. The degree of salinity affects the density and thus the buoyancy of the water, an important operational factor to a submarine.

Scroom!: (A) (M) Abbreviation for "Screw 'em!" Rarely if ever used by line naval officers; however, some CPOs and petty officers have been heard voicing it.

Scuppers: (S) Fittings on weather decks that allow water to drain overboard.

SECDEF: (G) Secretary of Defense.

Sheep screw: (G) A disorganized, embarrassing, graceless, chaotic fuck-up.

Sierra Hotel: (A) What pilots say when they can't say, "Shit hot!"

Simple servant: (G) A play on "civil servant" who is an employee of the "silly service."

Simulator or sim: (A) A device that can simulate the sensations perceived by a human being and the results of the human's responses. A simple toy computer or video game simulating the flight of an aircraft or the driving of a race car is an example of a primitive simulator.

Sit-guess: (M) Slang for "estimate of the situation," an educated guess about your predicament. Rarely used by submariners, who eschew such contradictions for fear they could be misunderstood.

Sit-rep: (M) Short for "situation report" to notify your superior officer about the sheep screw you're in at the moment. Rarely used by submariners. (See SIT-GUESS.)

Sked: (G) Shorthand term for "schedule."

Skimmer: (S) A submariner's term for a surface ship.

Skunk: (S) An unidentified surface ship contact.

Snivel: (A) (M) To complain about the injustice being done you.

SP: (G) Shore Patrol, the unit put ashore during liberty to maintain law and order among the ship's crew. SP works closely with local law enforcement authorities.

Spook: (G) Slang term for either a spy or a military intelligence specialist. Also used as a verb relating to reconnaissance.

Staff stooge: (G) Derogatory term referring to a staff officer. Also "staff weenie."

SS: (G) Untied States Navy designation for a submarine.

SSCV: (G) Aircraft carrier submarine.

SSF: (G) Fusion-powered fast attack submarine.

SSN: (G) Nuclear-powered fast attack submarine.

Strakes: (S) Continuous lines of fore and aft planking or a raised thin rib or fluid dynamic fence running lengthwise along the outer hull.

Submariner: (S) A person who serves or has served in a submarine and is qualified to wear the Double Dolphins. Always pronounced "sub-mareener" because "sub-mariner" implies a less than qualified seaman.

SWC: (S) Scalar wave communications, a highly classified communications system that allows a submerged submarine to communicate with other submarines and shore facilities.

TAB-V: (A) Theater Air Base Vulnerability shelter. Naval aviators consider all Air Force bases to be vulnerable. Air Force pilots feel the same way about SSCVs.

TACAMO!: (G) "Take Charge and Move Out!" Also a radio and scalar wave communications relay aircraft stationed at critical points for the purposes of communications integrity.

Tango Sierra: (G) Tough shit.

Target bearing: (S) The compass direction of a target from a firing ship.

TBS: (G) Talk Between Ships. A short-range communications system. Originally a World War II short-range radio set. The submarine service now uses a scalar wave communications set designed especially for this service with a range of about a hundred klicks.

TDC: (S) Target data computer. Originally "torpedo data computer." However, the tendency of the traditionalists to hang on to acronyms resulted in this one being held over and converted for use with any of the many weapons systems on an SSCV.

TDU: (S) Trash disposal unit. The garbage dump on a submarine. A vertical tube that ejects packaged garbage which is weighted to sink to the bottom.

Tech-weenie: (G) The derogatory term applied by military people to the scientists, engineers, and technicians who complicate a warrior's life by insisting that the armed services have gadgetry that is the newest, fastest, most powerful, most accurate, and usually the most unreliable products of their fertile techie imaginations.

Tender: (S) A logistics support and repair ship. Like lighters and log birds, SSCV crews who have been long at sea and are running short of everything love to see these. Not much good for liberty, but a chance to go topside for sunshine and fresh air while the ship is tied up alongside.

Three-Dolphin Rating: (S) A humorous reference applied to a submariner who has paid a visit to the Dolphin Club. Refers to the fact that three dolphins are required for two of them to mate underwater. The "Two-Dolphin

Rating" is the right of a person to wear the two-dolphin badge of a qualified submariner.

Tiger error: (A) What happens when an eager pilot tries too hard.

TO&E: (G) Table of Organization and Equipment.

Topsiders: (S) Rubber-soled cloth shoes worn in a submarine and when going topside on a surfaced submarine. Also known as "Jesus creepers" because someone wearing them can move with almost total silence.

TRACON: (A) A civilian Terminal Radar Control facility at an airport.

Trick: (S) A helmsman's watch at the wheel.

Umpteen hundred: (G) Sometime in the distant, undetermined future.

U.S.S. Tuscarora: (S) An imaginary ship that has been in commission in the United States Navy since World War I. Somehow, it never makes port when any other ship is there and is never re-fitted or dry-docked. Yet it always seems to have officers and a crew. Every seagoing naval person claims either to have served aboard the ship or to have actually seen the ship in some far-off port of call. However, usually it has departed just the day before.

VLF: (G) Very Low Frequency radio wavelength. Rarely used by the Navy in its submarine service in the twenty-first century.

VTOL: (A) A vertical takeoff and landing aircraft type utilizing surface blowing or Coanda Effect (surface blowing) to achieve lift at zero forward airspeed.

WAG: Acronym for "Wild-Assed Guess" or, in polite shore society, "Wildly Assumed Guess."

XO: (G) Executive Officer, the Number Two officer in a ship, air unit, or Marine unit.

Yaw: (S) The port-starboard rotation of a ship around her vertical axis.

ZI: (G) Zone of the Interior, the continental United States.

Zip gun: The retractable radar-directed high-rate fully automatic 50mm gun that is deployed topside by an SSCV when necessary to take care of approaching close-in unfriendlies or targets. Progeny of the twentieth-century Phoenix CWIS or the Goalkeeper system. Zip guns can also detect and handle incoming targets directly overhead, thus providing defense against space-launched anti-ship KE weapons that can go right through a submarine from deck to keel. Zip guns can't penetrate the armor of some surface ships, but can make life difficult for anyone topside on such a ship. Zip guns all have the 1775 Navy Jack painted on them, the flag with the thirteen red and white stripes, the rattlesnake, and the legend "Don't tread on me." And for good reason.

FANTASTICAL LANDS

If you and/or a friend would like to receive the *ROC Advance*, a bimonthly newsletter featuring all the newest and hottest ROC books and authors, on a complimentary basis, please fill out this form and return it to:

ROC Books/Penguin USA
375 Hudson Street
New York, NY 10014

Your Address

Name _____

Street _____ Apt. # _____

City _____ State _____ Zip _____

Friend's Address

Name _____

Street _____ Apt. # _____

City _____ State _____ Zip _____